THE BURNING LAKE

THE BURNING LAKE

Jon Thurley

THE BODLEY HEAD
LONDON

British Library Cataloguing
in Publication Data

Thurley, Jon M.
The burning lake.
I. Title
823′.914[F] PR6070.H7/
ISBN 0-370-30855-7

Printed in Great Britain for
The Bodley Head Ltd
9 Bow Street, London WC2E 7AL
by St Edmundsbury Press
Bury St Edmunds, Suffolk
Set in Linotron 202 Sabon by
Inforum Ltd, Portsmouth, Hants
First published 1985

To my androgynous friend
DUMA MALVA DIJEN TOBAD whose help and support
have been equivalent
to that of at least eight people.

'But the fearful and unbelieving, and the abominable, and murderers, and whoremongers, and sorcerers, and idolaters, and liars, shall have their part in the lake which burneth with fire and brimstone: which is the second death.'

Revelation of St. John the Divine
Chapter 21, Verse 7.

PROLOGUE

Spring, 1983.

It was a wild night. I had moved into the studio as the first stage in the slow process of leaving, and was woken by the shrieking wind. The glowing dial of the clock indicated 2.30. When I woke again at five it was quiet, and I heard the vixen call harshly, two or three times, down by the willow at the end of the first terraced lawn, followed by the high, excited yipping and barking of the dogs giving chase. I listened for a while to the distant sounds, surrounded by my shrouded paintings on their easels. Then it was silent again, except for the rheumatic creaking of the house, and the occasional, almost inaudible drone of a car moving up the hill past the gates. At seven the paperboy called, forcing the newspaper through the steel-sprung letter box so that the echoes reverberated down the hall. When the milkman arrived twenty minutes later I decided to get up.

As I dressed I could hear the sounds of the waking house. Footsteps on polished pine, the sniff and whiffle of the dogs down the corridor. The traffic was heavier now, a slurring low boom which ebbed and flowed. Miranda was screaming excitedly, 'Mummy, mummy, I want to show you something,' and I heard Caroline answering in her irritated morning voice, but the words were indistinguishable. I looked out of the window as I buttoned my shirt and began to knot my tie. Outside the lawns were sugared with frost, the white trees like lace against the brilliant white-blue of the morning sky. The thrushes and starlings moved with rapid, eccentric steps across the glittering grass, like drunken mourners after a wake. As I watched they flew off and a moment later Caroline and Miranda came into view. Miranda was dragging Caroline towards the hothouse, gesticulating furiously with her free hand, her face animated with excitement.

I examined myself in the mirror. My teeth felt furred, and my dry smoker's cough had returned. Without conviction I made my daily pledge to myself to stop smoking, but it had an even greater feeling of empty ritual than usual. My face looked a little pouchy and grey, and my hair had begun to show more white than brown. To me it looked the same face as it had since I was twenty, some twenty years before. A reviewer of one early exhibition of my paintings had said, 'The artist himself is like a young Byron.' I preferred to remember that phrase, and to forget that she had later referred to my 'finely chiselled profile', a statement which indicated the level of the review. I had changed since then, of course, towards maturity or decay, depending upon my frame of mind.

I finished dressing and steeled myself to go downstairs. Though there had been no wild scenes between Caroline and me recently, there was a sullen, brooding quality about those times when we could not avoid one another, and I felt like an unwelcome stranger in the house full of women; my wife, my daughter, Ingrid our au pair, Mrs Haddon, the housekeeper. When I went into the kitchen the back door was open, and a thin, chilling wind whipped past my ankles and into the hall. I shivered and went to shut it. As I took the handle I looked down the garden towards the hothouse. It seemed, in a trick of the brilliant light, that several of the windows were broken, and it was a few moments before I noticed several branches from the rotting silver-birch lying on the paved slabs around the hothouse base. As I ran down the garden following the two sets of prints, I cursed Thompson for not cutting the tree down before. We had discussed it weeks ago. The dogs ran at my heels, full of undirected excitement.

I reached the door and heard Miranda say, 'It's all right, Mummy. Don't cry,' and I saw them standing together, Caroline looking around her as if she had just woken from sleep, and Miranda clutching her arm, looking up pleadingly.

I said foolishly, 'What's happened?' and Caroline gestured

hopelessly towards the vaulted roof where several panes were missing. Glass lay all around her feet, rasping and crunching under them as she moved.

Miranda ran to me and I picked her up. Faced with this adult tragedy, all her excitement had gone. 'They'll be all right, won't they, Daddy?'

It was too easy to lie, but I was tempted briefly. 'We'll have to see.'

I put Miranda down and followed Caroline round the path, pausing to watch her as she looked abstractedly at this and that plant. The heater still pumped out its energy, distorting the vision for a short space around it, but the air felt cold and there was frost on the black soil. The orchids looked fresh and graceful, opening their waxy flowers to the morning sun. The Strelitzia still stood proudly, like ancient knights in brilliantly coloured, beaked armour. Aechmea, Peperomias, Dracaenas, Saxifraga, Cissus, Sansevieria, Calathea, and the brilliant red Poinsettias, all seemed to glow with life. The Hibiscus my brother Jonathan had given us still leaned elegantly towards the light. This was Caroline's hobby, and I knew that she loved these plants. It seemed important that they should not die. But even I knew that the killing cold which had entered their root systems had already begun to work, and we were seeing the last flowerings.

I said, 'I'll call in the greenhouse people to repair the panes,' and Caroline looked at me listlessly.

'It doesn't matter,' she said, her voice heavy with depression, 'they're only flowers, after all.'

She was still there two hours later, when I left to drive up to London.

1

When I no longer needed to make excuses for my frequent absences from home, I had taken to dropping in to Rachel's flat. I still slept at home, seemingly unable to make the final, irrevocable step. 'Shall we live here when it is all over?' I asked her once, and took her silence for a tacit assent. After a few weeks the habit of spending part of my evenings there two or three times a week had grown upon me, and I assumed that Rachel must find the same comfort in it as I did. Sometimes I felt a pang of regret that the illicit, secret meetings were over, and our times together lacked the urgency of the first few weeks. But the new rhythms seemed more permanent, more in keeping with the prospect of a life together; which is how I saw the future.

When I found Rachel packing I couldn't at first understand what was happening. I had arrived after six one evening in early March and let myself in, glad to be out of the rude wind. She and I had been at odds for a few days, not seriously it seemed to me, but enough to explain the absence of a greeting. I fixed myself a weak whisky and water from the cabinet, and put on Klemperer conducting *Die Walkure* while I sat sorting out the mail I had collected from Walter, my agent's office.

At first I thought she might be pressing me into taking a decision which she felt I could not reach unaided. I had been deluded into that state of mind so common with lovers at the outset of an affair, in which I imagined that every facet of her behaviour was motivated by her relationship with me or, at the very least, was conditioned by her regard. So I said nothing and watched her covertly from my armchair as I pretended to be busy with my mail.

After half an hour I began to realise that there was a more serious sense of purpose in her remoteness. She moved methodically around the room, removing a picture or an ornament after a moment of consideration, and the flat slowly began to assume a dispossessed and abandoned air. She had a habit of throwing back her long hair with a slender arm, and her face was like that of a child in repose — intent, serious, wholly preoccupied with the matter in mind. She stopped in front of a picture I had done of her and bit her lip, half turning as if to say something to me, but she said nothing and merely took it down and went into the bedroom with it. When she came back to collect further things for packing, she paused with her hand on the imitation T'ang horse, her other hand propping her chin, and one instep resting against the other leg. Even if there was artifice in the unconscious grace with which she did these things, I didn't care. I watched, and she behaved as though I were not there.

Slowly the realisation grew upon me that I too had been cast aside, that there was a terrible certainty in her movements which excluded me. I could not break the silence now, even as I felt the beginning of a sense of loss. I knew then that my uncertain possession of her was in the past.

When she had finished packing and through the open bedroom door, I had watched her label the brown cases, she came in and spoke to me as to a stranger. If I wished, she said, I might keep the keys and stay at the flat. I felt like a caretaker, entrusted with the sheet-covered furniture, a few carpets, some ornaments to dust. Like the flat, I was dispossessed, vacant.

After that we talked, of course, but it was to no avail. Something I said affected her and she opened the cases, carefully taking out the things I had given her, and putting them into the empty cupboard. She avoided my eyes, and I knew that she was crying. But no words could bring her back.

I did not know why she was doing this. There was no one I could ask why she was doing this. There was no explanation.

A month later, in April, I arranged to meet Brian O'Donnell for a curry at a small restaurant I knew off Oxford Street. I had been so unhappy since Rachel left that I felt it must show, at least to Caroline and Miranda, if to nobody else. At times of great stress I was prey to two contrasting impulses, both as irresistibly potent as I knew them to be a flight from reality: to leave the grey shores of England behind, to sunbathe and wander around archaeological sites in some unfamiliar locale; or to reach back into my past, to see people I had known years before, perhaps in the hope of recreating the untroubled happiness of those years.

It was a long evening and we sat in the restaurant well after the other diners had left. It was almost possible to maintain the fragile illusion that we were undergraduates at Cambridge again, enjoying our curry as a respite from the interminable Latin grace and jocund high spirits of eating in Hall. Except that the last twenty years had created lines which bracketed Brian's mouth, and I could see the faint purplish sheen of tiredness under his eyes. During the meal it had been easier to talk of the distant past, groping blindly back to the submerged comradeship of those days, but I knew that those old memories were, at best, tenuous and temporary props which would have to be replaced if we were, in any real sense, to resume the forward momentum of our friendship.

There was an edgy, uneasy quality to the conversation. After we had ordered Brian said, 'Willey was a very bad influence on Jonathan, you know. It was all that father–son thing which Willey wanted. So that Willey had to tell him in the end. That it had been a game, that he couldn't do it.' He had looked across at me and then realised I couldn't respond. It was too soon.

I reflected, in one of the attenuated pauses of the evening when we busied ourselves with the food and unspoken things lay heavily between us, that we had become poor, bare, forked animals now that the juvenile distractions of college were past. We were ill-at-ease faced with the unacknowledged fact that there were forbidden subjects. The silences underlined our separateness rather than being full of the peace I felt there should be between old friends.

Perhaps I began something when I asked after Brian's companion of five years. I think he felt it was an enquiry made with full knowledge of the situation, rather than a nod to convention. Lorraine had gone off to Greenham Common, he said, wounded and raw at the memory. Just packed her bags and left him a note. There had been a row before she left, that was true, and she'd accused Brian of being materialistic and lacking in any appreciation of the wider issues. I could see that the accusation had hurt him more than anything else. She'd always seemed to me a vicious little vixen who had monitored his life like a prison wardress: the sort who consulted her watch if his train was five minutes late, and kept a running score of imagined slights. But my query had stung him into a combative frame of mind, in which it seemed his humour must be satisfied in scoring some victory off me. With his fourth lager in his hand he told me teasingly that he had received two letters from Rachel, and there was an element of malice in his glance over the rim of the glass. I shrugged and affected disinterest, and was glad when he dropped the subject with evident disappointment. Just as I felt that we had returned to safe ground he threw me off balance again:

'I always wondered if you were aware of your competitiveness. I mean, where Jonathan was concerned?' I felt angry with him then, too angry to answer, and he continued:

'Just look at it. Both at Cambridge. Married within six weeks of each other. A child late in both marriages. And . . .' I knew that he had intended to say something about Rachel, but had realised, even in this mood, that there was a limit to what I would accept. One thing Brian could never stand was ridicule. Using a heavy mock Viennese accent, I said:

'Dear good Doctor. Surely it might occur to one as learned as you that siblings reared by the same parents might have a not dissimilar view of life conditioned by that upbringing . . . that a congruence of taste, attitude and maturing might be the product of nurture and, to some extent, of nature? Of course,' and I warmed to my theme, determined that he would not escape unscathed or feel constrained to return to the subject, 've poor artisans, earning our living from the labour of our hands, must rely upon such simple insights without the benefit of ze great book learning available to you great pioneers of the hidden frontiers of the psyche.' I gazed at Brian in pretended awe, hiding the pain and anger his words had caused behind a mocking face. For once I knew he would not pursue the matter further, discomfited by the attack. He laughed and made a placating gesture, and we moved aside to talk of politics and other generalities.

We ate in a leisurely fashion. Finally Brian pushed his half-empty plate across the stained linen tablecloth with a faint grimace of disgust. Looking at the saffron rice, a chicken leg with a strip of bloody meat attached to the bone, I suddenly felt I didn't want to eat any more either. The attentive Indian waiter moved forward, his hands behind his back and an expression of solicitous concern on his face.

'Is everything all right, sir?' he enquired anxiously. Brian smiled at him and nodded, indicating how full he was by patting his stomach with his right hand and blowing out his cheeks. The waiter returned to his servile vigil by the melamine bar, his expression unreadable in the soft red and green lights. In the background the taped Indian music suddenly stopped.

'It looked so good, too,' Brian said, and I answered without thinking, 'Well, that's advertising for you. Provide the image and to hell with the truth.'

It was an unguarded movement towards yet another subject we had avoided, and I was relieved when he merely laughed good-humouredly. Despite the needling which had been an intermittent feature of the evening it seemed to confirm the slow progress towards a resumption of the old friendship of Cambridge days. I ordered barfee and coffee for both of us, not from hunger but because Brian's guilt about his sweet tooth would be diminished by my joining him, and because I wanted to rebuild the mood of the evening in some way that would buy back the lost years.

When the coffee was in front of us Brian leaned forward, his elbows on the table. His glasses, slightly blurred by condensation, had slipped down his nose, and he pushed them up again with an automatic reflex of his forefinger. Despite my earlier thoughts I had noticed a considerable change in him, not so much in twenty years as in the four months since I had last seen him. The fact that he hadn't shaved might be excusable in another man, given that it was the weekend, but in Brian this, the untidiness of his dress, the hair growing lankly over his collar, the extra weight which showed at his jowls and round his belly — all suggested some agreeable entropy of the sharp-suited, glossy image he had presented at our last meeting. As if there had been no break in our previous conversation he said reflectively, 'Two months ago I had a terrible shock. A model we had used for a commercial over ten years ago came in to play a mature mother.' He smiled briefly, and looked down at his hands. 'When she came in the first time I thought she was the most beautiful woman I had ever seen. I didn't talk to her then —' he laughed — 'probably making the coffee. I doubt if she even noticed I was there. But I've seen her picture over the years in magazines, and occasionally she's appeared in an upmarket TV commercial . . .'

A couple came into the restaurant, the girl running her fingers through wind-blown hair, and Brian stopped to look at them. The waiter glanced at his watch and ushered them to a table before turning the sign on the door over to 'Closed' and locking the door.

'Well,' Brian resumed, turning back to me, 'every time I saw her picture it reminded me of how I felt at that moment. And over the years I would occasionally indulge in a little fantasy of meeting her, of the things we would say.' He paused, and looked at me, perhaps willing me to guess the end of the story, but I was still in no mood to play the disciple in his Socratic dialogue.

'A couple of months ago, as I said, she came in again. This time, she was brought in to see me as Creative Director.' Here his voice dropped into self-mocking, umbrageous tones to indicate how important this position was in his world. 'Suddenly, as I looked at her in the cold light of day, I could see that there was really nothing behind the ruin of that beauty. She was hard, domineering, avaricious, sterile, only interested in how she would be lit, how her hair would be done, which profile would be used. And I thought what a fool I'd been, though my illusion had given me a certain pleasure.'

He gestured round the restaurant, indicating the red flock wallpaper, the cubicles fronted by plywood arches, each containing a garish, illuminated photograph of some Indian scene. The waiter writhed obsequiously to the table in response to the gesture, and Brian waved him away with an absorbed smile.

'I thought I could transform the inner nature of things by presenting beautiful images. That if Coué could make people live more positively by thinking of themselves constructively, so I could use beautiful imagery to enhance the intrinsic value of things.' He paused for a moment, smiling at some thought: I felt mildly irritated by this abstract passion which seemed so ephemeral beside all we had shared, and particularly beside my own, more prosaic problems of the moment. In the same instant I realised that this was Brian's flight, his means of dealing with far more intimate hurts.

'It's taken me years to realise that soap powder only ever washes clothes,' he went on. 'All those beautiful women, those witty scripts, those thousands of misspent pounds to advertise something which these people —' he moved his hand rhetorically to indicate the waiter (now in an agony of uncertainty about what was required) '— have done as efficiently as anything in the West, for centuries, on flat stones, by some dirty river, with the sun for bleach.' He seemed profoundly downcast at the thought.

'We all thought advertising was the thing when we came down,' I said, adding hastily lest I sounded too patronising, 'we've all got to live.'

He looked at me quizzically for a moment over the top of his glasses. 'Don't be smug,' he said, 'you're in no position to cast stones,' and added, so quietly that he might have been talking to himself, 'and then we should have so much more time, but how should we use it?'

It was a relief to leave the stuffy atmosphere and step out into the sharp air. It had stopped raining and we sauntered down Oxford Street, occasionally stopping to look at a window display. Brian asked diffidently if I had arranged to move yet, and I responded, equally as diffidently, that I still had arrangements to make before I could move out.

'Don't leave it too long,' he said. 'That is, if you've really made up your mind.' Sometimes I felt a flicker of hatred for him because he left nothing decently hidden. It had always been so.

When we reached Oxford Circus we paused by unspoken mutual consent. An old woman, dressed in several layers of clothing, her coat secured around the waist with a piece of sisal, walked past at a furious pace, pushing a pram in which sat a variety of plastic bags. As she walked she spoke to an unseen companion, vehemently hissing and dribbling a farrago of nonsense. Brian shivered, watching her go. After a moment he said, 'I've given in my notice. I've decided to sell up and go to Egypt.'

I knew then that this was what had lain under the surface all evening; and, immediately, that Brian had recognised my trips abroad for the flights they were, through a corresponding sympathy. 'Why Egypt?' I asked, and he answered as if he had rehearsed the words many times, 'Oh, that was Rachel's idea. She has an uncle in the travel business there who has some connections with Cairo University. He can fix me up with digs and make some introductions.'

I was touched by his use of the word digs. It was such an undergraduate word, with all those carefree connotations.

'Funny to think of an Irishman lecturing on Averroes and Avicenna to Cairenes,' I said, trying to keep my tone light. 'What about money?'

He gestured impatiently, almost contemptuously. 'With the sale of the flat and the car I'll have quite a bit of capital. And I've some savings, and a few shares to cash in . . .'

A plane banked high overhead, making the turn to take it down over the Cromwell Road towards Heathrow. Brian's voice was that of an old man, bleak and weary: 'I'm tired of the dark, and the rain. And I don't like what is happening here, the feeling of decline . . .'

I couldn't let it go at that, even at the risk of losing the ground we had regained during the evening. 'Why, Brian?' I said, 'why?'

For the first time he looked at me as if he really saw me. I was surprised by the bitterness in his face, and detected a sense of regret that he could not avoid the consequences of his own thoughts, could not resume his comfortable, ordered life because it no longer provided him with what he needed. 'Somewhere new to hide, I suppose. I couldn't take much more. The absurd meetings, the expense-account lunches, the perverse, filthy waste of money, people, time, myself. It isn't a sudden decision.' He forestalled my next question. 'Next week,' he said with an air of finality, and I knew the matter was closed.

We walked down the steps. The Asian ticket-collector looked perfunctorily up at us from his copy of *The Standard* as we walked through the turnstile. When we were on the escalator, moving smoothly past the advertising posters, Brian turned to look up at me.

'I shouldn't really say anything,' he said, 'but who can resist the opportunity to meddle? I think Rachel is very unhappy.'

I felt a moment's fierce resentment at his presumption. I had tried to believe she was dead to me and, until that moment, I had been able to think of her as someone I had once known but knew no more. Then I saw that Brian was genuinely concerned, and I felt overcome by fear and nausea.

'Did she say anything to you in the letters?' I asked, and he turned to walk off the escalator, his face momentarily hidden from me.

'Nothing direct,' he said as we walked, 'but I feel there is something wrong at the moment.' He looked at my face and laughed reassuringly, putting his hand on my arm. 'It's probably my imagination. Seeing my own preoccupations reflected in everyone else. Don't worry!'

It was like someone starting to confide a secret and then thinking better of it. Nothing could surpass my imaginings now that he had opened up this rich seam. On the platform he said, 'You must come out to visit me,' and I nodded, unable to trust myself to say anything. I watched him standing at the window, clutching his plastic bag full of papers, his ungainly bulk braced against the jerky movements of the tube, and was moved again.

All the way to Wimbledon I sat feeling fearful and apprehensive: it seemed to me that I should have found some way to stop Rachel going, and Brian. I envied the small man opposite, quietly reading his book, investing him in my imagination with a full and tranquil life. When he got out at Southfields I saw that he had a grotesque hunch back.

I picked up the car at Wimbledon and drove home to the darkened house. Here I was only the man who could not control the wind, the processes of decay in trees, the forces of nature. In the hostile lounge I undressed in the dark and, on impulse, slept on the sofa.

2

I wrote to Brian, care of Rachel's uncle, Mr Davies, at the tour company address in Falouga Street, Agouza, two days after he left, and surprised myself by addressing the letter as from her flat. The days passed with no reply, and I felt abandoned and resentful as, day after day, I found only circulars, addressed to Rachel, in the front hall. Sometimes I dropped into the office to collect my mail, and once even had an uneasy cup of coffee with Walter.

'Don't try to start painting again until you're ready,' he warned, but I could sense the fear and thwarted cupidity underlying his apparent concern. He showed me some canvases by a new protégé, and seemed disappointed when I lavished praise upon them. 'Do you really think he's that good?' he asked, taking one over to the window and slanting it to catch the light. I knew that he was only attempting to spur me into action, to suggest that I might not be his most important client for much longer unless I made haste to resume our old relationship. He was discomfited when I laughed, his smooth, professional sympathy marred by an anxious look, but I had only laughed at the memory of myself some twenty years before, seated before him in this very office, awed by the lavish décor, the constant interruptions of phone calls from Rome, or Paris, or New York. I was amused too, at this minor coup de théâtre, knowing that it would be years before this new painter could command the prices my work fetched, however good he was.

Returning home, as I did each evening for the first month after Rachel had left, seemed like a visit to a world whose existence I had forgotten. I did my work slowly during the days, taking hours over the arrangement of catalogues, the provision of copy for future exhibitions, and worded and reworded the letters I dictated on to a cassette and dropped in to Walter's secretary to type. In the end I would feel reluctantly compelled to return home. A casual observer there would have noticed nothing exceptional in the outward ordering of our lives, save perhaps a certain distance between Caroline and myself. We no longer had those set dinner parties which featured so heavily in our previous life, but I paid the bills, and chaffed Ingrid, and we walked with Miranda and the dogs over the rolling Surrey countryside. We saw my sister Jean and her husband Alan — and Charles Deterding, my patron of sorts, dropped by for drinks. I resumed the exchange of letters with my parents in which each side retailed anecdotes about local life which could mean nothing to the other. Though Caroline seemed to have lost interest in the hothouse, I had arranged for it to be repaired, and found an entirely unexpected pleasure in ordering exotic plants from a variety of brochures: the brilliant Indian plants of my childhood, and frangipani, and bougainvillaea, in addition to replacing the casualties. But Caroline and I, having on the one and only occasion in our lives together discussed everything with passion and hatred and regret, now discussed nothing. The price of items, the repairs needed, Thompson's requests for the garden, yes, but nothing of a personal nature. It was a time when it seemed that we had taken all the decisions, but lassitude, or the fear of the unknown, prevented us from putting them into practice.

One evening in May there was a letter from Brian. I had almost decided not to make the detour to Rachel's flat on my way home, convinced by now that he would not write, but some intuition prevailed, and I parked outside and let myself in. I read it in the car, oblivious of the traffic streaming noisily past, in the spring sunshine which had brought young girls out in bright, flimsy dresses. It was a long, enthusiastic shout of joy about the experience of Egypt. He had toured the sites — Abu Simbel, 'a monolithic reconstruction in fibreglass and concrete which reproduces *in every detail* the original Temple of Rameses'; Philae, 'moved and rebuilt by the Italians: I thought they only produced bad governments, soapstone ashtrays and illuminated plastic gondolas'; Esna, Edfu, Kom Ombo, Luxor, The Valley of the Kings, Saqquarat, Gizeh — the litany of names ran through the flimsy pages in his loose, sprawling hand. There was a denseness here in the experience which ran counter to the Brian I had known for so many years, as though he had finally found something, some place in the physical world which had stirred him more than abstract ideas. He begged, urged, demanded that I come. It would be an experience I could never forget. I could stay in his pensione. He had found a post attached to the University starting in September, working with an American professor of philosophy on Al Farabi and Canon Medicinae. Of Rachel he spoke only at the end, and I could make small sense of his cryptic comments:

> She is not quite as I presumed when you and I had dinner in London. She takes some of the English tours during the season, and we have been to a few lectures at the Archaeology Faculty, and once to Cairo Museum. It is not so much unhappiness I sense as the feeling that she is waiting for somebody or something (though I feel she does not know what) which will free her from this withdrawal from life, this psychic paralysis. At least I can give you the assurance that she is physically well, thinner perhaps, browner certainly, but healthy. I feel that she is suffering, but it is in the mind and spirit and not the body. You will know that I cannot make any direct approach but, who knows, she may finally decide to confide in me. I have always cared for her too, in my own way.

I cursed Brian for his obliqueness, but I suddenly felt happier than I had for months. It was a general feeling of well-being, so undirected and diffuse that I found myself feeling warmly for Caroline, and guilty for my recent growing detachment from her. As I drove back I planned to take her out for a meal that evening. Though the gesture would not significantly affect the growing estrangement between us I felt it might take away some of the brooding sourness — at least for a while.

It was early evening when I arrived back. The daffodils lining the drive nodded and bobbed in the light breeze.

Thompson was just leaving and acknowledged me with a slight nod as I drove past him up the drive. There was a small white van bearing the legend 'Exotic Foliage' parked outside the front door, and I drew the car into the lee of the bay hedge in preference to putting it away in the garage, so that it would be accessible for the evening. The air was sweet with a touch of damp still where the trees sheltered the grass from the sun. I walked through the side gate around to the back of the house and the dogs rushed up to me, barking furiously at first, and then fawning around my legs with ecstatic leaps and bounds, and small, throaty noises of delight. I said 'Squirrels!' in an urgent tone, pointing to the copse at the end of the garden and they raced down to the trees to forage excitedly around the undergrowth. Ingrid's bicycle was propped against the wall, and I made a mental note to ask her to keep it in the shed.

The hothouse door was open. As I walked down towards it to see how the new plants and creepers were doing I felt a sense of pride. Though the work of planting and fertilising had been done by the experts, I did feel that I had taken some part in the re-creation of the steamy interior. The windows ran with condensation. I heard voices as I reached the door; as I looked in I felt a strange sense of unreality followed by a sensation of dizziness.

The inside was devastated; plants had been torn and slashed apart and it looked as if a marauding band of hooligans had systematically destroyed everything. The plants I had replaced so lovingly were lying in heaps on the floor, bent, twisted, the petals shredded. A begonia lay on the paving, the imprint of a ribbed sole clearly marked in the soil which still clung to the crushed roots. Further down the aisle a ginko oozed white sap from a broken stem, its palmate leaves creased and folded. At the end of the passageway, past a pile of black peat speckled with pebbles and sharp-edged slivers of clay pot, Caroline stood talking to a man in a white coat. She barely acknowledged my presence, her eyes flicking across for a moment whilst she continued talking. He stood in green Wellingtons, taking notes and nodding as she talked; a small, red-faced man with the blue, far-sighted eyes of a countryman.

I could hardly speak. The ruin seemed a greater loss than the death of a few flowers, the assault somehow menacing and violent in contrast to the orderly, planned replacement the two men had carried out only a couple of weeks before.

'What happened?' I asked, but she ignored me, though the man shot me an uneasy glance as he continued to write. I stepped over the pile of earth and ruined plants and touched her on the shoulder. 'What happened, Caroline?' I repeated, and felt sick when I saw her face.

It was under iron control. She would not let go, would not say anything which might betray her feelings, but I knew that her anger, her hatred, her belief that I had blighted her life would remain with her until the day she died.

When she spoke, her voice was tight and higher than usual, the voice she used to hide her anger with me when we were in company. 'It was thoughtful of you to try,' she said, 'but we always agreed that this could be my hobby, and I thought I'd like to set it out entirely differently this time.' She looked at me for a long moment, and I could see triumph and uncertainty in her face. But mostly triumph.

Miranda joined us for dinner and chattered on, seemingly oblivious to our silence. When I looked at her, sadness crept into my heart. Her best friend had told her about the Christmas pantomime her family had gone to. Could we go to a pantomime next Christmas, and have dinner in a real restaurant with proper linen cloths? I sat mute, and looked at her. It seemed my heart must break. I had never seen this, lurking in the shadows, and obscured from my attention by my struggle with Caroline. I had never known a child could hurt so much. When she began to tire, and her eyes drooped from the effort of being grown-up and sitting at the table with us, mimicking the conversations she had heard between our dinner guests, I picked her up. She put her finger in her mouth and her head on my shoulder and was a little girl again, her arm around my neck. I took her up to bed and watched her undress and make a gesture towards washing and cleaning her teeth. When I had tucked her in, with her doll on the pillow beside her, she put her arms out to be hugged.

I said, 'I may be going away tomorrow.' She said, 'Will you

be gone for long?' her eyes opening slightly as she fought against sleep. I hugged her for a moment and said, 'I don't know. I love you,' and she smiled with sleepy trust. 'I love you, Daddy. Goodnight.'

I looked back from the door and saw that she was already asleep, one arm thrown across the rag doll. I put out the light and walked down the stairs again to the dining-room. It was this I had never anticipated, the betrayal of trust and the abandonment of love.

Caroline looked at me and said, 'Don't worry, I'll explain it all to her,' and I thought I saw a momentary softening, a flicker of compassion. There was a part of me which observed what was happening with detachment, like a wounded man whom nature at first protects from a knowledge of his own hurt.

'Don't make her think I am a monster, will you?' I said. 'Give her a chance to make something better.'

I went upstairs to pack. At first indecisive, as I relived the exchanges we had just made, I finally decided to take only what I might need in the near future. So much of what we had bought together already carried the associations of a past life. Most of it wouldn't go well in Rachel's flat anyway. In the end it was almost easy to leave, like a death which could not be avoided.

The school stood in a quiet, tree-lined Wimbledon avenue. When my brother first told me that he and Beth had decided to send James there I had been mildly amused. It was one of those pretentious, mock Gothic buildings, surrounded by 1950s prefabricated concrete classrooms discreetly cached behind the main house. The grey uniform with burgundy piping, the copious list of 'extras' which sorted the wealthy parents from the struggling, even the motto 'Work and Pray' carved in a scroll beneath a griffon rampant over the chapel door by a loving Victorian craftsman, all suggested a subtly élitist middle-class attitude. But James had been so proud of his uniform that he had insisted on wearing it when I took him and Miranda out to the zoo. The school had accepted him very young at Jonathan's insistence.

'Look at my badge, Uncle David,' he had said, clutching

desperately at his cap which the wind threatened to whisk away. 'That's gold thread.' I had nodded gravely in deference to his awed tones. Alone with the two of them, I had no adult to share my amusement.

The car was instantly recognisable, so I had parked it down a side road. I stood in the leafy shadow of a horse-chestnut, wearing an overcoat and a hat which I hoped would disguise me to a careless glance. At 3.30 the children started coming out of the gates. A harassed master came out with the first wave, all of whom were shouting and shrieking at each other and at him, and proceeded to roar at some of the departing boys. 'Jones, *Jones*, remember the Green Cross Code! You stupid boy, didn't you see that car coming?' There was a great burst of laughter and a small boy shouted over his shoulder, 'I was too busy listening to you, sir!' as he hitched his satchel to a more comfortable position and walked deliberately into the road.

I saw the car draw up and Beth stepped out to stand by the side of it. She was still wearing unrelieved black, and her posture looked stiff and awkward. The boys streamed past her, some of them obviously making admiring comments about the Rolls, and one of the smartly dressed women stopped for a moment and spoke to her, inclining her head and touching Beth's arm in a gesture which betokened sympathy.

James was amongst the last to walk down the gravelled drive. He had his hands in his pockets, and his school cap was already in place on the back of his head. Right up to the gate he kicked a pebble, following its erratic flight, and I could see his lips pursed as if he were whistling. At the gate he walked through, turning to shut it behind him with exaggerated care, and walked slowly up the road towards Beth. By the car she looked at him for a moment, her arms folded in front of her, and then shut the door behind him as he climbed into the back seat. When they had gone I realised that they had not exchanged a single word. I need not have worried that they might see me. They were sunk in some dark, despairing world of their own in which the rest of us were as insubstantial as shadows.

In those last few days, as I organised my visa and found my way around the unfamiliar back-streets near the flat, buying convenience food for my indifferent appetite, I began to realise the extent to which I had misjudged the past. The enormity of the mistakes I had made appalled me and seemed, in this heightened mood of despair, to extend to my views of all those closest to me and well beyond. I had misjudged Caroline, and my brother Jonathan, and Beth, and Brian and Rachel; I had looked upon my dealer, Walter, as a friend: I had failed to see those underlying tides and currents which had been the true arbiters of the events of the past few months. I had no doubt, too, that this blindness would extend into the future, and that the course of action I had now put in train would be judged faulty and ill-advised in the passage of time.

When we were children (in another life, it seemed), the lounge of our forest-side house in India was hung with pre-Raphaelite paintings of my father's choice. After tea we children sat in the lounge with the adults as they listened to the news and discussed in grave grown-up voices the portent of events. Before we were born my parents had listened to the views of the advocates of the Muslim division of British India put forward at the early Round Table Conference of India in the Thirties, and had followed the fortunes of Gandhi, and Quaid-e-Azam, of Bhose, and Nehru, and Jinnah there.

It was a time and a place for seriousness, for realising that great events were taking place outside our small enclave. As soon as I was old enough to sit quietly, those times spoke to me of history and the unknown, of warring armies clashing by night and day. When Slim averted the threatened invasion of India in three months in early 1944, and when the re-conquest of Burma was begun in January 1945 and completed by the fall of Rangoon three months later, I was old enough to recognise the cadences of great movements motivated by great passions. When the tides seemed against us as colonials in India, and in Europe the Allies seemed to be making no progress against the Nazis, I felt the pressures of unknowable events reaching into the very room where we sat; at such times I remembered, as a charm against misfortune, that the East India Company had held sway in India since the taking of Bengal and the defeat of Suraj-ah-Dowlah's army at Plassey in 1757. The feelings I had for the pictures, and the views which grew up within me over those years of wars and rumours of wars, which culminated in the unimaginable horrors of Hiroshima and Nagasaki, were inextricably bound together. The pictures represented something beyond, greater than the temporary and specific present, and the childish preoccupations of the moment, something to do with heroism, chivalry, beauty, and the rise and fall of nations.

Narcissus gazed at his reflection in the water, amidst brilliant Arcadian foliage. Dante Gabriel Rossetti's Pandora, in slightly garish reproduction, looked from her frame into the room, her right hand poised upon the fatal box from which she would release the winged mischiefs. Burne Jones' King gazed up from his horse at the Beggar Maid. On the wall above the fireplace Rossetti's Proserpine endlessly contemplated the fatal pomegranate whose eaten seeds had condemned her to remain as Pluto's consort, Empress of Hades, while the incense burner which denoted her deity sent a light wisp of smoke into the foetid air. Ophelia floated down river, singing her requiem, surrounded by symbolic flowers; loosestrife, pansies, violets, roses. Chatterton lay upon his couch, his face turned from the light and his manuscripts scattered around the room, and there was a picture which I had never since rediscovered, 'The Silver Swan', which carried Orlando Gibbons' veiled commentary upon Mary, Queen of Scots:

> The Silver Swan that, living, had no note
> When Death approach'd unlok'd her silent throte
> Bending her breast against the reedy shore
> She spoke her first and last, and spake no more . . .

While the rest of the family listened to the well-modulated accents giving us, as the war progressed, (with the merest hint of propagandist bias), the news of the inexorable march towards victory of our brave forces, and my parents exchanged glances of adult understanding and relief, I looked at the pictures and saw a world of great issues, of courtly knights, fair maidens, and gallantry. All of which, despite all that had happened and the things I myself had done in envy, hatred, and darkness of spirit in the intervening years, had underpinned in some measure my views of everything: of Rachel most of all at this time, but also of the way in which others thought, and lived, and acted. As Jonathan used to say, I was seduced by pictures, by the images they concealed. I had never realised that true revelations often came in ugly clothing and without warning, and that beauty was no guarantee of anything beyond itself.

A week before leaving I sent Brian a card, giving my flight number and time of arrival, and asking him to arrange a room for me at his pensione. I hired a secretary with her own typewriter, and we sat awkwardly in the empty flat while I dictated a series of letters to her. I directed my brokers to remit dividends to Caroline, and my solicitors to draw up papers transferring the title in the house to her and instructed my bank about standing orders, the funding of Caroline's account, and the remittance of funds to me. I gave Walter permission to commit the sixty-odd canvases he still held to two further exhibitions, and informed him on the sending of statements and funds. She did the letters in silence over one day, and left to cool the coffee I had made her to go with her lunch-time sandwiches.

I checked the World Health Organisation recommendations, arranged to have injections against a variety of maladies, and carried out the remainder of my shopping in a feverish and slightly unreal state of mind. A tropical jacket and two pairs of light trousers from Simpsons, two safari shirts, two pairs of lightweight brown shoes, a straw hat, five pairs of aertex underpants, five pairs of light socks, ten moon-tiger mosquito coils, three packets of water-purifying tablets — and so on down the list I had prepared from my memories of previous trips abroad. As I packed I still hoped for some crisis to arise which would turn me aside from this flight so that I could shrug, and say to myself in later years, 'Well, if that hadn't happened . . .' with only the mild regret one has when bowing to the inevitability of fate.

I left on a morning in late May. The sky was dark and louring, as if a November day had accidentally misplaced itself. On the drive to the airport I had been far more aware than usual of the topography of my surroundings, glimpsed through the rain-spattered windows of the speeding car. I felt like a dying man, experiencing his familiar world for the last time, before being claimed by some desolate world of rocks, of sand, of unbearable newness.

I'd written to Caroline, detailing the arrangements I had made and saying that I would write in due course. I had posted the letter late in the evening the day before, guiltily franked with a second-class stamp to make doubly sure it would only be delivered after I had left.

The taxi driver broke in on my sombre thoughts.

'Holiday, guv?'

'Sort of.'

'Somewhere warm?'

'Egypt.'

He cleaned his ear with the tip of his little finger, shaking his head to clear it.

'I was in the desert,' he said, 'two years during the war. We used to take our leaves in Alex. Sometimes in Cairo. There used to be a marvellous place called Groppi's in Cairo.' He fell silent for a moment. 'Watch out for the salads. That's what gets you. They wash it in the Nile water . . .'

We turned off the motorway down to the tunnel. A Mercedes sped past, its wheels throwing a shower of water onto the screen, and the driver swore softly: 'Bloody foreigner.' It was 7.30.

The stewardess on the Egyptair baggage counter gave me a weary professional smile, her eyes moving beyond me as she mechanically recorded details on the tags and fixed them to the cases. As soon as I had checked in I went through Customs to the departure lounge and sat reading my paper over a coffee until the flight was called.

Some time after the plane had taken off and the seat belt light had gone out, I squeezed apologetically past my neighbour's knees and walked down to the toilet.

There, surrounded by a litter of wet paper towels on the floor, gagging from the smell of cheap perfume, and to the accompaniment of periodic rattling of the door as people tried to enter despite the 'Engaged' notice, I wept. I hoped Brian would be at Heliopolis to meet me in three hours' time. It felt, then, as if he were my only slender link with the past.

3

A November evening. Francis Thompson had a lot to answer for. Master in my own house, surrounded by the Gadarene herd my wife had assembled for dinner to advance my career, I sat like some Zoroastrian corpse atop his Tower of Silence watching my predatory guests devour vast mounds of the delicacies Caroline had prepared with such faultless ease.

The occasion was a party for me, nominally, at any rate. After fifteen years of reasonably well-paid hack portraiture I had received a series of grossly flattering reviews in the fashionable press for my fifth exhibition, three months before, in Charles Deterding's Montmartre Gallery. Since that time I seemed to have become a celebrity. Witticisms I never uttered were imputed to me in gossip columns; a picture of me in the midst of an orotund address (looking, by some trick of the camera, extremely drunk) seemed to have become the official photograph when no more apposite one was to hand, and was published with monotonous frequency; obscure and inaccurate biographical details appeared in the popular press, and I was pursued by a variety of journalists to give my views on a wide range of topics. None of the eager fresh-faced lads and lasses who turned up hopefully with their notebooks poised seemed to have any doubt that my comments on the Bomb, or abortion, or football violence could be anything other than well-informed and cogent.

I felt naked, like a hermit crab caught in the open without its shell. They had even got Caroline; she was doing a cookery column for one of the glossy women's journals. But she was entirely in her element, and looked upon all this as a positive bonus. So far the media had failed to track down my sister-in-law, Beth, the subject of most of the paintings in the exhibition — but that would undoubtedly come. It was the series of nudes of her that I had painted almost five years before which had caught the attention of the media.

This was a party to finalise as convivially as possible the details for another exhibition in three days' time. It had started well. My elder sister, Jean, and her husband Alan had come early, as was their custom. Alan, in business management, was, as always, a little ill-at-ease in our house; figures and the golf-club were more his métier, though I suspected he had a shrewd appreciation of the sudden increase in value of the five paintings I had given them. Jean threw her arms around me. Despite four children and the approach of matronly middle-age she was still childishly excited and affectionate.

'Darling, I knew you'd make it. We're delighted for you.'

'My clever brothers', was how Jean referred to Jonathan and me, and she basked in the reflected glory of our success. She swept off to the kitchen to talk to Caroline, and I asked Alan to fix the drinks. He looked relieved; here was a job he understood and which freed him for the moment from attempting to make artistic small talk. I doubt if he appreciated that his attempts were as awkward for the listener as for himself.

Jonathan and Beth arrived a few minutes later. I heard the Rolls crunch through the gravel on the drive and come to a stop, tucked in by the privet-hedge. Beth looked elegant in cream. Jonathan followed her to the front door. Their son, James, was being looked after by Beth's mother. Jonathan looked tired, and I remembered, with a stab of guilt, the dinner party we had both been to a few weeks ago. I knew enough about business to realise that he was in considerable trouble, from what he had shown me, but he seemed to have weathered many storms before. I hadn't given his problems much further thought, dismissing them from my mind as being of no real consequence.

He smiled at me and put his hand on my shoulder. 'Well,' he said with a wry smile, 'the reviews were certainly brilliant.'

I laughed. 'It's because all those horny old reviewers fancied the nudes of Beth,' I said lightly.

Miranda came rushing to the door. Jonathan spoiled her

outrageously, and she had pestered us all day to stay up because he was coming. He picked her up and gave her a big hug.

'So, how's *La Belle Dame Sans Merci* today?'

'What does that mean, Jonathan?'

'That you are going to grow into an ice-cold breaker of hearts. That men will throw themselves at your feet in droves. That —' he threw her towards the ceiling and caught her '— I shall be your Prospero and find you a wealthy Ferdinand with a Swiss bank account and a yacht and castles all round the world to fulfil your every wish . . .'

Miranda giggled delightedly. Beth looked at me and raised her eyebrows to heaven. Jonathan hid a good mind behind a display of buffoonery which often, in adult company, became embarrassing. He was capable of the most obscene comments, the most heartless witticisms, but for me, and I think for most people, his charm robbed the words of any offence.

Alan was spinning out the drinks performance, holding the glasses up to the light to gauge the measures. He greeted Jonathan and Beth a little warily. Jonathan had too often turned the savage, biting edge of his tongue on business and businessmen for Alan to feel entirely safe. He started to prepare scotches for Beth and Jonathan, while Miranda mock-wrestled with Jonathan's legs.

'I saw that report on your building plans in New York in the FT last week,' Alan said.

I glanced at Jonathan. His face had momentarily become closed, guarded, as he said, 'That report about me was about as accurate as the coverage for David's exhibition. Though at least they did have a good picture of me.'

I felt a little sorry for Alan, and an obscure feeling of hurt, as if Jonathan had diminished even the small achievement I felt I had secured. He smiled at Alan and took his drink. To me he said, 'Sorry, it's been a bad week, but I didn't mean to bring my problems here.'

I said, 'Have you managed to sort out that business with Mandeville yet?' Miranda almost pulled him over and he put his drink down on the glass-topped table to free his arms. He held her arms behind her back while she fought to get away.

'In a way, yes,' he said slowly, 'I have reached a decision about what needs to be done.' Something in his tone prompted me to look quickly at him. He seemed to be engrossed in his game with Miranda. The dogs came rushing in from the kitchen, shaking themselves to get rid of the rain on their coats.

During the evening I noticed Beth watching Jonathan anxiously. Once I intercepted a look between them as she talked to Caroline at one end of the lounge and he was in conversation with Charles and Lady Deterding. He raised his glass to her in a mock toast, smiling as if he hadn't a care in the world. But I could see she was not convinced, and that in the subtle signals which must have grown between them over the years, his brittle gaiety tonight was not a good sign. I knew that too, but I had known him all my life.

We didn't sit down to dinner until 9.30. Ingrid had taken Miranda, protesting volubly, off to bed an hour before. Caroline had asked me to delay people because the oven element hadn't been plugged in, so the dinner would be late. Though the hard-drinking crowd from the BBC arts department had only come for drinks, and left just before nine o'clock, I could hardly keep up with filling the glasses of the dinner guests.

By 10.30 Walter Jeffrey, my dealer and agent, was having a largely incoherent (but marvellously splenetic) argument with Charles Deterding, equally drunk and voluble, about Elias Cannetti's 'Crowds and Power'. Walter, in some tortuous argument which I could only catch in snatches, was drawing some parallels with Riesman's 'The Lonely Crowd'. Lady Deterding, I noted with jaundiced eye, had drunk a considerable amount of vintage claret, to judge by her rapidly closing eyes and her unconcern at the repeated clack of her top set which had probably retained some pieces of Caroline's splendid *boeuf-en-croûte* between the plate and her palate.

Jonathan and Beth, Jean and Alan were doing their sterling familiar best with the five others, (Walter was, pro tem, wifeless) whom I vaguely remembered as having attended one or other of the business parties prepared at metronomic three-monthly intervals by Caroline. They remembered my name and I nodded in their direction occasionally with a vacant and expansive grin, intended to convey simultaneously appreciation of their presence, and a mind preoccupied with lofty thoughts. Though I watched Jonathan from time to time he gave the impression of being at ease and, as the evening wore on I convinced myself that he must have sorted out his problems.

I felt oddly depressed. It seemed to me that my appreciation of our life had become subtly altered over the past months. In part it was a realisation that I was in the open now, without any shelter; but more than that there was a sense of spiritual desolation, that in the end all I had tried to do equated with these possessions which, now that they were part of our everyday lives, seemed to mean less and less to me.

In terms of pure mechanics the evening had gone well. Walter had managed to conclude an arrangement under which there would be a restrospective exhibition early the following year in London, followed by a transfer on to New York and then Chicago. The victory, so long sought, had been achieved. Curious that it should feel like a defeat, an annihilation of some part of me, as though I had been walking through a forest towards home, my mind full of expectations and excitement at what I would find there. Now that the terrors of the dark woods were behind me and I saw the house before me I was assailed by a sense of anti-climax — the terrors themselves had become the source of excitement and life. But, in practical terms, the evening had gone well.

Walter was entitled to his customary insensibility, and I had reached the first few tentative rungs of the ladder climbed before by the great Mark Rothko and my other idols. All based upon a bag of tricks, a sleight of hand I could no longer dignify to myself by any other name, a facility to reproduce time and time again in my canvases the emotional responses and sensations gleaned from the secret, wonderful, magical lantern slide of my childhood. That, at least, I had done without whimsy or condescension.

It was after twelve, and Jean looked at her watch and went to get her coat. Though the children were growing up, she and Alan were always the first to leave. Beth looked across at

Jonathan, who nodded, and they got up. It was a general signal for people to look at their watches and prepare to leave. I reminded Jean and Alan of their promise to come to the opening of the new exhibition in three days' time. Then they were gone.

Jonathan was helping Beth into her coat in the hall. I felt that there was some tension between them, but nothing that I could readily grasp. Beth kissed me and said, 'We must go now. Jonathan's got a lot on his plate and he's very tired.' I nodded.

Behind me Jonathan said, 'You're a big girl now, Beth. Why can't you just say you want to leave instead of making me the scapegoat? I was rather enjoying myself.'

Beth flushed, but said nothing. I felt awkward, as if I had intruded into a private dispute. Jonathan put his arm around my shoulder. I realised with a sense of shock that he was rather drunk.

'Well, little brother,' he said, 'if I believed the papers I would be looking at you as the glass of fashion and the mould of form.' He laughed unpleasantly and went on, 'Personally I wish somebody would pay me to push my faeces round on canvas . . .' He swayed in front of me, mock punching me on the shoulder. 'Isn't that how the good doctor from Vienna describes your activities?'

Beth caught him by the arm and together we took him to the car. She got into the driving seat and put the window down.

'I'm sorry,' she said with a lift of her shoulders.

'It's all right,' I said. 'Hope he feels better in the morning.'

The car started off as I walked back into the house. I felt angry and hurt, but somehow triumphant too, as if I had made some independent mark of my own for the first time.

The others were leaving now as well. It was cold in the porch as we saw them off.

'Goodnight. See you on Thursday.'

'Mind the step. Isn't it freezing. Drive carefully.'

'Goodnight.'

'Goodnight.'

Already the grass was like shards of steel in sugar and the iron ring of Walter's heels echoed as he stumbled towards the car. Charles Deterding combed his few remaining hairs as he walked behind Anne to their car. I wondered briefly if they still made love; that gesture was for no-one else. Her ravaged, voluptuary's face was illuminated by the torch she held for a moment as she searched for her key. Charles touched her hair with a gesture of genuine affection. Down the black dog of cynicism. The moon had a halo, and the stars were brilliant.

Caroline closed the door, her smile fading as the departing cars boomed and disappeared one after the other down the drive. She leaned in an exaggerated rag-doll posture — eyes turned to heaven — for a moment before gathering herself to face the devastation. I remembered, O curse it, that Mrs Haddon had gone to bed. Caroline still had a residual puritanism about taking on the staff we could now afford. We would have to plough through the wreckage ourselves or leave it congealing for the morning. As I watched Caroline's determined bustle I picked up the message, wordlessly, that we would, indeed, be doing it tonight.

As I loaded the dishwasher, bending my knees to keep my back straight, she said, 'I wonder what Walter meant . . .'

'Why? What did he say?'

She frowned, wrinkled her forehead in an effort to remember the words. 'He said that now you had beaten Jonathan you only had to beat yourself to be really successful.' She looked quizzically at me. She didn't like Walter, in part because she sensed some meaning inaccessible to her in his gnomic comments.

'You obviously caught the few coherent words he uttered tonight. This — and I picked up the half-empty brandy bottle, '— was full two hours ago and no-one else drank brandy.'

But she persisted. 'You weren't listening, but he addressed the remark to you. He was leering in that knowing way of his. Why can't the man speak in plain English instead of turning everything into some sort of mystery?'

'I don't know. Are we going to do all this tonight?'

We certainly were. Her anger towards Walter had given her access to a fresh fund of energy. I did know what Walter meant, and I was surprised at the sharpness of his perception. In some atavistic and instinctive way Walter ignored the ebb and flow of the surface, but knew the movement of the dark tides beneath; the lies, evasions and deceits which moved within and far, far below the polite dinner-table conversations and salon dealings. That instinct had brought him wealth, and brought him enemies. It had, too, brought me to him, still, after many years, a friend, despite his exaggerated percentages, the deliberate bad manners, the swaggering rodomontade.

I knew, too, that in that rich earth a richer dust lay concealed. Walter had changed his surname to Jeffrey, perhaps to escape the past. His father, Arnold Weinberg, had died in Auschwitz and his mother, Sophie, saved for some years by Oscar Schindler had, ironically, died some two years after the war of pneumonia aggravated by incipient silicosis. A year before my present success I had gone with Walter on a tour which I hoped would free me from the artistic rut in which I then felt myself. This had been two years before my successful exhibition.

As we left Heathrow behind us, Walter began to lose the bullying braggadocio he used in the office. Several evenings later we sat in a small bar in the Wola district of Warsaw. Lech Walesa had been imprisoned or spirited away, Glemp had given an ambivalent sermon, and we had seen, all day, the drably dressed, dispirited queues standing patiently outside dingy shops with no apparent merchandise to sell. I felt depressed and helpless as the rosy light died on the façade opposite. The sheer enormity of the problem, and my own inability to help in the face of it, made me begin to question my life and the things I took for granted. It was an unease compounded by a realisation that the certainties expressed by the English press and media were not valid here. That these people, standing in the rain to purchase some commodity they might or might not get, were denied the things which I took for granted as basic essentials.

I felt, too, the sensation that we in England could never really appreciate such deprivation, and my sense of exclusion from some vast area of suffering was further compounded by the sudden realisation that Walter knew how those people felt, and shared with them a heritage much deeper than he and I shared together in the fashionable capitals of London and New York.

Before the trip I had felt, if the truth be known, some slight contempt for what I saw as the superficiality of Walter's life. I had felt that I had suffered, both in my life and in my art, and that Walter, despite the experiences of his parents, danced above the surface of life like some insect hovering over the shallows. As the trip wore on I began to realise, both with a sense of self-disgust and a rising sense of panic, that I was the water-boatman, condemned to dance in the eddying wind above the river. It was an uncomfortable and persistent insight which has never entirely left me since. Like a tongue exploring an abscessed tooth, I returned again and again to the discomfort. More and more, during the course of those two weeks, I realised that Walter had embraced his past whilst I had thrown mine away; that he was the richer for what he had done, and I the poorer for what I had done.

The trip was now almost at an end. As I sat there with Walter he seemed, in his unaccustomed silence, to have become part of the alien city, which made me feel uneasy. After we had been there for perhaps an hour, a young man came towards the table and shook Walter by the hand. To my surprise they began to talk together in Polish. After a few moments' conversation, Walter took the hotel room key from his pocket and gave it to the youth. They shook hands and the young man walked away, the dusk swallowing his figure. Walter told me he was the son of an old friend of Sophie. Both mothers had worked together in the ceramics factory, and then in the ersatz munitions factory which had never produced any munitions. She was now ill, and he had brought some things for Pavel to take to her. It was safer that we did not go to her house. I saw that he was profoundly moved. He said, very quietly, 'That she should die like this, and I could do nothing.'

We talked late into the night. I felt then that it was the most honest sight I have ever had of another man's soul, laid bare without any hint of embarrassment or evasion, and I like to think that my response was in kind. Since that time I had been unaffected by the rough manners, the studied aggressiveness. They seemed to me in part an attempt to steal back, to demean, the seriousness of that evening. To me the comment he had made to Caroline seemed a reminder of what we had shared. I knew what he meant and, remembering Jonathan's outburst and my own feeling of triumph, I had an uncomfortable feeling that he might be right.

Mrs Haddon would be happy the next day. Caroline's method was to employ a housekeeper for whom we did all the work. If I ever pressed her with the absurdity of this arrangement she would become quite angry; if we didn't treat these people right they would leave us. It was the same with our gardener. He would take his heart pills while I sawed the branches off the alder tree. '*Arbeit Macht Frei*' read the legend over the gate to Auschwitz — Work Will Make You Free.' In a different sense it did, it did. My work in the studio, our constant battles with the house to keep rain and decay at bay, my ever-growing need for constant movement were my excuses, and my sacrifices to the fear that if I stopped I would begin to think. If I began to think I might begin to feel uncomfortable. And, worst of all, I might begin to piece together the veiled hints and comments I had heard. Then I might not like the finished picture.

The dogs were curled asleep in their baskets, grunting and snuffling as they dreamed. Upstairs, Miranda cried out in her sleep, but did not wake. The birds began to sing with growing confidence as we ascended the stairs to bed. At least it was a day of rest tomorrow.

4

It was 1946. Jonathan was eleven, two years older than I, and James was one year younger. Jean, six years my senior, was already immersed in the remoteness and mystery of early adolescence by the time I was being initiated into the differences between boys and girls in the dark recesses of the gardener's shed by Lilee, daughter of our near neighbour, Mr Bulant Singh, who taught physics to the sixth-formers at our school. Over those few weeks my pants had gone up and down like a yo-yo and, although the invitations to feel and touch produced some mild sensations of pleasure, I had become a little bored and mildly surprised by the obsessiveness of the game when Jonathan unexpectedly came in upon us one day. I was surprised and frightened by his violent reaction. He had shouted at Lilee, using words which I did not understand at the time, though the anger behind them was very plain. When she had gone, shaken and crying, he had taken me by the shoulders and made me promise not to play that game again: 'It's very dirty,' he kept repeating. Bewildered and perplexed, I had agreed.

Jean was slender and fair, peremptory with the servants, given to romantic fantasies about any visiting man under thirty, and a precociously avid reader of grown-up novels. Partly, I suppose, because the fashions in the colonial backwaters of India lagged some twenty years behind England, she grew up on a diet of attitudes, both in terms of moral precepts and behaviour which — if social historians are to be believed — prevailed in the England of the Twenties. Everything was judged by her, and by my parents, in terms of moral values; good or bad, worthwhile or worthless, right or wrong. There was no room for shades of colour or nuances of meaning. Everything was absolute.

Jean was so far beyond my understanding that I classified her as grown-up, and therefore an unknowable example of an alien species. As with them, so with her I lived in fear of her displeasure, and propitiated her whenever it seemed possible to do so. She frightened me with tales of witches and goblins, and once left me in the forest, deriving, as she later confessed, a sense of power from my terrified howls. But I suppose there are things for which to thank her. When I was three I read laboriously aloud. After her mocking comments, I painstakingly taught myself to read silently. As we grew older the years seemed to deal more kindly with us, and the balances and emphases changed between us. That is, they did for me but I cannot speak for her now. Certainly she forgot those childhood cruelties, and, when she did remember, adorned them with uncertain laughter robbing them of their true reality. The caricature disguises and distorts the true features of experience, and perhaps that is as well. By such devices we can attain a tolerable equilibrium.

Why Jonathan and I drew so much together in those early years is still obscure. In part, I suppose, it was because we each recognised in James some threat to our own positions within the family. Even then, Jonathan showed an unevenness of temperament which defied any attempt at categorising him as this sort of person or that. He was, at times, capable of seemingly dispassionate cruelty, at others of generosity beyond my understanding. I came upon him in the garden once, holding the head of a harmless grass snake under a forked stick. He called me over to look at it, both of us squatting in a dusty patch of mud amid the burnt grasses of summer. We were both soaked in sweat and dirt-streaked. Jonathan, burnt umber with straight black hair, myself mouse, freckled and much smaller. We both watched, fascinated. The scales under the rough bark of the fork had begun to slough as the snake wriggled to free itself. The basilisk eyes stared balefully. The tongue slithered nervously in and out. Jonathan took his bowie-knife from the sheath at his belt. I felt sick, unable to turn my eyes away or speak. With an intent, serious look, he pulled the blade hard across the body, just behind the head. The body writhed in what I thought must be agony.

Jonathan pointed to the severed head. 'That's still alive,' he said. 'The brain synthesises oxygen in a different way for about four minutes before brain death occurs.'

That was grown-up talk; I couldn't understand it. But I knew something which had just been alive was dead, and for no reason that I could see.

'Why did you do it?' I said. He laughed.

'You are a softie,' he said. 'It can't feel anything any more. That's just reflex action.' He pointed to the body which thrashed its coruscating coils in the dust. In a mock serious voice he said, 'Don't you remember that the serpent ruined us all?' He kicked the body aside indifferently. The red ants had already begun to gather. Jonathan cleaned the knife on some grass, then plunged it into the red earth two or three times. He got up, putting it back into the scabbard at his belt. It was over for him, if not for me.

The summer of that year in which I reached my ninth birthday was perfect. The snows had been heavy at the beginning of the year, and the chowkidar who guarded our estate said that it would be a very hot summer. Our small house nestled in a forest clearing on the side of a foothill in the Himalayan range. Across a vast valley the mountains stood clear against the sky, eternally snow-capped, and fissured with violet shadows. Day after perfect day the sun glowed from a clear, blue sky. Father travelled a lot, as a lawyer seconded to the ICS to administer a large area, and to instruct the Indian magistrates in the execution of their duties. Mother often went with him, one car taking them and the second following behind with the heavy, initialled leather trunks. The smell of mothballs pervaded the house for days after the trunks had been packed. When they were at home they often went to bridge evenings with friends, or to tennis parties, or to dances in the hill town of Hasooth Gali, perched atop the massive escarpment over the valley three thousand feet above and six miles away from our little colonial enclave. Veroo of the soft eyes, our adoring ayah, looked after us at such times. She was childless, and treated us almost as if we were her own children. Jonathan took advantage of her shamelessly, and I followed his lead, sheltering behind the dispensation he received. Eight-year-old James was a model of good behaviour. His favourite picture, Reynolds' 'The Cherub Choir', hung above his bed, and his odious near-divinity seemed to us confirmed both by his looks and by the treatment accorded him by our parents. I would not have known what the odour of sanctity was then, but in later years the phrase has always recalled James to me. He knew infallibly what adults expected of him, and furthermore, did it. Jonathan and I stood, like dirty urchins with noses pressed to the window pane, permanently envious, amazed, and separated by a vast gulf from such unreachable virtue. But even this constant source of irritation seemed less painful, that summer when I was nine.

If I could choose one year when, to me, the world was full of unspoilt promise, when anything could happen, then that would be my year. It was not that anything spectacularly different or dramatic occurred: possibly in retrospect I hearken back because nothing had happened then to disturb the fragile certainties of childhood. That summer was my summer; the sky bluer, the sun warmer, the gentians more profuse than ever before or since. But when I look at it now, I do know, through hindsight and experience, that the memory of that time is falsely enhanced and enriched by it being the last summer of innocence, before the stains of age and the growing darkness of living began to supercede and dull those clear and brilliant primary colours. I side with the Manichees.

One day remains particularly in my mind, reminding me in its precise recollections, of the general, unburdened happiness of that time.

It was a Saturday morning in early June. Father had hired a large car, complete with syce, for the morning. That in itself, was a treat, and the fact that we were going on a mystery tour was another. Mother and father sat in front with the syce, and we four crowded into the back. At first we listened solemnly to the snatches of adult conversation we could hear above the noise of the engine and the wind whistling past, almost afraid of this unaccustomed closeness to our parents.

Father said, 'The talk is that Mountbatten is using two cartographers who have never been to India before to draw up the divisions. How it will work in practice, nobody knows. But I think there will be bloodshed . . .'

It was 1946 and my parents were often serious when they talked together now. But to us it seemed that they both knew and could control everything, so we were safe. They were too engrossed in their adult conversation to notice us, and their voices, and the meaning of what they were saying, receded into the distance, whipped away by the exhilarating movement of the car. The road wandered past patient black buffaloes with long, backward-curving horns, standing knee-deep in stagnant water. The sun glittered on the wet surface of the fields. Suddenly we came to a clear run of white road running straight down between two fields, the green of the fields sharply demarcated from the mauve range of hills and the blue sky running like macramé across the horizon, and fading to the white-blue of the curving skyline. For the minutes it took the indifferent car to cover the white road to the hill far, far ahead, it seemed to me in my exalted state that this must be as close to heaven as would ever be permitted upon earth. When it was past, and my exultation had faded a little, I was surprised to find Jonathan apparently unaffected by the experience. As for the others, I knew they would never have seen it.

That afternoon, when we returned from the drive, Father announced that he had arranged a picnic. In a life of strictly measured treats this was a hard-to-believe richness. For me, our seasonal returns to the same clearing in the forest, our ritual and entirely unnecessary collection of pine-cones for winter fires, and the fishing for tadpoles were, from year to year, the promise of continuity and security fulfilled. The pine-cones we would gather into mounds which the servants would then store in gunny sacks to make the resinous blazes of Christmas. Too often the tadpoles would fry in their jam-jars on the porch, when our games, or the alternative interests supplied by snails or stag-beetles, took our minds from them. We would remember them weeks later, only to find them stuck to the algae-infested green sides of their glass homes, but the guilt was only momentary. That afternoon we had it all. Two married couples, friends of my parents, and their children; two bachelors who lectured at the local college, and our family. Behind us as we walked through the forest to the familiar clearings — seven children and eight adults — came the servants in starched white uniforms with green trimmings. They carried the picnic baskets: plates, embossed linen, cutlery, cups, glasses, thermos flasks, scones, sandwiches, cakes. At the end of the line the chokra carried the wind-up HMV gramophone with a collection of often-played 78 records: 'The Holy City' and 'Jerusalem' sung by Richard Dawson; 'Hark, Hark the Lark' and 'Who is Sylvia?' sung by Ernest Lough; 'The Ash Grove', 'Kathleen Mavourneen', 'The Cobbler's Song', 'The Mountains of Mourne', 'My Rosary', 'A Perfect Day' — enough to add nostalgic music to the sounds of the forest all that carefree afternoon, the distant songs filtering through the woods to us as we ran with our two cocker spaniels, and waded in the cold swift-running stream.

I remember that day as a series of pictures, through the eyes of the painter I have become. The feelings of contentment, the sense of permanency in the wildness about us, and the scenes, now sepia in my mind and beginning to show the muted and discoloured tones of age, of the picnic table. In a wider sense I suppose that such feelings stemmed from the powerful visions of our colonial predecessors, their absolute belief in the moral rightness of the British presence in India, the security and the ownership conferred upon us all by our indissoluble, if tenuous, link with the King-Emperor, all conspiring to confirm us in our feelings of well-being. It was as well we had such a day, and, in lesser degree, many more to follow during that summer. For things were happening in the country, and even less predictably, in our personal family life, which would put these days forever beyond my reach, except as a tormenting memory of paradise lost beyond regain.

As I settled into bed that night I had to share the happiness I felt, but couldn't find the words to express, with Jonathan. I said, 'That was the best day I ever had. Better than anything.'

There was a long silence in the darkened room. I could just make out Jonathan, lying in bed with his hands behind his head, staring at the ceiling. Then he spoke: 'It was a nice day. I wish it could always be like that.'

Something in his tone made me feel uncertain. Though I did not want to change the feeling of the day by admitting any hint of the premonitions his tone of voice made me feel, I couldn't help a note of anxiety entering into my voice.

'It will always be like this, won't it, Jonathan?'

'I don't know,' he said. 'I don't know. Go to sleep.'

'Goodnight.'

'Goodnight.'

But I knew that he, too, was lying awake in the dark; some tremor or vibration, some feeling that happiness must be paid for in pain, beset both of us. Though it could not outweigh the things of that day, it remained — a small, gnawing, unidentifiable unease, and it was a long time before I slept.

5

Three days after the dinner party, on a stormy November evening, I went to my own exhibition. It was a strange sensation.

Major Mordaunt wrote one memorable verse. I remember my father in tears at a party where a blond youth in a Fauntleroy suit declaimed Sir Henry Newbolt's *Vitae Lampada*, and I remember his readings to us as children from *Le Morte d'Arthur*, *Idylls of the King*, and *Sohrab and Rustum*. But on the evening of the exhibition when — for a few hours — I wandered around in a dazed condition listening in near delirious delight to the hyperbolic conversations of the viewers at the private showing, it had to be Mordaunt. Perhaps, given his lowly place within the serried ranks of great departed poets, this bore some symbolic relationship to my achievements.

> Sound, sound the clarion, fill the fife
> To all the sensual world proclaim
> One crowded hour of glorious life
> Is worth an age without a name.

That was how it felt at first. It had been a fantastic evening. Ten years before I would have spent the next week going over in my mind the details of each sycophantic conversation. Even the slightly sour congratulations of one of the more senior academicians present had only served to underline the fact that I had arrived. I took a glass of champagne from the tray proffered by the betailed waiter, and sallied self-importantly into the room.

Walter came up with a slight frown, looking at his watch,

but I forestalled him. 'I'm here now, who do I have to meet?'

I was led across to the Royal party where the lady in question was surrounded by three ladies-in-waiting and an immaculately dressed gentleman with patent-leather hair. Standing in front of a rather pudendic view of Beth while we engaged in hesitant small talk, I felt a little embarrassed, as if a total stranger had walked into a lavatory where I was engaged in evacuating my bowels. After that was over I was taken around to meet a number of lesser dignitaries. I still had to maintain my air of polite interest, but at least I could feel that a burp, or cough, or fart would not condemn me to immortal displeasure.

I've always had a penchant for low life. Arthur, the caretaker, sidled up to me and whispered out of the side of his mouth:

'Bloody 'ell, Mr David, you artists have a rare old time. All those naked ladies, and getting paid for it. I've never seen the missis like that!' — and gave me a sly wink and a nudge in the ribs.

'You've got it all wrong, Arthur. We painters are like doctors. If we weren't, we'd die of sexual exhaustion before finishing a picture.'

Arthur had known me twenty years, and I had become used to his views.

'You trying to tell me that you didn't fancy her, then?' he said. 'Pull the other one.'

He moved off to galvanise into action the two waiters lounging in conversation by the table.

'Christ,' said a voice at my elbow, and I turned round to find a familiar face from Cambridge. I couldn't remember his name, as he pumped my arm furiously up and down.

'Miles Sinclair,' he said, 'you remember . . . the little spotty one who planned to be a great novelist . . .'

I remembered. We had all planned to be a great something or other in those heady days; and it had all seemed possible. I remembered that he now wrote up exhibitions for one of the national newspapers. Very floridly and without much perception. He had evidently learnt something of an exhibition-side manner, though, as he deftly took me by the elbow and steered me towards the refreshment table, where he put two canapés in his mouth and picked one up as a reserve.

'You know,' he said with his mouth full, 'I've always thought there must be little more gratifyingly self-indulgent than walking around a gallery covered in your paintings, virtually all adorned with a red sticker, with a glass of champagne in your hand — listening to the tones of awe, admiration and envy . . .' He trailed off on a questioning note and I felt obliged to reply.

'I'd be very green indeed to take people's comments at their face value.'

He nodded briskly. 'Still,' he said with a trace of wistfulness in his voice, 'whatever people might say behind your back, they can't take it away from you.'

I had few illusions about Sinclair. His reviews invariably had an overblown Swiftian acidulousness, the overkill of the impotent man.

I saw Mark Oldroyd's slight figure across the room and made my excuses to Sinclair. Possibly a mistake to leave him, I thought, as he indicated for me to go ahead with a wave of his hand, his mouth full of yet another wodge of canapés. I was really delighted to see Mark. He didn't much care for these functions normally, but we had been friends for twenty years, since the occasion I had interviewed him for *Granta*. He was, according to prevalent gossip, terminally ill, and as I got closer to him I realised with a shock that the flesh seemed to have fallen away and that his skin had an unhealthy, greyish pallor. He shook my hand and looked steadily at me.

'I'm glad to see you,' he smiled wryly. 'I see that Walter has catered for the fleshpots, as usual.'

I said, 'How are you, Mark?'

My face must have indicated the concern I could not hide. For a moment he looked round at the noisy assembly. Caroline was talking to the Royal party. Charles Deterding hovered in attendance, his arms clasped behind his back and his feet moving slightly like a ballet dancer remembering his steps. Walter, wearing a vulgar tie in green and yellow patterns which contrasted oddly with his sober, pin striped suit, was conducting a couple of earnest Austrians on a detailed tour of the pictures. God knows what he was telling them, but it must have made sense for they nodded ceaselessly.

'I'm dying. I didn't believe the doctors when they gave me only a couple of months ten years ago. I was right then. But — he gestured against the proffered tray — 'this time I know that the end is coming though they tell me I will recover. One realises how little they know . . .'

It was hard to think of anything to say. If I were as honest as Mark I could have accepted the statement, but some social habit, the inability to cope with anything truly serious, without evasion, had grown upon me since I had left Cambridge.

Then he said, 'David, I don't know why you are giving in . . . doing this sort of thing. You are capable of something really good, but this is trivial.' He saw my involuntary flinch and said, quickly, 'I'm sorry. When one doesn't have much time left one develops a morbid belief in the validity of one's observations, as if impending death confers some absolute insight.' He laughed harshly, clearing his throat.

I said defensively, 'I was surprised when these attracted so much attention. I had really only done them years ago as an exercise in technique. But then Walter saw them and persuaded me that they would form a unified theme for an exhibition . . .'

Mark listened, pondered a moment and then said, 'I know how seductive this kind of success can be. You have the talent and insight to do something really remarkable. But your biggest problem is still your need to comply with other people's wishes, isn't it?' Without waiting for my response, he went on, 'By the way, is Jonathan here?'

It was not as disconnected a sequence as it might have seemed to an outside observer. Mark knew, as I did, the extent of my psychic subordination to Jonathan. There was no sign of Jonathan or Beth yet, but his business meetings often went on far into the evening. We would probably end up eating with them later in the evening.

I was glad that Mark Oldroyd was there, though there was no longer the warm and comforting feeling that I would see him again and again. When I had first visited him in Cambridge he was, arguably, the most eminent and copied artist in Europe. I had gone, full of my Berenson and Kenneth Clark, anticipating the sort of exchanges I had come to associate with Cambridge intelligentsia, where it behoved one to know one's references and to be able to develop a coherent counter-argument off the top of one's head. After a few minutes I had discarded all those preconceptions in the face of a man who seemed to live a life of amazing simplicity and directness. I had spent an entranced afternoon with him at his house on the outskirts of Cambridge, past Girton on the Huntingdon Road. It was the first time I had met a real painter who had lived amongst painters and saw them as people with a working life which was as natural as that of an accountant or a solicitor. The house was filled with paintings by his friends. Two beautiful Jack Yeats portraits hung on either side of the hall fireplace. A small Modigliani of a woman in a red dress hung in a niche in the study, it had been given to him by an English girl who had been with the painter in the weeks preceding his suicide. There were early Augustus Johns, Gwen Johns, a Kandinsky, Gebler, even some Picassos. Sculptures by Giacommetti, Lyn Chadwick and David Butler stood on white plinths around the pine-floored rooms. His reminiscences had none of the studied, bookish flavour I had come to associate with artistic biographies. Without attempting to confer meaning upon his observations he made them live.

We talked for some time, and I was reluctant to move away from him. Finally he said, 'You mustn't neglect your duties,' and (with a conspiratorial smile) pushed me towards a group who had been eyeing me for some time.

As I talked to the little group, whose names I had forgotten as soon as I had been introduced, I looked around for Jonathan. Jean waved from the corner where she and Alan were painstakingly doing the rounds of the pictures, catalogue in hand. Alan looked worried, like a doctor unwillingly ensconced in a party of avid smokers. I waved back, and they resumed their earnest scrutiny.

It seemed that Jonathan had not come to see the triumph confirmed. I had never known what he would do when faced with any particular set of circumstances. With most people I had found that there was — quite quickly — a discernible pattern in their behaviour, the ability to mentate models of how they might behave, within limits, in any given situation. But not Jonathan. His absence was in part a relief, and in part a disappointment, not unmixed with anxiety. I had wanted to impress him, wanted him to appreciate the flattery and adulation of the evening, but had sensed, too, that he would find some way to destroy my feelings of achievement. Since childhood that capacity he possessed had remained a constant in our changing relationship, and I knew that those darknesses which existed within me were products, in part, of his devising, and that he always knew where they might be found within me.

Sinclair brought a tall, very beautiful girl over to meet me. I suspected that he was trying to entice her back to his flat, and that I was expected, in some spirit of solidarity with an old university acquaintance, to play my part in the scenario of his evening; by professing close friendship and hinting at good times together in the past, so that she would hang rapt on my every word and fail to see how often he signalled the waiter to fill her glass. I thought she was rather fanciable myself, felt sorry for her, and treated him like a stranger. It gave me some pleasure, though I knew it would have repercussions.

I introduced Jean and Alan to Mark Oldroyd and was surprised to find how easily they got on together. I had introduced Jonathan to Mark in Cambridge many years ago. It was a sort of pride — I could bask in the warm glow of Mark's approval of Jonathan, and derive some spurious stature in Jonathan's eyes by the association. I was still at King's and Jonathan had come up to Trinity for a reunion of some kind. It was the morning after his dinner and he was plainly the worse for wear. I had felt a slightly disloyal unease that Jonathan's muttered responses might not impress Mark (I was very young, evidently) but, once we had arrived, he had risen to the occasion with that same effortless charm and genuine interest which had always, for me, far outweighed the black moods. But they had not taken to each other, or that was what I inferred from the oblique comments each had subsequently ventured upon the occasion. Mark had said, drily, 'I think you should warn him against spending too much time with Willey. All that ridiculous cloak and dagger stuff . . .' Again, I had ignored the innuendo.

Charles Deterding came up to me, smiling widely. I liked Charles.

'Amazing,' he said, 'simply amazing. We've sold everything. I'll talk to Walter about the next show as soon as possible.'

I'd often wondered why Charles was in the art gallery game. He had no real appreciation of painting, and the thirty-six thousand acres in Ayrshire his agent controlled for him, plus the majority shareholding left to him in a chain of international hotels, amply provided him with the means for a lifestyle in which three stately homes and an extremely healthy collection of nineteenth-century water colours seemed not to have noticeably depleted his resources. Perhaps the very fecklessness and improvidence of the artists whose work he showed gave him a secondhand appreciation of the desperation, the hunger for recognition, of those he sponsored so generously. And in some small measure the warm approval of the evening washed over him. He was so enthusiastic, so flushed with pleasure, that I felt like hugging him.

Instead, I said, 'I owe you and Anne an enormous amount. I couldn't have achieved any of this without you.' He reddened immediately, but I could see he was touched.

'Nonsense, old man. You're the one with the talent. I only exist to show you off . . .'

There was nothing more to be said. I suddenly felt tired.

Caroline was talking to Walter in a corner. I squeezed Charles' arm and moved on. Suddenly I saw Beth standing by the door. She was very pale and seemed bewildered, distressed.

There have been a few moments in my life when I have felt that something so monstrous, so cataclysmic is about to happen I know nothing will ever be the same. Something in Beth's stance, in the way she was looking with expressionless eyes at some inner scene which no one else could see, as the party moved indifferently about her, overwhelmed me with an impression that some pattern, uncoiling according to its own laws within me, had been abruptly broken. Even as I moved towards her — in those few steps — a number of selfish first thoughts had taken hold, to be instantly replaced by even wilder fantasies. Later I was to remember those instinctive thoughts, summoned beyond recall, with guilt and self-hatred. Only, as some measure of recompense, I can recall that the pleasure of the occasion was instantly cast aside. In those moments I felt the punitive threat of death offered to me; for it seemed that whatever was to come must, in some obscure yet validly causal way, be my fault.

I stood in front of her, both of us wordless. Her regular prettiness had quite gone and her face was distorted — whether with grief or anguish, the distinction was too fine for me. She leaned towards me and was violently sick down the front of my clothes. In between the bouts of retching, and before she fainted, she merely said, 'He didn't have the right, he didn't have the right.' She seemed very angry.

It would have helped, later, when the overwhelming horror was past, if one could have found comfort and refuge in the echoes and resonances of some old and comforting myth. If one could have felt the slow, sad music of humanity, or could have seen the shape and the cadence of what had happened repeated in some organised and understandable form. The eagle's gift in Rome which had told halt-footed, stammering Claudius that he would be Caesar. The proof, as in finding a watch on some remote walk and being certain that it was manufactured for a purpose, that there is a design and balance in the dazzling diversity of human activities. But at the time there was nothing, and the rooms of Jonathan's house gave nothing back. It was all in pieces, all coherence gone.

6

1945. On his tenth birthday father had given Jonathan an air gun. As we came down to breakfast that morning there was the usual slightly envious excitement. I guessed immediately from the shape of the package that stood by Jonathan's chair what the present was, and felt a momentary jealousy. Jonathan was speechless. He held the package for a long moment, looking at it with almost disbelieving eyes, and then at the rest of us. He looked as if he might cry.

'Go on, open it,' my father said. It was the best present he could have had.

After breakfast we went out into the garden, and Jonathan let me hold the gun for a few moments. It had a polished teak stock, a break action loading, and the waisted lead slugs were fed into a tube which unscrewed from the muzzle. It even had a ring calibrator and wind adjustment lever on the back sight. He took it back from me after a few seconds, as if he thought I might break it, and again I felt a twinge of jealousy. We took the cardboard targets which had come with the rifle to the flat ground in front of the training college. I put a target on the wire holder and set it into the earth. Jonathan threw himself face down on the ground some ten yards away, the line of his right leg carrying through the line of the rifle. Veroo and her husband, Kajan, came to watch. Kajan smiled approvingly, but Veroo screwed up her face and put her hands over her ears each time the compressed air popped out of the barrel with the noise of a bursting paper bag. After an hour I was the only faithful spectator left, but the targets now had slug marks in fine central groupings a couple of inches in diameter. I had been allowed two attempts but both had gone well wide. The mechanics of the front and back sight eluded me completely. Then even father came up to watch, grey-suited and carrying his light malacca walking stick. He had brought two used light bulbs with him which I propped with stones so that they stood proud. Jonathan fired and the first one shattered with a loud, popping sound. Father shot the second one.

For a week Jonathan took that rifle everywhere with him. At night it would stand by his bed, and sometimes he would reach out to stroke it, as if it were some living creature which responded to his touch. Then, one morning, when we went out to the midan in front of the training college again to shoot at targets, father came up the steep path. I couldn't believe my eyes. He was elegantly dressed, as usual, in a grey pin-striped suit, but was carrying two potatoes in one hand and a carrot in the other. Jonathan sensed what was to come more quickly than I did, and his face took on a dark brooding aspect. Father asked for the gun and, withdrawing the muzzle-tube, plunged it into a potato before screwing it back in and cocking the gun. He fired it at the baked brick wall nearby, and a fine spray of disintegrating potato made a mark some two inches wide.

'You see,' he said, 'it works just as well with this. Take a shot at my hand.'

There was obedient resignation in Jonathan's whole posture as he loaded the gun again and screwed in the muzzle full of potato. He took careful aim and fired, his arm jerking slightly upwards as he did so. Father staggered back, holding his right cheek. I rushed forward, but he put a reassuring hand on my shoulder.

'It's all right,' he said, 'I would really have been hurt badly if that had been a slug.'

I couldn't understand how Jonathan had missed father's hand. Jonathan apologised without looking at father. We picked up the targets and all walked together in silence back to the house. To my knowledge, he never used the gun again. It lay in a corner of the verandah until mother gave it to the children of one of the servants. Jonathan never seemed to notice that it had gone.

7

I could not sleep the second night. Jonathan's death, and the manner of it, had brought the channering worm ever closer. It is curious how death affects one with visions of one's own mortality. Even without this I had felt, and more and more of late, the slowing of the blood, the wasting of the sinew, the slow attrition of middle-age. It happened mostly at night, when Caroline's regular untroubled breathing, the slurred tick of the electric alarm, and the settling creaking of the cooling house produced a trance-like state. The little death of sleep. I regretted the cigarettes, and even the modest amount of claret I had drunk, and made magic and childlike bargains with my Maker, if there is a Maker. But even I, capable always of the most extravagant self-deceits, realised briefly that the validity of such bargains erodes with time, that out there, in the unfriendly darkness, my appointment could not forever be delayed.

Caroline groaned, and threw her arms above her head. I used to tell her she slept like a chimpanzee, but at such moments she entered my heart in a way which her tight and brittle control prevented in consciousness, returning me briefly to the memories of her little flat in Kensington, before the slow beast which had brought us to this place had bestirred its torpid limbs. She slept a sleep full of small noises, grunts of alarm or pleasure, occasional mutters. I envied it, recognising that I was condemned to a sleepless night — part worrying about the arrangements, the funeral baked meats, the niceties — part harrowing through the past like a treasure hunter, seeking amidst the siftings some small objects which might restore my unstable equilibrium.

It was impossible to face what had happened directly. Though I had already begun to reach into the past, to draw the connections out of their hiding places, like tendons from the flaccid limbs of a Christmas turkey, I could not bear to think of what had happened. It still had the uncertain texture, the mad illogicality of a nightmare, and it seemed as if I must have some power to reverse it, to return our lives to the way in which they were before; if only I could find the key. The only valencies I could ascribe to those early years, the only conclusions they could lead me to, were those that I had drawn myself whose force had led me down the roads I had followed. It seemed to me that what happens to us is what we most desire; or that was how it had seemed before.

When I heard the church clock strike three I got up as softly as I could and went downstairs. The dogs came over to me as I walked into the kitchen, but returned to their baskets after a cursory show of affection. Outside, the wind moaned through the pines like the keening of a mother for her dead child. Perhaps such imagery was the concomitant to the horrors of the previous night. Caroline always made lists; for shopping, for the seating arrangements at dinners, for the packing for a tour or a holiday, for Miranda's school uniforms, for everything. All our life was recorded in her neat, small hand on scraps of paper in the drawers of the office. It was as if the making of them, and the ticking of each item that went on afterwards (with a pause for inward thought), held together the undisciplined and instinctual blind groping forward of our lives. I felt then that I must make a list, knowing somewhere that it was a defence against my thoughts in the too-silent house, a way of occupying myself until the welcome sounds of getting up began to bring life back in again.

By six o'clock I had begun to feel sleepy again. My list ran to over twenty items — parents; funeral preparations; newspaper announcements; undertakers; letters to friends and relatives abroad; food and drink; information for coroner; schedule of meals and visits; the will; Beth's insurance arrangements; any unfinished business at the office, etc. When I had written out each item, it had contained a sense of fullness, the reverberations of the minutiae which went into the few black words on the white paper. As I looked at it again with the ragged treble of the dawn chorus in the background, it had no meaning, as though the words had become dislocated and disengaged from the processes of thought which had spawned them. My back ached, and I felt a spasm of pure hatred for Jonathan. Just at the moment when success was within my reach he had stolen the focus of attention.

As 1946 wore on it became evident, even to us children, that something was in the air. At first it was nothing tangible, nothing which could be defined and expressed to account for the feeling of unease that we all felt. It was like growing pains, that then current prognosis for the mysterious aches of childhood which were without clinical significance. The symptoms were contained in a look, or a comment, as we passed a villager on the road or were jostled in the bazaar. The very ephemerality of the changes had its own sinister shapelessness.

One day that summer we went down to the races in Rawalpindi. As ever, this was a great social event in the colonial fraternity, and we were all got up in our best clothes. Mother was elegantly dressed in white linen, with a large, floppy-brimmed hat, and my father wore his tails. My father's deputy, Mr Stanton and his wife Frances were in the box with us. I adored her in the way that small boys fall in love with older women. She was like a frailer version of Cophetua's beggar maid. Her body was almost wasted in its thinness but her cheeks shone with what appeared to be febrile good health. She always joked with Jonathan and myself. Two years later she was dead from tuberculosis, and Stanton himself, grief-racked, died less than a year after her. No foreshadowing of those future events marred that day.

Father had a box where the twenty seats were filled with friends and business acquaintances. Below the box the concrete terraces teemed with Indian racegoers, beggars, sweet-vendors, ice-cream wallahs, tic-tac men and bookies. The sparse turf was brown and worn and each race brought gritty clouds of dust in its wake. From where we sat we could just see the beginning and end of each race, but the foreshortened perspective gave us no indication of who had won.

Modest gambling was socially acceptable, and the box had clubbed together to hire a runner whose job was to check on the winners, collect the winnings, and place the new bets. It was an onerous job, since he had to make his way to the winning-post, some half a mile away, after each race, and then back to the start of the course to collect the winnings. But, in doing this for the sahibs, he made enough to feed his family for a week. So, with the mandatory grin on his face, he toiled backwards and forwards. The afternoon wore on, hot and oppressive. The monsoon was due soon, and the air was still and heavy. Jean sat with the grown-ups; three seats away Paul Edwards, three years older, kept glancing across at her. She affected not to notice, but I knew she was putting on a grown-up act for his benefit. I wondered if he had kissed her, though it still escaped me why people went through such elaborate games when there were so many more interesting things to be done. James was on hand to pass the stengahs to the adults, laughing at their jokes and making himself generally agreeable. I played at the back of the box with one of the little girls, until we were told to be quieter. Then we played boxes, and noughts and crosses.

Suddenly there was a flurry of shouting in front of the box. People rushed forward to look at something on the ground. I wriggled through the standing adults to see what had happened. It was our poor runner who had collapsed on his way back with the winnings from the last race. The cloth in which he had wrapped the rupees had fallen to the ground, and coins had spilled all around. Someone from the box shouted in rage, but in a few moments they were all gone. Under his dark skin the runner had an unhealthy pallor and seemed to be unconscious. Dr MacKenzie, the estate doctor, vaulted over the wooden frame and rushed forward, shouting for people to stand back and give him air. In ones and twos the crowd drifted back to the rail where another race had started. Two men with official armbands came up, gesturing furiously to the stretcher tent. Finally two stretcher-bearers ambled up, chatting to their friends as they made their way over without haste. Our poor little man was loaded unceremoniously on to the stretcher and taken towards the tent.

'How was he?' I heard my father ask Dr MacKenzie who had returned to the box.

'Dead, I'm afraid. He'd had a massive heart attack. They've taken him off to the tent to avoid disturbing the crowd.'

The afternoon resumed, seemingly unaffected by this little tragedy. Without the runner the younger members took over his duties, with much good-natured squabbling and grumbling over whose turn it was now. Our servants brought tea, and laid the little folding tables with linen. Father, who had lost consistently, was coming in for some good-natured ribbing. I went to find Jonathan in the other corner of the box. Something seemed terribly wrong. He was looking at the laughing group of adults around father as if he would gladly run amok with an axe amongst them.

'I just don't believe it,' he said in a low, intense voice. 'That man has just died and they carry on as if nothing has happened, as if they weren't to blame. What's going to happen to his wife and children?'

I felt immediately obscurely guilty, tarred with the same brush. I had gone back to my game in a similar spirit of indifference. Men died in India all the time, rabid dogs were shot, our household pets disappeared. This man had been only an afternoon hireling; we hadn't even known him.

But for a brief moment I believe that I saw what Jonathan saw, and felt what he felt. That monstrous indifference that India encouraged towards suffering, and even towards individual death, could in turn be reflected back on each of us, could diminish each of us to a momentary pause in events on a hot afternoon. Years later I remember Jonathan saying about something else, 'It had no more significance at the time than the contents of a butcher's shop.' But all that was yet to come.

'Come on,' I said. 'It's buttered scones.' He looked as if he had not heard me. Momentarily I was aware of the vast, unbridgeable space between us. I felt afraid and closed my mind to it.

We left the race course as one of those spectacular Indian sunsets began. The crowds were thinner now, and we walked over the ground covered with red squirts of betel nut, with bidi ends, and the prodigal wrappings of sweets and ice-cream cones. The muezzin sounded far in the distance, but the remaining punters took no heed. They, like us, were dissociated from all that, were part of the new and liberated consciousness. A leper came towards us, his skin covered in silver scales, holding out a hand without fingers. One of the party threw him some small coins, and he scrabbled to pick them up, holding them awkwardly between the stumps. We walked back to the cars. Now that the afternoon was over a light depression hung over the party. It had been so good, despite the unpleasantness, and was already receding into the past, the realms of idealisation and distortion. We said our goodbyes and the cars began to move through the unconcerned stragglers with much beeping of horns. It was a thirty mile drive into the mountains for us, and the roads were loose shale and snaked treacherously round the ragged rocks.

As our car began to move, a group of well-dressed young Indians moved into the road in front of us. When our syce sounded his horn they laughed and jogged one another with their elbows, as if we had unwittingly made an uproarious joke. Suddenly, and without anything being said, I sensed something ugly and menacing in the scene. As the car came to a stop, a tall youth indolently stretched out his hand, palm open, against the radiator. His eyes were glazed, as though he were not looking at the scene before him but at some private vision. He spat, quite elegantly, a comet of red pan upon the windscreen, and shouted 'British go home.'

As if this were a signal, stones started to crash into the bodywork of the car. One hit the windscreen, which fractured into lines immediately, like ice cracking under the weight of a foot. The syce slowed down to avoid hitting the press of bodies. We were surrounded by grotesquely grinning faces: the car began to rock, first softly, then with increasing violence.

Father shouted to the syce, '*Jaow*, Saeed, *jaow*,' and punctuated the words with a heavy slap on Saeed's shoulder.

The car surged forward, knocking one of the youths into the gutter. I saw little Ram Singh, a friend of Jonathan's, watching the scene with wide, terrified eyes. As we accelerated away, a few more rocks hit the back of the car. Then the shouting died away and we were left with the sunset, the trees skimming past us and the distant sound of shouts over the car engine. My father was shaking, though whether with anger or fear it was hard to tell.

'You see, Jane,' he said, 'after all we have done for them, you see how they treat us?'

Mother didn't reply. Her family had been in India for four generations, and she and my father did not agree on the rights and wrongs of the British policies in that country.

Jonathan said vehemently, 'They were right to do it. We treat them so badly,' and when I looked at her face I could see that she agreed with him.

'I hope Ram was all right,' I said, but nobody answered. Nobody talked after that, all the way home.

I began to lose Jonathan that summer. I knew that he no longer found our games exciting, though he would still condescendingly join me occasionally in playing badminton on the lawn, or in looking for stag-beetles. He spent a lot of time with Ram, who was the same age but was very small and looked much younger. Father frowned on the friendship but Mother would say pleadingly, 'They're only boys. They'll grow apart.' So Ram was accepted around the house like a little brown ghost who only spoke when he and Jonathan were alone together. I would hear them laughing and feel a sense of exclusion. Jonathan had gone somewhere I couldn't follow, into that remote and separate part of himself which made adults so different. He began to spend more time with James, too, which seemed to me the greatest perfidy of all. It was Jonathan who had led me to despise James, to mock and taunt him for his ingratiating ways with adults, for his blond curls and his good manners. Now I was left out, and felt uncouth and brutish in my exile.

I suppose it was significant that I resented James because Jonathan sought him out and in doing so pushed me, who had been his constant companion, into some minor role in his life. I could not see then that his leaving and returning would be a feature of our relationship in the future. It seemed then like an absolute loss which could neither be shared nor mourned. It seemed, like the illusory permanency of all things in childhood, to be part of a new regimen which would never end.

James had never really impinged upon my life before then. Looking back I can see that, secure in my complicity with Jonathan, I had tended only to look upon him through the perspective Jonathan offered me. 'Father's pet,' Jonathan had called him scornfully, and he had seemed to me to epitomise all the things that we were not, and could never aspire to be. In addition to his blond good looks he possessed an undeniable grace — at least for adults — though from my vantage point it seemed to shade over into a readiness to please which carried more than a hint of subservience. James always looked neat and his hands never needed to be examined before meals. He accepted without question the role of shining example offered to him by our parents. Looking back into the uncertain and murky memories of childhood I recall, still with guilt, my childish hatred of him. He was not overly intelligent, but was possessed of emotional understanding far beyond his years. I remember Jonathan saying, years later, of that period in our lives: 'I was looking for the secret quality in James which made most people love him.' Then he had laughed, that bitter and ironic laugh, before going on, 'But needless to say, I never did find it.'

8

Sunday morning. Three days since Jonathan had died. That morning, in the normal course of events, would have been a slow rising to the surface through readings of the papers, spread out upon the bed. Time for thinking, a stasis between one week and the next, a time for indexing the events of the previous few days, for shaping some of the themes for the following week. As it was, I knew from the moment I was awake that it was the day to visit Beth, to find within myself some means of trying to restore the forward momentum of reality.

Caroline was downstairs talking to Mrs Haddon. Their voices echoed thinly up the stairwell, Caroline's sharp and authoritative, and Mrs Haddon's low, intimate, full of a confidential behind-the-hand gossipy tone. The smells of toast and bacon hung sharply in the air. Ingrid had already taken Miranda to the park with the dogs. It had been impossible to miss their whining and racing around the hall, colliding with radiators, legs and chairs in their frantic joy. I lay in bed for a few moments more, savouring the dying associations with normality.

When I came downstairs I realised Mrs Haddon had been to visit relatives and, blessed with total recall, was taking Caroline through a detailed account of the previous evening. 'Well,' she was saying, 'I said to her, it wouldn't be right, not with my Norman out, I said. After all,' this in appeal to Caroline, her eyes raised anxiously while her hands scrabbled ineffectually with the dishes in the soapy water, 'it's a small place and you know how people talk.' As the conversation went on I gathered that Mrs Haddon once more believed that some elderly man friend was lusting uncontrollably for her ample and accommodating frame.

As I ate my eggs and bacon I spared a thought for Jean. She had undertaken to break the news to our parents. 'I'll find a way,' she said, when we had discussed it and reached no firm conclusions about how to respond to the questions they would undoubtedly ask. She would call and let us know how they had taken it, and when it would be convenient to fetch them.

How could Caroline and Mrs Haddon find interest, at such a time as this, in discussing the relative merits of cleaning liquids? I had finished my breakfast, and Mrs Haddon had paused in her monologue to clear away the plates, when Ingrid brought Miranda back from the park. The dogs tumbled into the kitchen, mud-covered and joyful.

'Mummy, the deer were shouting at each other.'

'Were they the ones with horns?'

'Yes. They were chasing the little ones. We were frightened that they would hurt them.'

What would Spock suggest for a five-year-old at this stage?

'They're really being friendly. Those are the daddies talking to the mummies.'

Well, I supposed so. Sometimes I felt that I was entirely unsuited to be a father. Caroline could see no problem. Miranda would only take in as much as she could comprehend. The rest would pass her by. None the less we avoided the more salacious excesses of gossip and language in front of her. Though, for all I knew, Ingrid might be a reincarnation of Elizabeth Bathory. Could one safely entrust the welfare of our child to a girl who persisted in calling Buck, our labrador, Buick, doubtless perpetuating the myth that I was an overpaid capitalist with an overdeveloped love of cars? Malmo seemed disappointingly unlike my fantasies of Sweden if Ingrid's descriptions were to be believed. In the Cambridge of my day we thought the Malmo bookshops carried only maps to show you to bordellos where, for a modest sum, your youthful appetites might be slaked upon etiolated Swedish girls with the voracious sexual appetites of consumptives. Ingrid, weighing in at around seventeen stone, had dispatched that myth. Though, on reflection, there would have had to be some of her sort to redress the balance.

Yet at this moment, as I watched Ingrid's large jaws champing ruminatively at a piece of toast, her pale eyes fixed upon some spot at the end of the garden, I would have gladly changed places with her. Even the prospect of carrying myself around encased within that pillow of guts for the next fifty years seemed preferable to what was now left to me to do. I could not conceive what to say to Beth. But that was my role in this whole sad affair, Master of Ceremonies during this interval in normal life.

9

By the middle of 1947 we all knew that something far-reaching and incomprehensible was happening. The sun still shone from a cloudless sky; we still went on our picnics at weekends. But some indefinable shift had taken place which blurred the bright edges of the future.

Our nearest neighbours, the Bulant Singhs, lived with their daughter Lilee, some half a mile away through the encroaching forest, in a small, garishly painted and furnished house. Since Jonathan had discovered Lilee and myself in the garden shed, deeply engrossed in each other's private equipment, relations between the three of us had cooled. But Bulant Singh was an excellent bridge and tennis player, and my parents, unaware of the events taking place at our level, still maintained cordial, if somewhat condescending, relations with the family.

Bulant Singh, for his part, strove to emulate the British, almost invariably provoking smiles or open laughter. Jonathan and I were 'jolly fine chaps', Jean 'an edible young lady', and my parents would return from dinner at their house with tales of the recondite meats Singh had managed to obtain from the Hindoo butchers run by Farmer Sharpe, some five miles down towards Rawalpindi. Jonathan and I saw Rajoo and Gopal, Mr Sharpe's Hindoo helpers, quite a lot; to use Bulant Singh's vernacular, they had 'taken quite a shining to us'. We often knew what my parents were going to get for dinner with the Bulant Singhs before they did. 'Tripe', Jonathan would whisper, and we'd both almost weep with laughter. I had no idea what any of these exotic foods were: tripe, hodge, trotters, sweetbreads. But the idea of my staid parents being faced with the prospect of politely eating such outlandishly named meats always engulfed us in paroxysms of mirth.

One school-day morning I arrived down late. I had been reading Pinocchio into the early hours and slept through the chowkidar's alarm call. When I arrived at the breakfast table everybody else was seated around the unlaid table. There was an unnatural silence and father was sitting at the head of the table, drumming his fingers on the cloth. He liked the household run to a precise schedule, and any deviation from the long established timetable provoked him to a furious show of anger that smouldered for days after the event. I sat down, thankful that he didn't vent his annoyance on me. It was often expressed in sarcasm. 'Ah,' he would say, 'so you have deigned to get up to eat with the rest of us. Doubtless you have overslept because you stayed up late immersed in your profound study of the Georgics . . .' and on and on in this vein, picking away at the parts of my education which he felt were weakest. But on this morning his anger had passed the point where it could be deflected by my slipping into the room. He rang the little service handbell sharply. Silence.

Then Veroo appeared from the servants' quarters. She looked dishevelled and dazed and, as father opened his mouth to roar at her, she burst into tears, leaning against the lintel. It was a shocking yet curiously fascinating sight. It was the first time I had seen an adult cry and it aroused in me a momentary insight that they might, after all, be related in some way to me. Father, red-faced and embarrassed, looked at mother as if to say 'this is your business,' and then gazed out of the window with affected unconcern. I could see the pulse beating in his throat; the cold, unseeing blue eyes, staring glaucously into the sunshine.

Mother took Veroo gently by the arm and they walked slowly through to the kitchen. We sat uncomfortably in silence, occasionally catching one another's eye, but not daring to say anything to disturb the tension or draw my father's attention to us. Through the wall we could hear muffled voices, and the sound of Veroo sobbing. Even James was at a loss, and sat, pale and frightened, looking down at the tablecloth.

It is a terrible and fearful thing to be a child, dependent upon adults for affection and for life itself. The five minutes we sat there seemed like an eternity, and my father's threatening silence an indictment upon all of us, but upon me in particular. I felt shrunken and without a will of my own; I could no longer grasp what I must do to propitiate his anger.

Finally mother returned. She was obviously extremely distressed and shocked, and her voice quavered. She said, 'Could you come here a moment dear?' and to us, 'Just stay there for a little while. Veroo will bring you some breakfast in a minute.' We heard her talking to father in low, urgent tones in the corridor. A few moments later they both went out.

Veroo made us a makeshift breakfast which we ate in silence. Her brooding distress discouraged any questions, and we felt too subdued and uneasy even to talk to each other.

Bulant Singh wasn't at school assembly in the morning, and his classes were being taken by Mr Parker. When I met Jonathan at lunch break we made no connection between these facts and what had happened that morning. It was only when Kajan came to pick us up for the walk back home that we learned what had happened.

Kajan was an Afridi, and by nature almost indifferent to death. It was the natural end to man and the gateway to Eternal Life and thus of consequence only in a speciously Eastern way. This attitude did not, in any way, diminish his exuberant and tangible affection for us, but it had, in the past, created a complete barrier to understanding between him and my parents. Our small community had no Anglican priest, and my father, with his High Church background, had gladly stepped into the breach. He had even worn elaborate vestments. Two years before, at Christmas, Kajan had come forward as the presents were being distributed and handed my father a brown-paper parcel. When my father had opened it he found a cassock and surplice enclosed. Through the breast of the garment was a large rent, encrusted with rusty black stains. When father asked where Kajan had got this we were told that his tribe had sacked and raided a small monastery in the north. The priest had unfortunately died, he said with a shrug. He could not understand why my father showed horror, and would not accept the gift. But he loved us and hid the insult he felt.

That evening he was not exuberant. At first he was grim,

surly and uncommunicative. But as we walked it was obviously welling out of him. Too good a story to leave untold. So, with many admonitions against letting my parents know he had told us, we heard the story.

Apparently Bulant Singh had gone down to Sharpe's Piggery the previous day to get some pork. He prided himself on his Westernised liberal attitudes and was inviting Parker and his wife over to dinner. When he had arrived at the farm he had been surprised to find it very quiet. Farmer Sharpe was not in the fields, there were no teams of yoked oxen ploughing; just the light breeze riffling the sedge-grasses, and the occasional boom of the quarry in the distance.

Singh had left his car in the yard outside the shed where Rajoo and Gopal prepared the meat and walked to the house to pay his respects to Mr Sharpe. There was no reply so he walked to the abbatoir to give his order. As he knocked on the shed door it swung away from him. After the blinding white light it took a few moments for his eyes to get used to the darkness of the interior. The hut smelled, as always, of blood and sawdust. As his eyes became accustomed to the darkness he realised with horror that what he had taken at first as two giant carcases of beef hanging from the butchers hooks was something else. Rajoo and Gopal hung limply from the meat-hooks forced through their throats. Their faces were livid and congealed blood glistened in runnels down their naked bodies. Rajoo's left arm had been savagely broken, and splinters of white bone showed through the mutilated flesh — the limb bent at an unnatural angle. Both men had been castrated.

At this point Jonathan was violently sick in the small ditch running alongside the path. Kajan squatted sympathetically by his side, patting his back. 'Do you feel better now, Jonathan sahib?' he said. Jonathan retched again, and Kajan wiped his face tenderly with the end of his puggaree. We began to walk on, torn between horror and fascination. Kajan resumed.

The story had been retailed to Kajan through Bulant Singh's chokra, and had undoubtedly been embellished in the retelling. Bulant Singh had arrived back home like a man possessed by devils. All his servants were immediately called in to pack up the entire contents of the house. As they worked, fearful of his mood, and wondering what this would mean for each of them and their families, he told his story. Not as a sequence, but in pieces, and with sporadic excursions into anti-British and anti-Muslim sentiments. He kept putting his head in his hands, or leaning against the wall as if exhausted; a dozen times he said to Sita, his wife, 'You have no idea of the horror of it . . . the horror of it.'

All afternoon the servants and the family bundled everything into tea-chests brought down from the attic. At about four o'clock Bulant Singh had locked himself in his study and begun to make telephone calls. At 9.30 a lorry arrived and Bulant Singh himself helped load it with the household furniture. Bulant Singh had wept when he said goodbye to Mohammed Zaban, his bearer. He had, said Kajan enviously, given Mohammed Zaban a note in a sandalwood box. When Mohammed Zaban had taken the note to the scribe to be read that morning he had found it was a promissory note for six months' salary. Singh had also given him various letters to deliver. Father had one. It thanked him, in florid and profuse terms, for having been a good friend for so long 'to one as unworthy as I', and apologised for leaving so abruptly without saying goodbye. There was no forwarding address.

Two days later Bulant Singh's house was burned to the ground. The fire had started mysteriously in the night and, equally mysteriously, had not been reported to the police until the house was far beyond saving. I went over with Jonathan and James. The heat was still intense, and the trees beyond seemed to shimmer and wave as if we were looking at them in a distorting mirror. A blackened beam crashed to the ground, sending a shower of sparks glittering into the air. The twisted frame of a metal pram, which Lilee had used for her dolls long before, lay like a skeleton outside the fire-burned bricks. For once we listened to James, whose acceptance by the grown-ups gave him access to information we would never have.

'It's about something called partition,' he said importantly. I couldn't understand this at all. Partition referred to the division between the rooms in houses; nothing else.

'Partition of what?' asked Jonathan, frowning with concentration.

'Well, I heard Daddy say that Lord Mountbatten was dividing India up so that the Muslims would all be in one place and the Hindoos in another —'

'Don't be silly,' said Jonathan, 'they can't just get people to give up their homes and move —'

'Well, that's what Daddy said,' enjoined James with precarious dignity. 'Anyway,' he added fractiously, 'they'll only have to build another mud hut somewhere else.'

Jonathan was holding a thumb-stick, whittled and smooth so that his thumb fitted into the 'Y' at the top. He turned on James and jabbed the stick hard into James' calf. He was almost incoherent with rage.

'You silly fool,' he shouted, 'why don't you just drop dead.'

There was such venom in his voice that I felt afraid. James stood in front of us uncertainly, rubbing his leg; his eyes were bright with tears of pain. He looked at Jonathan as if appealing to know what he had done wrong. But Jonathan was implacable. I was afraid he was going to attack James. In a few moments James limped away.

Jonathan stabbed viciously at the large rock on which I sat. 'He can't really help it. That's what they all say at the club. They treat them like animals.'

In Jonathan's darker moods he could withdraw for days. They came and went without any logic that I could perceive, though I could instantly tell when they were upon him. Once mother had tried to make a joke about his anger. He had turned on her with such fury that she was shocked.

'You'll grow up to be a murderer,' she said to him, and to my father, 'I don't know what we are going to do about that boy. He's so sulky and moody — I can't do anything with him.'

Some weeks after this incident, during a French lesson, we were responding to the teacher's litany of questions. Monsieur Alain was a romantic who had come out to India to sustain his fantasies of the East. He was in love with the under-matron, a pretty Anglo-Indian girl in her early twenties, and we all followed the progress of his courtship with interest. The interest didn't extend to the lessons for me.

'*Où est Toto?*'

'*Toto est dans la salle à manger*?' I intoned dutifully, along with the rest of the class.

'*Où est Bobette*?'

'*Bobette est dans le jardin*.'

On the playing field outside, two men were running very hard towards the houses which bordered the field, beyond which the jungle stood black against the sky. The younger of the pair was ten yards clear of the second one — running as though his life depended on it. Spurts of red dust sprang from between his toes. He grimaced with the effort, and his arms flew wildly. The older man behind him ran fast, too. They seemed to be competing in a race to see who would reach the line of houses first.

In those few moments the class had moved to the window, ignoring M. Alain's shrill protest, '*Messieurs, asseyez-vous immédiatement*.'

Suddenly a group of men came into view behind the two runners. They were led by Karam Deen, who supplied horses to the colonial community and ran a stables on the road above the village. They were nine or ten strong, most carrying staves, and one or two carrying ferocious *kukris*. As they ran they shouted, but the words were distorted. They were gaining fast on the older man, and I heard him scream despairingly to the other. The younger man looked around and, as he did so, lost his balance and fell. In a moment the pursuing group were on the two figures. I saw Karam Deen's stick slamming home, and sunlight flashed on the knives which were raised and lowered into the mass of bodies.

One of the masters, Mr Majid, ran into our vision from the right. Over the sickening thudding we could hear his voice screaming '*Bas . . . bas*.' The crowd broke apart and stood sullenly round the two motionless figures. There was blood in the dust, and Karam Deen's white kameez was covered in red. Majid began to speak to the men. He seemed to be arguing with them passionately.

M. Alain called us back to our seats. Ram said, 'Why were they doing that, sir? What had those men done?' We were all profoundly shocked.

M. Alain stood braced against his desk in front of the

blackboard. His face was very white, and he was shaking uncontrollably. He said nothing for a few moments. When he spoke he had gained a measure of control.

'When the bell goes you will remain here. I rely upon your class monitor to see that you remain quiet . . .' He looked out of the window and spoke as if to himself. 'I cannot understand what is happening here and therefore I cannot explain anything to you. It is the end of this life as we know it. It is the end of the dream.'

Over the next months such incidents became commonplace. Houses were looted and burned to the ground. Villagers were killed. Whole families were wiped out. A young Sikh lecturer friend of my parents had become a Christian and was convinced he was safe.

'These people are all my friends. Why should I leave my home?' he had said when father tried to persuade him to leave. He was found crucified upside down in his bedroom one morning.

One Saturday afternoon my parents took us all up to the tennis club. Here, nominally at any rate, colonial life followed the time-honoured pattern.

We arrived in time for tiffin. The adults ate inside the cool clubhouse, served by the club retainers dressed in white with blue trim. The punkah wallah sat on the verandah outside, rhythmically moving the large rush fan to create a draught. The contestants for the afternoon tennis match were already in their white shirts and long white trousers. For dinner they wore their compulsory club blazers. The wives were mainly in white or cream linen suits with small wrist-buttoned white gloves. Lunch was accompanied by gaseous beer from the Rawalpindi breweries or, for one or two of the more social members of the club, by large stengahs of whisky. We children were served on long trestles on the immaculate lawn by the side of the clubhouse. The tables were laid with crisp starched linen, embossed with the gryphon rampant which was the club's mascot. From inside the adult voices rose and fell, punctuated from time to time by boisterous laughter.

After lunch I sat in the shade of the clubhouse verandah to watch the opening matches. Mother sat in a Lloyd Loom chair with her face in the shade, with Frances Stanton, Helen Porter and Doreen Parker. The sun burned down. Dr MacKenzie was playing against one of the young lecturers from the training college. Though MacKenzie was well into his forties he was the clear favourite to win — a slim athletic man of middle build, with grey wings to his black hair. The ladies watched appreciatively, commenting on the play. At three o'clock the barman brought over a jug of iced lime-water for them. Some of the children were playing French cricket on the lawn at the side. Jonathan lay on his stomach, playing chess with Roger Swinton, a year older, and very superior towards me.

'He's a marvellous player,' said Helen Porter, referring to MacKenzie and turning to Frances for approval. Helen was one of nature's spinsters. Quite pretty, quite well turned out, but somehow imbued with the ephemeral qualities of her lonely life.

'He's an even better dancer,' Frances Stanton commented. 'But, as my mother used to say, never trust a man who dances well . . .'

There was a short burst of appreciative laughter. Mother said, 'It's a pity old Bully isn't here. At least he'd give Mac a run for the cup . . .'

Doreen held her hand up theatrically, the other hand against her forehead. 'I knew there was something I meant to tell you. Mr Majid's bearer came back yesterday from visiting his family in 'Pindi and he said that a Sikh and his wife and daughter were murdered and thrown into a nullah a few weeks ago . . .' She became conspiratorial, so that I had to strain my ears to hear what she was saying. 'Of course it's very hard to tell one of them from another, but from what he told my servant it seems very likely that it was poor old Bully . . .'

The game was forgotten, and suddenly the afternoon seemed filled with menacing shadows. The idea of Mr Bulant Singh, his wife, and Lilee lying dead in a nullah seemed absurd and unthinkable. I imagined him on his back and saying to his unseen assailants, 'This is not cricket that you are playing, chaps. Give a fellow a chance, I say,' but even this caricatured rendition in my head failed to shift the image that had formed in my mind. I imagined Bulant Singh fighting with his attackers until he was beaten to the ground, but I could feel nothing.

Mother was saying, 'But Dee, where did he get the story from? Are you sure he hasn't made it up?' But Doreen was adamant, immovable. Her face was set tightly, defensively, as if she felt under siege. She beckoned imperiously to the waiter, '*Chokra, pani lao*,' and he padded off obediently into the clubhouse. She folded her arms, ignoring the enquiring glances from the others, and gave the impression she was interested in the tennis. When conversation resumed it was desultory, and the spirit had gone out of it.

As the afternoon wore on and the shadows lengthened an air of quiet melancholy came over the party. Even tea, normally punctuated with light-hearted laughter and good-natured flirting, was subdued.

Father got into the semi-final after tea, but was despatched in straight sets by Dr MacKenzie. He came off court perspiring, and wiped his face on the towel hung over his chair before joining the ladies. I saw mother whisper to him and guessed she must be telling him the story.

His face became set and hard. I heard him say quietly, 'It's only a rumour. We mustn't allow this sort of unsupported story to prey on us. Do the children know?'

Mother glanced at me, and I affected to be engrossed in my book. She shook her head.

'Good,' said father. 'Whatever happens they won't touch the British. They wouldn't dare.'

The weather changed unexpectedly a few weeks later. We woke to heavy louring clouds in place of the bright sun. The air was still, and even the tops of the pine trees outside the bedroom window showed no movement. It seemed as if we were breathing through a blanket. I felt apathetic, without energy, and could find no enthusiasm for anything. The rioting of the past few months had affected all of us.

Jonathan often awoke screaming in the night, and it was now a familiar sight to see mother sitting by his bed in the grey light, waiting patiently for him to wake up. 'You've had a nightmare, dear,' she would say, stroking his forehead with slow, unhurried movements. It would take him some time to struggle awake, thrashing and grunting. Then he would look around for a moment before settling down. It had happened again in the night, and lack of sleep added to the lethargy we felt.

It was a Saturday. Jean was going to spend the day with a girlfriend a few miles away. Father was rarely at home at weekends now. Though the authorities were completely unable to cope with the scale of the rioting, a number of arrests were made, and these men had to be tried and sentenced as speedily as possible in order to relieve the pressure on the overflowing gaols. We had seen very little of him over the preceding few weeks, and he would arrive back with his briefcase full of notes which he worked on late into the night.

I walked into the garden with Jonathan after breakfast; mother and James had gone riding. The birds were quiet. Even the cat, normally active in the morning, lay listlessly in the shade of the verandah. We walked down the path to the edge of the nullah at the end of the garden, and squatted down to watch the tadpoles wriggle through the heavy weed in the stagnant rock pools above the falls, their transparent bellies showing the whorls of intestines. The muezzin call came faintly down the valley, 'Allah il Allah, Mohammed Rasillalah Allah.' At the end of the garden, Shawkat Khan, our gardener, knelt to face Mecca. The air crackled with electricity and every movement I made started drops of perspiration trickling down my chest.

Everything seemed suspended in an agonising waiting. The stillness was unnatural. Apart from the trickle and drip of the dried-up stream over the falls twenty feet away, it was silent. Jonathan stirred some weed with the end of a twig, and the water was instantly full of wriggling tadpoles. On the surface water-boatmen skimmed and scuttered, and a brilliant blue dragon-fly hovered for a moment over the water upstream, before skimming away.

'Do you remember that picnic?' Jonathan asked, and I nodded. There was no need for him to place it more carefully. He sighed, his suntanned face heavy and sad. 'It seems like years ago.' He tucked his head further down towards his brown knees. An ominous crackle of thunder sounded, like the tearing of a giant sheet of paper. A light wind sprang up, riffling our hair, and then as quickly died away.

Suddenly — it seemed to take only a moment — the sky darkened. The wind rushed through the Douglas fir at the edge of the nullah in a fury of whipping branches. A dead limb flew past my head and crashed on the rocks below my feet. The dust blew proud and red and angry across the garden, pitting into our faces. We could only just see the house. A vast boom of thunder sounded above our heads, shaking the ground, and simultaneously lightning forked into the forest in a ragged thrust. Jonathan grabbed my arm and began to haul me up the bank after him, as the red friable soil crumbled beneath my feet. Another huge clap of thunder and then it was raining in warm, teeming drops. Within seconds we were soaked to the skin as we battled through the screeching wind towards the house. A rattan chair came bowling past us, tumbling bumpily head over heels like a rusty acrobat. The door into the house from the verandah flapped frantically. Jonathan picked up the cowering, soaked cat under one arm and pushed me in front of him into the house. We were streaming with water, and the red earth from our legs and shoes ran in trickles on to the carpet.

Jonathan slammed the door behind us and bolted it. It was as though a tap had been shut off, with only the hissing patter on the skylight to remind us of the fury outside. I suddenly remembered mother and James out riding, and could see from Jonathan's expression that he had just remembered too.

'You'd better go and change into dry clothes,' he said, 'then wait here. I'm going to find them.' He took his raincoat from the cupboard in the hall, and put his wellingtons on. Before I could say anything he had opened the door and vanished. I looked through the window, but the grey rain hid everything, and his figure had already disappeared.

Normally I loved to lie in bed in the safe, warm house and hear the sounds of the storm outside. That was when we were all safe inside and the morning would dawn again, warm and bright. It was not the same that day. The cat huddled shivering under the table in the corner of the lounge. The electricity line must have come down, so that I was forced to sit in darkness except for the butterly fluttering of white light which blazed into the room from time to time, like the flickering of an old movie projector.

I don't know how long I waited, straining my eyes into the garden for some sight of Jonathan, or mother and James returning. After about an hour the rain began to die down, and I could see the road in front of the house as it went up the wooded hill. Water streamed down in rivulets, carrying the red mud of the verge over the slick macadam. For the first time I can remember, I felt afraid; not because of the creaks and whispers of the beams in the old house soaking up the rain, but at what might have happened in the storm outside.

It must have been a couple of hours before I saw Jonathan and mother coming down the road. I could see, behind them, a dandy carried by two coolies. I ran down the path to the gate. James, very white faced and seemingly asleep, lay in the dandy, wrapped in a blanket. There was a livid sickle-shaped scar on his forehead. Behind a syce led the two horses.

I hardly dared ask, 'Is he all right?'

Mother smiled wanly, her exhaustion evident in the stoop of her shoulders and her dragging walk. 'He's all right. His horse bolted when the thunder first started, and he fell down the *khud*. But he'll be fine after a rest.'

Much later Jonathan and I went up to see James lying in bed. Dr MacKenzie had been, and had put some stitches in the cut. 'He'll be fine, don't worry,' he said to father and mother as he came out, shutting the door behind him. To father he said, 'Well, let's have the return game when the court dries out, eh?'

To me, James looked far from fine. He was asleep and seemed to have scarcely more colour than the linen sheet. Mother had put some wild gentians in the vase on the window-sill. They looked pale and sickly in the sallow light. I stood at the end of the bed, by Jonathan's side, scarcely daring to breathe.

I realised Jonathan was crying and heard him say, under his breath . . . 'I didn't mean it, God. Please let him be all right. I'll do anything you want.'

It was very quiet that evening. The wind blew steadily, and by sunset there were only a few clouds trailing darkly against the brilliant horizon. The air smelt fresh, the heavy smells of earth mixing with the lighter scent of wet grass. The nightjar began to tune his song, and deep in the forest we could hear the first hesitant calls of the jackal pack. Jean arrived back for dinner at eight o'clock, and mother quietly told her what had happened. Father didn't work that evening, and after dinner we played charades in the drawing room. Jonathan excelled himself, and was the first to score five correct guesses. At nine o'clock we were allowed to listen to the BBC news, a treat normally reserved for Christmas Eve and New Year's Eve. The spokesman said some things about Lord Mountbatten and India, but the quiet voice, distorted through the crackle of static, seemed to have little relevance to us and what was happening.

Mother came up to wish us goodnight, and father called up the stairs. James coughed and she went over the landing to see him. Jonathan put out the light and we settled down to sleep.

Many years later I went to an exhibition of Landseer at the Tate Gallery. It was a Sunday afternoon in November, drab and cold, and the floors were covered in watery mud imprinted with sole marks. There were the usual collections of tourists being taken round by their guides: a party of neatly dressed Japanese, weighed down by cameras and airline bags; an earnest American girl with bleached blonde hair trailing a geriatric assembly behind her, most of the men in lumberjack shirts and sporting baseball caps in bright colours, wedged atop grey hair; the women in a variety of solid WASP tweeds and classics.

We had dropped in because it was raining, and because I wanted to look at the Bacon triptych again, but Caroline had said impulsively, 'Oh, let's just have a quick look at the old boy,' and we had trailed through the turnstile. The American girl must have majored in Landseer, for she took the group through, picture by picture.

'Gee, isn't that beautiful,' said a stout matron, grasping the arm of a cadaverous man standing beside her, as they looked at 'Dignity and Impudence'. 'I wonder how Blossom is getting on without us.' Caroline squeezed my arm and I felt her shake with an explosion of silent mirth.

Like cheap music, cheap painting carries for me sometimes, and in unexpected ways, a power out of all proportion to its significance. When the Americans had finally shuffled off, and the blonde girl had begun her high-pitched nasal dialogue a little further down the hall, we stopped in front of a picture depicting stags in a Highland setting. Caroline muttered, 'When the pods go pop on the broom, green broom,' and we stood for a moment looking at it. It was the title I found arresting, which is what I mean about being surprised in unexpected ways — 'Coming Events Cast their Shadows Before Them'. It crystallised in a phrase for me the feeling of some malign purpose immanent in the future which I had carried with me since childhood.

The morning after the storm was sunny and tranquil. Jonathan and I left early for a swim. I envied his proficiency in the water. My own competence was limited to two or three widths of the little pool, swimming with an undignified quick breast stroke, my terrified neck held at full stretch to keep my head out of the water. The clubhouse was near enough to our house to be considered safe for us to visit unattended, and two armed guards in immaculate khaki shorts and crisp khaki shirts stood stiffly to attention at the gates of the compound.

When we returned for breakfast Dr MacKenzie was in the hall. My parents were listening to him as he explained something to them. They all looked very serious.

Father said, 'You boys had better go in and get your breakfast,' and turned back to carry on the discussion. I felt a twinge of remorse that I had not given James a thought since the day before.

Late that afternoon Dr MacKenzie came back. Shortly afterwards the old ambulance trundled down the hill, and two stretcher-bearers went up the stairs to bring James down. He seemed to be asleep, his hair lying in damp curls against the white forehead gashed by the livid scar. They carried him gently, and my parents and Dr MacKenzie climbed in and sat on the seat opposite. The three of us stood behind; Jean began to cry, and Jonathan put his arm around her.

Mother said, forcing lightness into her tone, 'Kajan and

Veroo will be here to look after you. We'll see you later.' Then the doors closed and the stretcher-bearers swung into the cab. The ambulance moved slowly up the hill and out of sight between the trees.

Jean was crying bitterly. 'He'll be all right,' Jonathan said, but his tone lacked conviction. Veroo stayed with us all afternoon; she showed Jean how to make barfi, and Jonathan and I sat with them in the dark kitchen, none of us wanting to be alone. After tea Kajan left to walk up to the hospital.

Late that evening we sat in the glazed sun-lounge playing records. The moon was bright, silvering the road, and throwing the foliage of the trees into sharp relief.

Jonathan pointed through the window. 'Here comes Kajan,' he said quietly.

Veroo ran up the road to meet him. Something in his appearance told us what had happened before he reached the house. He stood in front of us and said, 'Jimmy Sahib is dead.'

10

I have always been a master of prevarication, and of giving widely discrete needs the same valency, the same weight. Although beneath my blood boils, this balancing, this subconscious even-handedness, gives to others the illusion of calm, of the ratiocinative faculties holding sway over the bestial. But in time even I am forced to submit to the pressures of things which must be faced, or done. Caroline was not coming with me to see Beth, because Miranda was going to a birthday party in Richmond. Balloons were tied to the gate, as if all the invitees wouldn't know where Richard and Anne lived; a conjuror, and exhausted parents looking at their watches from four o'clock onwards. I could not blame Caroline. She was always for life and the living, and weeds and the phrases of condolence were not her métier.

Caroline said, 'You'd better go, darling,' her hand on my

shoulder, but I knew that she was already immersed, behind those preoccupied eyes, in details of the afternoon, the meals, the arrangements for the New York trip consequent upon my success, and all those myriad daily concerns which she used to remove so deftly from my shoulders, leaving me time to worry about the fundamentals; the paunch, the falling hair, the carious teeth — and now this. Like a small boy faced with the joyless prospect of the term ahead, with the last minutes ticking away, I tried one last plea, knowing it had failed before it was uttered. But the trying was all. (So his game heart pumped and he put on speed.)

'Perhaps it would be easier for Beth with you there. I just don't know what to say —' I trailed off lamely, aware that my pleas were falling on deaf ears.

'Now you know I can't come,' said Caroline, as though humouring a child. 'There really won't be much you can say. But I know you can listen, and that is what she will need now. Remember to tell her she can stay here if she wants to, though I know that her mother is with her at the moment.'

So Custer went out into the garage, after kisses all round. Miranda was already planning for the party, Ingrid and Mrs Haddon had resumed the mysterious female knowingness of their respective régimes, Caroline had begun the preparations for ensuring the household ran smoothly for another day. I felt sometimes that our inferior sex was indeed a different race, saved from the fate of the dinosaurs by being adopted as unwieldy pets with some limited usefulness, but cut off for ever from the spaces in which women lived and moved and had their being.

Now that I was on the road and the car had started, I could no longer interpose further activities as bulwarks between the present and the dreaded meeting with Beth. Now my saving levity deserted me. My mind still shifted away from looking at the scene I saw together with her when we returned after the interrupted launch party. Yet I knew that scene would, in time, become in some distorted and oblique way a part of my future work, and would work like a dark mole through my disordered psyche.

As I drove along the unadopted road, scattering a fine spray of gravel into the laurel hedge running behind the browned grass, the house came into sight between the Scots pines. 'Jonathan's folly,' we used to call it. There was an air of neglect, even after this short time. On the still immaculate lawn James' toys lay listlessly scattered. He had gone to Jean's for the moment. The curtains were drawn and, despite the cold, no smoke issued from the chimneys. '*Tempus edax rerum.*' Time, the devourer of all things.

Mrs Gardner, Beth's mother, opened the door. She had been crying, the make-up marked by dried rivulets on her cheeks where the tears had passed through the powder, and her clothes looked tired and creased. I had always liked her; bright, fiercely protective of Beth, outgoing. But today she had shrunk, her eyes were dull, and even her perfunctory embrace was a parody of her usual warm clasp. I followed her down the hall to the kitchen. The house smelt stale, fusty, airless. She poured me a cup of coffee.

'Beth's asleep. It's the first time since . . .' She let the sentence trail away with a tired gesture.

'Has the doctor been?'

'He tried to talk to her, but I think she's still too shocked to take things in.'

'Did he give her anything?'

'Something to help her sleep.' Then, seeing my look, she said, 'Something safe, he said. He told me there wouldn't be much that could be done. It would take time. He said to ring if I were worried, and he would come out.'

The next bit was more awkward, but better Margaret than Beth.

'Is she all right for money? I mean the mortgage, food, things like that . . . until everything is sorted out?'

She shot me an oblique, puzzled glance. It would be hard for her to know that, like everything else about Jonathan, I would know little of this side of his life. That despite the evidence of the affluent house, the two new cars in the garage, the lavish furnishings, and the soon-to-depart nanny, my images would grow and be nourished from childhood memories. Jonathan protecting me from two older boys at school. 'I know judo,' he had said menacingly, and they had moved reluctantly off. I had said from the safety of his protection, half convinced myself, 'But you don't . . . ,' and he had laughed and ruffled my hair. 'Never let them know what you have or haven't got.' In the narrow vault of my head were many things known but not acknowledged.

I busied myself making a lunch of sorts for us. It was plainly beyond Margaret, even if it had occurred to her. The Morning Service on the radio provided a funereal background to my preparations. The vicar delivered an unctuous and orotund address constructed around 'As ye reap, so shall ye sow'. I thought briefly, 'They have even taken the words now. The mystery is replaced by the new technocrats.' The dead eyes of the trout looked up at me as I prepared them messily for the grill.

Margaret said, 'I will never understand why. They had everything, everything.' What could I say? I looked at the pictures of murderers on the television, in newspapers, with amazement. Given the curl of a lip here, a wart there, I could sometimes have been looking into a mirror. 'There's no art can find the mind's construction in the face.' That goes for marriages, too. I remembered Frances Stanton and Dr MacKenzie sneaking off to his house one afternoon, unaware of my seven-year-old eyes watching them from my thicket hiding place. Yet I had heard my mother often talk of their perfect marriages. Perhaps now that Freud had overtaken the old ecclesiastical canons, such straying could be looked upon as beneficial, a deceit entered into for the benefit of the duped partner.

I said, aware of the pontifical tones, 'We can't blame ourselves. The courts always give the verdict as "while the balance of the mind was disturbed".'

'That's only a formula because they never really know,' she said mournfully. 'I saw them only the day before. They were planning a trip to India in the summer. I know that people do hide things — but they seemed so normal. We went for a walk on the heath only yesterday, and Jonathan and James flew the kite. He talked about his business. That seemed to be doing well.' She paused for a long while, her lips moving as if to find the shape of the right phrases. 'All the old business seemed to have sorted itself out. He never talked about it any more. Even Beth said, only a few weeks ago, that he seemed to have forgotten.'

Today, emboldened or made incautious by pervading unreality, I asked, 'What do you mean by "the old business"?'

Then the door opened and Beth came into the room. I had no warning of how she would look, and my face must have registered my shock that a few days could have so destroyed and sapped her. She was in a white overgown, her hair unkempt and her eyes as black and expressionless as olives. She acknowledged me with a listless 'Hello,' and lit a cigarette. She hadn't smoked for years, but I saw that her fingers were now stained a deep yellow. All the speeches I had rehearsed in the car fell away. I wished that Walter or Caroline were there to take responsibility for the moment. Or Jonathan. But this time it was I. Even in the midst of my rising panic I felt sorry for Margaret. She needed to sleep.

'Margaret, why don't you go and have a bit of a rest? You look as though you could do with it.'

The sub-text of such occasions suddenly protrudes, awkwardly, like the bones of a dinosaur uncovered by the receding tide. Beth intercepted Margaret's worried look with a faint smile.

'Yes, Mother. Go up and have a rest. I've got a lot to talk to David about. Don't worry, I'm quite all right.'

Sunt lacrimae rerum, et mentem mortalia tangunt. There are tears in things and they touch the mind of man. It is never the big things; the holocausts, the famines, or the multiplicity of monstrous disasters that flesh is heir to which bring home the finite nature of existence. As Margaret walked to the door, I realised for the first time, in all its awful truth, that Jonathan was really dead.

11

1947. In later years I often talked to Jonathan and Jean about the hours, days and weeks following James' death, but they remain vague and insubstantial, impervious in the sense of chronology to the conscious assaults of memory. From time to time a smell, or a colour, or a chance remark will gnaw for a second at the frayed edge of the veil. But the coherence of that time is lost, perhaps irretrievably. Since we all felt this, I can only conclude that we dealt with James' death, and the daily reports and evidences of violences, by a denial that they existed. Reduced to picture-book dimensions they were robbed of their terrifying and incomprehensible sadness. There was no authority to whom we could turn for an explanation of what was happening. Nor could we take refuge in the distancing devices which are the stock-in-trade of the politician in every adult. Like any child I could understand the dialectic of assault and counter-assault, of wrong-doing and retribution; what I could not understand was the massively impersonal injustice of what had happened and was happening.

Dr MacKenzie had assured my parents that James would recover; yet he had died. The radio and the newspapers had said nothing to suggest that there would be bloodshed and massacre of the most inhuman kind; yet I knew that the people who had killed my friends in Sharpe's piggery had lived side by side with their families for ages. The safety and refuge I had felt in our community had been destroyed by the riots, and I had drawn myself into the smaller circle of home. That, too, had now been made unsafe. My vision of the estate awaiting me when I too, like my parents before me, became an adult, was altered and diminished. The sadness soaked indelibly into every corner of my life, and it seemed to me, and to the others as I gathered later, that we carried a guilt which could not be expiated because we had continued to live and James had died. Each word I had said against him, each joke I had shared with Jonathan about him, became in memory an almost intolerable burden. I wanted to run, and run, and hide, and hide, from the demons that pursued me. But there could be no escape from them.

After Kajan's flat statement, we carried on as usual. In the first few hours it seemed that life had returned to normal. Mother was very shocked, and remained in hospital. Father arrived back late the next morning. He was unshaven and his suit was badly creased, the leather of his right shoe scuffed. As he sat with us at lunch I noticed that the nail on his index finger was badly torn. He sat in silence, hardly touching the food put in front of him. He talked briefly, but only to ask for salt or pepper, or to instruct Veroo to clear the table. He said nothing about what had happened after they left in the ambulance, and none of us ventured to ask. He left to prepare himself for the office, and came down a few minutes later shaved and changed. Though I felt doubts, he seemed so normal, and so did Kajan and Veroo, that I could almost dismiss the sense of depression which prevailed in the house. When he had gone the atmosphere was better, though a curious uncertainty about what to do next seemed to take hold of each of us. Jean went to her room and slept. Jonathan went out to see Ram. I lay on my bed and tried to read, but I kept drifting off to sleep, and eventually gave in to it.

Three days went past in this way. Father was rarely at home, and the feeling of indecision prevailed.

Father had ordered the servants to remove every item associated with James from the house. His room was stripped of all his books, his pictures; they even removed his toys from the communal box under the stairs. It was as though he had never existed. Once at tea-time Jonathan started to say, 'I remember when James . . .' He got no further. Father stood up abruptly, catching the table in his haste. As he almost ran out of the room the tea cups and plates clattered to the floor. We looked at each other, open-mouthed with shock. Veroo came in to help pick up the pieces. 'I think your father is very sad,' she said.

On the fourth day we walked up with father for the funeral service. We were all dressed in our best clothes, and father wore a black suit. As we walked up the lonely mountain road to the little English cemetery by the church we were joined by other silent families. Father walked ahead; it seemed he had noticed nobody. Mr Majid fell in behind us, in black kameez and white trousers; then came the Parkers, the Stantons and Miss Porter. Father Muldoon had come from Rawalpindi for the service, and walked behind us. Then, like silent ghosts, came the servants. At first those that we knew; our own servants and those from the college. Then more and more. Men I had never seen before silently joined us. In ragged, dirty clothing, some carrying guns and sporting bandoliers. The bell tolled out mournfully across the valley, a counterpoint to the shuffling sound of our feet as we walked forward. The small coffin was already in place beside the newly dug grave, the trestles and ropes ready to lower it into the ground.

Father Muldoon cleared his throat and began, 'Forasmuch as it hath pleased Almighty God . . .' The bell had ceased and the only sound was his thin, reedy voice. His hands were blue-veined and papery, and the Bible trembled. I noticed Karam Deen standing with the group of men I had not seen before. When the service was over father sprinkled some earth on the coffin, and stood back. Jonathan went forward, threw in a handful of dirt and then dropped something on the coffin with a dull thud. When I moved forward I saw that it was his bowie knife.

The coffin looked very small in the dark red earth. I could imagine James inside it, lying as if asleep. It seemed awful to think of him left in that cold earth alone in the graveyard. Behind me Mr Majid coughed, and I realised that I was holding up the long procession who were coming to throw earth into the grave. I threw in a handful of earth and moved forward to join the family. When Veroo's turn came she held the corner of her saree to her face; as she threw the earth in she wrenched her head aside as if she could not bear to look down. Tears were streaming down her face. Father shifted his weight on his feet and I looked at him out of the corner of my eye. His face was stern, expressionless.

Karam Deen was the last to come forward. He leaned his rifle against his side and made the greeting of *namaste*, then stooped to throw his earth onto the coffin. Then he lifted his grizzled head to look at his ragged band of followers and held his rifle above his head. Without a word they followed him through the gates of the churchyard and down the valley road.

That melancholy evening Jonathan and I were in the playroom. Father had gone up to the hospital to see mother after the funeral, and we had walked home with Kajan and Veroo, down the metalled road and through the tall pines exuding their resinous tang. Overhead a pair of golden eagles wheeled and circled on the thermals in their gyres, questing for food in the vast woodland stretching above us. A hoopoe flew across the path and into the dark wood. But nothing could afford a moment's delight.

I tried to read my book, but it had lost the savour of a week before, and I found it hard to concentrate on the words. Jonathan sat on a stool in the other corner of the room, his chin resting in his cupped hands. It was hard to break the silence which stretched between us. As the brown night-mist began rising from the lawn, father came down the hill, Kajan walking a few paces behind him. Their voices in the hall had a hollow, sepulchral ring. Then I heard father go into the lounge and Kajan went through the kitchen door, the bang reverberating down the hall before dying down. The silence of nothing to say descended again, claustrophobic and smothering.

Jonathan moved over to the records spilled in their sleeves over the floor by the desk. He put a record on the turn table. With a rising feeling of horrified fascination I heard the opening bars of James' favourite song, 'My Rosary', sung by John McCormack.

I heard the door from the lounge open, and quick steps in the hall. The playroom door slammed open, and father burst in. Even in my apprehension I could see how dishevelled he looked, almost dirty, with stubble glinting on his chin. He had always seemed to be in control, even when he was angry, and it was shocking to see him like this. He stepped on the pile of records, cracking several under his foot, and pulled the arm of the record-player off the record. Then he broke the record in half and threw it on the ground. Jonathan sat watching him in sullen silence. I hoped father would realise that he had broken the rule, and not I.

Father shouted in a high, strained voice, 'I don't ever want to hear any of his records again.' His head moved from side to side, and he was shaking uncontrollably. He looked at us, and I seemed to see contempt and hatred in the look. In a low voice he said, 'Why was it James who had to die?'

Neither of us moved as he went out of the room. At first I couldn't grasp the significance of what he had said. It was the use of the words 'had to die' which puzzled me, as if James was the sacrificial victim in some arcane rite which was designed to protect us from harm. It was only later that it occurred to me that he might, in that moment, have preferred one of us others to have taken James' place. Jonathan began to sort out the broken records and put the pieces into the waste-paper basket.

'I wonder when mother's coming home,' he said. 'I hope she comes soon.'

12

It was hard to imagine that outside Jonathan's house that afternoon, life, in the words of the old cliché, went on as normal. That way lies paranoia, or at least the belief that everyone else is having a wonderful time whilst one is the only absentee from the party. It was hard to feel deprived of words which, containing no comfort, might help to inch forward into that black fog of ignorance about why it had happened. Beth put on Fauré's *Requiem*, and for the first part of the afternoon we sat in chairs on either side of the hearth, immersed in our own thoughts. From time to time Beth would reach for another cigarette, and the air became heavy with the rank smell, the smoke curling with motes of dust in the shafts of sunlight which moved slowly across the pattern of the Persian carpet. Her lips moved, as if she were going over old conversations, or reminding herself of what she might have said, long after the events of which she was thinking had taken place. But those are my associations and, for all I know, she may have been trying to come to terms, as I was, with what had happened. Her body looked slack, untidy.

When the light had gone, and I had drawn the curtains and put on the lamp, she turned to me as if we were continuing a conversation momentarily set aside and then resumed.

'He knew about us, you know.'

I felt as if I had been hit in the face. 'How?' I said, and then, 'When did he find out?'

She went on in a flat monotone, as if delivering a lecture whose contents did not interest her enough for her to invest light or shade in the tones of her voice. 'The day it happened. It's hard to know why I said it, and I hated myself as I did so.' She reflected for a moment, then resumed, her hand describing limp shapes in the air. 'It was something to do with how sure he seemed about everything. It had been happening for a long time. It seemed that I had become irrelevant, like a piece of furniture or an old possession. We'd gone to the Heath in the afternoon, and mother and I watched him fly the kite with James. He even had to take that over, and I watched James look at him like some sort of god. Then he talked to mother about going to India. He hadn't even discussed it with me at all. He talked about all the places he planned to take us, implying we'd spent ages going over the travel brochures together. It was a fait accompli in his mind. Mother of course believed him. She couldn't see beyond the picture of the perfect marriage — but then, nobody could.' She paused for a moment, to light another cigarette, and drew her feet under her on the chair. 'I suppose I wanted to get at you, too. It seemed to me that you had done the same thing, that you had used me when it suited you, and had pushed me away when you had no further use for me. Oh, it was fun at first, and I wasn't unwilling. It was my secret to hug in the face of Jonathan's indifference, a little part of my soul which he couldn't possess and overrun.'

I sat silently, suddenly drawn from the wings on to the centre of the stage. I used to tell myself I was hurting nobody, save myself, when in the dark reaches of the night I thought of the absolute injunctions of the Church against what I was doing. Now I could see not Nemesis, but an avenging God behind what had happened. I had assumed that retribution would be exacted upon me, when my wavering disbelief temporarily shaded back into belief, but had never envisaged that the pattern would work out in this tortured fashion. After a few moments Beth went on.

'I used to plan different scenarios when I would tell him what had happened. It was my game. It often came to mind lately . . . he would come into dinner in an unusually dismissive mood, full of self-confidence, and I would let him carry on while I worked through my scenario. He would continue talking in the way I found so brilliant at first, full of profound statements about literature and life . . .' she gave a brief, snorting laugh, 'until I realised it was a hollow sham, that something had gone wrong at university or even before, that he didn't really believe in himself any more. In a way it was quite sad. But what I couldn't face, above all, was the fact that he wouldn't acknowledge that, wouldn't clear it out of the way so that he could start from the bottom again. He seemed to be cheating me of something real when he retired into himself — seemed to be giving me an act without substance. And I thought, finally, *that* might shake him.'

I said bitterly, 'It certainly did that. It was years ago, anyway. Didn't you know about the trouble he was having with Mandeville?'

The words had no effect upon her. I had to strain to catch her voice.

'I'd got so low that I didn't care any more. I'd lost the ability to discriminate between the things one could say, and the things one couldn't. It all went really wrong, not like my fantasy at all. It suddenly seemed as if I had to say everything. I'm sorry, I can't talk about it any more . . .'

I wanted to break her neck, to smash her against the wall in my anger and frustration. Instead I said, 'And I suppose you built it up into some kind of grand passion, instead of a momentary whim which became a convenience. Did it never occur to you what you would be doing to all of us?'

She didn't reply. It was as though she had sunk into some subterranean chamber where sound couldn't reach her, where the preoccupations of the moment had no interest or relevance. There was silence again, except for the loud tick of the grandfather clock in the corner. It was hard, looking at her now, to recall that there had been physical passion, on my part at least. She had offered to sit for me for the series of nudes I had, in an aberrant moment, agreed to produce to a deadline for Walter's partner in Paris. Beth's fascination for me was because Jonathan had chosen her in preference to someone else. In time I found that the openness I had found so attractive at first had a superficiality about it, that there were no receding depths behind. Her personality seemed largely shaped by being the centre of attention all the time, and after a while her endless self-absorption showed through the smokescreen of issues which she discussed with scant knowledge.

Certainly she was attractive, and it was difficult to keep my mind preoccupied with the problems of light and texture, the arrangement of planes. In some sense I realised that this attraction was because of her relationship with Jonathan. When he had approved the arrangement he'd smiled, 'You don't mind getting another leg up from a philistine.' It was a reminder of his introduction of Rachel to me, the precursor of these subsequent, less accomplished and heartfelt canvases.

One day Beth had arrived late. Jonathan had asked her to give him a lift to a meeting, and she had done so, knowing it would make her late. I could imagine his slightly mocking attitude, as if what she and I were doing was of small account beside his meeting. So, out of anger for both of them, it happened. That anger had overcome the moral scruples inculcated by a lifetime governed by parental value judgements. I had already transgressed in achieving a degree of material success ('Lay not up treasure for yourself on earth where moth and rust do corrupt . . .') and when Beth and I made love that day I had set some sort of seal on my decay. She had responded with a fierceness which surprised me, and with an abandon which suggested a liberated and inventive mind.

Though my studio was forbidden to everyone while I was working, the sound of footsteps in the corridor — Ingrid, or Mrs Haddon dusting, perhaps — was occasionally sufficient to induce detumescence or premature ejaculation in me; for her, the proximity of someone not party to our feverish activities, lent an added zest. Sometimes, when the house was empty, I would feel gratified to hear her call my name as she subsided, sobbing with mingled pleasure and exhaustion. On other occasions she would giggle when the muffled sounds outside brought on a mechanical failure. We never needed to talk of love to each other, since we both knew that what we were doing had little relationship to love.

It seemed we were both indulging, in a secondary, tangential fashion, in expressing our feelings for Jonathan through these actions. The paintings, which I somehow managed to produce in very short order, and often through a pleasantly replete haze of sexual exhaustion, must have benefited from this extra mural activity. Though I found something missing in them the critics liked them and, with Walter's eye to the main chance, I knew it would not be long before I was asked for a further series. It seemed as if we had enjoyed a pleasant interlude. No more than that. Ironically enough we had not exhibited the nudes immediately. It was almost five years before Walter felt the time was right.

The Fauré had long since finished; the light had truly gone. I heard Margaret moving outside the door. I felt the need to do something, to get away from the house, to go out to dinner or to a theatre; always aware that such external journeys were merely the outward show of those mysterious inner journeys which began and ended somewhere beyond the level of control.

As I started to get up Beth said, 'He left you a note, you know. Perhaps you'd like to look at it!'

It wasn't a question, nor was a refusal possible. She went to the door and returned from the hall moments later, a bulky envelope in her hand which she gave me without comment. Though I knew that these words would not produce any solution or answer any questions, I was afraid to look at them.

The letter began with a series of instructions relating to bank accounts, life assurance documents, instructions on foreign account holdings and details of executors and solicitors. As I read the neat type I began to feel a sense of unreality. The sheer normality of the instructions in the face of what had happened provided a bizarre contrast. The second sheet was different. It was typed on a different machine. The capital 'I' was partly blurred. Symbolically enough, I thought, with a half-hysterical gasp of laughter.

Beth watched me curiously. For the first time her features betrayed some life. I began to read.

13

1947. The fragile sense of normality which I had felt in the hours after James' death had turned out to be an illusion, and in the following weeks it felt as if the sun had set forever. Mother returned from hospital a month later looking frail, and with dark circles under her eyes. She seemed serene in herself, though the rather muscular vivacity with which she had dominated us in the past had disappeared, and it often seemed, to me at least, that she was not really present in the room with us. She had the look of a sleepwalker, gazing upon an interior scene denied to the rest of us. Sometimes whatever she saw made her smile, but it was a smile that spoke of regret, and loss, and sadness.

In that month father had aged visibly. He gave off a feeling of hostile coldness, of distance, and I felt the presence of traps all around him when I was in his company. That mordant quality in his observations which had made me shrink in the past, reappeared fitfully from time to time, and, such was the tenor of the moment, I almost welcomed the sting as a symbol of the return to normality. He had slowly begun to look after his appearance again, but his cheeks were hollow, and the skin around his eyes had a white, pinched, look. From that time on it seemed that my parents crept closer together for warmth and comfort, taking with them the good things to a place beyond our reach. By now we knew that James could not be discussed in any way, and that no one could even acknowledge that he had lived with us and been our brother for some years.

The great plan which Jinnah had forced on Mountbatten with Gandhi's characteristically ambivalent consent had begun to misfire badly. Outside the confines of our narrow estate, reports filtered back of the savage and bloody rioting which spread throughout the frontier lands. Not that I have ever found in subsequent years any acceptance that the British in general, or Lord Mountbatten in particular, had acted without proper consideration of the likely consequences. At first the assumption was that this was a *jihad*, a holy war, in which the Muslim was driving the unbelievers from his land. But as month succeeded month it became evident that such readings were grotesquely naive. The repositioning of people from fertile and arable lands which their ancestors had occupied for centuries, the primitive fear of the unknown of those forced to leave, the greed of those who saw an opportunity to increase their holdings, occurred at a grass-root level, and exacerbated the conflict.

It could hardly be reported back to Cabinet in London, because it was not known in Delhi. England, wearied by the long war against Fascism, was absorbed in beginning to make the repairs of peace, and now that a decision had been taken to quit India, what did it matter how the civil riots were described to the British populace? It was further proof, if proof were needed, of the unreasonableness of the brown man. Perhaps, if Gandhi's policies had not proved quite so effective in blunting the edges of the Imperialist presence, the British in India could not have tolerated such an affront. But they left it, given a journalistic impulse here and there to probe into other areas, just as in a holy war. And, by the time the historians moved in, the issue was substantially closed as far as Britain was concerned.

Our birthdays passed with token celebrations. In previous years they had been occasions of great excitement. As in the days before Christmas, one would be aware of covert whispering and teasing glances for days before the event. Much of my early excitement had been the yearly anticipation of a bicycle for my birthday. Though this was inexorably followed by the sense of anti-climax when in successive years a train set followed an aeroplane (with electric motor), the days of waiting were a reward in themselves. There was always the hope that this time, the process of wishing, or a wordless divination by my parents, would result in the right present. By the time my birthday arrived in the autumn there were few friends left to celebrate with, in any event. To compensate for Jonathan's slow defection, I had made friends with John and Diana Parker, twins of around my own age, and with Paul Sutcliffe, a few months older. But by this time all of them had long since gone, the Parkers to New Zealand, and the Sutcliffes to England. There was no excitement in anticipation, and now that the bicycle finally arrived I could not find in myself the enthusiasm of former years.

It was not only within the family that change and distortion were taking place. As the preludes to Partition began it became obvious that, whatever the outcome, Bulant Singh had acted wisely in leaving. The tragedy of Sharpe's Piggery had been repeated many times elsewhere, and some of the rioters and looters were taking advantage of the authorities' inability to cope with the scale of the disorder by paying off old scores of their own. One of our acquaintances was in charge of awarding large catering and supplies contracts for the government, and, over the course of some twenty years, had managed to build himself a considerble fortune through accepting bribes. Early in the year his magnificent house on the Mall at Hasooth Gali was burned down, and he and his wife and daughters barely escaped, dressed as washerwomen, and driving an exorbitantly expensive donkey and cart purchased from a delighted contractor. It was not an unamusing picture — given his vast bulk.

The number of buzzards circling around below the road cut into the mountainside which led to Hasooth Gali had increased enormously, though we could still only see the tops of the dense pines when we looked over the iron railings to the drop below. Reared on 'Westerns' shown in the flea-pit cinema in

Hasooth, we had our dark suspicions of what lay under the trees, and it seems likely that our wildest imaginings were correct.

Many of the boys began to leave the local schools, and the Hindoo servants from local families disappeared in dribs and drabs. The organisation of the school, and of the entire community began to break down, piece by piece. A widespread epidemic of food poisoning was traced to a local contractor selling tainted meat. In the riots even the farm animals belonging to Hindoos had been killed and left to decay in the sweltering sun. Saeed Ahmed had gathered such cadavers as he felt would pass muster from the valley and had his coolies take them to the cold-store. He complained when caught that they had been over-assiduous in their collecting. He was blameless, intending only to use such meat as could have come from an abattoir. And wasn't he, after all, helping to provide a nutritious diet at a time when meat was scarce and hard to come by? And at a very good price? He was unrepentant, even when father took him on a visit to the school hospital.

'Very bad luck,' he kept saying as he passed through the wards, and, raising his eyes to heaven as if to castigate God for this injustice, 'I don't know what went wrong. We have very clean factory.' His case never came to court — through those mysterious processes which underpinned justice in the Punjab at that time. But after the incident he was observed to be poorer, though his warm and all-embracing smile never wavered for an instant.

The club had become a refuge, where anxious Europeans could exchange worried information. At first everything was a bit of a joke, a laugh, a temporary inconvenience. Some of the memsahibs had even had to try their hands at cooking, creating much hilarity in the clubhouse as they circulated their favourite stories, embellishing them day by day with additional detail.

Dr Mac's wife, Joan, was expert at the droll portrayal of her disasters in the kitchen. Used to a gas cooker in her native Scotland, she had found the open hearth cookery used by Indian *khansamahs* incomprehensible.

As she said dryly, to the accompaniment of appreciative

laugher, 'First Mac had to go without food for two days, while I learned to light the damn thing. Then —' pausing for effect, her arm raised in exaggerated gesture, the other hand on her hip, 'he had three days of becoming used to charcoal offerings. It was like getting a new pope elected. He knew when dinner was ready when the black smoke started pouring out of the kitchen shed!'

Dr Mac stood smiling at his wife, his pipe in his mouth. No one took Joan's comments seriously; she was far too competent to have found many problems, and Dr Mac too sleek and well-fed to suggest a man on the point of starvation.

But the jocular high spirits of the club could not disguise the worsening situation. Some two months after James' death a young teacher, Agnes Pollitt, had been attacked and raped in the school grounds, only yards from a lighted verandah. Her assailant had used considerable force, and she had been in hospital for almost a month before returning to work. I noticed the servants looking at each other when she came in; it was not the servile blandness of former years, but a knowing, and silently triumphant glance.

Jonathan said to me, 'They know who did it.'

'What is rape?' I asked him, buttressed from the grown-ups by the rattan partition behind which he and I were playing a desultory game of caroms.

He made a circle with the index finger of his left hand and his thumb, and pierced it with the index finger of his other hand.

Oh well, I thought, grown-ups always seem to be trying to do that to one another. Jonathan had shown me a pair of stag beetles mating in the summer, and it seemed a curious and inexplicable activity. In a wider sense the incident had exposed the hollowness of English security in the new situation; the English had failed to curb the riots, and in the new mood which prevailed the old fear and respect had been replaced by a realisation that such communities as our own were weak.

On the evening that Agnes Pollitt returned, the club was full of sympathetic faces. I had heard father talking to mother in their bedroom as they prepared for the evening. Jonathan and I played on the landing, each covertly listening without admitting so to the other.

'Poor girl,' said father, but there was a tinge of disgust in his tones, 'That will blight her marriage chances.'

We could hear mother rummaging in the wardrobe. 'Why should it?' she said. 'It wasn't her fault.'

'That may be so, but no decent man would want to touch her after an Indian had . . . done that to her.'

'Sometimes,' mother said slowly, 'sometimes I'm glad I don't understand the way men's minds work.'

Jonathan looked puzzled, but the sounds from the bedroom indicated that my parents would shortly be coming out. We walked down the stairs and out into the garden. Mother came out shortly afterwards, her face set and hard, and her lips a grim line. Father locked the door and we walked towards the club.

Father stood at the bar with Dr MacKenzie, both chatting and watching the group of women around Agnes. Dr MacKenzie's family had been in India since before the Mutiny, and it was rumoured that there was Rajput blood in the family from a runaway marriage in the early nineteenth century. But though he tanned easily, and his hair had the oily blue-black sheen of an Indian, his eyes were startlingly blue and his voice, even now, had the cadences of Scotland and not the chee-chee sing-song lilt of the Anglo-Indian. I had noticed, in the way that children do, some cooling, some wariness in the relationship between Dr Mac and my parents since James' death, but, on an occasion such as this, father appeared to prefer his company to that of the younger men present. Jean fancied herself in love with Dr Mac, and stationed herself on a high stool at the bar with her ginger beer, in a position where she could gaze at him. The two men talked without paying her much attention.

At the other end of the room Agnes Pollitt appeared to be crying, and Frances Stanton put an arm around her shoulder and led her to a chair in the corner, indicating with her eyes, over her shoulder, that they should be left alone. There was a rustle of sympathy, and the women exchanged glances. Someone said, 'The only thing she could remember was that he smelt of horses.' (Karam Deen always smelt of horses, I remembered). Another voice said, 'I lock all the doors now. You can't even trust the chowkidar . . .'

I beat Jonathan at caroms twice. He was only playing half-heartedly, his whole demeanour indicating boredom. He had changed over the past few months. Where he had been outgoing and rebellious, he was now quiet and watchful. I had long since ceased to mourn his departure, since it had dawned upon me that he had not gone as a result of anything I had done. It seemed he was storing everything he saw and heard; that he had lost faith in the omnipotence of our parents, and was determined to understand everything for himself. I knew that our childish games no longer interested him, though he submitted to playing them with a good enough grace. He watched, and listened, and something in his stillness made me feel strange. Even then, I think, I sensed that it was not the stillness of repose, but of enormous tension curbed with a tremendous effort of will.

'I've won again,' I said, and he smiled at me, stacking the counters into the centre of the board. I could see his indifference to playing again, but there seemed nothing else to suggest, so I waited for him to complete the cluster. Jean came across with a smile of smug satisfaction on her face.

'I know something you don't,' she said, pirouetting on her toes and taking a sip of her ginger beer.

Jonathan smiled. 'You've been listening to your pin-up talking to Daddy, haven't you?' he needled her.

Jean flushed. 'He's not my pin-up,' she said. 'Anyway, if you don't want to hear —'

Jonathan said quickly, 'Yes, I do.' Jean looked at him teasingly, calculatingly, her tongue held between her front teeth. 'All right then,' she said, 'I bet you didn't know we're going away?'

In the background, the air was blue with coils of smoke, and the laughter rose and fell. I looked at the familiar scene, the chair that had always been just so, Mazuffar standing behind the bar, his watchful eyes moving around the room to see who needed him, Dr Mac resting on his elbow on the bar talking to father. The fan stirred idly, moving the heavy ferns in the jardinière. The spirit of place, the genie had caught me in its coils. I did not want to move from here, to relinquish the call that even the dead objects scattered around this room had upon my affections. That was the least of it, for outside the breathless valley sheered up into the blue and everlasting range which cut like a swathe across our horizons to the North. I could not voice the feelings that those white and violet ranges evoked in me, the sense of eternity and of unchanging peace. In a moment I felt all this slipping away.

'Where?' asked Jonathan.

'They didn't say. But it's getting too dangerous to stay.'

'Why? Because of what happened to Miss Pollitt?'

'No,' said Dr Mac who had ambled across and heard these last exchanges. He put an arm loosely around Jean's shoulders and gave her an affectionate squeeze. She blushed with pleasure and looked at Jonathan to see his reaction. His dark face betrayed nothing as he waited for Dr Mac to go on.

'We're all at risk here, to some extent. It's true that the Indians have no specific grievance against the white community here —' he gestured to indicate the club members, '— but as with any crowd, they could alter the focus of their anger very easily. Remember that these people are seeing themselves as the arbiters of their own future for the first time for over two hundred years. It's a very heady sensation . . .'

Dr Mac never talked down to us. Somehow we were given direct access to the mysterious world of adults by him, and when I was with him I found thoughts which would never have formed in the company of my parents.

He took Jean by the shoulders gently and sat her down in the chair by Jonathan's side.

'Your parents have had a terrible bereavement,' he said, 'and you may find the next months very hard. None of us knows what lies ahead, but it will not be easy for any of you.' It was like a Sibylline oracle, offering an obscure thread running whitely into the dark of the disordered future. My father came over and stood by Dr Mac's side, watching us. He looked far-away, the stengah in his hand shaking slightly.

'Do you remember, Mac,' he said, 'we played our first game of tennis at this club on the day that Chamberlain came back with his little piece of paper?' He swayed a little, and held the screen to steady himself.

Dr Mac smiled wolfishly, 'And wasn't I brilliant. Brilliant!'

he crowed, self-mockingly. 'You trounced me in straight sets.'

Mazuffar had begun to dim the lights. Two or three couples had already gone reluctantly into the velvet night. Cicadas shrilled and droned in the massed pelargoniums. Mother and Frances Stanton had collected their wraps and were walking up towards the bar. Frances put a hand on Dr Mac's arm. She gestured towards Joan who was walking up the room towards us.

'Your wife has had us all in stitches. She should have gone on the stage . . .' Dr Mac permitted himself a small smile. He caught Joan in his arms and took two or three steps with her, humming one of Lehar's tunes.

'Come on, ma wee haggis. Time tae goo hame!'

We all drifted away from the clubhouse. As we walked the warm yellow light lay comfortingly around the building. Outside the sky was inlaid with cold stars, and the familiar landscape seemed remote and foreign.

The following morning I heard Veroo run into the house calling for my mother. She sounded so distressed that Jonathan and I scrambled into our dressing-gowns and ran downstairs. The door onto the verandah was open and mother was standing on the path leading down to the lawn, with Veroo. Mother was in her night wrap, her hair loose and down her shoulders, and they were both bent over something which lay on the edge of the flower bed. Jonathan reached the scene before I did, and turned back to me, saying, 'Don't look.' But I had seen our cat Smokey lying on the path with her throat cut.

There was no lobby for the noes when father told us we were leaving over breakfast three days later. Jonathan, inexplicably, seemed to be excited and full of energy. I suppose it was indicative of the way we were then that I didn't want to go, having never known or wanted anything other than what we had, while Jonathan saw the future as a great adventure, full of movement, and bustle, and activity.

Two days later, with the servants weeping as they carried our cabin trunks to the Army lorries, we prepared to leave. There were a few friends to see us off. Ram had brought

Jonathan his copy of Fitzgerald's *Omar Khayyam*, wrapped in rice-paper. We climbed into the back of the lorry, where our trunks had already been lashed down to provide rudimentary seating. The lorry began to move slowly down the hill, and the group of waving figures receded into the distance. Some six miles to the north-east James lay dead under the earth in the Christian cemetery.

The first night in Rawalpindi, thirty miles towards the plains, we slept on the floor of the Phoenix ballroom, a decaying 1930s building. Dinner had been served in a makeshift canteen, on battered tin plates supplied by the Army.

Jonathan came back from the lavatories looking disgusted. 'You need wellingtons in there,' he said, pointing to his shoes which were ringed with damp.

When I could contain myself no longer I walked in to them. They reeked of ammonia, stale beer and vomit, and the stalls were stained a deep brown where the water sprayed out from metal nozzles. The drain was clogged with bidis and pan leaves, and water dripped down the walls in long stains. Under the cistern some wag had written: 'Our aim is to keep this place clean, your aim helps', and another legend read, 'The management should provide the users of these facilities with braille fly-buttons.'

The night was punctuated by noises — by whispered conversations between people unable to sleep, others caught in nightmares crying out in their sleep and the heavy stertorous snoring of the few to be envied who could, it seemed, sleep through anything. Throughout the night there was the whisper and squeak of shoes on the polished floor, as people moved across the ballroom floor to go to the toilets, or went outside for a breath of fresh air. We slept, fully clothed, in a small ring. Mother and father were under a woollen blanket, and the rest of us had one Army issue khaki blanket each. I felt dirty already, with an oily sweatiness which left my skin feeling clogged.

Near us, Miss Preminder, a light-skinned Hindoo teacher who was trying to escape with us, tossed and turned. She had removed her caste mark, and in her floral print dress could pass for European. As it turned out, she needn't have gone to such great trouble; four days later she was left by the railway track, repeatedly raped and then mutilated almost beyond recognition.

We spent three nights in the Phoenix dance hall, setting out in military convoy each morning, only to be turned back because the train hadn't yet arrived. The ballroom had begun to take on the aspect of a transit camp. Some families had rigged up lines, hung over with towels, curtains, sheets to demarcate their private area. For security reasons we were required to remain inside for most of the day, and, with the heat at its highest just before the monsoon, the smell in the hall was a mixture of stale odours, which the inadequate windows and skylights were powerless to dispel.

Our liaison officer, Captain Prescott, was plainly tired of his responsibilities for the civilian refugees. All his early attempts at imposing military discipline upon the disorderly crowd in the ballroom had come to nothing. His neat listings of cleaning details, and procedure for collecting meals were completely ignored. By the third day there was no evidence of any structure of command; the floor was littered with paper and wrappers, and the line-up of patient families waiting for their meals spread well into the mornings and afternoons.

On the fourth day we climbed again into the open-backed convoy lorry to drive down the dusty road to the station. We could hear sporadic firing in the distance, and the smoke from burning buildings hung like a haze over the poorer part of the city. Jonathan helped Miss Preminder up, and carried her cases over, leaning sideways with his arm out to take the strain. He had cried out in his sleep the night before, and mother had walked him out into the hallway to comfort him. His face looked sallow, with dark smudges appearing under his eyes. We settled down on the sacking provided for us in the back, and the lorry started to jolt and start down the track.

Some lean chickens ran into the road from a mud compound on the verge, and a woman in a soiled saree came running out, imploring them to stop. The truck stopped with a jolt, the driver cursing at the woman through the open window. She spat at him, her saree gathered under her arm to save it from the dust, and drove the squawking chickens back towards the compound. We started again. The sun baked down and the khaki metal burned to the touch. Jean sat in the corner behind the driver's cab talking animatedly to one of the daughters of another couple we had met at the Phoenix. Her face was streaked with dust and perspiration, and the light cotton dress she wore was grease-marked and dirty. Father stood in the body of the vehicle holding on to a roof strut and bracing his body against the movement of the vehicle. Mother lay with her eyes closed against the bulkhead.

At the station we were made to wait in the lorries while Captain Prescott and my father disappeared into the huddle of dirty buildings. A train stood there with some twenty cattle trucks straggling behind it. Some goats tethered to a small tree in front of the station foraged endlessly for food on the baked earth. I desperately wanted to find a toilet. In the past days I had been able to keep little down; between constant diarrhoea and being sick I felt empty and light-headed. A military policeman came out of the small station and undid the metal bolts of the tailgate, inviting us to follow him.

Prescott was standing with father and an Indian in station-master's uniform. He gestured worriedly towards the carriages standing by the station. 'I'm afraid it's all we can get with any certainty.'

Father laughed, 'I don't think any of us expected luxury.'

The station-master spread his hands and shrugged his shoulders expressively. He was apologetic, but unable to offer any alternative. 'There have been no trains for three days. This driver told us the train was stopped many times. They had to stop for rubble on the track, then they find a man on the rails . . .' He looked as if he were going to cry. 'It is not possible to run a good service with these problems.'

Prescott nodded soothingly, opening his mouth to speak and mouthing without words as he waited for this peroration to end. 'Nobody blames you, Mr Das. These things happen in wartime.'

Das seized upon the words avidly. 'That is right, sir. It is the bloody war. This bloody war —'

Prescott straightened imperceptibly. 'Mr Das. Please remember there are women and children present.'

Das stopped, his mouth open. The waiting-room was now full of our party, standing resignedly by their belongings.

Prescott and father went off with Das to see if they could improve the situation. So many of us were by now suffering from diarrhoea or dysentery that it was vital that some kind of toilet facilities were available on the journey. Prescott had started to argue that no one could possibly object to regular stops in the Gobi Desert, but father's face had assumed a look which it would have been difficult to misinterpret.

I took advantage of the pause in events to find a toilet myself. As I sat there in the foetid darkness I strained my ears for sounds of what might be happening outside. My hold on the future had become so tenuous that I was uncertain of what might happen at any moment. The logic of events had gone, and the calm and ordered existence of a year ago seemed to belong to another world. It seemed to me, as I sat there, that I could emerge blinking into the bright sunlight to see the train disappearing into the distance. The uncertainties of the past few months seemed to extend into the heart of the family, and it felt I could no longer rely upon my parents to wait for me, to ensure that I was safe.

The train stood idle in the fierce sun. One party grouped themselves in the shade of the station verandah and settled down to wait. Already the faces bore a look of resignation, an absence of expectation which the experience of the last few days had given each of us in some measure. Late in the morning, a small shunter appeared down the track, and there was a quickening of interest from the younger members. A few railway hands sauntered down to the points and the shunter began to remove the cattle trucks. Over the next hour some ancient third-class carriages were shunted down to the waiting engine, and coupled together with much puffing and clanging. The bogies were red with rust and the windows scarred and pitted with scratches.

Das appeared from his office, beaming, with father and Captain Prescott in attendance. He indicated the dilapidated wagons proudly, like a businessman showing off a new car.

'You see? Even within this dire emergency you can witness our ability to give you good service.' Despite the quaint English and the strangely accented diction, he had, for a moment, a quiet dignity. He shook hands gravely with father and Captain Prescott, and then walked back to his office, his small fat body erect with pride at his achievement.

'It's the best I can get,' said Prescott, and father nodded acceptingly. 'At least it has toilet and washing facilities. I would say that each carriage will be filled to twice capacity seating.' They turned aside to talk about how the accommodation could best be shared.

By the late afternoon, after a makeshift lunch organised by Mr Das, all Prescott's military suggestions for dividing up the compartments had been rejected, and people began to arrange themselves roughly into groups on the midan, with their friends. Jonathan, Jean and I sat with mother under the shade of a banyan at one end of the station compound. Miss Preminder had crept shyly closer and sat a few yards away, looking covertly across to us from time to time.

The group who had diffidently moved nearer to us, giving their half-hearted commitment to joining us for the journey ahead, comprised some five families and several individuals. There was a clergyman, his wife and two daughters; a tall, fierce-looking old gentleman whom I judged to be an ex-Army officer from his military bearing and curt turn of phrase; a Miss Violet Terry, a spinster in her late sixties or early seventies, fluttered uneasily to and fro, holding a pink parasol edged with white lace, to protect her from the sun.

'We've got all the best lookers,' muttered Jonathan, digging me in the ribs and indicating Miss Terry.

By nightfall we were all loaded into the compartments. Our carriage, like the others, had wooden seating for maybe thirty passengers with metal and cord luggage storage racks. The tattered brown lino was split and torn, showing the weft and warp of its string backing. The seating was blackened and shiny from generations of travellers, and the carriage smelt faintly of carbolic soap. There was a closed doorway at one end which led, over a flimsy walkway, to a small toilet which we were to share with the next carriage up the train. The children, including Jonathan and myself, were stowed in the luggage racks, and the adults found themselves places on the wooden seating below.

Miss Terry was among the last to get on. She seemed bewildered, smiling uncertainly round the carriage without looking at anyone in particular. The porter had pushed her cabin trunk through the open door and it had been forced to one side as people came through to claim their seats. There seemed nowhere for her to go. She took a small handkerchief from the sleeve of her dress and held it to her face. I realised, with slight embarrassment, that she was crying.

Jonathan swung over the edge of the luggage rack and lowered himself to the ground. 'I'll find you a place,' he said firmly, taking her by the elbow. He took her down to the corner where Miss Preminder was sitting with my parents. My father looked approving, and a space was made. When Jonathan returned, dragging her trunk behind him to stow under the seat, she was happily exchanging memories of Sialkot with Miss Preminder.

The ten days of that journey from Lahore to Bangalore remain a hazy memory. Mornings looking out of the train window as the sun rose red through the Gobi dust. The metronomic chatter of the rhythm of the wheels, and the change as we clattered over points. The dirt, and the greasy pervasive smells which took over from the carbolic by the third day. Behind all this lies the memory of the fear of that time, which underpins the fragmented details which still recur, seen obliquely and for a moment only, through the corner of an eye. Of violence, of violence, of death.

Miss Preminder's abduction and rape occurred in the night, during one of our frequent and lengthy stops. By the time we had woken in response to her screaming and the violent flurry of activity in the door of the carriage, there was nothing to see. Despite mother's fears, father went out with Colonel Fotheringham, the military gentleman, to return with a grim face half an hour later.

At the time I could only hear snatches of conversation, though I learned the rest later. 'Nothing we could do . . .' he whispered to mother. 'No chance . . . too late by the time we came.'

I looked across at Jonathan, who lay back on one elbow watching them talk. His eyes were wide, but I could not sense what he was thinking, and fell asleep. But, this aside, I have one memory which cannot fade, and which will stay with me until the day I die.

It was the third or fourth day. The previous day we had progressed very slowly, the train chugging gently through the arid sands and shrubs of the Gobi. Occasionally we passed groups of scavenging jackals, who raised their heads to stare with unfrightened curiosity, and then returned to worry at their bloody meals. Once we were going slowly enough to look closely at a corpse, a few feet away in a pile of buzzing flies. Decay had given a deliquescence to the flesh, the mouth gaped like soft rank fruit, the eyes had gone. He was a boy of fifteen or sixteen.

In the morning we had made good time. Somehow the speed of the train had communicated a sense of well-being and purpose to the carriage, and there was much laughter and joking from the adults below. I had spent the morning playing canasta with Jonathan and Miss Terry. She had an infectious laugh and a fund of anecdotes about her childhood as the daughter of missionary parents on the North West Frontier. The hesitation and bewilderment she had shown on the first day had quite gone, and she was often now the comforter of distressed children. Over the past few days I had seen her helping one of the younger mothers, whose little son was badly affected by diarrhoea and vomiting. My own condition varied from day to day, but the tablets I had been given seemed to help.

Just before lunch-time we came slowly into a station and pulled to a halt, with a great hiss of steam and a powerful jolt. The attendant came down the train to announce that tiffin would be served on the station, and we all disgorged the metal plates we had been issued, battered and dented from long use; the metal cup, and the fork and spoon. Mother told us that we were to have a treat of curry and rice. She seemed anxious, as though she had something to say but could not find the words.

As Jonathan and I were about to leave she asked us to wait a minute. When the press of people had moved away from the door she took Jonathan by the shoulder and told him that he was in charge, that we must not look to the left when we got off the train, and must look at our plates when we brought the food back to eat in the carriage. She stood by the door to watch us go. Something gleamed large and unfamiliar, brown and white, at the corner of my left eye as I walked up the platform. Our resolution gave out at about the same time. At first I saw what appeared to be a pile of sandbags. Suddenly I realised that they were naked corpses, stacked neatly layer upon layer, head to foot. There must have been three hundred of them, stiff in the regimented layers, shimmering with buzzing flies. A slight carious breeze flicked across our nostrils, and was gone. We both stopped and stared, any presence of obeying mother lost in the enormity of the vision.

Jonathan said wonderingly, 'It's just like a butcher's shop. Is that all there is to it?' Past us came lines of people returning from the canteen, their lunch bowls full.

Jonathan didn't have any lunch. I ate his share, but then I've always reacted slowly. We saw many more bodies. Six days later we reached Bangalore. My mother had lost two stones in weight. I had amoebic dysentery. Jonathan had ringworm and bacillary dysentery. We all had lice. Those were the only results which could be weighed, measured, diagnosed, assessed, calibrated.

There was a letter waiting for father at Bangalore Station from Stanton. We had left just in time to avoid the sharp escalation in fighting. The church had been vandalised. Dr Mac and Joan had left for a break in Delhi. Stanton's servant, Lal Din, had heard a rumour of a Sikh and his wife and daughter escaping from an ambush in Rawalpindi some months before, and getting safely across the border. From the descriptions it might have been Bulant Singh. We sat on our trunks at the station while father read the letter, first to himself and then, in edited form, to us.

Miss Terry came past with a porter bringing her bags on a trolley. Somehow she had managed to find a fresh dress and, with her white hair and pink face, she could have been going to attend a garden party. She thanked father and mother effusively for all their help, and shook hands gravely with Jean. She turned to Jonathan and me, a gentle smile turning up her mouth at the corners. 'I wanted to thank you boys,' she said, 'It was the best journey I have ever had in my life.'

14

The light was gold through the window. I looked up from time to time as I read, to remind myself of the prosaic normality of my surroundings. Margaret had been right. Beth was a wealthy woman; that much I had culled from the bundle of documents I read first. I turned to the letter from Jonathan. My hand shook and I put the paper on my knee to steady it.

> My dear Beth,
>
> I know you will find it hard to accept that what I have done is nothing directly to do with what you have told me, but that is the truth. You have given me more happiness than I believed possible, and that incident, to me at any rate, is an irrelevant postscript, in that I was unaware of it. If it gave you some happiness or fulfilment which your relationship with me lacked, then I am happy that it happened to you. In the final analysis we all steer a lonely course to wherever we are going.
>
> I don't think the balance of my mind is disturbed, though that is arguably a subjective statement. It has seemed to me that my choices for action have become more and more limited as the years go by, that I have destroyed people, things, relationships rather than preserved them. Now I feel that I am standing in the dark, cut off by my own will and actions from all those I could have loved, and fearful of the demons which seem to pursue me, though I know they have no independent existence outside my own mind. I know that these words will give you little comfort, for though they

have a precise meaning for me they will not for you. I can only say that this action has not been taken because of your unfaithfulness, or because of any failure in you, nor for financial worries, fears for my health, or any of those sane, normal, attributable things. It is because I have run my course, and I cannot face day after day without the sustaining influence of some hope or dreams . . .

There was more, but I couldn't read it. Margaret had come in and sat down. Beth was looking at me, perhaps hoping I could offer her some insight. I had to leave. Perhaps tomorrow, when I saw her again, I could ask some more. There was so much unanswered, and I knew the pieces of the puzzle which I did not already have might be to hand here.

Margaret came with me to the door. Her face was twisted in an expression of distaste. As I put my coat on she quietly said, 'How could you do that to your own brother? I couldn't help hearing . . .'

What could I say? Does it really matter what people think, or is it only that elusive thread of what, at any one time, is right or wrong in some absolute sense, that matters. It rose to my lips to point out that her daughter was not guiltless in what had happened between us, but I knew that what she said had really no more relevance than a belch to relieve the pressure of an over-extended stomach. It occurred to me that she wouldn't tell Leonard, her husband; but I knew that she would spend many dark hours agonising over Beth's part, because she was too intelligent to sustain for long the notion of Beth's complete innocence. I buttoned my coat and walked over to the car. As my tyres crackled down the gravel, two cats screamed at each other somewhere in the garden.

15

1948. It was a year of unhappy exile for Jonathan and me, surrounded in the main by grandmother and aunts, cramped into the city suburbs on the flat, featureless plains of Southern India. We were the guests in a family unaccustomed to boys. Grandfather had died some years before and our grandmother's tendency to treat men as unpleasant and inferior creatures had been allowed to grow unchecked. She was a woman of profuse and diverse talents, bound together chaotically into the personality of a temperamental prima donna.

'I'm going blind,' she announced one day. 'I must have light.' She strode around the old house putting every light on. When mother absent-mindedly put the dining-room light off during a brilliant lunch-time, grandmother turned on her accusingly, 'You don't care about my eyes, you children. Soon I won't be able to see at all.'

Mother and her two sisters were up from their chairs to comfort her. For the next week we had the lights on day and night, and grandmother carried on her intricate needlework with a triumphant smile on her face. It never occurred to mother or Aunt Violet or Aunt Patricia to question their mother. She dominated the household like a squat spider, running to each area of the web as the threads moved — mending, removing objects, watching.

It was a year of convent schools, and learning the responses. 'Hail Mary, full of grace,' I would chant dutifully.

'Take that smile off your silly face,' Jonathan would sing, a few rows behind me.

Reverend Mother would smile benignly, full of distrait other-worldliness. It was rumoured that some of the South

Indian nuns were from a tribe of cannibals, and an apocryphal story was told of a nun at the school who, some years previously, had been found eating a child and had led the authorities to her storeroom in the vaults under the altar where the skeletons of several children were discovered. Whether or not it was true, if those simple nuns found some confusion in a religion whose most sacred rite suggested a glorious union with the Divine through cannibalism, they were not alone.

The doctrines of the Trinity, the Transubstantiation, and the Virgin Birth were concepts which I could not grasp intellectually. At the same time we lived in a household of converts, where the concept of moral values attributable to each action, which my parents had taught us, was intensified into a narrow codification which had a powerful effect upon young minds. Here for the first time was a set of regulations which permitted expiation through a series of simple acts. No longer would I have to hug the knowledge of my own wickedness to me. If the grown-ups could pay for their sins, whatever they might be, by pious attendances at Mass, Confession, and prescribed penances, then this might work for me too.

Jonathan came upon me one afternoon in grandmother's chintzy lounge. He had been out flying kites with Ashok, who lived further down the road, and I had taken advantage of his absence to find out a little more about Catholicism. Grandmother's library contained some gems of Victorian philosophy and sentiment. Ranged alongside Arthur Mee was Samuel Smiles *Self-help*, and by the side of that was a slim, brown leather-bound volume entitled *Some Thoughts About Religion and the Divine Soul* by Revd Arthur Atkinson. It was this that I guiltily pushed under a cushion when he burst in, his kite and the spool of string tucked under his right arm.

'What's that?' he asked, his interest immediately aroused.

I protested that it was nothing, but he was on me and had the book in his hand before I could fend him off.

'Ah-hah!' he shouted in mock triumph, holding the book beyond my reach. 'What have we here. Our earnest young Christian is denying his anthropoid origins.' He threw the book onto the sofa and advanced towards me in an attitude of mock menace.

'Do you repent, you terrible young sinner? Do you plan to spend eternity clad in white raiment and seated upon a cloud playing a harp, or . . .' his voice lowered to a sepulchral guttural '. . . will you be condemned for what you have done to eternal hell fire and damnation?'

I couldn't stop him, and it was some time, and several speeches, before he realised that my eyes were not fixed upon him, but upon my grandmother who stood, quivering with suppressed rage, in the doorway. When we had fallen silent in front of her she surveyed us with a grim look. She addressed her remarks to Jonathan.

'I suppose you think it funny to blaspheme. God is not mocked, young man. I've told your mother that you show a complete disregard for the teachings of your elders.'

Neither of us had anything to say. Our downcast looks seemed to drive her to greater fury. For half an hour she walked up and down the room haranguing us for our shortcomings. Somehow my table manners and Jonathan's appearance entered into it. I came to realise that, in some way, her anger was not directed towards us but was obliquely aimed at my mother.

It was the first time I recollect my father standing up for us. Though nothing was said in front of us we could hear him, late that night when we were meant to be asleep in our shared bedroom, talking to mother. The anger made his words more clipped than usual, and betrayed itself in the inappropriate laughter which often accompanied his explosions of pure rage.

'Well of course I told her. None of her business.'

My mother's response was inaudible. Father must have gone to the drinks cupboard for the next sound was the chink of the decanter on glass. His heavy tread sounded across the parquet flooring.

'You must realise that her whole attitude was an implied criticism of the way we have brought our boys up. I won't have that.' The little explosions of laughter began, and I pulled the sheets tighter around me. I could see in the half darkness that Jonathan was awake. He lay with his hands behind his head, looking at the ceiling. Though it was hard to see his face in detail it seemed that he was smiling.

In the next room father continued: 'She's permitted her own

daughters to absorb the stupid, bigoted prejudices of this cloistered community.' His voice rose, 'How can we expect them to cope with life in an English public school if this is what they're taught? Tell me that.'

Something had struck a chord in him, and I could hear him raging on and on after I had ceased to pay attention, secure in the knowledge that we were safe from his wrath. In the end it had not escaped my attention, or Jonathan's, that this had been no defence of us, but rather that the incident had obliquely criticised the wisdoms by which we had been raised.

In the morning I waited for Jonathan to finish cleaning his teeth. Outside grandmother was supervising the milking of the cow which was brought around and tethered to the side of the house where she could ensure that the milk wasn't watered. We could hear her raised voice: 'Krishna, how often have I told you to wash this bucket properly?' There was a loud clang as she hit the bucket with the end of her walking stick. The cow gave a mournful low.

Jonathan spat the waste out into the bowl, and washed his toothbrush. 'They don't own us, you know,' he said.

Grandmother had never forgiven Jonathan or me for being the unwitting instigators of father's quarrel with her. After the incident she merely ignored us. Any necessary business with us, thereafter, was done through one of our aunts, a servant, or even the dog.

'Well, Towser,' she would say, leaning down to play with her spaniel's ear affectionately, 'If those boys don't leave for school they'll be late.'

Only once did either of us rebel against the convention. Grandmother was seated at the breakfast table in her wrap, a cup of coffee cradled in her plump white hands, her malicious eyes never still. I was ready to leave but Jonathan was finishing his toast, so I sat and waited. The elderly house servant, Gus, shuffled in to clear the table and grandmother leaned forward confidentially. I felt the familiar crab of tension in my stomach as she started to speak, knowing that her remarks would contain some barb intended for one or other of us.

'Did you sleep well?' she asked Gus.

Gus thought about this for a moment, scratching the sparse

hair on top of his shiny brown head. Finally, having given the matter due deliberation, he volunteered that he had. 'Yes'm. I sleep very well now I'm —'

Grandmother cut him off with a smile. 'You're lucky. Just as I got to sleep there was a terrible screaming which woke me up, and I wasn't able to get back to sleep at all!' She leaned back triumphantly, looking carefully away from us.

I saw that Jonathan had gone very white, his head shaking slightly as it did when he was angry. 'I had a nightmare,' he said, getting up quickly so he stood right at her side. She gave no indication of having heard, and he yelled into her ear at the top of his voice 'I had a nightmare!' and ran from the room, sobbing with rage and frustration.

Grandmother called Towser over and gave him a piece of toast. 'There's a good boy,' she said. 'who's a good boy then?'

After we had been in Bangalore for about nine months father returned to the Punjab to see whether conditions had improved. During the next three months his letters were infrequent and heavily censored, but a succession of people came to pay their respects and to say they had seen him. When he returned he looked tired and thin. He had been offered a job which would involve arranging an orderly transition from British to Pakistani administration. He warned us that we must not expect things to be as they had been when we left. People had gone, and everywhere there was evidence of the war. We had about ten days to prepare for the return.

With the prospect of being rid of the twelve-month domination by women, Jonathan and I took on a new lease of life. The servile acceptances of our stay could be shrugged off, now that we saw the end in sight. Jonathan brought in the frogs he had kept in the bamboo plantation in the garden and put them down grandmother's toilet. Her histrionics were gratifying. We rampaged around the gardens like little arabs, ignoring the shocked faces at the window.

When the time came to leave we said our goodbyes to grandmother and our aunts dutifully, outside the station, but the sense of mutual relief was almost tangible.

'I hate women,' Jonathan announced to me with feeling, as the train slowly moved out of the station with much hissing of steam. On the station the small figures waved, almost hidden in the vapour. Then we were out from under the great canopy and into the blinding sunlight. As we walked to the compartment Jonathan kept digging me in the ribs saying, 'We're free, we're free,' and he skipped down the corridor shouting his glee past the startled passengers.

The boat trip to Bombay, after the train, was a desperate affair. Above decks we were the only family. Below decks, in conditions the cargo of live-stock could barely tolerate, some twenty Indian families lived — in all senses of the word — cooked their meals, and were copiously sick. The excitement at the prospect of our return began to be modified.

Five days after leaving Bangalore we were on the bus driving up the winding road from Rawalpindi. I held my breath, convinced that some savage change would have been wrought upon the hills and forests but they were unscarred and as they had always been in my memory. There were changes, but they were within me, and not within that eternal landscape.

Kajan came to meet us by the gutted brewery at the bottom of the hill. He seemed thinner and less ebullient, but otherwise unaltered. Accompanying him were some coolies to carry the baggage, and a dandy for mother. We walked slowly up the winding road, savouring the resinous smells, and the familiarity of the landscape. Jean and father together behind the dandy, while Jonathan and I went ahead. Above the road, on the fleshy swell of hills covered in couch grass, the gentians swayed in thick, disordered ranks to the edge of the dark pines.

As we reached the polo ground which marked the lower edge of the estate I saw a solitary figure standing by one of the pine trees, one hand resting against the rough bark.

By my side Jonathan shouted 'Ram, Ram,' and ran forward with his arms outstretched.

Behind us I heard Kajan shouting urgently, 'Nay Sahib, Nay, Sahib.' I began to run after Jonathan. This more than the hills and trees was the real sign that we had returned. Ram stood still by the tree. I was just behind as Jonathan put his arms around Ram and hugged him. Something seemed strange, unnatural, strained.

Ram stood limply as Jonathan hugged him. His face bore the

vacant, absent look of someone who has no awareness of his surroundings. As Jonathan stepped back and started to talk, Ram suddenly smiled. Light shone into a pink, empty cavern. He had no tongue any more, and only a deep gargling sound came out. Jonathan fell back against me. There was nothing to say as we watched Ram walk away through the trees until he was lost to sight.

Kajan came up behind us and took Jonathan's arm. Almost pleadingly he said, 'He was warning people. Karam Deen's men came one night . . .' he left the sentence unfinished. We resumed our walk up the hill.

So we came home.

Ram had not been the only casualty of the war. Blackened ruins dotted the landscape where once fine houses had stood. In the year we had been away most of the people we had known had left for England. Joan and Dr Mac had come back, and the Stantons had remained throughout the rioting. It was a sad little assembly, on our first evening back, around the clubhouse bar. It was dusty and run-down. A broken window had been carelessly patched with plywood and the tables stood in listless disarray, each covered in a complement of chairs. The new barman, Ali, was willing enough, although there were very few supplies. But the first half hour was exciting as we all exchanged information about the last year.

Dr Mac had received a letter from a cousin in London who had run into a 'substantial Indian gentleman' who, on finding out in conversation of the relationship, had hugged him in Veeraswamy's restaurant, shouting 'English proverb very true. It is a small world. Please tell my friends you have met me.' Unfortunately he had been dragged away by his friends who were in a hurry to leave, and hadn't given his name.

'It must be Bully,' said father, and Dr Mac smiled, filling his pipe.

The events of the year had hastened Frances Stanton's decline. Her skin looked so thin and fine that we were afraid even to shake her hand. She sat in one of the low chairs, and it was evident that even this was almost more of an effort than she could make. She had already some tenuous connection with death which expressed itself in her slow, patient smile, and in the feeling she gave of having sunk into some region beyond the reach of our excited exchanges. Jonathan sat by her side and said very little. Once, when her shawl slipped, he rose immediately and put it around her shoulders. Stanton smiled across at him. The year had aged him, too. There was little flesh on his big frame, and he watched his wife constantly with a kind of helpless tenderness.

Dr Mac came over from the bar where he had been talking to father, and they both joined us round the table. Mac looked over at Jonathan and said, 'Ram doesn't suffer, you know,' as though the comment were a part of a dialogue which had been going on between them, unheard by the rest of us. Immediately I saw Jonathan's face contort, and he brushed the back of his hand across his eyes. It took a moment or two before he could control himself enough to to speak. 'Is he mad, Dr Mac?'

Mac concentrated upon filling his pipe, then lit it with a match, drawing deeply until the tobacco glowed an even red.

'He isn't mad in the conventional sense. He has gone into what is called a fugue state — a flight from reality. He denies the reality of everything that has happened to him, and so shuts out the pain.' There was an embarrassed silence. Dr Mac was breaking an old convention in talking in these terms. Our community had understood honour and courage and moral virtue, but ideas about behaviour which were not rooted in the heroic virtues were suspect, particularly those which suggested that self-interest was acceptable.

Jonathan smiled gratefully at Dr Mac, who smiled back at him as if he had not noticed the silence which greeted his remark.

Father cleared his throat. 'As soon as we're installed in the new house we must have a house-warming,' he said, putting his hand on mother's shoulder, and this moved the conversation into other channels.

Jonathan said to me, 'Let's have a look at the pool,' and we slipped out into the moonlight. I didn't say anything because I knew he was embarrassed to show emotion and wanted to recover himself.

We walked up the asphalt road past the tennis courts. As we neared the baths there was the sound of splashing and laughter. We reached the grassy hill above the baths and could see, in the bright silver light, several of the estate servants swimming in the pool. One or two of them waved to us, and then went back to the rudimentary polo game they had been playing when we arrived. The water looked black and uninviting, and a fine scummy froth speckled with dead leaves and pine needles lapped and sucked at the hand-rail channel which ran around the bath. We stood for a short while watching the game. Then Jonathan turned towards the clubhouse and we walked back in silence.

When we arrived back in mother said, 'Where have you been?' Her voice sounded anxious, as if the trees around the estate still bristled with murderous bands.

'We've been watching the servants playing water polo in the pool,' said Jonathan with a laugh.

Father stopped his conversation with Stanton in mid-sentence. He looked incredulous, as if he could not believe what he had heard. 'What did you say?' His colour, always high, had darkened his face immediately.

Jonathan, surprised, repeated the information.

'We'll see about this,' said father, striding towards the door, but Dr Mac barred his way. 'A lot of things have changed now,' he said, 'we must go carefully.'

Ali smiled with a fleeting knowing look. Father stood before Dr Mac for a moment as if he would push him aside, but Mac stood firmly planted in the doorway, the relaxed smile never leaving his face. 'Another round, please, Ali,' he said, leading father back to the table.

We walked back up the road to the new house where all our packing cases still stood in empty rooms. As we passed the swimming baths we could hear laughter and voices, and Jonathan nudged me in the ribs. Ahead of us I heard father say to mother: 'Mac's gone native, more's the pity.'

Mother looked down at the pool. 'Where's the harm in it?' she said, and took his arm.

They walked in silence for a few steps, and I heard mother start to talk about Frances Stanton. From her tones it was obvious what she was saying, without attempting to distinguish the soft sibilants.

Jonathan said to me, 'She's dying, you know. She's very young to die.' He sounded hurt and puzzled, like a child who cannot understand why his favourite toy won't work any more.

In 1949 we left India. Jonathan had preceded us and had been at school in England for some months. Father had finally decided to retire and we settled in a small hamlet in Cornwall. By then I had joined Jonathan and my jealousy of him added to the misery I felt, exiled to this strange, grey country, amidst this barbarous collection of strange boys with their cruel institutions. It began slowly, a small canker which went into remission from time to time, depending upon the way Jonathan behaved towards me. But the school gave me a perspective on Jonathan within which I could see his need to win, to be first or at least ahead, which denied our relationship a sense of peace and affection. The years between us separated us far more within the school than they had formerly. I knew that the rules governing that society precluded him from helping me when, within the first month, I joined the other new boys, naked and trembling, to push a pencil around the changing rooms with my nose while the previous year's victims flicked me with wet towels. I knew that he could not intervene in the system which forced me to fag, or which permitted the contents of my tuck-box to be distributed between the older boys. My turn would come, and these were the laws which Arnold and his successors believed were the making of men and of captains of industry. What separated us was that I could not complain to him in private of the injustices I had suffered, could derive no solace from him for the abuses under which I led my daily life. If he had been different he could have helped but his eyes were looking beyond.

During the holidays we maintained an uneasy peace of sorts, more for the sake of Jean and my parents than from a natural inclination to do so. Such an abyss existed between their ideas of school life and the reality that there was little to say to them, and the bonds became weak and tenuous, decayed by the half-truths and compromised statements we were forced into uttering.

Only once did I attempt to tell Jean what really happened, to convey the flavour of the experience to her. We walked down the disused railway line with the dogs at our heels. From the distant quarry came the boom of detonations, and the summer vacation traffic roared ceaselessly past on the raised embankment some thirty feet above us. We had been talking about games.

'Go on,' she persisted, when I had drawn back from the brink of telling her what had happened after we had played cricket against a neighbouring school during the summer.

'Well,' I said lamely, 'they offered us beer, and we were allowed to smoke in their studies. The masters knew . . .'

'Is that all?' she said scornfully. Stung by her contempt I gave in to the temptation to tell her everything, knowing, as I said it, that I was making a mistake. As she walked by my side and the dogs rushed ahead, sniffing through the meadow grass and buttercups, I felt with part of my mind that nothing could be the same after the revelation I was about to make.

'When we came back from tea,' I went on, 'the corridor outside the dining-room was lined with small boys.' I could see her stiffen. 'And we were told that we could choose any one we wanted.'

Jean stopped and looked at me, her face showing her horror. 'You mean . . . for that?' she asked, and I nodded. 'But if they didn't want to?'

'That's nothing to do with it at all,' I said. 'Everything's like that at school.'

The sky darkened as a cloud moved across the sun. Jean stood for a moment, looking up at the hills beyond the road. 'That's horrible,' she said, and began to cry. We walked back ten yards apart, and her shaking shoulders ahead of me reproached me for having told the story.

I did realise at school that I had power over Jonathan, even if it was only power of an indirect and unusable nature. Though he tried to disguise from me the nature of the requests when he made them, I knew that he portrayed himself as the good son to my parents, and was anxious to preserve this image at all costs.

Two incidents occurred during our school-days which prompted him to approach me to ask if I would keep my silence. 'It's really nothing, but I don't want to bother them. They're getting on, you know, and they don't really understand what goes on here . . .' Though each time I acquiesced, I had found at last a weapon which, unused, had some unseen future potential.

The first occurred when I was fourteen and Jonathan sixteen. Though I think he was indifferent to sport he had, nevertheless, got into the 1st XV at rugby. The school was not academic, but had a considerable reputation at games, and once we had reached the Senior School at the age of twelve we were forced, willy-nilly, to devote any Saturday afternoon on which the 1st XV were playing at home, to watching the rugby.

On the occasion in question we were playing a west country crammer, many of whose teams were virtually club members; older, more powerful and jealous of their unbeaten reputation. It was a cold, damp day, and our breath smoked in the dank air. Whenever the players wheeled and ran past the touchline where I stood with Thomas and Pulford, my particular friends, I caught the reek of mud and sweat. Being the last match of the season the mayor of the local town and his wife were in attendance with the headmaster. The head had played for Cambridge thirty years before, and constantly broke into his own conversation with the Mayor to yell advice.

'Get it out, Watkins, out, out . . .' then a few moments later, 'Don't hold on to it, man, pass it down the line.' It was hard to comprehend such passion.

By half-time we were a try and a penalty down. There had been an ugly fracas in the first half, and our tight head prop had a bad tear at the top of one ear. As the second half started it was obvious that tempers were frayed, and, after three very bad-tempered loose mauls the referee whistled up and talked to the two sides. For a short while everything seemed to be more controlled. Then Watkins, the scrum half, kicked up the field towards their twenty-five, and our forwards streamed after the ball. Their full-back, unable to clear the ball, fell upon it, and the pack, including Jonathan, formed around him.

As the maul rucked and swayed a voice could be heard from the middle of the press of bodies: 'Oh God, my head, my head!'

The referee ran up and blew his whistle, and the wrestling mass whirled and pulled apart. All save Jonathan, his face a contorted mask of fury, who was grinding the aluminium studs of his boot into the face of the full-back. He seemed not to have heard the referee's whistle, and, even when he had been pulled back by two of his team mates his face wore an expression of committed fury, as if it were legitimate for him to vent his anger in this fashion. He was sent off, and we lost the match.

Later he said to me, 'No need to say anything about that,' but this voice carried a note of anxious query. I said nothing. He was mildly reproved by his house master, but as a potential Oxbridge candidate, was afforded the best protection possible.

In the summer of his last year Jonathan was captain of cricket. In retrospect his application to these games was amazing, since he genuinely had no stomach for group activities, but the record was still there in gold letters on the board of the school assembly room for all to see when last I went back, unwillingly, to give the prizes as a distinguished old boy.

The most important match of the season was against Downham who, that year, had an unbeaten record for three years. We batted first under a cloudless sky, and for once I found I was interested in the game, and my pulse stirred and quickened as the runs were scored. At tea-time Jonathan declared at 185 for 7, having contributed a graceful 48 not out himself. But after tea it was rapidly apparent that the story was by no means over. Their opening bat, a solid, blond six-footer, plodded steadily and slowly towards his 50 without giving a chance, while his three partners put on 140 between them.

The cheering grew more intense from the small group of Downham spectators segregated with their master on the far boundary. Then the fifth man and the opener settled in, and the score stood at 143 for 5 by the time a catch at silly mid-on and an LBW decision dismissed both of them in the same over. By the time the last man came in there were only seven runs to get, and the Downham supporters were cheering and nudging each other in expectation.

Henderson, the slow spinner, who had dismissed most of

their batsmen, delivered a slow off break and the batsman stepped forward to the pitch, squaring his shoulders, then stepped back and poked at the ball. It went straight up in the air towards mid-on and Jenkins, a sixth form contemporary of Jonathan, ran towards it, squinting into the sun. The ball hung in the air at the top of the parabola — almost held up by the hundreds of eyes watching from the boundary and the field. He couldn't miss it! There was an audible hiss of triumph. Then the ball dropped through his fingers and bounced a few feet on the turf. Jenkins picked it up — his face already reddening in confusion — and threw it towards the wicket. It went wide and the batsmen stole two runs. A lucky four and a grabbed single and the match was over.

Jenkins was taken to sick bay that evening with a suspected fractured collar-bone and bruised ribs. Whilst a certain amount of 'horseplay' was tolerated in the interests of what the headmaster called '*mens sana in corpore sano*', this could not be overlooked.

When a request for information produced nothing, the headmaster announced that members of the 1st XI were gated until the ringleaders owned up. A day later Jonathan went to see the head. At assembly the following morning the head announced that Jonathan had taken entire blame for the incident, and had shown by his behaviour how a true leader should behave; that he would accept this symbolic act though he personally knew that Jonathan, who had won an Open Scholarship to Trinity College, Cambridge, was not the type of person to carry out such a brutal act upon a defenceless boy. That he knew that Jonathan would ensure that those responsible would reap some appropriate punishment 'within the time-honoured framework in which these things are settled at our school'.

When I travelled home with Jonathan on the train that holiday I was suddenly aware he hated me, but as we were brothers he could never openly acknowledge it.

16

'What are you going to do, son?' was a comment which had nagged at my ambitionless progress since I was thirteen. Usually my father would make such a start to a conversation from behind his *Daily Telegraph*, some three days into the holiday, before my school report had arrived. A vague sensation of guilt would irritate the back of my mind. So many of my contemporaries had known for years what they would do. They were destined for flourishing law practices in Cardiff, or merchant banks in the City. It seemed that Jonathan and I alone had failed to offer ourselves for the Law, the Church, or the Services, in the absence of a family profession or firm into which we could thankfully fall. I would sit motionless, praying for the moment to pass without incident, or for some cataclysmic happening to divert my father's attention and expunge thoughts of my future from his mind.

'Well, er . . .' I would start, mistaking the rhetoric for a genuine question. How I could have been repeatedly mistaken in this is hard to understand now. The ritual was always the same.

In retirement, father's tongue had assumed a sharper edge. He would get up from his chair, removing his spectacles, and would close the door. I can only guess that some secret grapevine had warned everyone else to be out shopping, or be out for a walk, or be absent on some other business, for no one ever came to my rescue. He would then pace across the gold Tabriz carpet which lay across the centre of the lounge, while he speculated aloud on what the future might hold for me. I am surprised, now, that I never felt angry, only humiliated and diminished by what was said on these occasions.

'Let's see —' his spectacles folded in his right hand, tapping his lip with the end '— you paint, of course. It won't cost too much to set yourself up . . . two pairs of white dungarees, a couple of paint brushes. Perhaps there'll be a vogue for ex-public school painters. People might use you in preference to a genuine artisan because it will give them something to talk about . . .'

I would sit mute under his flailing tongue. Though the exact details differed from time to time, the themes that he drew out of these long monologues remained the same: the way in which he and my mother had scrimped to send 'you children' to private schools; my seeming indifference to the needs of the progressive future; the way in which I let the family down. After an hour the sarcasm would ripen into disgust. A contrast between father's childhood, dogged by early responsibility, the selfless chopping of wood and the paper round, and my own cushioned existence, would be made. Finally, with a gesture of washing his hands he would end up.

'There seems little point in talking to you. Your interests seem to be confined to girls and asinine music — neither of which will stand you in much stead once you are cast upon your own resources.'

My isolation was underlined when Jonathan got his scholarship to Trinity to read History. 'I'm one of Willey's boys,' he said, and told me that Willey was his moral tutor and had — in his time — been a famous Marxist historian at Cambridge in the thirties. Willey was an old friend of the headmaster and they had both won Half-Blues at squash.

During the vacations in those long two years, when Jonathan came down from Cambridge and I from school, to pursue our divided and increasingly mutually secretive lives, father would introduce Jonathan with pride. 'This is my elder son. He has a scholarship at Cambridge.'

Though it was not Jonathan's fault, I felt embittered by his success, as if he had stolen some portion of my birthright from me. It was hard to comprehend his new existence, full of strange expressions and reeking of the strange odours of the outside world.

It began more and more to seem that Jonathan stood between me and the sun. I envied him and hated him. The divisions which had appeared and vanished, only to reappear again, in our childhood in India and then at school, were now emphasised and scribed beyond deleting. I sensed in the way Jonathan listened to me, with half-closed eyes and a small smile on his mouth, his feeling of superiority over me. He began to join in adult discussions, to contribute with considerable and amusing ability, his own anecdotes and points of view. Each day that I passed in his company accentuated my clumsy and inarticulate oafishness. During his second long vacation he had saved almost enough for a small second-hand car. At breakfast one morning father slipped a cheque on to the table for the balance of the purchase. I took the dogs for a long, long walk, unable to join my friends and hardly able to be civil to the villagers I passed. Two days after Jonathan bought the car, my parents invited the small amateur group over for a few drinks to celebrate the end of their production of *Dracula*.

Falling in love at seventeen is a serious business. When Jacqueline arrived at the door I could only gaze at her for a moment, before fumbling to help remove her coat. As the other players crowded into the hall I could feel my heart beating wildly, and hardly noticed the people who were introducing themselves. Amidst the theatrical conversations and the bubbling laughter, Jonathan and I threaded through the groups, replenishing their glasses. I kept taking her canapés and peanuts for the first hour, until she shook her pretty dark head at me with a smile, and laid one white imperious hand on my sleeve.

'I couldn't possibly,' she said in her deliciously throaty voice. 'I'll put on weight.' I stammered my apologies and rushed to the kitchen to double up in wincing embarrassment at my inept display. Later in the evening I sat by her side. She seemed a little tired, as if she needed a rest from the babel going on around her.

'What do you do?' she said, leaning towards me, so that the curve of one enchanting breast swayed into view down the deep divide of her white, swathed neckline. Mesmerised by the sight, I was desperately trying to find some witty response which concealed the true state of affairs, when I heard my father's voice behind me.

'He's still at school,' he said, and I turned to see him smile momentarily, before resuming his conversation with Dracula. I saw the interest die in her eyes, the almost imperceptible shift as she looked around the room. In that instant I felt my world had ended, and, for the first time, felt a passing instant of pure hatred for my father.

'Have you met Jonathan?' said father, and Jonathan stood before us, assured, well-groomed, at ease. I left him the field, muttering some face-saving formula about seeing to the glasses. The evening rolled interminably on, and I smiled and made polite conversation until the last guest had left. When the house was quiet I lay in bed and wept, stuffing the corner of my pillow into my mouth so that the sounds wouldn't penetrate into my parents' room.

But I, too, got to Cambridge without expectation or any other thought for the future.

'He's always hidden his talents from us,' said father to mother.

During my second year I felt disillusion steal over me. The importance of the first year, and, above all, the opportunity to draw level with Jonathan again, had now dulled before the realisation that Cambridge provided no answers for the questions which nagged at me with an increasing persistence.

I had digs in Maid's Causeway. Through the window of my room I could watch the fanatical oarsmen taking their fours and eights out from six o'clock in the morning. Belinda, the landlady's voluptuous daughter, brought me an early morning cup of tea in bed every day. Her transparent willingness was underlined by the pink towelling dressing-gown she wore, cinched loosely at the waist, whose neckline barely contained one of her large white breasts when she leaned over to put my tea on the bedside table.

'Anything you want?' she would enquire with a fleeting, tempting smile, but though she sometimes occupied a steamy place in my thoughts, I had a suspicion that she was seeking a more permanent liaison than I had in mind, and might be prepared to further her ambitions by 'falling pregnant', a nice euphemism which was in vogue at the time.

So I would say, 'No, thanks very much,' and, after breakfast, would troop off for the round of the morning's lectures. I had begun to move away from the schoolboy dream of a permanently available — and aroused — stream of glossy fantasy women. My encounters over the past few years had been hastily consummated in the backs of cars, in nettle patches on woodland walks, and, on one occasion, my trousers round my ankles and my shoes still on, in the marriage bed still warm from the departure of a husband for the day shift. Though these activities had their excitements and their fulfilment in a limited sense, I felt, more than ever, the division between the nasty, brutish, and short things I was doing with a variety of women, and my idealistic dream of how I would like life to be with one.

One day in the early November of my twenty-first year, I came out of Hall, and decided that I would not, for once, go round to The Eagle to meet up with the members of the Moral Sciences Faculty who were, by way of revision, discussing the aims of philosophy each night to the accompaniment of several pints of Abbotts Ale.

Philosophy tended to win through in the early part of the evening; by the end, save in the rare cases where somebody was actually sick in the oak-settled lounge, the landlord undoubtedly did. The previous night we had done some fairly serious revision. Brian O'Donnell, a poker-faced bespectacled Irish post-graduate student, well over six feet tall and with a considerable capacity for beer, took it upon himself to discuss the idea of the Good with me. Such conversations often provoked hilarity in the assorted group of engineers, zoologists and natural scientists who joined us.

'Can you prove anything, Brian?' Chris Newman, a pragmatic, second-year mechanical engineer, mocked. Brian faced these assaults with a precarious dignity. One large hand in front of him, the other cradling his pint on the stained round table, he would stop the conversation.

'Dear boy, you scientists have such vulgar minds. Unless

anything is capable of proof it seems not worth consideration. Though, I might say, by way of diversion, that I understand you seem not to have one entirely consistent and irreducible theory relating to the behaviour of electricity. Nor can you reconcile the general Theory of Relativity with Quantum Mechanics.' The ensuing jeers had no effect upon him. 'Can you absolutely prove the innate goodness or badness of the rules by which we choose to live as a society? No. But nevertheless, we no longer hang witches, or anyone for that matter. We no longer have rotten boroughs. We will soon be permitting homosexuality between consenting adults in private —' with a humorous glance at Newman, who had recently decided to admit his homosexuality. 'None of these things would have evolved and our culture would be immeasurably poorer if we did not constantly question the assumptions upon which our society is based.'

Nobody felt much like taking it further. Brian could argue all night, with passion and conviction. He turned to me, his wide blue eyes owlish behind the heavy round glasses. 'Well, David. Do you believe in the Platonic Idea of the Good as an absolute quality which has an independent existence verifiable by argument? Or do you believe that the Good is found in those actions which tend towards promoting the greatest happiness of the greatest number?'

It seemed to me, suddenly, that the quasi-serious question crystallised my feelings of disillusion about Cambridge. I did not want Brian's basilisk eye boring into me all evening as we interminably discussed these arid ideas. In the corner a girl with a red blouse leaned towards the heavy-set undergraduate with whom she sat.

I said flippantly, 'Whatever is, is right. Isn't that the post-Freudian message? Within limits there is no evil and no good. Only self-interest in all things. Even the highest form of altruism can no longer be considered pure or sacrosanct. Only a desire to see oneself in a particular way.'

As Brian opened his mouth to reply, Jonathan came in with a group of people, a girl on his arm. I recognised some of the Trinity crowd. Giles Mason, President of the Union, with his thin, clever mouth. Simon Molyneaux-Templeton, a prominent debater and one of the leading lights of the Amateur Dramatic Club. A number of the others I had met, from time to time, at cheese and wine parties at Jonathan's rooms in Great Court, Trinity.

The girl was small and dark, with an olive skin and long brown hair hanging down her back. She seemed calm, involved in herself and her own quietness, amidst the babel around her.

I went over, and Jonathan introduced me to her. 'Rachel, this is my brother David.'

He looked around the bar as if searching for someone else and I smiled and shook her hand. She glanced at me for a moment, and then turned away.

Mason was shouting from the corner to Jonathan, 'He isn't here. Shall we try the Little Rose?'

Jonathan nodded. 'Do you want to join us? We're off to a party in London.'

Brian said to Jonathan, 'Not tonight. I'll come next time.'

I didn't feel too confident, looking at the flushed faces, and made my excuses. They walked out into the night, talking loudly.

It is only in retrospect, that one can see a moment which changes one's life. Perhaps Rachel had arrived at the moment when I felt most keenly the hollowness of my earlier affairs. It may, too, have had some connection with her being with Jonathan which provoked me to think more about her. She had a foreignness, a strangeness which had immediately attracted me. Her very withdrawal from the noise and bustle of the group was remarkable in itself.

Brian looked at me when they had gone, an amused grin on his face. 'I never thought I'd see it,' he said wryly. 'L-U-R-V-E at first sight.'

Hiding my embarrassment I countered, 'You've been reading too many Wittgenstein romances. Why don't you go and write me a first person Apologia for suicide?'

He laughed, and punched my arm with a mock aggressive gesture. 'So I was right. Get you one for the road.'

After that I joined the general conversation in a desultory way. Half my mind was preoccupied with Rachel. Jonathan's relationships with women were a closed book to me, so I had no idea of what may or may not have happened. She had not been in evidence when I saw him at a party a week before, so he may well just have met her. From time to time Brian shot me a sardonic glance, as though to imply that I had fallen into a trap which he had avoided.

At 10.40 we spilled out into Bene't Street. Miles Sinclair's large car stood ostentatiously outside the Bath Hotel. Wealthy, clever Miles had to use his money to ingratiate himself. He carried within himself something oleaginous, some whiff of putrescence which alienated all his year in the faculty. Brian and I began to move slowly down towards King's Parade when suddenly, with a wild whoop, he turned and ran towards Sinclair's car. With a spring, he was on the polished bonnet which creaked and dented under his weight. Another spring and he was dancing on the roof. A group of undergraduates stopped in amazement on the other side of the road, and their laughter prompted a pushing scrum of men in the doorway of the Bath Hotel.

'Come up,' roared Brian at the top of his voice, holding out his hand to me, 'the view up here is fantastic.' He drawled the words out, grunting with the effort of hauling me up. As we swayed, arm in arm, the metalwork of the roof began to buckle.

Miles appeared at the door, pushing his way through the crowd and Brian shouted to him, 'Ask not for whom the roof buckles, Miles. It buckles for thee.'

Down the street I noticed the Senior Proctor approaching with his bulldogs. Brian was past running, and I doubted I could out-distance them the three miles to Maid's Causeway. They moved ponderously forward, and stood just beyond the crowd of undergraduates on the pavement watching the proceedings.

'Mr O'Donnell, I believe,' said the Senior Proctor in a silky voice.

Brian swayed on his feet, and, taking the ends of his gown in his hands, made an exaggerated curtsey. 'Dr Willey, I presume. Though it may be hard for you to believe, sir, my presence here is a complete accident. I was passing by this venerable establishment with my friend here —' he clasped me around the shoulders, indicating the Bath Hotel '— when an apparition of singular repugnance appeared in the doorway and my autonomic nervous system took over. Before I knew what had happened I was up here taking refuge. I plead justifiable self-defence.' He delivered all this with such good humour that I fancied I saw Willey smile under the mortar-board. It didn't extend to the dry voice.

'Thank you, Mr O'Donnell. I do not believe the Arts Theatre will be requiring your further services for the moment. Now, if you and your friend will please give your names to Mr Jebson here we can carry on with our business, and leave you to yours.'

When he was out of sight, walking magisterially behind the bulldogs, I asked Brian, 'How do you know Willey?'

I fancied he was a bit shifty as he answered, 'Oh, I've known him for years. I go along with Jonathan to his Monday evening meetings.'

Brian was philosophical as we walked back to college for a coffee before I returned to my digs. It was a fine and perhaps a gating for a couple of weeks.

'But don't you find it ludicrous that we should be treated like this?' I said incredulously.

He shrugged. 'For what I've done tonight the law would prescribe a much tougher sentence,' he said. 'As it is, I've had a bit of fun and dented Sinclair's self-esteem and his car for a meaningless fine.'

I would never have managed to convince him that this was precisely the point I was making. That we were robbed, by a paternalistic and patronising university legislature, of the right to adult punishments for adult offences. As if we were all retarded in some sense.

As I arrived back at Maid's Causeway, Mrs Richards was peering down the lane anxiously. 'Ah, there you are,' she said in a relieved way. She was a stickler for university discipline and we were meant to be in by eleven unless we had an exeat.

Belinda lounged at the bottom of the stairs, in a tight sweater with pink mules on her feet. My slight stirrings of lust were guiltily dampened by a memory of Rachel.

So, for all these reasons, this evening I had forsaken my usual haunts in favour of going to a coffee bar in the Market Square and from thence back to my room. Not that this was an entirely virtuous occupation, since the coffee bar was normally occupied by the sleek continental girls from the language schools. For company I had persuaded Peter Garster, a third year economist, to join me.

The Market Square was yellow under the sodium lighting, and the rain drizzled down as it had all day. Small groups of undergraduates hurried towards the Arts Cinema, huddled under umbrellas, or rushing from door to door to try and keep dry. The Criterion Coffee Bar, standing at the corner of the square, served terrible coffee at exorbitant prices. But few people were there for the coffee. Peter got a table and I went over to the counter. I could feel the evening was a mistake already; the girls in their brilliant plumage were as unassailable as the pictures we had passed from hand to hand at school. Peter, a compulsive worker, was already surreptitiously peeling back the cuff of his rather grubby sweater to look at his watch.

'Thanks,' he said, as I slopped the coffee down beside him and offered him a cigarette. 'Don't mind if I do.'

Across the crowded tables I saw Giles Mason talking to a pretty girl with blonde hair. He acknowledged my presence with a vague wave of his hand, and the girl looked round, as if fearful of missing something of importance.

Peter said, 'I was sorry to hear about Jonathan,' pulling me sharply back to the present.

'What about Jonathan?'

He eyed me uncertainly. Anxiety had lent an edge to my voice. 'Aaah . . the story that's going round is that —' he looked round him as if he would like to escape, desperately embarrassed to have brought this up. To give himself time he picked up his coffee cup, but his hand shook, and he placed the cup back in the saucer.

'What is the story, Peter?'

It transpired that Jonathan had attacked and beaten up a fellow student. They had been in a group in the Great Court at Trinity some evenings before, and one of the fellows' wives had walked through on her way to the Master's Lodge. One of the group was a student named Atkinson who, by all accounts, was bright and witty but tended to be abrasive. He, apparently, had made a barbed comment about her morals. In the general laugh that followed Jonathan had grabbed hold of him and truculently asked him what basis he had for making the comment.

Atkinson had chosen the wrong line in attempting to turn the feelings of the group against Jonathan, making some comment about 'immature schoolboys who behaved as if every woman was the Virgin Mary.' Jonathan had taken him by the throat and smashed his face into the wall of the cloisters, eventually having to be pulled off the near-unconscious Atkinson. Atkinson was now in the college sick-bay with a broken nose, and there was a rumour that the Master had received a solicitor's letter and that Jonathan might be sent down.

Peter evidently knew little more, and had begun to waffle. I excused myself and walked over to Giles' table. His thin, politician's face had a wary look as I pulled up a chair, acknowledging the girl's presence with a quick smile.

'I've only just heard about Jonathan,' I said. 'Perhaps you can fill me in on the latest news.'

He laughed uncomfortably, shifting his bottom from side to side on his seat. A lock of black hair fell over his eye, and he flicked it back with an impatient gesture.

'There's very little to tell. We've got together a petition to say he was quite justified and we're putting it in before he sees the Master tomorrow. He'll be all right.'

'How's the victim? Atkinson?'

'A bit bruised around the nose and eyes. Slightly shocked, but nothing serious.'

The girl watched us with blue, serious eyes shifting from face to face as we talked, like a spectator at a tennis match. Giles put a hand over hers, in a gesture which indicated that this interruption would soon be over, and that they could then resume their conversation. Though he was too urbane to show his annoyance I could sense that he wanted me to go.

'There's no danger that he'll be sent down?'

'I shouldn't think so. The worst that could happen, in my opinion, is that they'll rusticate him until the end of term. But I think he'll get away with a warning. Don't worry, Willey will get him off.' He turned back to the girl pointedly, turning his back on me to indicate that the discussion was at an end.

Peter looked up as I arrived with a questioning look. 'Nothing more to add, really,' I said, affecting a nonchalant voice. 'It seems to have been a storm in a tea cup.'

He looked disappointed. 'Well, that's a relief. I must be off to my books.'

As he walked out, two girls came past the cashier's desk. One was tall and rather heavily built. The other was Rachel. As they looked around to see if there was a place to sit I got up, and the movement attracted Rachel's attention. She smiled and came over, the other girl following behind her. 'Please, allow me to get you some coffees,' I said. I was aware that Giles was looking at our table with curiosity. It was my turn to ignore him.

Three weeks after term started, I found a note in my locker at college.

'I can run fifteen times around the "quad" in three minutes.' There was a B under this message, followed by a half-hearted attempt at calligraphic curlicues. A little perplexed by this, I carried on with the business of the day, dismissing it from my mind. Two days later I found another note when I arrived at the porter's lodge just after breakfast, to see if my grant had arrived. The first three weeks of term were often lived on tick.

'I can run twenty-five times around the "quad" in two and a half minutes.' This time the note was signed 'B.O. your friendly, neighbourhood smell.'

I went up to Brian O'Donnell's room. A voice screamed, 'Bugger off,' when I knocked, and this was followed by the sound of furniture falling over. There was a long silence, and I knocked again.

'Brian, it's me. David.'

'Go away.' His voice sounded strangely old.

I said, 'I'm not going away until you've given me a coffee.'

There was silence for a few moments and then I heard the key being turned in the lock. I opened the door and walked into the room. The windows were shut and there was a heavy smell of gas in the air. There were clothes on the floor, carelessly flung around, and the bed was unmade. Brian walked over to the bed and sat down. He was wearing wide-striped pyjamas in blue and white, and his hair was awry as if he had just got up. His eyes, without the heavy glasses, were unfocused, giving him a vulnerable look. The floor was covered with books and papers, Wittgenstein's *Tractatus*, Russell's *Principia Mathematica*, Kant's *The Critique of Pure Reason*. Working papers in his small, neat hand lay all around. Brian huddled his shoulders in his arms, silent, like a child who has been rebuked. I felt uncertain of what to say, sensing that something was very wrong.

'Well,' I said, with an attempt at jocularity. 'What happened to the Idea of the Good?'

I was totally unprepared for the effect my words had on him. He threw himself face down on the bed, his big body racked with sobs. When I asked him gently what was wrong, he turned his face towards me as if I were his accuser.

'I have been good. I have . . . but I can't make it make sense any more.'

He began to weep again in earnest, the heavy sobs shaking his frame. I waited for him to calm down, my mind racing ahead with ideas of what I should do. When he stopped I went over to the gas ring to make us some coffee. As I washed the crockery in the washbasin, Brian moved over to the books on the floor and began to pile them up. Even this seemed to defeat him in its complexity; several times he shifted sheets to specific places in the pile, as if this ritual contained some inner meaning of deep significance to him.

Finally he put the pile on the floor again, the books sliding across the floor. He sat looking at them helplessly. 'I'm so tired, so tired,' he said in a dead voice, to himself.

I'd already missed the start of my first lecture, but I could not leave him. He took the cup of coffee I gave him, and sat back on the bed. I had always thought of Brian as totally in command of himself, capable of dealing with everything. As I sat there it occurred to me that this sense of completeness and imperviousness which he projected was his defence, a defiant gesture against the forces which threatened to overcome him. It was cold, and I draped his dressing-gown around his shoulders and lit the fire.

There was a knock on the door, and his bedmaker, Mrs Hackin, came in. She was one of the college gossips, and undoubtedly news of what had happened to Brian would be around the college in no time, but it couldn't be helped. I asked if she would see if Wilkins, the college chaplain, could come across when he had a moment as Mr O'Donnell wasn't very well.

'What about the room?' she asked, wide-eyed and avoiding looking at Brian directly, as if to do so would infect her with his malaise.

I said, 'Leave it for the moment Mrs Hackin, if you would,' and when she had gone I asked Brian if he wanted to talk.

He said nothing for a long time, staring into the fire vacantly. Then he laughed without humour. 'Gave myself a fright.' He pointed towards the fire. 'I woke up in the middle of the night lying in front of that. The gas was on, but I couldn't remember lighting it. The room was full of gas.' Then he added, 'I can't go on, but I don't know how to stop.'

Wilkins finally came, his equine face showing a strained concern, and between us we got Brian dressed and over to the college doctor. In the afternoon I packed some clothes for him and took them across to the psychiatric annexe of Addenbrooke's. A young nurse took me in to see him. She was red-haired and very pretty.

'He's had a breakdown,' she whispered to me outside the door of his room. 'Don't be too surprised if he seems a bit strange.'

But, apart from his quietness and evident depression, Brian didn't seem strange at all then. He thanked me gravely for having brought his clothes. Yes, thank you, he did have everything he needed. Yes, he would like to see me when I could spare the time.

When I went to see him the following day, he ignored me. He sat in front of a mirror, painting a picture of himself. I hadn't realised he could paint so well. The features were well executed and the face was undoubtedly Brian's. I talked for a while as he painted, just giving him general college gossip, though he gave no indication of having heard anything I said. When the pretty nurse came in to bring him some tea, I went to look at the picture. It was black all over, only one eye shone through the thick layers of oil paint on the canvas. I left him, painting furiously.

Two days later Brian was moved to a hospital in Surrey.

His going, coupled with the incident Jonathan had been involved in, made me feel profoundly depressed for a few days. I had met up with Jonathan, who had made light of the incident. He was reprieved after his tutor had interceded on his behalf.

'It was just one of those things,' he said lightly, indicating dismissal with a wave of his hand, as we stood on the freezing touchline watching St Catharine's beat Trinity at rugby. But I knew that there was more to it than he was prepared to admit. He was very concerned to hear about Brian. 'We must visit him,' he said. 'He mustn't feel abandoned.'

I didn't, for some reason, tell Jonathan about Rachel, though she had told me that there was nothing serious in their relationship. I didn't, in those black days, even want to see her. It was hard to feel optimistic about the future, and I felt I wanted to find a hole to hide in until things became better.

At the beginning of December, Jonathan reminded me that we should go to see Brian, and we arranged to drive to the hospital after breakfast the following Saturday. I felt a fluttering sickness in my stomach the whole week, whenever I thought about the visit. It was not an apprehension with any solid base, beyond the last memory I had of him, seated before his mirror in his dirty tartan dressing-gown, obliterating the portrait of himself he had painted so carefully, with thick, savage strokes of black paint. What I assumed to be the symbolism of his actions had not been lost on me, and since that last meeting the three letters I had written to him remained unanswered. Jonathan made the arrangements with the hospital.

Saturday morning had the brightness of a Spring day, though the morning grass was beaded with hoar. I went into college for breakfast and joined the undignified mêlée for hot toast. It seemed a conspiracy, fuelled by the resentment of the college kitchen staff at our privileged life, that breakfast toast would be thrown to us much as Nero's legionaries must have thrown Christians into the Colosseum arena. To vary the chances, the tray, piled with hot toast, would be brought in through one of three doors and, as with the three-card trick, most of us were caught unawares. That morning the normality of the procedure contained some feeling of affirmation.

'Saved you a piece,' said Peter Garster, holding it in his rather grimy hand. I felt grateful for the contact. The coffee tasted dreadful.

I didn't really want to spend the day with Jonathan. Since meeting Rachel and her friend Sabena at the coffee bar some four weeks previously I had seen her a number of times. We had gone to a couple of Bergman films together, and spent two Saturday afternoons punting on the Backs. She was quite unlike any girl I had met before. Remote, mysterious, unconcerned. She lived with Sabena, who was studying at the Bell School of Languages, and two other girls, both student teachers, in a small house in Madingley. After the second afternoon on the river she asked me to have a coffee with her in the Market Square. Though she eluded me still, in some essential sense, I had learned some of the facts about her.

She was an only child of wealthy parents. Her mother was half-French, her maternal grandmother Spanish, her father English. Her parents were divorced and her mother had remarried. They had attempted to dissuade her from leaving home, but she had decided she must, at the age of eighteen, assert her independence and had been accepted by Homerton College to do a teacher's training course.

'Facts, facts,' she teased me as we punted down the Cam in the sunlight. 'Why do you want all these facts?'

Before I could stop myself I said, 'Because they are all you will let me have.' She fell silent at that, trailing her hand in the brown water.

I had never been able to think of her as I thought about other girls. It was then, I suppose, the beginning of the sexual revolution which created freedoms, and intense problems, for so many of my generation. For me, and for many of my friends, it felt casual sex was almost expected of us. With Rachel it was different.

'You know,' she said gravely to me as she brought the tea tray into the little front room, glowing with late afternoon sunlight, 'Jonathan is just a friend. He talks to me about things that bother him . . . like this business with the boy a few weeks ago.' I felt better for that. She was freeing me from any sense of guilt. As she handed me the cup her slim brown hand brushed against mine for a moment.

'Jonathan tells me you are a painter. Why did you come to Cambridge?'

As the sun slowly faded out of the room I told her about the opposition to my plans. How my parents did not feel that painting was a fitting occupation for a grown man, and how it felt almost impossible to break out of the habit of making myself into what I thought they might want me to be. She sat on the floor with her legs drawn in under her, an elbow on the sofa supporting her head, and watched me with her dark eyes. I was weak under her gaze, feeling I was presenting myself as an unmade man, a composite of others' expectations. I wished I could show myself as strong and resolute, but my faculties for deception have always been limited, and I knew that she would, in any event, see through an attempt to deceive her.

'It's your life,' she said. 'They don't own you, you know.'

I was reminded, instantly and for a moment only, of Jonathan cleaning his teeth in grandmother's house, and the sounds of the cow being milked outside.

'It's not as easy as that.'

She smiled apologetically. 'I know. But isn't life and maturing about self-realisation too? Even if it seems a little selfish sometimes.'

She seemed so sad and grave as she said this that I felt an impulse to walk over from my chair and hold her in my arms. She may have sensed this for she stood up and held out her hand. 'Come and look at the garden. Leave the tray, I'll take care of all that later.'

We walked into the garden hand-in-hand. Something in the gesture had robbed me of the will to impose myself on her for the moment. As we looked at the wilderness of vetch, campion, and bindweed, she leaned unselfconsciously against me. 'I think you'll make a very good painter,' she said.

I had only missed seeing her on three days following my last visit to Brian. When I was away from her I felt restless, unable to settle to anything. When she was in my rooms, reading or listening to records, I found that I didn't need to talk, and could even concentrate on work in the comfortable silence between us.

However, despite her oblique reference to Jonathan, I still felt uneasily that I was in the wrong, that I should either declare myself to him or walk away from Rachel. I felt powerless to do either, and the prospect of a day nursing my secret was depressing.

I went out into the quadrangle. There were a few wispy clouds, and the sun was wintry, without strength. Jonathan waved from the car parked outside the college. 'Come on, little brother. We've got a long drive ahead!' He was animated, vivacious. I regretted my decision to go down. Though it had seemed the right thing to do in principle, now that the time had come to carry out my resolution, I could only wish that the day, with all its uncomfortable promise, was over.

Outside Royston he pulled out to overtake a large lorry. Ahead of us the hill stretched for perhaps half a mile. As we began to move past, the car engine screaming with the effort, the lorry driver's arm came out of the driver's window, frantically signalling us to drop behind. Ahead I could see a faraway speck of red growing larger, second by second. I felt sick, measuring the distance between us. Jonathan breathed hard, twice. We moved with agonising slowness past the flapping green tarpaulin of the lorry. The car ahead turned on its headlights, and drove over almost to the grass verge. Just as it seemed to me that a collision was inevitable, we moved past and Jonathan pulled sharply into the side. I didn't have time to look at the other car as it sped past, horn blaring.

Jonathan said, 'I'm sorry. It must have looked terrifying from your seat.' I agreed with feeling, and he turned towards me with that small down-turned smile with which he protected himself. After that we drove more sedately.

When we were almost at Finchley, and I had heard Jonathan's plans for getting into property development when he came down, and had recovered from the fright of the near accident, he said casually, 'Giles said he saw you with Rachel.' It was almost an enquiry. Before I had time to answer he went on, 'She's an interesting girl, isn't she? Very mature for her age.'

I nodded mutely, trying to gauge from his tone how I should respond to any further discussion of Rachel. We negotiated the Swiss Cottage intersection in silence, and I felt that some comment was expected of me. A feeling of being in competition with Jonathan, it seemed Rachel represented some prize to be awarded to the victor in a race we were running.

'Did you know that her grandfather had an affair with La Pasionaria when they were fighting Franco?' he asked.

I wound the window down; despite the cold air it suddenly seemed very stuffy in the car. 'She's an unusual girl,' I said. 'I like her.'

Jonathan took the car through a yellow light across Oxford Street, and a taxi moving towards us at right angles braked sharply. In a flat, sharp tone he said, 'I think we should both be careful.'

As I had found so often with Jonathan since our childhood, there were areas I dared not enter and obscure challenges which I neither comprehended nor wished to pursue. I could glean nothing from what he had said, beyond the impression that he was warning me against something. It was not said as if he were declaring an interest in her himself, but as though he were suggesting that Rachel were, in some way, a potential danger to both of us. Now that the subject had been aired, albeit in such a circumspect fashion, I felt easier. Brian was much more of a shared problem.

As we drove up the long gravelled drive, flanked by dense conifers, to the Dickens Hospital, I was reminded irrepressibly of my youthful ideas of Dotheboys Hall. It was pure Victorian wedding cake, far enough from the grime and soot of Central London to have preserved the Minoan red and soapstone finish. It gave the impression of airlessness, of poverty of soul, and the small windows which looked out upon the grounds were all closed, their panes glinting in turn as we swept in an arc into the parking bays.

Jonathan led the way into the large, gloomy reception hall. Above the mock Scottish baronial fireplace, an austere Victorian figure gazed down from a sombre portrait. The hall had been cannibalised to provide a reception desk and telephone exchange, behind which sat a girl, busy with the telephones, and an older woman in nurse's uniform wearing octagonal glasses.

'Yes, can I help you?' she asked, looking up at us sharply. In the background I could hear the sound of exaggerated laughter from the lawns behind the building. A woman in a white coat walked past the end of the hall with an old man on her arm.

Jonathan said, 'We've come to visit Brian O'Donnell. My name is Hardy and this is my brother. I called you and made an appointment.' She looked down at her register and started to follow the names and messages across. The girl on the switchboard answered a call. Jonathan looked at me with a brief smile.

Finally the receptionist grunted her affirmation of the appointment. 'I'll just confirm with Dr Cardwell that it will be all right.'

I walked over to the french windows at the end of the hall and looked out across the grounds. A young woman got up from a wooden garden seat and walked towards me. She was very pretty in a dishevelled sort of way, with blonde wildly blown hair and a rather stained pink wool dress. She looked at me through narrowed eyes. 'Are you Dr Bearman?' she asked.

I shook my head, and as she opened her mouth to speak again, a white-clad nurse hurried up.

'I'm sorry,' she said to me, and took the girl by the arm and led her unresistingly away. As I watched her go, Jonathan came up behind me and touched me on the shoulder. The receptionist stood behind him.

'We can go up now, David,' he said. He seemed nervous suddenly and this, paradoxically, made me feel more relaxed.

We walked up the wide oak staircase. On the first floor there was a large open landing with faded chintz armchairs surrounding a battered round table covered in magazines. A woman sat in one, feeding a child with a bottle. Next to her sat a man, looking out of the window onto the grounds. Neither spoke as we walked past. When we got to the top, the receptionist held up a hand to indicate that we should wait, and knocked on a door at the corner of the landing, bending her ear to the panel to listen for a response. Satisfied, she beckoned us forward and walked back towards the stairs.

I felt my heart hammering against my ribs, and my mouth was unpleasantly dry. The hospital had oppressed me in prospect, and even more so when we had entered the funereal hall. Jonathan walked quickly forward and pushed the door open, and I followed him into the room. The curtains were partly drawn, permitting only a diffused haze of grey light into the room.

Brian sat in a corner of the room, in an armchair. He was thin to the point of emaciation, and his face had a greyish-white pallor. He looked vacantly towards the door, and then at his hands which lay, limp and fleshless, in his lap. In a chair in the other corner of the room a black-haired, squat man of forty or so sat, weaving furiously at a basket, his lips moving incessantly. Four iron-frame beds were grouped around the room.

Jonathan walked towards Brian. 'Hello, Brian,' he said quietly, but the figure in the chair made no movement. I sat on the edge of the bed by Brian's side, and Jonathan pulled up a wooden chair. He said, 'I've brought you something,' and took a photograph out of his wallet.

It was a shot of a group of us taken the previous year in The Eagle, just before closing time on the night the exams ended. Brian stood in the middle, his college scarf wound around his head like a puggaree, and his tankard raised towards the camera. Jonathan put it in Brian's lap, but Brian did not even move.

The man in the corner started to laugh. 'It's no good,' he shouted, still weaving away furiously. 'He won't talk to you. He won't talk to anyone.' He grinned across at us furiously.

'Does he ever talk?' Jonathan asked.

The man was immediately wary, his eyes flicking around the room, and his tongue moving across his lips. 'Got to be careful,' he said. 'All enemies here.'

Jonathan looked at him, and then back at Brian.

I could no longer associate the figure in the chair with the Brian I had known. Without the witty erudition, the hard intellect which underpinned the sly asides, he was like a stranger for whom it was hard to feel anything. I was shocked at the ephemerality of the friendship we had, which I had once believed could transcend anything. It occurred to me that I could have stood his being gravely ill, or involved in an accident, because these would have permitted me to feel something. Faced with this still, withdrawn figure, it was hard to associate him with the past we had shared at Cambridge.

There was a movement from the chair, and I glanced over to see Brian straining forward. His mouth was open, and his eyes seemed to be bulging with the effort to say something.

'Yes?' said Jonathan, leaning forward to catch the words.

Still Brian continued to strain forward. Suddenly a gush of yellow liquid dribbled from his lips down his face, and into his lap. His lips moved. 'Sorry. Dirty boy. I'm sorry,' he whispered.

Jonathan took a handkerchief out of his pocket and cleaned Brian's face with it, cradling his head with his other hand. 'It's all right. Nothing to worry about,' he said. Jonathan's eyes were bright. I moistened a flannel in the wash-basin and helped him to clean up Brian's dressing-gown.

'He always does that after lunch,' said the other man triumphantly. 'I usually clean him afterwards.'

We sat there for another half an hour. Jonathan talked to me, almost with desperation, of times we had shared together with Brian in the past. I responded mechanically, aware that he was trying to reach some spark of memory within that inert figure, but feeling in some absolute way that Brian had gone beyond our recalling.

When we left, the basket weaver paused from his ferocious activity for a moment to wave feverishly to us. 'It was nice to meet you. Goodbye. Goodbye.'

In the hall the hard-faced receptionist looked up. Her face softened briefly as she looked at us. 'I'm sorry. Was he having one of his bad days?'

'I suppose so,' said Jonathan. 'He didn't speak, didn't seem to remember us.'

She nodded sympathetically. ‘Yes, he does have days like that. But sometimes he seems to rally a little.’ She raised her shoulders in a shrug and splayed her hands expressively in front of her. Then, as we were about to leave she called us back.

‘Before he became like this he talked to another patient who seemed to know you.’ She searched through files on her desk, but the papers were evidently not there and she turned to us again. ‘There was an old Indian gentleman who was here for some time who said he had known you in India. I was walking in the garden with Brian when he told me. Brian kept saying, “What a coincidence. I must tell them when they come down”.’

‘What was his name?’ I asked.

She wrinkled her forehead. ‘I knew you’d ask me that,’ she said. ‘I can’t remember, and his papers have gone over to Head Office.’ She stood up and clamped her hands around her head. ‘He wore a turban and had a white beard.’ She laughed reminiscently. ‘He was very funny. Everybody liked him.’

We thanked her and walked back to the car. ‘Bully, I suppose,’ said Jonathan, and I nodded.

As the weather broke we drove without speaking through the rain and up the North Circular. Only once did Jonathan speak. ‘It’s not worth loving anybody. They all break, or leave, or die,’ he said. The rest of the journey was silent.

17

Just before we went down for the Christmas vacation, something happened which, in more ways than I can discern even now, changed the pattern of my life.

I was now twenty-two and still could not have answered my father’s question with any degree of accuracy. I felt that the tripos I was taking was enjoyable, but bore little relationship to the cloudy future. The letters from my father usually contained hints in the last paragraph. Though I am sure he intended to convey a note of subtle concern, the paragraphs could have stood out no more clearly if they had been written in red ink.

'You remember John Carwardine,' he had written in such a paragraph earlier in the term, 'he joined the Foreign Office and has now been posted to Washington. Apparently he is enjoying himself thoroughly. His parents came to dinner last week, and said how much he had been changed and broadened by the experience of working there.'

By October, when I was trying to sharpen some ideas about what I wanted to do, I had already received another letter, this time from my mother, in which the last paragraph carried the phrasing and sentiments I knew could only have come from my father. 'Mrs Colquhoun came round for bridge the other night. Martin has passed into Sandhurst with flying colours . . .' and there followed precise details of career structure, pay, length of contract, etc., until the letter began to read like an Army recruiting brochure. A thought which, I suppose, had struck my mother as she had then gone into a couple of paragraphs of horticultural detail about the garden, and a few generalisations about the local people.

Rachel laughed when I told her, her small, even white teeth startling in the brown face. 'Why are you so afraid?' she mocked. 'You're old enough to stand up to them now, you know!'

We were sitting in an Indian restaurant opposite St Johns. The waiter came over with the bill, with the curious servility of his calling. As I fumbled to pay, a thought which had come to mind when some months ago Rachel asked me about painting, returned again as it had done many times before.

It was an effort to ask it of her, but something in the mechanical process of paying the bill, and some feeling from the wildly overdone surroundings and the sheer ordinariness of what we were doing, prompted me to say, 'Rachel, if you let me paint you I would try to enter the picture for an exhibition.' I had thought of this so many times before that it was almost a shock to see the surprise in her face. She sat silently for a moment looking down at her hands in front of her.

When she spoke her voice was studiedly impersonal.

'If you like,' she said, indicating it was a matter of no concern to her.

I felt a little hurt, assuming she might have seen how much it had cost me to say it.

'I want to,' I said, and she nodded.

When we walked up over the bridge and got to the traffic-lights she took my arm. It was a gesture that was both intimate, and controlling, for it suggested familiarity as between friends and not lovers. We walked up the hill to the house, and she stood under the street light, fumbling in her handbag for the key.

'Come in and have a coffee,' she said. 'We'll have it in my room.' I had never been inside her room before, and she indicated the door to the left at the top of the stairs as she went to the kitchen to make the coffee.

It was a feminine room, decorated in greens and golds. On one wall there was a reproduction Graham Sutherland landscape, and above the bed a Corot. The bookcase by the small antique writing desk was full of Jane Austen and Trollope. On the open writing desk there was a silver-framed photograph in sepia of a darkly handsome couple. The woman was seated in a chair, regally swathed in silk, with her hair piled upon her head. The man stood behind her with one hand on the back of the chair, the other resting on his hip, the eyes serious and the mouth unsmiling under the heavy moustache. Grandparents, I supposed. My eyes strayed from the frame to a note lying by its side. It was in Jonathan's writing and I only had time to register, with shock and fear, the words 'My darling Rachel' when I heard her walking towards the door.

I made every effort to keep the knowledge of what I had seen from my face. Thoughts rushed through my mind feverishly as I opened the door for her and took the tray to place it on the occasional table. The words did not necessarily mean that she and Jonathan were having an affair . . . or did they? She would not have left the note where I could see it if it were not entirely innocent . . . or would she? I wished that I had bid her good-night on the steps outside, and gone back to my digs in Maid's Causeway in ignorance. I could see no way to put my mind at rest, beyond the bluntest question which I knew I could never frame. We talked lightly about the evening, the film we had seen, the curry, but my heart felt as heavy as lead. Rachel slipped off her shoes and curled up on the bed leaning on her arm.

'Bergman must be a curious man. A mixture of clown and depressive,' she said. 'Clowns react against their own self-destructiveness,' I said, thinking of Brian. She caught my thought, as she often did. I felt guilty in using my real sadness for Brian to bring Rachel closer, but was aware that I was over-emphasising my melancholy. I felt that I needed some sign from her, however slight, to show that she cared for me in some way.

'You were very fond of him, weren't you?' She had a trick of making words and phrases I would avoid, because of the naked sentiment they revealed, acceptable and wholly appropriate. I noticed with surprise that she had got the tense right, even if it were only a slip of the tongue. I put my cup down on the tray and sat on the floor, leaning against the chintz sofa.

'Brian somehow gave me the feeling of being of value,' I said. I felt almost surprised to find myself saying it, but it was true. Rachel nodded. Her face was shadowed from the light and I could only guess at her expression.

'You never value yourself enough,' she said, and her voice sounded warm and comforting.

I was surprised to feel a prickle of tears in my eyes, and moved my head to avoid the light. Rachel stepped across from the bed and knelt beside me. 'I suppose you feel that men mustn't cry,' she said softly, stroking my head.

Wordlessly, the tears now streaming down my face, I wept uncontrollably. For Brian, for Ram, for the decaying pile of bodies on the station platform, for Frances Stanton, and most of all for James. It surprised me. I thought that I would never stop, but slowly I felt a sense of the present returning and with it a sense of shame. I did not want to leave Rachel, and clung to her while she whispered meaningless comforting words and kissed my head with small kisses.

I put my arms around her. Her face was a few inches from mine, serious now, her dark eyes looking at me expressionlessly. I kissed her on the eyes, and then on her mouth, a long, long kiss.

'Ah,' she smiled. 'Don't hurt me,' and I realised that I had been holding her in a fierce grip. Still looking at each other we walked towards the bed. I kissed her again and put my hand against her breast. She held my hand for a moment and then began to remove her clothes.

I looked at her as I undressed. Her brown body showed faint bikini marks. I was suddenly struck by how small and delicate she was, and felt fiercely protective for a moment. I was ready before she was, and stood awkwardly watching her as she removed her underclothes and placed then neatly over the back of the chair. She smiled at me, and I was overcome with tenderness for her as we slipped into the bed and turned towards each other.

When we had made love, with seeming hunger on her part, and desire such as I had never known on mine, and made love again, and then again, she had settled down to sleep in the crook of my arm, her damp body pressed against me. I looked down at her in the soft light of the bedside lamp. A small pulse beat in her throat, and her mouth was half open. A strand of hair lay along the line from her high cheekbone to her jaw. Once, in the long moments that I watched her, trying to absorb what had happened, she stirred against my shoulder and smiled. Slowly, as I relived each gesture, each caress, I realised that whatever Rachel's reasons might have been in bringing me home and making love to me, the sense of commitment which I sought from her was still as elusive as it had ever been.

At three o'clock I slipped silently out into the grey, deserted streets. Belinda let me in, yawning hugely but with a conspiratorial smile. Evidently she did sleep naked. I slept like a dead man and woke at 10.30 with a parched throat and a blinding headache. I only went home for a few days vacation — eager to return. Though we had not spoken of it Rachel came back early too.

In some mysterious way this incident — so important in itself to me — disappeared for the moment, without a ripple, under the surface of our relationship. We resumed our meetings and separations as if nothing had happened to disturb the calm tenor of our friendship. I say friendship, because that was the word Rachel most frequently used to define us, as though she wanted to set a seal upon the way we were or to create a shape in the way we saw and spoke and touched each other. It was, I see now, the safety of ritual that she sought then, and I was forced to comply with the rules which governed our meetings. Men were 'boys', reduced to a pre-sexual level; if I was distant I was 'being horrid' to her. I often thought I could stand it no longer, but when once I briefly took a girl I had met to a party and returned with her for the euphemistically named 'coffee' of those days, I found that I couldn't carry out my intentions.

A month after Rachel and I had slept together she said, quite abruptly, 'Do you still want to paint me?' We were in the Fitzwilliam Museum, looking at the collection of Turners. In the dusty silence there were only the keepers, warily watching us, and one old lady scribbling copiously on a lined note-pad. I had until then forgotten my original clear intention.

I remember even the smell of that room, the dusty coverings, and I remember the bright, leaping feeling as she said this; it seemed she had, in some near-divine way, sensed that I needed a guidance and direction from outside.

We would start the following Saturday, after lunch. 'You mustn't be angry with me if I can't remain absolutely still,' Rachel said.

It was curious to me that something which seemed so small, so remote, that I had barely thought about it at all for a long time, should suddenly become a feverish near-obsession. I realised on the first day that it should be a nude study, largely because I knew from the exhibitions I had been visiting recently that these were the conventions in which dealers were most interested. I had always loved the clarity and mystery of Manet's 'Olympia', and, uncertain of my own taste in such things, had resolved that I would use the pose as the basis for my study.

On the Wednesday, running from the Lecture Rooms at Mill Lane for a tutorial, I bumped straight into Jonathan, walking with Giles and a couple of other friends towards the Lecture Rooms. He had heard from father, and imparted the news from home, such as it was. He also told me that a mutual acquaintance had dropped in to see Brian and had found him much as we had. As I turned to go he caught me by the arm, smiling without humour as he sometimes did to hide his embarrassment.

'I hear you're going to paint Rachel,' he said, and I nodded. His grip was beginning to hurt. He looked at me for a moment longer, and dropped my arm with a short laugh. 'Don't say I didn't warn you,' he said.

Those weeks are still like yesterday. Rachel had evoked in me an ambition which I had felt destroyed by the opposition of my parents, and I felt I was growing every day in secret, as if I could at last begin to present myself in the world with the beginnings of a coherent inner structure. Such was the nature of the beast that I was able, during the course of those long sessions, to detach myself from Rachel herself, despite the memories which the sight of her, naked and slender, recalled to me at first. We became quite cosy, with a shared familiarity suggestive of a much longer association, and as time went by I learned more and more about her, though the knowledge was gleaned through my inferences and not through her revealing herself to me in any deliberate sense.

I remember one afternoon, with the sounds from the river drifting through the open window, coxes shouting, and the megaphoned instructions from the coaches on the bank cutting through the low boom of the traffic. It was warm, with that sticky, sleepy summer warmth which lowers one's guard, social awareness, call it what you will. We had drunk coffee, Rachel decorously clothed in a light housecoat had then settled back into the august pose, mocking its style by wrinkling a lip superciliously and closing her eyes.

In an hour the basic style I wanted had begun to form, still more in my mind than on the canvas. For some reason the letter I had glimpsed from Jonathan had simultaneously begun to prey on my mind, like a worm below the surface, just as I had solved the stylistic problems in front of me. At first I fought against it, still immersed in portraying the line of her neck against the green cushioned background, and wiping the sweat from my forehead with the back of my hand as I stood back to see what I had achieved. I knew that any questions would disturb the fragile bond between us, and though I knew that change must come if I were to reach a deeper relationship with her, I shrank from taking the first step.

For the first time since I had begun to paint her I found that her nakedness disturbed me. Questions which I could not ask, nor ever believe the answers if I did, began to trouble me; about former lovers, if there were any, and about Jonathan. Finally, inevitably, I asked the question.

'Do you see much of Jonathan now?'

A lorry rumbled by somewhere outside, and a light wind stirred the curtains. I placed two more brush strokes on the canvas, and was surprised to find that they were subtly and infinitesimally wrong. A bumble-bee hit the window and droned back into the room, before finding its uncertain way into the sunlight outside.

Rachel yawned, stretched like a cat, swinging her legs over the edge of the bed. She turned to pick up her wrap and threw it around her shoulders.

'Not much,' she said, her eyes looking past me at the scene outside. 'He seems to spend a lot of his time in secretive activities.' I made no comment. She carried on conversationally, as if the abrupt change of key were a continuation of some conversation we had left aside before. 'My mother once told me that any woman could entrap any man by showing a fascinated interest in anything he said.' She laughed, white teeth showing momentarily in a brown face.

'I see,' I said stiffly. 'I'll try to make sure I don't bore you too much.'

She came over to me, suddenly contrite at what she had said and put her arms around me, her head on my shoulder. 'I don't mean you. You read too much into things. You're my friend.' She gave me a final squeeze and took her pile of clothes to the bathroom to get dressed.

I felt suddenly depressed, aware that she had, yet again, relegated me to some warm yet asexual role in her life, in which I could not escape from the safe and brotherly image she had permitted me.

In the two weeks that followed I felt a slow excitement unwinding within me. In the second week Rachel came over to look at the picture for the first time. I watched her face, divorced for the moment from only seeing her as an image to be painstakingly transferred to canvas, and was suddenly aware that her approval of what I had done was of tremendous importance. She had no giveaway habits that I had been able to discern, no unconscious gestures which signified secret approval or disapproval, but, as I watched her following the lines of the painting, and then standing back to see it totally, I saw a small smile on her mouth. It seemed to me to express satisfaction, even pleasure, in the way she had been portrayed.

She stood back on one naked foot, curling the other foot against the back of her calf, and looked at me. 'It's very good,' she said, and I felt that she believed for the first time that I was capable of doing something she had never really felt I could.

It had that quality of enigma that I have always associated with Rachel. So often I felt that I had gained a genuine insight, had seen some naked and vulnerable part of her, only to find in some later incident a contradiction which returned her to her impenetrable self.

'Aren't they beautiful?' she commented once, in the early summer days, as we skirted past a hedgerow of wild poppies on our way to Grantchester for tea. We had stopped and looked at them for a long moment, and I had felt my heart stir with tenderness for her.

But a month later, as she tramped through the fields by Fen Causeway, she had a hazel switch in her hand. I had been asking her about her past, trying to discover, without her knowing, about past lovers. She had seen though the subterfuge in my questions, had caught the note of suppressed anxiety in my voice when I asked about a name that had come up three or four times.

'My past is my own. No one has any right to it except me,' and she strode ahead, flaying the wild flowers with her switch. I hurried to placate her, but, so fragile and tenuous was our relationship that her uncaring destruction made me shrink inside.

As the painting progressed I persuaded myself that there was a change in her feelings towards me. I knew that she had put aside other arrangements in order to sit for me, and she had never shown any impatience for me to finish. Many years later I recognised that people can tolerate almost any degree of discomfort and inconvenience when they are the complete focus of attention.

But at that time I felt grateful to her because I felt that she was doing this for me; and I felt this must indicate some depths of feeling in her which, eventually, would return us to a state where we could resume the unfinished business which had begun when we made love. I never thought we had entered upon an affair, because the word indicated a finite state with a defined beginning and end. At least it did in my mind then, and conjured up a picture of seedy hotels, of furtive meetings between people long married to others but unable to commit themselves to another beyond the secret moment.

Those weeks were too intense to recall most other events of the time. I went to lectures, but remembered little of their content at the end of each hour. Peter Garster was rusticated for the term for climbing into college late one night, very drunk, and landing on the roof of the senior tutor's car. Had he not broken his leg he might have got away with it, but he was discovered by the night porter, and the convocation decided that his offence was sufficiently rank for rustication. I went to hear Jonathan debating at the Union. He was one of the proposers of the motion 'This House believes that the End justifies the Means'.

Once I had overcome my apathy at dressing up I felt a certain excitement. It was one of the few times I had heard Jonathan speak with real passion, and I was surprised and moved by the demagogic power of his oratory. But it was not just that which had moved and surprised me, but the solid, crafted underpinning of his arguments, the eclectic sweep and assurance of his knowledge. When he had finished, the chamber stood and applauded him; hundreds of young men, some shouting and whistling. I could see that he disregarded it, and that moved me most of all, for I saw that it was not a performance I had seen, but a voluntary exposure of deeply held convictions. But these things were just punctuations of varying importance, and I longed for the time to pass when I would again be absorbed in Rachel's little room in taking the painting a few fragile and precarious steps further towards completion.

It remains one of the best things I have ever done. When it was truly finished I restrained the impulse to protract the time by making more and more additions. We stood hand-in-hand looking at the easel in the afternoon light which slanted through the big window.

'Oh, David, —' she looked up at me momentarily and then back to the canvas, 'it really is me.'

I burst into Lehar's 'Though I say not', picking her up and dancing her around the room, ignoring her laughing protests. There was a moment when, breathless, we stumbled on to the bed when I thought that it was possible to start again. Something in the widening of her eyes and the imperceptible pause as we looked at each other. But I was too slow, and she moved from under my arm and gathered her clothes to get dressed in the bathroom.

That evening, a little drunk after our celebratory dinner, we walked arm-in-arm over Silver Street Bridge. In the courtyard outside the Anchor a group of undergraduates were playing bridge by candlelight, their voices carrying across the muddy brown Cam to be lost in the foliage of the opposite bank. I felt light-headed, sad and relieved all in the same moment, and I could see dimly and for the first time ever, the shape of the future beginning to form ahead of me. The very air seemed full of mysterious promise. We strolled up King's Parade under the glitter of the lights and the clock of Great St Mary's chimed ten o'clock and, on an impulse, I suggested a drink in The Eagle.

As we walked across the cobbled courtyard into the crowded bar Rachel let go of my arm, and I could feel an imperceptible withdrawal in her attitude. She sat in a corner and I fought my way to the bar to get our drinks. Suddenly I spotted Jonathan with Giles at the corner of the bar, with a group of Trinity undergraduates. He looked pointedly over at Rachel and raised his glass to me. He didn't come over to our table and we finished our drinks quickly. The excitement of a few moments before had evaporated, and we spoke little on the long walk back to her house.

Towards the end of term I had seen less of Rachel. Exams were imminent, and I doubted my ability to scrape through without a lot of revision, particularly after the lost weeks of painting. Each day I trudged up to the university library with Miles Sinclair and Harold Abrahams, a third year engineer, who gave every indication of being a new Einstein.

The library looked like a monstrous charnel house, squat, functional and ugly. The air inside, dry and dusty with the conscientious air-conditioning, had the febrile, artificial feel of some monstrous intensive care unit. But what I disliked most of all, particularly as Part One of the tripos drew nearer, was the silence and the deliberate appearance of the undergraduates as they walked firmly back to their places with the books of their choice. Each one of them seemed to have some secret certainty I lacked, some security for the future. When Miles and Harold left me to join the purposeful seekers after knowledge, I felt truly alone.

After a week of this régime my confidence was partially restored. On the Friday we met for coffee in the canteen. 'Jesus,' said Harold, as we queued patiently with our cooling coffees, 'you know that moral sciences freak, Warner?' referring to a lank and etiolated third-year undergraduate who affected a lofty and disdainful air.

I nodded and Harold resumed, 'I've just overheard him talking to someone about incest in fishes. Would you believe it? No wonder there's an outcry about our grants.' He carried on, muttering to himself and shaking his head in profound disbelief.

I had submitted the picture of Rachel, together with several smaller pictures, for an exhibition to be held in a prestigious gallery in Whitechapel. After a few days of anxious fantasising, and looking into my pigeon-hole several times a day, the ripples of excitement gradually passed, and the more mundane demands of life reasserted themselves. In a weak moment I had agreed to row in an eight, so I would cycle from the university library at two o'clock each day to present myself at the boathouse at 2.45. I had already regretted the decision, but there was no way out of the commitment, so I heaved and sweated and strained in the pitching boat for seven miles each afternoon and comforted myself with the thought that it was doing me good.

One afternoon Miles, who was coxing the eight, momentarily lost concentration as we rounded a bend, and the boat crashed into one of the house-boats moored alongside the bank. As we slowly sank, each man desperately freeing his feet from the buckles, I joined in the general moaning whilst secretly rejoicing that there were insufficient eights available for us to continue with the present daily regimen. It gave a week's respite for me to apply myself to my studies.

I had not seen Rachel since the last outing. It was, in part, because I was genuinely unsure of the direction we were to take from here, and in part because I daily hoped to confront her with the tangible evidence of our joint success.

In the third week of my voluntary exile I received a letter from the gallery. I couldn't at first bring myself to open it, convinced that it would be a rejection. After two hours at the library, I knew that I could do no work until I knew what the decision was, and, trembling with fear and anticipation, tore open the envelope. I could hardly believe the florid letter, profuse with praise. Four of my pictures had been accepted for the exhibition, including Rachel's picture — 'a veritable masterpiece', as the writer, a Mr Rubinstein, assured me.

I can recollect childhood moments when I could see, with piercing sharpness, the fragile and chance-laden dynamic of my life. If James had not gone riding with mother, if there hadn't been a thunderstorm, how different our lives would be; but the randomness, and the overall sway and governance of blind chance reached into every corner of our lives, and often denied any conscious choice in taking a particular direction. 'People make their own luck,' Jonathan used to say, but that statement of a partial truth failed to take account of the haphazard meetings and chance events which so often seemed to be prompted by the workings of some malign agency.

All day I thought of how I would surprise Rachel. I did not want to phone her, for I knew that she would glean my excitement from my voice, and I wanted to enjoy my triumph. I decided that I would go round to the house that evening with a bottle of champagne to celebrate, and take her out to dinner if she were free. My excitement grew through the day, bringing with it a suspension of ordinary reality. It seemed to me that everything had a clarity and a perfection which I had lost for some time, and had now regained. Miles was gratified and a little mystified when I laughed loud and long at one of his jokes; even Harold's never-ending diatribe over lunch, inveighing against the stupidity of a social system which gave the arts a fine edge over the hard sciences, did little to dampen my spirits. It seemed I had quite depressed them with my exuberance by the end of the meal.

It was a crepuscular, murky evening, with a light monotonous drizzle seeping from a leaden sky. As I walked by the river, a soaked sculler was lifting his boat from the water, his singlet sodden with rain. Before the hill I paused a moment, savouring in prospect Rachel's reaction. The lights in some of the houses were on, reminding me fleetingly of the sensation of coming home to cosiness and warmth.

When I rang the bell Sabena answered. She seemed momentarily perplexed, as though unable to place me. Then she said, 'I don't know if Rachel is in . . .' ending on an uncertain enquiring note. I remember as I walked up the stairs that she stood in the dark hall, watching me . . . I knocked on Rachel's door and walked in.

There was a swift movement from the couple in the room. Rachel's hair was wild and disordered, and I could see the heavy flush of blood under the brown skin of her cheek. Jonathan was lowering his hands from where they must have rested around her body.

I felt immediately cold, and tired. There was no question in my mind of their degree of complicity, and with a painter's imagination I immediately conceived them passionately embracing in the act of love, as I was to imagine them, time and again, in the weeks and months that followed.

With an effort, I moved a few steps to put the champagne down on the occasional table. 'If you have something to celebrate,' I gestured towards the bottle, 'please be my guests.' Somehow I summoned a smile, and moved back towards the door.

As I went through it I heard Rachel say, 'David, don't go,' but I was already running down the stairs and a moment later was in the grey streets again.

*

Jonathan left Cambridge that year. He and Giles both got Firsts, and Giles departed to a sinecure job with a family merchant bank in the City, while Jonathan moved into a property development company in the West End. Dr Willey had arranged the job for him.

At first I found it hard to forgive his perfidy, for that was how I saw it, but as the rhythms of the new year slipped back onto the patterns of pre-Rachel, and the hurt became anaesthetized, I wrote to him once or twice. The replies shed little light on what he was doing. I had one or two brief makeshift affairs with nurses from Addenbrooke's. We talked more of contraception than of love.

'Christ,' said Wendy, a Northern staff nurse, 'it's exciting when you do it that way. Colin never bothered to try that sort of thing.'

She clung to me at the station in her nurse's cloak and uniform as I left at the end of the year, my degree safe if unspectacular. 'I know you don't love me,' she kept repeating, turning her tear-stained face to me, 'but can I come to see you in London?'

'Yes,' I said soothingly, my arm around her limply, hoping that none of my friends could see me. 'Let me know when you are coming up.'

That was the flavour of that last year. I remembered Brian declaiming in a mock heroic voice as we sat in The Eagle at the end of our first year, 'My way of life has fallen into the sere, and yellow leaf.' I felt so old, so old, but I see now that it was only the posturing faux cynicism of youth.

18

Seven-thirty. The lark may be on the wing and the morning dew-pearl'd, but frankly, I would have preferred to leave the delights of such sights and sounds to others. I could never understand why the cat (known by sly and accurate association as Walter) chose to lie athwart my feet so that I awoke to a numbing feeling of paralysis. I supposed it was preferable to his habit of slavering while he shredded my knee-caps with spasmodic movements of his unsheathed claws. In the morning I would gladly have dispensed with the entire menagerie, and that sweeping statement would have included Miranda, Ingrid, Mrs Haddon and, above all, the dogs. Myself apart, all other living things in our house appeared to feel that they must do justice to the new day by making loud and joyful noises about it from the crack of dawn.

('Look, Miranda, aren't the house-martens sweet? They sing so prettily in the morning.')

Mrs Haddon yelled up the stairwell to say breakfast was ready; Ingrid screamed at Miranda to hurry up 'because your daddy wants to have his bath'. Caroline turned the radio up to full blast, the dogs raced ceaselessly up and down the stairs intent upon the walk they felt must be imminent, and there was even an overhead jet rattling the leaded panes to usher in the joyful day. From where I lay I could see it was raining heavily, Daddy certainly didn't want his bath, and were there any chance of a further couple of hours of oblivion from the encroaching demands of the day, he would joyfully have accepted it. In being half-awake I could shut out the harsh outlines of reality, could veer and swim like a fish away from the shapes that threatened, the shadows that approached. But not today.

As I gloomily surveyed the toothpaste-devastated wash-basin which Miranda had just left, I reflected that I did not want to go in to the studio today. With such an uncertain self-image as mine, my chosen occupation seemed, on one day, to attain the summit of the *Scala Perfectionis*, on the next day to be a ridiculous pastime for a grown man to pursue. In the early days, when I was pursuing the round of sycophantic society portraits, I was forced to attend sittings on time, neatly dressed in a subtle parody of a city gentleman, to remove the moustaches from the top lips of society matrons and insert some dignity into the portraits of jumped-up entrepreneurs and film producers seeking a spurious respectability to go with the leather-bound books bought by the yard. The doing of those things had not left me untouched. How I wished I had possessed the courage to remain a bank clerk while writing *The Waste Land*; and, in some sense, I saw that it was not courage, or simple self-abnegation, but that my paintings were indissolubly linked with these performances.

I saw that my love for material things, for houses, cars, good food and wine, antique statuary and Russian icons, had not perverted my art, but had been an essential constituent in the forming of it from the beginning. Today, whatever tantrums I intended to hint at in my meeting with Walter and his prospective buyers, I had a certainty (which would change again the next day) that I was part of the ephemera of our decade, an Etty or an Alma Tadema whose fashionable life would merely be an object of curiosity in the future; that, however much I wanted it to be different, the reasons which had brought me to paint came from some source far closer to the surface, and thus less significant and important, than Mark Oldroyd's paintings. It was part of that distressing mechanism within me which was always measuring, always calibrating my own abilities and talents against those of my contemporaries. But while I still felt, secretly, my own pre-eminence in one field, I could play the fool with the best.

Perhaps I had too much of the courtesan or even the butler within me to eschew entirely the facile flattery of what the newspapers would call 'my public'. I wanted to know that the dish was well prepared and served. Often I would take the lead, thus showing some cunning sympathy with an embarrassed would-be patron who could not understand what I was trying to say, in laughing at my own work. That reassurance seemed to convince such buyers of the essential and clubbable amiability of our relationship, and to remind them that they were buying an investment, not something to be considered seriously in any other terms. And in these things I supported them, partly with belief but partly, too, with contempt. That I still held in my mind and spirit, to explain something to myself of the pity I feel for things. That often vague and ineffectual desire to help someone in distress had become more and more a private and an incommunicable thing.

Over breakfast I caught up with the day I had missed. I had briefly talked to Caroline about Beth the previous night, with the obvious omissions, as she lay half-aware in bed. 'Oh good,' she said sleepily, 'you see, I told you it wouldn't be too bad.'

Miranda told me that the party was all right, but that Richard got angry when Justin bit Susan. Children are marvellous in their matter-of-fact retailing of such incidents. How would it be reported if I decided to savage Walter at the New York opening?

'But,' Miranda said, 'Justin was quite right.' Gravely looking at her toast soldier covered in yellow egg yolk, she took a large bite, her eyes closed with the effort of cramming in as much as her mouth would accommodate. 'She took his piece of birthday cake from his plate.'

Faced with such irrefutable reasonableness, I could only nod, whilst the babble of morning life carried on around me. I realised that Miranda was trying to delay her departure for school. She watched Caroline getting into her coat and donning her gloves, and began to tell me a story about school.

'Daddy. You know Miss Pringle at school?' I nodded vaguely, and she continued. (Was Miss Pringle the one who smelled as if she had just done two miles in an unventilated PVC tracksuit at the height of summer?) 'Well, she told me I must learn to concentrate. But the sums are so boring. I finish them and then I've got nothing to do except look out of the window. Then Miss Pringle gets angry and tells me I'm not concentrating. But I always get them all right.' This last phrase was on a rising note of appeal.

Well, which was Scylla and which Charybdis today? How could I endorse the remorseless logic without giving Miranda the ammunition to face Miss Pringle triumphantly with 'my Daddy says'. I had always found if one waited long enough all choices for action are overtaken and removed.

'Come on, Miranda.' Caroline had spotted a hint that the mutineer was attempting to win my support.

'Mummy, I think I've got a stomach-ache.'

'If you have to think about it you haven't got a stomach-ache.'

'I mean I have to think where the pain is.'

Christ, the ingenuity of the child went well beyond my youthful attempts to avoid going to school. She could, faced with a resourceful player of stamina, carry this on for hours. But Caroline, too, was an old hand at this game.

'Well, whether or not you have a pain you are going to school *NOW*.'

Tears, a refusal to put on her coat. Even I was included in her 'I hate you', delivered from the door. Mrs Haddon looked on, her posture ambivalent, hands tightly clasped together to prevent herself from clipping Miranda around the ear or, perhaps, from gathering her into a comforting embrace.

Caroline called over her shoulder, 'Remember you must ring your mother to make the arrangements,' and the door slammed behind them. What could I use now to delay the moment when I must look at the next piece of the future, to decide what must be put in and what left out when I made the call? Sometimes (pace Brian) it seemed to me that bliss would consist in being held in a straitjacket in a permanent bed in a mental hospital, released forever from the requirements of decisions or even of social exchange.

There was plenty of time before my lunch with Walter and the German buyers. I should, nevertheless, have started the day in my blue, pinstriped suit, instead of which I was in my brown gardening cords, stained with sump oil and creosote. Still, that would only take me ten minutes. Plenty of time.

Mrs Haddon asked, 'Which room are your parents going to use, Mr David?'

Mr David, indeed! I felt like Max de Winter. 'I should think it will be the blue one, as usual, Mrs Haddon. Could you get some flowers nearer the time?' I was used to the look of withering contempt when I made suggestions of this sort. Better to make them and make sure the lily was gilded.

In the garden, Thompson was wandering around the bushes with the fork, searching for other shrubs to dig up. His squat, hunchbacked figure seemed to quiver with suppressed fury at the prodigality of growth. The previous week a Hammamolis Molis disappeared under his ferocious onslaught, and I saw that he had already gouged a great lump from the underside of the St John's Wort. God knew what he had his sight on now, or what prompted his mysterious desire to reduce the garden to a clinical state of neat perfection, unsullied by the untidiness of Nature. I walked around the garden with him.

Now that he had me I knew that I would shortly be pressed into service. Sure enough, he walked slightly ahead of me, virtually nudging me like a recalcitrant wall-flower at a dance, towards the honeysuckle against the old wall of the kitchen garden.

'This should come up.' He gestured with his fork. 'It's draining the soil of goodness. It's too heavy for me to manage on my own, but if you give me a hand with this piece of rope tied around the trunk we'll manage between us.'

I was a bit dubious about 'goodness'. It didn't seem to have a very scientific ring to it. It reminded me of the medieval humours. Thompson was undoubtedly both choleric and phlegmy.

'All right, Mr Thompson. If you're sure it needs to come up.' To me it seemed like an inoffensive old friend, and Thompson's ministrations in the surrounding shrubbery had left little to divert the eye from the bare wall.

Thompson didn't dignify the query with a response. His fork was already deep in the heavy soil. It bent alarmingly as he put his weight on it, but the honeysuckle hardly moved. Plainly my contribution was going to be heavier than I had anticipated. The removal of the silver-birch the previous year had cost me five visits to the osteopath, and much ribaldry from my unsympathetic family. Nothing for it, though, if I were to retain Thompson's grudging respect.

I suffered a moment's indignation, a near revolt. Was Thompson's nihilistic desire to rid the garden of all living things more important than my wish to see my garden transformed into a Marvellian bower where I could contemplate ways of avoiding working on my next assignment? The man had fingers like blow torches; the grass curled and browned under his footprints. His ammoniac breath even blighted the spurge. I felt the root system start to give way. Too late, I failed to save myself, and dropped like a stone on a handy dog turd. Thomspon permitted himself a small, secret smile. Another bath seemed called for and leaving Thompson to hack at the remaining root, I limped towards the house.

'Phone, Mr David.'

'Shit.' Quick recovery. 'Who is it, Mrs Haddon?'

She fixed me with a disapproving look. Mrs Haddon was for flowers, shrubs, clean language, and could not understand my unwilling and servile complicity with Thompson. The language she affected not to hear, though a glance at her pursed lips gave the lie to that.

I cleaned my feet meticulously, buying time before this next instalment of my unwilling involvement in these unfolding events. I felt that I should be preparing myself, but was still running away from any proper consideration of what had happened, and did not know what I should be trying to say. This was far worse than talking to Beth. I had a picture of my parents, old now, and out of touch with the world I knew, bewildered by what had happened. Jean had told them it was an accident when she had called. But they would have to gain some information before the inquest and the coronor's report.

Usually the soughing sound of long distance calls filled me with the excitement of anticipation. Not that day. I heard my mother talking to my father as she waited for me to come to the phone. They would both be standing by the extension in the kitchen.

'Hello, mother.'

'Hello, son, how are you and Caroline?'

'We're all right. It's been a shock to all of us, of course.'

'I know, son. Jean has called us several times. She's very

upset. Have you talked to her?'

'Only very briefly. They're coming over tomorrow evening, so you'll see them then.'

I could sense mother buckling herself together, determined to be a good sport, not to be a burden to 'the children' as she still called us. Mother's phrases, recalling childhood instantly like a taste on the tongue, contained in them a distillation of all the reasons for our worries about both parents. In translation 'being a good sport' approximated to not calling the doctor out over the weekend when mother had fallen down the stairs and had broken her leg. 'They need time off, too, dear,' she had said weakly, white splinters extruding through the flesh as father carried her up to bed. Such self-denying martyrdom drove me close to insanity, for I could see the unreasonable and unarguable pleasure they got from it.

'I'll come down to pick you up tomorrow. Don't expect me until after lunch.'

'Are you sure, dear? We can have lunch ready for you. It's no trouble.'

'I'm sure. I'll get something on the way down. Probably be with you around tea-time.'

'All right. See you then. Love to Caroline.'

'See you then. Bye.'

I would probably be there immediately after lunch, having dawdled slightly to blur the fact that I could easily have made lunch. I once gave a time and was delayed by a traffic jam for half an hour. When I arrived I could see my father had imagined me dead a dozen times over. Whether such thoughts were to do with concern or some inadmissible hope I don't know. Whatever prompted the concern I never gave an accurate time again. I reflected that the day would come when I was lying in a ditch for several hours, with four wheels in the air, to the accompaniment of their blithe unconcern.

At least that was over. Mother had not asked the questions I had dreaded and could prepare no answer for. It seemed to me that the truth could not be acceptable currency for what had to be said. And the truth I thought I saw then is not the truth I see, or think that I see, now.

Caroline was back. I could tell by her expression that

Miranda had been difficult. Though Miranda had been told nothing of Jonathan's death, I knew that she could sense the unease, the tensions within the household. She had been more than ordinarily affectionate with me, and more than ordinarily difficult with Caroline.

'She was an absolute little pig this morning,' said Caroline, hanging her scarf on the back of the door as if it were a garotte she was tightening around Miranda's neck. 'She virtually had to be carried out of the car screaming.'

'She's probably disturbed because we all are. She'll settle down when it's all over, I'm sure.'

'God, I hope so. Did you ring your parents?'

'Well, we spoke,' I said defensively, glossing over my reluctance to positive action, a trait which infuriated Caroline, and I retailed the gist of my conversation, and threw in the exchanges with Thompson and Mrs Haddon for good measure. Evidently I had not done anything too wrong, judging by Caroline's distracted reaction.

I walked upstairs to the bedroom to change for my lunch meeting. Caroline had a meeting with the local Amenities Commission, and was going on to the hairdresser afterwards. She came into the bedroom to powder her nose, titivate, and to change her shoes. She needed stout sensible shoes to keep her footing while getting Miranda into the classroom, but the Amenities Commission liked a bit of style. So did Rogero (né Roger) who presided over a camp and gossip-ridden salon which seemed to charge what it pleased. As I hauled my trousers out of the press, pleased to have managed a knife-edge rather than tramlines, Caroline said,

'Miranda said something odd this morning.'

'What?'

'Well,' said Caroline, screwing up her face in an effort to remember, as she turned from side to side to assess the effect in the cheval mirror, 'she asked why Uncle Jonathan was so sad. I didn't want to question her too closely as we haven't told her anything yet, so I merely said that people did get sad sometimes. Then she said, "but not like Uncle Jonathan".'

'She doesn't miss much,' I said, 'and she adored Jonathan.'

We finished our separate preparations and dispersed in near silence, each preoccupied in our own thoughts.

19

Jonathan came down from Cambridge the year before I did, with a much clearer idea of what he intended to do than I had. His office was only an hour from Cambridge and, in the loneliness of that first year, as he gradually realised that a university degree was no absolute guarantee of success, he invited me down to see him once or twice. When I did see him I was struck by an ephemeral feeling of melancholy, a slight tarnish of the high spirits he had displayed as an undergraduate.

On the first occasion I drove down in a borrowed car. London seemed immersed in a marmoreal calm. Early snow had left the Finchley Road covered in a fine brown slush and there were few people on the pavements in the biting cold. I met him at the office where he was grandly entitled Executive Assistant to the Managing Director. The sign at the bottom of the stairs read: 'Morris Cohen and Partners, Property Consultants', and I climbed up a dark stairway covered in threadbare orange carpet to the fourth floor. There was no sign of any partner, just a sad-faced girl of twenty-two or three and Jonathan, sitting in a dusty outer office surrounded by grey filing cabinets. As I arrived at the door I could hear manic, braying laughter. The shrieking continued as Jonathan tried to introduce me to the girl.

'I can't leave yet,' he said, indicating the inner office with a grimace as he did so. The girl made me a coffee, taking the mug and condiments from a cupboard seemingly stuffed with hoovers and cleaning equipment.

The telephone was replaced with a crash in the other room and Morris Cohen slammed through the door. He was short, bald, and grossly overweight. At first it seemed as if he must be on amphetamines; he moved incessantly and delivered his sentences as from a machine-gun, in short stabbing bursts. Amidst the rambling misquotations which, apparently, made up his ordinary conversation, he managed to suggest that Miss Bowker was inefficient for not having typed a letter he had given her that morning, and that Jonathan was over-paid, because he and I were going to lunch together.

'Another Cambridge graduate, I suppose,' he said, pumping my hand, '*de mortuis, nil nisi bonum. Sic transit gloria mundi.* It doesn't pay to be mad in this office but it helps.' He then rapidly admonished Miss Bowker again, and told Jonathan three times not to be late back from lunch — 'a fair day's work for a fair day's pay, my boy' — before vanishing into his office to commence another call.

Miss Bowker shut the door between the offices. 'I hate him,' she said without rancour. 'He's been through my handbag again this morning.'

'It's a sign of true love,' said Jonathan. 'The only way the poor sod can show you how passionately he cares about you is to find out everything about you.' The voice in the other room rose and fell, and Jonathan warmed to his theme. 'Imagine the scene now, Mary. You've finally accepted one of those invitations he throws out to you. He invites you back to his sumptuous bachelor pad after an evening in which he has dazzled you with his virtuosity in five languages, his culture, his enormous physical attractions.' Miss Bowker shivered slightly, watching Jonathan with an expression midway between disgust and laughter. 'He pops out of the room to slip into something more comfortable. You're sitting in the lounge with a glass of chilled champagne. Vivaldi's *Four Seasons* playing gently on the music centre. Suddenly he appears at the door in a shift and rushes towards you, excited beyond belief to claim you for his own, and knocks over one of his priceless Toby Jugs . . . But even this is not enough to deflect him from his evil purpose.'

Miss Bowker covered her ears with her hands, giggling, 'I don't want to hear any more. You've been perverted by contact with him.'

We left her preparing her face to go out for lunch. As we

walked down the stairs I could hear Cohen charge through the door again. He shouted something and I could hear Miss Bowker reply in a low tone. As she came out I could hear Cohen roaring the Horst Wessel song in a rich baritone. Jonathan smiled at me wryly as we emerged into the sunlight of Oxford Street.

'He varies. Sometimes he creeps up the stairs in hopes of catching Mary and me locked in mortal embrace. But he loses his nerve at the last minute and gives a warning cough. He's clinically insane, but one doesn't have to listen.'

I felt depressed at the scene we had just witnessed. It was so far removed from what I had imagined his life would be. And by association it seemed as if I were diminished in some way.

We ate at the Bald Faced Stag. Once away from the office Jonathan seemed more cheerful. As he outlined his plans for the future I could only compare them with the scene we had just left. The squalid office furnished with cheap hired desks and filing cabinets, the sad-faced girl, the bizarre spectacle of Cohen haranguing the two of them. I remembered watching Jonathan when he had been about to deliver his speech at the Union; to my eyes he had seemed glittering, assured, and poised. I wondered again, and not for the first time, why Jonathan seemed to accept everything that Willey suggested.

He watched a girl with a very good figure teeter by on high heels. 'I'll have two of those, please,' he said with his mouth full, indicating the girl. He looked at his watch. 'But not yet. Time to go back before the old fool blows a gasket.'

When we returned Cohen was castigating Miss Bowker for 'taking an hour and a half for lunch.' He spoke through the pipe clenched between his teeth, the smoke spiralling upwards in furious little billows, and a fine spray of saliva showering onto the carpet. His grey trousers were stained down the front and I noticed that his elastic-sided boots had heels to give him height. Miss Bowker sat calmly at her typewriter, sorting out some papers before her, and occasionally turning to stare with flat indifference at the unappetising, grey rooftops which cut off all but a small square of grey sky.

'Oh, there you are,' Cohen shouted, turning on Jonathan and gesturing with the stem of his pipe at the watch on his other wrist. 'This is a work house, not a shirk house. You know what my motto is — another day, another dollar. Now, for fuck's sake, get on with your work — and that means you, too, pig face,' he said, with a gesture at Miss Bowker, before rushing back into his office and slamming the door behind him.

'A limited vocabulary, a thick skin, and total insensitivity to others is what you need in this business,' said Jonathan, with a slight smile of complicity with Miss Bowker. He looked at me, amused at my shocked face. 'Don't worry. This is only stage one in the master plan which is going to take me away from all this to a land of untold plenty.' He hauled Miss Bowker to her feet and pulled her into a jive step. 'Where I shall live a life of unparalleled luxury . . .'

The door slammed open and Cohen stood there, blinking angrily. 'You still here?' he said rudely to me. He looked aggressively at Jonathan, his small mouth working for a moment. 'This isn't the bloody groves of Academe, you know. Get into your office and do some work for a change.'

Under his discomfiting eye I bade my goodbyes. The air outside seemed fresh and sweet as I walked to the car. It had always been hard to understand Jonathan. Now it was harder still.

A year after I came down I was living in some squalor on the bottom floor of a house in Primrose Hill. It was owned by a very junior merchant banker and his formidable fashion designer wife, and had been conceived, designed, and executed with five girls sharing in mind. Since girls, then, were less well paid and Mrs Arnold was extremely greedy, she eventually decided to accept five men. By the end of the first party someone had broken the sliding door into the toilet, on the mistaken assumption it was hinged, and the flat generally had the appearance of an ageing courtesan who had finally decided to loosen her corsets and accept the ravages of time gracefully.

Nicholas Arnold would occasionally be dispatched downstairs to reason with us. Invariably this would follow the sounds of a heated argument upstairs, followed by her voice enjoining him to 'stand up to them for a change', or some similar exhortation, followed by his timid tread on the stairs.

Brendon, our resident red-haired advertising executive and self-appointed spokesmen, would take on the task of conciliation. After twenty minutes of coffee and grave-eyed listening, Nicholas would return upstairs, bearing another set of useless promises and we would resume our generally feckless existence. For me it had a transitory feeling in any event, since I knew that I must find a studio where I could work without interruption.

One morning I received an envelope with the impressive crest of a well-known advertising agency embossed on the cream linen. It was a Saturday and the rain dropped monotonously onto the tiny garden outside the kitchen window. John Ash, one of the other residents, had evidently had a successful evening, judging from the unmistakably feminine giggles issuing from his room. I made myself a solitary breakfast of toast and marmalade and coffee and sat down to look through my mail, saving the envelope for last. When I slit it open I felt a surge of pure happiness. It was from Brian O'Donnell, Senior Account Executive, inviting me to a party to be held the following Saturday.

I had often thought about Brian since the day when Jonathan and I had been to see him, but always in the past tense, like a friend who has died and can only be recalled through the memory of old times. When I remembered the visit to the hospital, it seemed then he had already died, and the figure in the chair bore no relationship whatsoever to me. From time to time I had felt guilty, and thought that I should try to find him again, but the feeling was without substance and without the strength to motivate me into tracking him down.

Brendan, it transpired, had met Brian a few times. His description of Brian was so at odds with the Brian I remembered that I felt a few qualms about meeting him again. 'He's a red-hot copywriter,' said Brendan, mentioning some of the television campaigns Brian had been working on. It was difficult to think of Brian selling soap powders, toothpaste and margarine, after the conversations we had had together in Cambridge.

The party was held in the agency's immaculate executive suite of offices in Baker Street. As I walked through the enormous chrome and glass doors into the interior, tastefully decorated and embellished with sprays of orchids, I felt the alien strangeness of the atmosphere. Though I had come in a suit, I felt that I lacked the steely glossiness of these confident men, braying at each other over their canapés and champagne cocktails.

Seeing Brian across the room was something of a shock. His hair was sleeked back, and his owlish glasses had been replaced by gold-framed spectacles in smoked plastic. He waved across with a gesture of recognition, and resumed his conversation with two heavy-set and ponderous men. I helped myself to a cocktail from the tray, and, knowing no one else, affected to be engrossed in looking at the pictures which hung in ostentatious overcrowding on the walls.

A pretty, tow-haired girl looked sympathetically at me, and when I smiled, detached herself from the group she was with and came over to me. She had an open friendliness which was at variance with the tenor of the party, and I felt her interest must be genuine, since no one there could mistake me for a person of importance in this world. When we had talked for a bit she volunteered her name. Caroline Madox. It had a nice ring, though her clipped county vowels (with just a hint of the North) suggested an upbringing more concerned with horses and coming-out balls than with things of the mind. She made me feel more at home, less alien, in my unfamiliar suit and tie.

'I can tell you don't come here often,' she said, smiling, as she took another glass of champagne for each of us from a passing waiter. She made it sound like a compliment, a moment of shared conspiracy against the glossy-haired young men in suits talking in loud and over-confident tones all around us.

'You should have been a detective.'

She laughed, throwing back the tow-coloured hair from her forehead. Her eyes were hazel, and the slight mongolian fold above her eyes gave her pale, English good looks a subtle and attractive difference. Even to my unpractised eye it was evident that the clothes she was wearing and the jewellery she displayed so casually were quietly expensive, and I was beginning, somewhat ruefully, to persuade myself that she was separated from me in ways which I knew were unbridgeable once the first friendly moments had passed.

Perhaps something of what I was thinking communicated itself to her. She looked at me with mock reproach and fumbled in her handbag, bringing out a piece of paper on which she wrote her name and telephone number.

'There you are,' she said gaily. 'I know I'm being very forward, but I'm new in London too, and I think this is the only way to keep contact with people one likes.'

I felt a warm, grateful glow, but something warned me against asking her out immediately. 'Yes,' I said, looking down at the paper to hide my confusion. 'I will be in touch.' It was nice to see that she meant it, that it was not an empty form of words used to navigate her way through a social evening.

As I stowed away the paper in my wallet, Brian came up. He caught Caroline around the shoulders and squeezed her tightly, planting a kiss in the general area of her cheek. 'You've got to watch him. He's always been a fast worker,' he said, with a stage wink in my direction. Then he grabbed my hand and pumped it furiously, but his eyes were moving purposefully around the room. 'I'm glad you could make it. It's years since we met.'

I felt in that instant that all the questions I had wanted to ask, the slow unwindings of our stories I had imagined over quiet drinks or dinners, would never be possible. From somewhere Brian had found himself an impenetrable armour, and the fee was this life of trivial meetings and small preoccupations.

He even had photographs of his flat in Chelsea — an arid geometric assembly of steel and smoked glass taken with a fish-eye lens. I had to listen hard, trying hopefully to find some trace of synthetic enthusiasm in his voice. Occasionally he paused to demonstrate his acceptance in this world by nodding, or laying a hand on a sleeve, or jerking his head towards one of the immaculately clad personages who walked past him.

After a time I was able to grasp and comprehend the change. Brian seemed now to see everything in terms of material possessions; he had a Porsche, a flat in Chelsea, a trendy girlfriend who lived in the King's Road, and whatever it was within him that might have wanted more than these things had been left behind in the years since Jonathan and I had seen him, a silent motionless figure in a chair in a hospital in the country.

He did say one thing before he was whisked off by his managing director. It was a phrase, dropped carelessly and almost as an aside which, in later years, returned to me as a possible connection in the crazed jigsaw of our lives. He had met up with Jonathan and Charles Mandeville, another Cambridge acquaintance of ours, at a party some weeks before. For a few moments the perfect confidence of his performance wavered, and I saw a glimpse of the Brian I remembered.

'It was odd,' he said reflectively, 'despite the fact that they are almost contemporaries they seemed like father and son. Mandeville kept advising Jonathan, and I could see that Jonathan really didn't like it too much, though he listened. Jonathan works for him, doesn't he?' I nodded and Brian laughed ruefully.

'Yes,' he said, with almost a trace of sadness in his voice, 'you soon relearn what the world is like, how it runs, when you come down.'

We exchanged promises to keep in touch after that, but I could see that I had already kept him away from more important contacts for long enough, so I urged him to return to the party. On my way out I passed Caroline. She was talking to a sharp-suited young man.

'And then what happened?' I heard her say, but was glad that her attention was not so taken up that she ignored my passing. 'Give me a call,' she said, waving her hand, and I nodded. The evening air had a clear, fresh feel as I walked past The Volunteer and into Regents Park.

Jonathan had met up with Charles Mandeville again through one of those coincidences that people look back upon as the start of their meteoric rise or fall. They had first met at a May Ball at Cambridge, where Jonathan and I were part of a large group. Nothing had distinguished that meeting in any way. They were perfectly polite to each other and talked briefly about all the conventional things one did talk about at May Balls. The future was not among those things, and by the time we were punting down the Cam as the sun rose, Jonathan had quite forgotten the meeting.

After eighteen months with Cohen, Jonathan was finding it difficult to cope. Cohen was compulsively inquisitive: private mail, often belonging to other offices; private conversations in which he could only have had the faintest idea of who or what was being talked about, were meat and drink to him. He was a ragbag of mismanaged motives; eager to spread slanders about anyone he saw as more capable than himself, which meant, with his painful lack of self-confidence, almost anyone, and compulsively secret about his own private affairs, such as they were.

'He turns the protection of nothing into an art form,' said Jonathan, and ventured that Cohen merely vanished when he had no audience, like Miss Gamp.

Somewhere, deep in the recesses of Golders Green, Cohen kept a small and lonely flat, to which he was occasionally able to inveigle an acquaintance for a game of bridge. He yearned passionately after Miss Bowker, but treated her as small children sometimes do their mothers, in his method of demonstrating his desire for her, screaming at her, abusing her, and humiliating her. Sometimes he would call Jonathan in to tell him, at tedious length, just how appalling she was, how little she worked, and how she bit the hand that fed her. Jonathan had learned, through noisy trial and error, never to take Miss Bowker's side overtly; this tended to drive Cohen into paroxysms of anger against her.

When she came back from lunch five minutes late he would round on her furiously — 'What time do you call this? Who have you been with? Where have you been?' — all delivered at the top of his voice, were the counterpoints in the manic times.

He had been married briefly, and had been deserted. Much of his life was given to squiring young and totally unsuitable one-time-only blind dates on extravagant evenings perhaps in an unconscious attempt to compensate for what he saw as his own unattractiveness. 'Even his mother couldn't love him,' muttered Miss Bowker viciously to Jonathan, ignoring the fact that love-hate phone calls from his mother were a daily feature of their office life.

Despite all this, Jonathan felt that he had used the time well. It was a field in which techniques, experience, and contacts could only be learned by living through the days of deals and meetings, and not through study. He had kept his eyes and ears open, always careful to distance himself in company from Cohen's wilder moods and more absurd behaviour. He had assiduously nurtured those contacts who he had begun to perceive would carry him on to better things, and had turned aside from the many who merely wanted to pass a pleasant lunch-time before retiring to sleep in their offices. He learned to distinguish those ephemeral marks which set aside people who were looking ahead from those who had given up. The signs were never easy, having nothing to do with the superficialities of dress, or even with the lavishness of office appointments. They were to be seen in the set of a head, the look in an eye; but to the initiated, they were unmistakable.

Though he was ready in himself to leave, he knew that he needed one major project to give him the security to start on his own. In the meantime he realised that relations with Cohen had reached an all-time low, in part because he could no longer enter into the farcical mock-serious frame of mind necessary to sustain comfortably a day in Cohen's company.

One morning, when matters had reached this stage, Cohen had surprised Jonathan by carefully bringing him a cup of coffee and placing it on his desk; a soggy digestive biscuit lay in the spillage of the saucer. Cohen seemed a little subdued and hesitant, as if he wanted to broach some matter of great moment but was, temporarily, at a loss for words.

He leaned up against a filing cabinet, in elaborately casual stage pose, and started, 'Please don't take this the wrong way, Jonathan . . .' The telephone rang, and he exited at a run, shouting 'Bugger it' at the top of his voice. He had evidently decided that whatever he had to say had to be prefaced with the same apology, for he managed it a further four times between telephone calls, only to blunder out on each occasion like an infuriated pachyderm to vent his spleen on Miss Bowker and whoever it was who was daring to interrupt him.

Jonathan meanwhile was finding it hard to control the small

but growing knot of anger in his entrails which was tightened by the uncertainty of what to expect.

Finally, just before lunch, Cohen came in to say that he would be very pleased if Jonathan would make up a foursome for the first night of *Lear* the following week. A couple of nice mature ladies, and dinner afterwards.

At dinner some weeks after the occasion, he told me the story. 'For once my instincts let me down,' said Jonathan, recounting the occasion. 'I thought that Cohen was proffering the olive branch, and decided to accept in the interest of cementing good relations . . .'

The following morning, through the thin partition dividing his office from Cohen's, he overheard Cohen, using his version of sotto voce, informing someone that he had found a replacement for Simon who had dropped out of the party going to *King Lear*. Jonathan felt mildly aggrieved, most of all at his own lack of percipience.

A few minutes later Cohen had come in. 'It's all arranged, my boy. I'll get the tickets, you get the dinner.' He went on to suggest a few restaurants which might be suitable. 'I know the maitre d'hôtel at the Savoy. Nobody can get in, but if you show him a tenner we may be able to manage it.' Jonathan, who had assumed the evening was a gesture to restore good relations, had booked at a modest restaurant near the theatre.

When Cohen told him, two days before the proposed evening out, that there was to be a third pair, Charles Mandeville and his partner, Jonathan's nerve had faltered. He felt that his desire to execute some oblique sort of justice through forcing Cohen to suffer the choice of restaurant would have to be modified.

Mandeville was just the sort of contact he needed now, and if the evening went right this could be the moment he had been anticipating for the past few months. Mandeville had been spectacularly successful since leaving Cambridge. Though the first years, now never alluded to by those who sought his favours, were full of dubious connections, and he had been unsuccessfully sued by several tenants for alleged Rachmanite practices, he had blossomed and flourished.

From a small office in a decaying Victorian house in Islington he had moved to a large Georgian house off Curzon Street in Mayfair. His tastes still ran to blowsy starlets whose appearances in the gossip columns were more frequent than their professional engagements, to revue bars rather than legitimate theatre, and to flashy sports cars which seemed incongruous when piloted by a plump man with greying wings to his hair. But he wanted to buy respectability if he could. Even if it meant commissioning a fashionable interior decorator to do up his house, and spending evenings with people he couldn't understand at events he didn't want to attend.

His entrance to Cambridge had been due entirely to his talents as a good tight head prop, and he had, in honouring his place, played in the Varsity team for three years and had been awarded a pass degree in each of those three years.

The evening had been even more bizarre than Jonathan had anticipated, though, as he succinctly put it, 'A glint of gold did finally shine through the shit.' Everybody else had been late and the first opportunity to meet had been in the crowded bar after a disastrous first act.

'The Fool was just like that sycophantic little twerp Sinclair,' said Jonathan, 'and Lear stumbled around the stage as if he was smashed and had just lost his glasses. The Gadarene bar,' he went on, 'was full of swine elbowing each other to get to the drink. Cohen was leaping up and down, gesticulating madly as if he were doing a preview of the storm scene, and Mandeville was standing with ——' and he mentioned a well-known and recently divorced star '— and two ladies *d'un certain age*, one of whom was undoubtedly to be mine.' I knew him well enough to see beyond the humour and his face told me it all. They had swilled with the best in both intervals, and then taxied down to the Savoy.

Jonathan poured himself a Perrier from the bottle in front of him, and looked around the restaurant where we were eating, with a reminiscing smile. 'Do you remember Guercino's painting, "Et in Arcadia Ego"?' he asked.

I was surprised by this seeming irrelevance, but nodded.

He resumed, 'Well, the point of the painting is that Death is speaking, reminding the revellers of his omnipresence even in Paradise.' He paused for a moment, his finger tapping against his lip. 'Bosch would have approved the revelling scene. It was the usual crowd of fleshpots, film people, a sprinkling of Americans, all gorging far more than they could possibly need or properly utilise. Morris loved it, of course, and so did the ladies. But I looked at Mandeville, at forty, with those dead, fish-like eyes, and was reminded of Guercino's painting.' Later, when I recalled such conversations with Jonathan, I realised how much he had hidden, even from me.

Jonathan had stolen a few opportunities to talk to Mandeville. Mandeville was, by now, so far removed from the day-to-day business of his company that he seemed stimulated by the discussion.

'Do you really think the lease would go that cheaply?' he asked, after Jonathan had outlined a plan to secure a building in a prime site.

Cohen, apparently engrossed in conversation with his partner on the other side of the table, leapt in. 'Now, Jonathan, you're dealing with the crème de la crème here. Why don't you talk to the ladies and let two old professionals chat about the business.' His attitude suggested an affinity composed of friendship and mutual respect between Mandeville and himself.

During this speech Mandeville had continued to look at Jonathan. When Cohen had finished, Mandeville shifted his gaze slightly and fixed Morris with a cold gaze. 'Morris,' he said softly, 'we were having a very interesting discussion. In fact I think I may be able to do a few things with Jonathan. Why don't *you* talk to the ladies?'

The evening began to take on a different aspect. Cohen, embarrassed by the snub, started to overact outrageously for the benefit of the three ladies. The waiter arrived to take the order for the dessert.

'Ah,' said Cohen, leaning back in his chair and fixing the waiter with a look which suggested he was not beyond chatting to his social inferiors. In a heavy Italian accent, suggesting the suburbs of Palermo as its origin, he went on,

'Now Giorgio, you have come to bring us our just desserts,' and crowed with laughter over his pun.

The waiter remained impassive, notebook poised, until the

explosion had died away. 'I'm sorry sir, I don't understand. My name is Franco.' Angeline, Cohen's partner, shot him a dark look, but he was unabashed.

By 1.30 Cohen had been sick and was quarrelling behind his hand with Angeline. She was embarrassed, darting frequent glances in our direction, and also at the other two women who were carrying on a desultory conversation. Cohen, however, was in full and oblivious spate. He appeared to be enumerating the many things he had lavished upon her, seeming to suggest that each gift represented some contractual step in the permanent purchase of her favours.

'Yes, I do like you,' she said defensively, in such a way as to suggest, beyond a shadow of doubt, that she loathed him. But her affirmation was not enough, and he ploughed forward remorselessly, occasionally pausing to take a large draught of claret, and to refill his glass to the brim.

By the time the party was ready to leave Jonathan had arranged to meet Mandeville the following week. He felt that the horrors of the evening had been repaid, if only just.

Once on the pavement, Mandeville's chauffeur swept him and the starlet away, and Angeline and Samantha, Jonathan's date, walked together in front in that time-honoured protective way women have when one lady is having problems with her partner. Cohen scuttled down the steps to where Jonathan waited, a large cigar clenched in his hand.

'It's the elbow for me. Probably just as well. She was getting very possessive indeed.' He took Jonathan's arm as they walked down the Strand to the car and he lowered his voice, as if imparting some confidence. 'Marriage is on her mind. You know how they get when they reach a certain age.'

As they walked down the road together Cohen tripped across the leg of a tramp protruding from a doorway out onto the pavement. 'Christ,' he said crossly, 'can't you move your bloody legs out of the way?'

The tramp looked up at him. 'I had polio when I was young. Can't straighten my leg.' Cohen passed him a tenpenny piece as if it were a banker's draft.

'Well, if you'd told me I wouldn't have complained,' he said benignly, putting his hand briefly on Jonathan's shoulder. In some unfathomable way all was right with his world.

Jonathan had felt a moment of compassion as he held the car door open for Angeline. In some aspect it was courage that kept Cohen going, time and again, through the same process of hope, illusion, disillusion and despair. But he always rose up again, indomitably pursuing yet another unconquerable hope. Jonathan had felt differently, this time, because he knew that his long apprenticeship with Cohen was finally over.

20

When Jonathan asked me to dinner to celebrate his engagement to Beth, I asked if I might bring Caroline.

I had followed up, a decorous week after the party at Brian's agency, and over the ensuing six months we had seen more and more of each other. I had found her to be an intriguing mix of the naïve and the sophisticate, and was amazed at her comprehensive knowledge of London theatre, and her corresponding ignorance of art and literature. She had a gift for the immediate, catching the wrong gesture in a play, or the right movement in an opera by an instinct; but her gift was not my slow one, for contemplation of a picture or a sculpture, and the working out of meanings. Her quicksilver lightened my lead.

'God, haven't you got that yet?' she laughed in mock exasperation as she stood at the bar in the first interval of a particularly abstruse German play.

She drove as she talked, the tow hair flying back from her alive face, and the car racing to undertake, overtake and squeeze through gaps in the traffic.

'Is it that important?' I asked once, breathless with fear as we had narrowly missed the back corner of a lorry, and she had turned to me and smiled.

'What are you afraid of? I was perfectly —' with a heavy accent, '— in control,' and she waved her hand airily to show her unconcern.

She gathered people around her wherever we went, dazzling them with the energy and vigour of her presence. That was how it seemed then and I, too, was dazzled. By the time Jonathan invited me to the celebration, an evening without Caroline seemed unthinkable, though even if she had not come it would have ended, as it had for the past two months, in her tiny flat in Kensington where we had first made love, as if by slowly reached mutual consent between old friends. If I had felt then a flicker of disappointment, a transient insight that this love-making was a token gesture only given because expected, it was swamped by the breathless rush of everything we did.

When I asked if I might bring Caroline along, Jonathan sounded momentarily disappointed, as if I had taken something from him.

'By all means,' he said, but his voice had a flatter register, and I felt again the sense of competition which had never entirely deserted our relationship.

He was now established in a West End office. It was uncomfortably smart, carpeted throughout in seaweed Wilton, and decorated with nineteenth-century watercolours, and some fine antique furniture. It was, to my taste, an office for looking at rather than working in, but I accepted that the image he presented was important. It was one of the ways in which I could reconcile these trappings with my changing view of Jonathan.

He had taken Miss Bowker with him after leaving Cohen, and she organised his life with a zeal with which I would never have credited her. I saw from the way she watched him that it had its roots in a fascination with him, and, looking through her eyes, I could see the impression of excitement he gave, of barely controlled energy. It seemed hard on her faithful boyfriend, who worked nearby and presented himself every lunch hour with doglike devotion (so Jonathan told me) to take her out. I think that the suburban future he planned in secret for himself and for her was distorted and undermined by her working for Jonathan.

Dinner was at a newly-fashionable restaurant in the King's Road, I liked Beth at first. It was only later that I felt differently. She seemed to have an awareness, a gutter sharpness which complemented her fine-boned, model's face, and a laugh which told of a broad and accepting attitude to life. She had given up modelling and acting, she confided in me, when she had become aware of how superficial a life based upon physical appearance was.

I was less impressed with the untutored enthusiasm with which she talked about Eastern philosophy. She had read Ouspensky and Gurdjieff's *Meetings with Remarkable Men*, wanted to see Katmandu, and had been to Transcendental Meditation classes. But underlying all the froth was a shrewd commonsense, and I was surprised both at her affection for Jonathan and her ability to see him critically.

There were six of us, Giles and his very county wife, Lavinia, making up the other pair. Giles had grey hair above his ears (probably orris root, I thought cynically) and had moved effortlessly into merchant banking. He had now been adopted as a prospective Tory candidate in a safe seat, and both he and Lavinia exuded a self-satisfaction, a smugly fundamentalist right-thinkingness which irritated and annoyed me.

'Well,' said Jonathan, flushed and mellow, holding up his glass of wine as he looked down the table at Beth. 'Wish us the best,' and we all solemnly clinked glasses and drank a toast. Beth got up from her chair and put her hands to his cheeks and kissed him on the forehead, before slipping back to her chair. Jonathan flushed, but I could see he was pleased. Beth signalled to the head waiter and he acknowledged her wave. Suddenly the lights went out.

'Not another power cut,' said someone in aggrieved tones, as the door opened and the candles on the tables gutted and swayed.

The chef came through the door, pushing a trolley on which sat a cake, blazing with candles. It all seemed, momentarily, like a reprise of our birthday parties of long ago. 'Oh, Beth. You shouldn't have . . .' exclaimed Jonathan, clasping his hands in front of him. His eyes shone. Beth looked at him for a moment, her face almost maternal in the soft glow. The lights came back on, and the diners resumed their conversation.

It had an effect upon me which I could not articulate. Not

the meal, or the restaurant, or the conversation, but the sight of Jonathan, briefly stripped of the layers of the years, and the sense of openness between them which Beth and he projected. The feeling persisted as we drove back through the near-deserted streets.

Caroline said, 'You're quiet. A penny for them,' but I couldn't explain in any way that communicated what I felt. 'Did you see that?' she said, breaking through my halting attempts at explanation as a car jinked at reckless speed past our nose from left to right as we drove round Hyde Park Corner. 'Swine,' she shouted through the open window, shaking her fist. It never occurred to me then that she avoided discussing feelings or states of mind — it seemed she merely found them uninteresting.

Two days later I proposed to Caroline. 'Do you really want to?' she asked incredulously, as if I had just made a suggestion which evaded lunacy by a hair's breadth.

I had been sure when I spoke, but the question raised doubts. Nothing tangible, nothing which could be put into a balance-sheet in black and white; merely a momentary disquiet, a flickering sensation that something was not entirely in focus.

'I wouldn't have asked otherwise, would I?' I said, feathering my oars so that we sat in the middle of the Serpentine lake, the seagulls giving their high, plaintive cries as they wheeled and swooped above us.

She looked out across the flat water, stippled with sunlight, towards the Knightsbridge Barracks for a moment, before answering. 'Why not,' she said reflectively. And so the deed was done, for better or worse.

Three months later I was Jonathan's best man in Hampstead and made my speech fearfully at a reception for two hundred. Six weeks after that, Caroline and I were married in a registry office in Chelsea and six of us had a Chinese meal.

One Saturday afternoon (both old married men now), I played one of my rare games of tennis with Jonathan. We went to the public courts at Wimbledon, immaculate in whites amidst the blue shorts and grey socks around us. On balance I should have won, being possessed of greater skills and having spent much more time than he had in perfecting my game to, admittedly, modest standards. But, as with everything we had done together, his passion for winning gave him the edge, and since it meant so much to him, I was perhaps less competitive in chasing the ball in the final points than I might have been against another opponent.

He glanced at me suspiciously as we gathered our balls and rackets together. 'It looked as if you weren't really trying over a couple of those points.'

'I just couldn't get to those three shots,' I said, only half-lying, and we went off to shower and change.

Afterwards, at the snack-bar where we went for a cup of tea, he shook me. 'Rachel is working for Charles Mandeville,' he said casually. What surprised me was the shock of hearing him talk of her, after all those years.

'Oh really,' I said, feigning lack of interest.

He looked at me with an ironic smile, as if to say 'You don't fool me, you know' and went on, 'It wasn't what you thought at all, that evening in Cambridge. Actually Giles had told me he thought she was having an affair with Mandeville.' His eyes were far away, and he seemed to be focusing upon a memory which was almost beyond reach. 'Remember, I'd warned you to be careful? I know a lot of people laughed at Charles, but he was always dangerous. He never knew where to draw the line.' He laughed, recollecting something. 'He finally put old Cohen out of business, you know. Cohen was so furious at my defection that he tried to get in on a big deal. When he couldn't deliver, Mandeville bought him out for a derisory sum.'

My tea was getting cold, a light scum of greasy residue covering the surface. I felt cheated in some way.

'Then what were you doing that evening when I came?' I asked, trying to keep the vehemence out of my voice.

Jonathan put both his hands on the edge of the table and spread his fingers, looking at the nails. 'I won't deny I wanted it to be something else,' he said, 'but she had some way of defusing the situation whenever I approached her.' He looked at me to see if I understood, and I nodded, remembering the feeling and textures of her ability to avoid my clumsy shows of tenderness and love.

'Just before you came I had tried.' He paused, searching for words. 'We had seen a lot of each other, as you know, and I thought that she felt something for me. When you knocked and came in, I knew that it was the finish. When you'd left she asked me to go. I remember something curious that she said. "People always think the worst because it is more difficult to cope with the best." I didn't see her again until a few months ago when I went in to see Mandeville.'

There are things within us which we can deny; old hurts which seem to have no potency any more, old loves which seem the products of less wise times, old deaths which seem to have ossified into the remote and separate structures of past time. When they are approached directly the mind can create defences which minimise their impact, or idealise them so that they do not have the bitter strength of reality. But the unforeseen and unexpected has a basilisk power, and against that the only defence is true indifference. In those few moments I knew that I had not reached that state so far as Rachel was concerned.

'How is she?' I asked, and was surprised to find my voice unsteady.

'She still looks the same,' said Jonathan. 'But she must have changed. We all have, haven't we?'

There was one secret triumph which I held for myself as we went out and walked back to the cars. That I had, in however limited a sense, momentarily possessed Rachel. It was only that which left the fragile balance of my relationship with Jonathan seemingly unchanged. Next time we played tennis I would not give any points away.

21

I remember joining Walter and a French art critic for a rendering of Beethoven's *Mount of Olives* at St Martin's Church one fine evening. When we came out into the courtyard into the summer evening the waxy magnolia blossoms were closing slowly for the night. We stood in the courtyard, the sky darkening moment by moment, still held by the memory of the music. The Frenchman said, '*de rien*' twice with a dismissive gesture of his hand, but I could see that he had been moved by the music.

People always say: never go back, particularly if, like Meaulnes, the seducing memories are enmeshed, intertwined, inextricably connected with the awareness and forgotten feeling of childhood. I knew that if I did not go back, there would be part of me forever consumed with yearning for the lost lands. They were small things that I remembered, which would have been of no consequence to anyone else; a crooked pine which stood upon the hills above our house; a view of the Himalayas from a vantage point above the vast, open valley. I knew, if only dimly after all these years, that these seemingly random memories were the repositories of feelings which I no longer had the keys to unlock. But, since I desired the odyssey, and since I could not feel that the things I must revisit could have meaning for anyone else, I chose to go alone.

Nor did Caroline complain when, prompted by some unconscious atavistic impulse, I decided to savour the delights of packing for myself.

A month later I knew that it had been a mistake. Since my family had left, the President's summer palace had been built a few miles from Hasooth Gali, and the steep wooded slopes had been deforested and built upon. Dr Mac was long dead, and his wife also, and as I trudged around the estate, determined to leave no stone unturned in searching for my past, I felt like a man who has returned to his home after an absence of many years only to find it altered beyond recognition, and peopled with polite strangers. Because such changes disturbed the totality of my recall, they remained irritatingly present, distorting my views, reminding me of the passage of the years.

There was one incident which didn't disappoint, which reminded me of the obliqueness and unpredictability of the India that I knew. (It is hard still, after so many years, to think that our home was in Pakistan, and not India. So much had happened before 1947 that the ideas and language of that time have not been superseded in my memory by subsequent events and arrangements.)

Three days before I was due to leave, I walked up the old road, now rutted and distorted, with campion and vetch and wild grasses growing through the remains of the tarmacadam, to Karam Deen's stables. As I walked towards the complex of buildings huddled under the trees, lizards and zonures scuttled away at my approach, to vanish into cracks in the dry stone walling at the side of the road. I felt hot and dusty, and the thin air seemed insufficient to take me up the slope any faster than the shambling pace I had adopted. My thin cotton shirt was soaked with perspiration, and I could feel runnels of damp coursing down my face, mixed with the gritty feeling of dust. The sheds were just as I had remembered them, mud-walled and crowned with sloping and discoloured corrugated iron, grouped around a central courtyard with a well.

In the fenced garden beyond, now in view as I crested the hill above the complex, and began the perilous, shaled descent, two horses cropped busily, their tails swishing over their backs to dislodge the persistent horse-flies. In the corner of the next field a chestnut dam, gravid and listless, stood with her head bowed, gazing patiently into the distance. A tang of resin filled the air and then was gone. On the sweltering air I could hear the small buzzings and rustlings of insects and birds, and a vast bumble-bee droned crazily across my path.

As I came to the white-washed adobe wall which housed the

cool-looking entrance to the courtyard, a man stepped out of the shadows and stood waiting for me. With a sense of shock I recognised Karam Deen himself. I had thought he must be dead long ago, but he stood lean and erect, giving no quarter to his ninety-odd years. He gave the gesture of salaam, and then joined his hands together, greeting me as if I had seen him only a few days before.

'Salaam, David Sahib,' he said, beckoning me with a courteous gesture into the shade of the colonnade cloister. On the other side a group of women sat in gaily coloured sarees involved in some activity, and looking shyly over their shoulders at us. I sat on the wicker stool he indicated, and he squatted easily on his haunches, his elbows resting on his knees, his hands clasped as in prayer under his chin. The last time I had seen him was at James' funeral, as he marshalled his ragged band and walked away into the valley, so many years before.

It was ironic in all the circumstances, that my one real link with this past should be Karam Deen, but over half an hour we had remembered many people, and had each learned something of what had happened. I felt easier with him, though it was impossible to separate him entirely from what he had done during Partition. He held the new settlers, the 'summer wallahs', in contempt. They were not really men, forced to flee the plains below to seek refuge from the heat, and, though he took their money and hired them horses, he left his sons to talk to them.

He told me that Dr Mac had been killed in a riding accident. 'He was a man,' he said with a fierce smile. 'His horse broke her foreleg at Pindi Point, and he fell over the edge of the rock. When they found him he was still alive, laughing and joking with them. When they picked him up the blood came out of his mouth and he died.'

He rocked and swayed from side to side, clicking his tongue against his teeth as he reminisced. A boy walked across the courtyard and Karam Deen called him over with pride. 'This is my great-grandson,' he said with pride, and the boy smiled uncomprehendingly. 'Go and bring us some tea and halva.'

When we had drunk our tea I asked him, 'Do you know where I can find Ram?' He sat motionless, the black eyes expressionless, then spat into the dust. 'He is dead,' he said, with a dismissive gesture of his hand. When I persisted, wanting to know when and how he had died, he said, 'You do not understand. He is dead to us. He was my nephew's son — and he betrayed us.'

When I was ready to go, he took me round the stables. Where there had been four or five horses, thin and hungry, there were now some fifteen, sleek and well-fed. As I made sounds of approval he watched me with a smile. When we had finished, I made the gesture of namaste. He stepped forward and clasped my hand between his two hands. His grip was so powerful that I winced.

'Please, David Sahib,' he said, 'send me a gold watch with my name inside when you get back to England.'

I began to climb the steep hill. The palpable earth hummed and shifted under my feet with scurrying insects, and a buzzard lazed through the azure sky in a wide sweep obliquely past me and down the hill. Everything was unchanged after all, save that I was now the stranger. All that I remembered was as it had been, the dry heat shimmering from the dark-red earth, the Mother-in-law Tongue plants sawing out of walls and crevices, the brilliant dragonflies darting their brief lives away on shimmering wings. It was as if time alone had taken me beyond this, and the grey skies and small rooms of England had made it impossible to return. I paused for breath.

Below, Karam Deen stepped out into the blinding sunlight. He shielded his eyes with one hand and waved to me, indicating I should wait, and began to climb up the hill after me. When he was abreast of me he stood for a moment, and we looked down to the soft mauves and blues of the haze which engulfed the villages on the way to Rawalpindi.

He said in Hindi, 'I almost forgot. Mrs Stanton gave this to me to keep for your father. She said he would come back. But I can give it to you.'

I picked up the oval cameo brooch hanging on its slender gold chain. Under the convex glass her sepia picture looked out at me, grave and unsmiling, the cloud of brown hair loosely arranged on her head, and her white neck rising from a swathe of white chiffon. I think I had always known, but had denied it, and it was too late now to do harm or good.

'I'll see that he gets it,' I said.

22

Three weeks before it happened, Jonathan had telephoned to ask me out to a dinner party. It had been a dark morning, the rain lashing in flurries against the house and the wind rumbling the pyrecantha to and fro across the mellow bricks. Walter had called to ask when I would be delivering my new set of studies for Charles. Miranda had found one of the goldfish dead and had been almost inconsolable over breakfast. Caroline had dreamed that I had walked out of a dinner party at the Connaught leaving her to pay the bill, and was still angry with me for behaving so badly. Thompson stalked the garden, a murderous crow in black, armed with the shears and waging his grim war against all living things.

I had accepted Jonathan's invitation with alacrity. It was one of those periods when coy domesticity had begun to pall, and I felt the need for the whiff of the bar-room, the psychic spit and sawdust. As usual I had no idea of what might be in store for me. The other guests might be city bankers, or actors, or opera singers, almost anybody from the miscellaneous ragbag of Jonathan's past life. We arranged that he would pick me up at about seven.

Jonathan arrived at 6.30. As usual his tyres skidded on the gravel drive and the car rocked as he braked heavily. It irritated me to see him lock the doors in my drive, but I recognised this instinct to be as much a part of him as the way he put his hand over his mouth when he was embarrassed. He irritated Caroline too, but when he was with us he could charm us both completely. It was only when he had gone, and the warmth of the bright smile had faded, and we no longer had to concentrate to keep up with him, that we both felt used and scorned; though we were never able to define exactly why.

He walked in past me and kissed Caroline on the cheek. Miranda ran past me and put her arms up. He swept her up and threw her into the air.

'How's old smelly then?'

'You always call me smelly, Uncle Jonathan.'

'Phew. I'm not surprised. Have you been rolling in compost?' His nose wrinkled in mock disgust.

'Course not. I don't smell.' Miranda laughed delightedly.

'Nice,' he said. 'You smell nice.'

We went into the lounge. Caroline fixed our drinks. Whisky for us, gin and tonic for Jonathan. Now that his face had relaxed, he looked tired. There was a pallor under his dark skin, and his face looked drawn. Caroline beat me to it.

'You look tired, Jonathan. Are you overworking?'

He laughed with genuine amusement, as if the idea of working hard was incongruous.

'Oh yes,' he said. 'I've been killing myself on a property deal. The gap between what I am and what I do widens daily. The people I am dealing with look upon a business breakfast on Concorde to New York as the *summum vitae*. It gives them a sense of importance. Any word over two syllables gives them tramlines on the forehead.'

'Is it worth it?' asked Caroline.

He looked serious for a moment. 'Someone once told me that value judgements and questioning the fundamental meaning of life were symptoms of depression. If I permitted myself to look at what I do *sub specie aeternitatis* I would stop tomorrow. But it is worth it because if I bring this off, I will never need to worry about money again.' He laughed shortly and looked at me. 'The parents wouldn't approve.'

I felt awkward, feeling this to be a covert request for support. 'Surely they'd be happy to feel you were doing well?'

'Yes, I suppose so,' he said, but his voice lacked conviction. He put his glass down and looked at his watch. 'We'd better go,' he said.

'Don't lead my husband astray,' said Caroline, an edge of

asperity in her voice. On a few occasions I had returned with Jonathan in the early hours, much the worse for wear. Drink and Jonathan together made me loud and garrulous. A recognition of all that was in her voice.

'Promise,' he said, and we went out of the door.

Jonathan seemed remote, abstracted, and to break the silence I said, 'Who'll be there?'

'You'll know them,' he said. 'Rona will be hostess.'

I was a little surprised. Walter's wife, blonde, precisely coiffured and made-up, beautiful in a glacial way, was the sort of woman who terrified me and prompted in me an inept clumsiness. I speculated upon Jonathan's involvement with her. Though Rona and Walter were still married, they had long since elected to lead their separate lives. I realise now that I was naïve to assume that there was necessarily anything in it, but it seemed to me then that Jonathan might be having an affair with her.

'I see you don't approve, little brother,' said Jonathan mockingly, and I realised that the silence had lasted for a couple of miles.

I said, rather pompously, 'It isn't up to me to approve or disappove. But you must see it is a little awkward for me.'

He roared with laughter. 'Walter is the most civilised man in the world. You don't think he is at home weeping into his whisky and soda, do you? Walter, at the moment, is probably with a young lady acquaintance of his in Soho . . . Modigliani, with just a touch of Picasso Blue Period . . .'

He saw my bemused look, and roared again. The car rocketed towards the Sheen roundabout, and wove through the traffic to the other side.

'After a certain age sex becomes less important,' he said. 'It no longer contains the potential of that elusive secret of life we searched for so assiduously years ago. It becomes just another incident.'

For some reason his words reminded me of Jung's savage and terrible dictum: 'The aspect of themselves which human beings sacrifice in the attainment of a given object in their lives is reborn alive and comes back after many years, knife in hand, demanding to sacrifice that which sacrificed it,' and I saw

Jonathan, knife in hand, bending over the headless snake, that summer, so long ago.

Dinner was at one of those restaurants which I would never normally patronise when going out with my own circle of friends and acquaintances. Everything was a shade too new, too assiduously copying the styles of other restaurants, too opulent. There was even a small, brightly illuminated rock-pool fed by a fountain where a small and indolent alligator gazed out indifferently at the expense-account diners talking animatedly at their small tables around the floor. The waiters had the dour, saturnine look of Mafia henchmen, and there was little warmth in the maitre d'hôtel's artificial smile of welcome to Jonathan. We had arrived first, followed shortly by Rona, and sat in a red plush embrasure with a pink pleated canopy fringed with gold braid.

Being an artist is often disconcerting. The visual imagery which bombarded me, of Jonathan and Rona in bed together, inhibited my small talk at the start of the evening. After a couple of drinks, it became easier. Rona made some reference to my last exhibition, and I was surprised by the knowledge she displayed of what was happening in the art world; not the ephemera of who was 'in' or 'out', or who had bought what for how much, but quick and perceptive comments on some of the new young 'fringe' painters. Jonathan was abstracted, silent, looking up whenever anyone came across the floor. I noticed that his hand shook slightly when he reached for his glass. Every so often he smiled or nodded when Rona made a point, but it was merely a polite reflex, and I could see his mind was elsewhere.

After we had been there for half an hour or so the maitre d'hôtel ushered in two men. With something of a shock I recognised the taller and bulkier of the two. Over the years I had heard rumours of Mandeville's wild living, his shady connections, and the fortune he had made for himself by, so it was said, extremely dubious means. He never seemed to have trouble in evicting people from his properties in the empire he had built for himself, predominantly in the ghetto areas of London, but it was rumoured that he employed rent collectors and minders who were indifferent to the methods they used provided that they worked. His properties were controlled through a network of companies, and tenants who dared to complain tended to give up trying to wade through the changes in registered ownership to find out who actually controlled their homes. He was even said to have had a part in the disappearance of two rival property tycoons, though this had never come to any issue, despite police enquiries. I knew that Jonathan was involved with some strange people, and felt, sometimes, that he had an awed and childlike respect for some of the semi-criminal fraternity. I had thought that he had outgrown a fascination for the Mandevilles of this world. In that, as in so much else about him, I was wrong.

The maitre d'hôtel brought them across with a real smile of welcome. Doubtless he recognised the ring of the true as opposed to the counterfeit this time. Halsbury, Mandeville's partner, was an undersized weasel-faced man with black, thinning hair, and the shadow of a heavy beard. His eyes moved the whole time, hooded and dark, assessing, speculating. Jonathan made the introductions and I could see he was under considerable strain. Their greeting of Rona and me was perfunctory, and I felt that I had failed when Mandeville's eyes flicked briefly over me, dismissing me from any importance in the future proceedings. Though Rona and I would still provide the audience which Jonathan needed so much, I feared that we would be witnessing a play which he no longer directed.

We ordered from a menu as baroque and overblown as the establishment itself. In the background a small orchestra had begun tuning their instruments, and a tall blonde in a white, low-cut gown was standing by the microphone. She began to sing 'Begin the Beguine'. Her voice came through the smoke-laden air with a hint of quality, of true pain. Mandeville looked at her for a long moment. 'Very nice,' he said, and I could almost see his thoughts.

He turned to Jonathan, who sat at the other corner of the embrasure. His manner was that of a confident and over-assured school bully talking to a new boy.

'Well,' he said, 'did you manage to get the draft through?'

Jonathan paused. Unusually, for him, he seemed to be at a loss for words. He looked down at the tablecloth, drawing lines on the linen with the tines of his fork.

'I'm sorry Charles. I'm afraid Schroders pulled out at the last moment. I'm talking to another potential investor —'

Halsbury's lips were moving before he had finished. 'We have a deadline with the builders. Penalty clauses both ways.' He leaned across the table and I felt the hair at the back of my neck prickle. Gripping Jonathan's arm he said, 'You agreed to come in with us and you knew the deal. We stand to make a lot if everything is completed on time. If it isn't . . .' He left the sentence uncompleted, but his eyes, unwinking now, gazed into Jonathan's with a flat stare.

Mandeville said smoothly, 'Jonathan, you know that we are in a very tough business. We like our friends to come in with us, but we have to take steps if people let us down . . .' His voice was soft, almost pleading, and I could sense in it some desire for forgiveness, even for absolution. He carried on, speaking confidentially to Jonathan as if we were not there. 'You've still got two and a half weeks before the deadline. See what you can do . . .' He put his hand on Jonathan's arm, but his smile didn't extend to his eyes. I remembered father, standing on the Persian carpet with my report in his hand, 'See what you can do, son . . .'

Rona seemed unmoved by these exchanges. I was frightened and surprised. It was disconcerting to see Jonathan cower before people like Mandeville and Halsbury. I knew Jonathan had brought Rona and myself to soften the proceedings; what it might have been like if we had not been there I could not imagine.

No imagination was needed to recognise the clear threat to Jonathan. It was uphill going for the rest of dinner. We found common ground of a kind in discussing the cinema. Their viewings seemed to have taken place exclusively on jumbos flying between international airports, and their tastes were certainly some way from my own. Even the red wine, dispensed in liberal quantities to accompany the meal, made very little difference. The singer moved somnambulistically through her repertoire of old numbers. The early frisson of excitement I had felt, the glimpse of quality, had long since faded. Everything about the evening, the food, the wine, felt stained and tainted.

Just before ten o'clock Jonathan excused himself from the table to make a telephone call. We had all abandoned any pretence of talking by now, though the general raucousness and the plaintive notes from the small stage in themselves provided a thin excuse for the lack of further exchanges. When he returned he appeared upset, but smiled and made a gesture of dismissal with his hand when he saw me look at him. He called for the bill.

Mandeville stood up. Jonathan could have been his son or his brother from the warmth of their embrace, but I knew that under the phoniness of the scene lurked the hard bone of reality.

'Two and a half weeks, Jonathan,' Mandeville said. 'If you're still going to Cambridge, look in on The Eagle for me.' He smiled. 'I'll wait for your call,' he said, and then they went out.

The most important things are those we cannot talk about directly. We had another drink together after they left. Then Rona looked at her watch. 'I must go,' she said. 'Walter's waiting for me,' and I caught Jonathan's smile. She refused his offer to see her to her car, kissed us both, and walked away elegantly through the crowded tables. We watched her out of sight.

I felt embarrassed to have been a witness to the evening. It didn't seem possible to ignore what had happened, to chat in a desultory fashion of other things; yet I dreaded talking about what I had observed. I knew Jonathan could not, would not, abandon the image he had forged for me, though I sensed his disquiet. I knew, too, that I could not find the words to break through.

Usually Jonathan forestalled any personal questioning with a flippant or facetious remark, turning the conversation away from himself with an ease born of long practice. I knew that he had created a situation which could not be dismissed in that way, in which the governing rules were harder and bleaker than those which operated in my softer, more sheltered life. If I missed a deadline, Walter might shout and rant a bit, but I considered it a legitimate return for his percentage that he should protect me from the consequences of running a few days past, and by and large the arrangement worked satisfactorily to the accompaniment of mutterings and grumblings on both sides. Here I knew that there were no such protections, no mediator, and the complicity which existed in Jonathan's arrangement with Mandeville and Halsbury, their complete disregard for Rona and myself as witnesses to the evening, suggested that they were unconcerned about any repercussions.

Jonathan said nothing, but pulled a letter from his inside pocket. It was heavily marked and creased, like a love letter which had been read and re-read. It was a letter from Mandeville, in which he reminded Jonathan of the penalties payable if a financing deal for a new hotel was delayed. It was strange to think that Mandeville had, for a time, shared the same cultural heritage as we had. There was little evidence of a love of language in the bluntly expressed letter. I noticed that the capital I's did not come out clearly, and that even the spelling was a little erratic. But the message was unmistakably plain.

Since the terms in the letter were expressed in percentages, I asked Jonathan to give me some details of what he was required to provide. For a wild moment or two I had wondered if I could help him in some way. When he told me, I knew that he was beyond such help as I could offer. The commitment ran into millions. With that sort of money at stake I could believe that any default would have serious consequences. Jonathan watched me, with a smile which seemed to me to paper over an abyss of despair.

I said, 'What happens if you can't get the money together?'

The smile vanished, and his face set into lines of bleakness.

'The unthinkable,' he said.

It was a sombre drive back. But, perhaps because the burden was shared, Jonathan seemed almost light-hearted. As he drove he talked about India, the India that he remembered. He reminded me of our game around the large estate. He had painted an old cardboard box as a car: fixed to a defunct carom board as a base, and with a rope attached, he used to drag me around the garden. As we went he gave me a commentary. Each flower bed, each tree, even the compost heap represented somewhere we had read about.

As he talked I remembered those sensations of childhood, watching Jonathan's brown legs moving purposefully in front of me as he grunted with the effort of getting the board moving. He was so convincing that, even watching the familiar garden go by, I was caught up in the spell of his descriptions:

'This is Gibraltar. Look —' with an arm outstretched, pointing, '— there are the Apes. When they leave the Rock, it will no longer be British.'

Sometimes, deliberately I suspect, though he always denied it, he would turn a corner too fast and the centrifugal force would throw me out of the box onto the lawn. As he talked, his face, illuminated by the green glow from the dashboard lights, was softened by memory. Gradually, I recognised that he was using this as a device to distance the present; and the scene I had just witnessed came back to me, together with half-glimpsed fantasies which fed off the unspoken words, the hidden intent, which underlay the conversation. I saw that his apparent carelessness, the discursiveness of his conversation, did not mean that he had come to terms with his present predicament. He had just dismissed the events of the evening and replaced them with the harder, brighter colours of childhood. But I knew that, unlike childhood, the consequences of failure here would be real.

Jonathan turned the car into the drive. The lights were off. He refused my offer of a drink, looking at his watch.

'I've got an early start in the morning,' he said. 'Lots to do.' His voice sounded light and confident.

I hesitated a moment, looking for some words to penetrate the darkness between us.

He laughed, brushing his hand across his face, but without malice

'Don't worry about me. I've survived a lot of problems.' The moment had gone. I said goodnight and made my way through the light drizzle to the door as the car moved slowly across the gravel. Upstairs a light clicked on.

23

The house was unusually silent the morning of the inquest. By unspoken mutual consent we even managed to eat our breakfasts silently. I walked into the garden on the pretext of watching Thompson working. Only Miranda seemed unaffected, and I blessed her for chattering on to my parents, forcing them to respond. The inquest was at 10.30 in a coroner's court near the City.

Brian O'Donnell was already in the waiting area when we arrived. His black suit was immaculately cut, and he gave an ersatz impression as if he had been hired to mourn for someone he hadn't really known. When I organised a place for my parents I left them with Caroline and made my way over to him. I could see that he was preparing himself, wary that I might catch him undefended in some way.

'God, what a terrible business!' he said, clearing his throat nervously.

'Yes,' I said, 'I suppose it is.' He looked at me anxiously, as if I were departing from the conventions of the occasion with this numbed response. His tongue flicked over his lips. I realised that he wanted to say something. Twice he started, and then seemed to be affected by some nervousness which paralysed his vocal chords.

'He came to see me, you know, about two weeks ago.'

I was surprised at that, so far as I was then capable of being surprised by anything. A group of people came in through the door — Walter, Mandeville, Halsbury, like a group of career politicians attending the reading of some minor Bill; then Jean, and Alan supporting Beth. Beth was in black, and the veil falling from the toque on her head couldn't disguise that she had been crying.

'Why,' I asked, and Brian swallowed convulsively, his Adam's apple bobbing down his long throat and then up again. I looked at his hand which had begun to shake; when he saw me looking he thrust it deep into his pocket.

'It was odd. We'd drifted apart, as you know, ever since . . . ah . . . coming down, and I really had no idea why he wanted to come. But he was very insistent on the phone — you know how he is . . . was . . . and we arranged to meet that evening.' He paused for a moment, looking at the door, and I saw Giles and his wife come in. Giles caught her arm and gestured towards us and we both smiled stiffly. Caroline went over to them and took them across to meet my parents. I turned back to Brian.

'Oh yes,' he said. 'Well, we had a couple of drinks and chatted generally about Cambridge. I began to wonder what it was all about.'

Brian was sweating profusely, and he looked pale.

'Then Jonathan asked me if I could put in a good word for him with Schroders. He knew that I was connected with the family in some way, and though he wouldn't normally dream of asking for such a favour it was a matter of considerable urgency, one might almost say life or death. He had that curious delivery, seeming to be only half-serious in what he was saying, and I tried to joke with him. I said they wouldn't even give me the pickings from their noses, that they were so mean that they had coin box payphones in their country homes . . . I really waxed quite eloquent. Anyway, he listened for a bit with that half smile on his face until I really thought he was quite amused. 'Christ —' he looked at me appealingly '— I've got some money but what he was looking for was beyond anything I could count . . . let alone raise. I gave him another drink, and everything seemed quite cosy. He drank it up and said he had to go, and I got his coat and walked with him to the door. When we got there he turned to me and said, "Thanks, Brian. My own fault really, I suppose. I should have realised it was futile to ask a semi-imbecile to understand what they were being offered." It wasn't until he had gone that I realised what he had said.'

'It doesn't matter,' I said. 'You know what he was like. A bit sharp sometimes.'

I thought Brian was going to cry. 'I don't mind that. What I can't stand is that I couldn't recognise his desperation. If only I could have listened to him a bit more . . .'

'It wouldn't have helped,' I said. I wondered how many other 'if only' stories I was going to hear; how I could get away from Brian without appearing brusque. I was saved from having to take any decision by Mandeville arriving at my side. He nodded to Brian and took me by the arm.

'I'm sorry,' he said. 'I'm truly sorry.' I looked into his narrow, mean-set eyes. He had the feral, animal hardness which I recalled from Cambridge, but to my fanciful imaginings it was overlaid and strengthened by the deals he had done since we had left. As I was about to reply I caught Rachel's figure in the door, out of the corner of my eye. She looked small, her hands composed in front of her, clasping her bag. She looked around the room uncertainly at first, then, seeing us, she moved towards us. Mandeville caught her by the arm in a gesture betraying intimacy which was not lost upon me.

'You know David, don't you?' he said, and she nodded mutely, looking up at me. It was the first time I had seen her since that summer over fifteen years ago when I had surprised her and Jonathan in what I had then thought to be a guilty embrace. For a moment I experienced that sensation of needless loss, an instant apprehension of the years between which might have been different, before the present crowded its black waters over the thought.

'It's a pity to meet you again in these circumstances,' I said.

Caroline came across quickly. It had always been easy to draw her to my side at any function merely by falling into conversation with the prettiest woman present. Rachel smiled, with the quiet merest lifting of the corners of her mouth which I remembered from Cambridge.

'I know what is going on here,' it said in gentle amusement, and, at the same time, I caught the familiar feeling that she was no longer fully present. That voluntary self-exile worked its intrigue on me again, as it had done so many times before.

She said, 'So this is your wife,' and Caroline looked across at me, her unguarded expression showing her calculation before she turned to Rachel, smiling.

'You two have met before, I take it?'

Rachel laughed. 'More years ago than I care to remember. In Cambridge . . .'

'Oh, then!' said Caroline, relief evident in her voice. Relief, I suppose that the meetings had not taken place unknown to her, and been hidden from her during the years she and I had been together.

The usher came out and called us into the court. To my surprise Sinclair was there, and a number of Jonathan's friends from Cambridge days. Jean and Beth sat with both sets of parents on one of the wooden pews in the centre of the courtroom. Before the proceedings started I looked across as the door into the chamber opened, and in the corner of my vision, saw Cohen arrive. I barely recognised him as he walked down with a brisk step, trailing behind him a rather heavily peroxided blonde, bored, petulant and much younger. Where once he had been round and solid, his clothes now hung off him, and even from where I sat I could see his suit had seen better days. Before he got to his seat an usher had indicated that he should remove the pipe stuck in his mouth, and I heard the raucous laugh which accompanied his unheard sally. That at least hadn't changed, though I could see from the usher's sour face that the joke was lost upon him.

The coroner had the harassed, no-nonsense air of a family GP who suspected his patients of malingering, and a habit of closing his eyes and passing his hand wearily over his forehead and nose. In some ways his attitude was a relief, conferring an impersonality upon the proceedings which made it difficult to feel that we were discussing the way in which my brother had met his death. But I could see that my parents were ill-prepared for the details of what had taken place. When Beth took the stand and began to give evidence I saw my mother put her face in her hands, and my father, arm around her shoulders, looked white and drained.

I never had admired Beth as much as I did that day. She looked terrible, with the haunted, withdrawn appearance of someone who had witnessed a scene so terrible as to be incommunicable and beyond exorcism. In a low, controlled voice she answered the questions put to her, occasionally pausing to sip from the glass of water on the stand in front of her. She could see no reason why Jonathan should have decided to take his life.

'Yes,' she said, with a glance towards the corner of the courtroom where Mandeville sat. She knew that he had business worries, but then he had always had those as long as she had known him. It was when she came to describe the events of the evening on which she found him that her control began to leave her. I felt the court willing her to keep going.

The coroner leaned forward and said in a dry voice, 'I realise this must be very painful for you. Please take your time.' She straightened her shoulders and looked out defiantly.

'I'd taken James to my mother's house for tea. Jonathan wasn't due back until much later. He had a meeting, he told me. Anyway, when I got back his car was in the drive. We walked into the house and James went off to play. I called up the stairs . . .' She paused, swallowing strongly, and a rustle of movement passed around the court. 'There was no answer, and I went up to the bedroom to change.'

Someone coughed, and Beth faltered for a moment, then resumed in a stronger voice.

'The first thing I saw was my dressing-room chair on its side. I couldn't understand what it was doing there and went to pick it up. Then I saw Jonathan —' she put her head in her hands and her shoulders shook. '— He was hanging from a beam in the bedroom.' In the silence that followed, I looked at my parents. They sat as if turned to stone, and I caught Jean's worried look before I turned back to look at Beth.

When the letter was produced, the coroner asked where Beth had found it. It had come in the post, she said, and I could see that he was puzzled. I hadn't realised this either, assuming that Beth had found it somewhere in the house. He asked Beth why Jonathan would have posted such a note, rather than leaving it at home, and Beth said a rather curious thing.

'First, he was always very businesslike in all his dealings. Second, I think it was his way of ensuring that he did what he had planned to do.' She delivered it like part of a lecture which she had memorised and I realised she had thought about it at length, puzzled and confused herself by what had happened. The coroner nodded, and made a note on the pad before him.

Plotinus called death 'The flight of the alone to The Alone.' I looked around the crowded chamber and wondered how many of the others were reaching the same conclusion that I was groping towards, with such open-eyed horror. When I had arrived back with Beth that night, her mother (called by Beth), had let the ambulance men in. I had had only the whispered, broken phrases offered by Beth, and the remains of the rope hanging from the beam to conjure up the scene. Later, when I had undertaken to identify him, steeling myself against the expected sight, I had felt he was strangely at peace, and the goitrous bruise on his throat held no terrors for me.

When the coroner returned an open verdict I knew that the same doubts had occurred to him. There was a sudden outbreak of incredulous whispering around the court, and I could sense the disbelief and incomprehension at the verdict. As I turned I saw Rachel looking at me, and something in her steady gaze convinced me, in some subterranean, intuitive way, that she, too, had the same uncertainties as I had.

It was time to go home, to resume the disturbed pattern of our lives. But first we had to endure another of those rituals which, even now, seemed almost risible. We stood in the large black and white-tiled hall, while the chamber emptied, to exchange meaningless condolences with people we hardly knew.

Jean and Caroline took mother away, and father followed them, his stoop more pronounced than ever before. I stood by Beth's side. She seemed remote, far away, her eyes gazing unseeingly across the hall and a small, formal smile painfully tugging the corner of her lips. Cohen was first, the wilted, pneumatic blonde in her mock ocelot holding on to his arm, her face twisted into the simulacrum of a sympathetic smile.

'Terrible,' he said. 'Absolutely terrible. He was like a son to me.' He exuded a smell of stale perspiration mixed with tobacco, and I noticed that his trousers had been badly mended. I murmured some conventional nicety, and endured a bone-wrenching handshake.

He walked past Mandeville with a precarious dignity, and out into the street. Behind him the blonde, released from the inhibitions of the occasion, wailed, 'Wait for meeee. Why are you going so fast? There's nothing urgent to do, is there?' But he continued walking, without a backward glance.

One surprise was Miss Bowker. She had her arm through that of a gangling, sandy-haired young man, and I could see that she was several months pregnant.

'I kept out of sight of him,' she said as she arrived, and I remembered that first meeting with her in Cohen's office. 'This is my husband, Andrew.' We shook hands, and murmured politely at each other, two people who would never meet again.

I walked down the hall to where Rachel was sitting. Mandeville was talking to Beth, and I could see her nod from time to time, though her body still held that stiff, unbending pose, as though cast in plaster. I sat by Rachel's side, and she looked at me calmly. I felt I had to ask her.

'Were you in the office when he came in for the last time?' She nodded, and I went on, 'That must have been when that letter was written.'

Her eyes slid past me to where Beth stood, still talking to Mandeville, but she made no reply. I waited, watching her, trying to divine some nuance of meaning, some hint, from the still face in front of me. All she said was, 'I think Beth has suffered enough, don't you?'

I asked if I could come to see her, and she gave me a card with her address on it.

'But telephone first,' she said. 'I'm often out.'

I said nothing to Mandeville, but took Beth's arm, and together we walked out to the car-park. The wake, for that is how it persisted in my mind, was to be in two days at Jonathan's house, Jean had suggested this as the best arrangement in the circumstances, rather than bringing everyone together after the funeral. We drove back in silence, our convoy interspersed amidst the speeding traffic.

It was two afternoons later, at Rachel's flat. Rachel said, 'He came to me that afternoon.' She had turned her face away from me, busying herself with mixing a drink, but I could see she was crying. I watched her mutely. After a few moments she composed herself, and the shaking of her shoulders stopped.

'What for?' I asked stupidly.

She turned around to face me. The wind blew the net curtain across, and it sank slowly down.

'He tried to force me to make love with him,' she said. I felt sick. She paused for a moment.

'In the end I gave in. He was too strong for me and I was frightened. He carried me over to the bed, and I just lay there. All the time he was going on about . . .' She raised her hands up, as if she couldn't find the words to express herself.

'Oh, Mandeville and Cambridge, and how he had always desired me, would always. It was awful.'

'What happened?' I asked, dully.

She brought the drink over to me and put it on the glass-topped table. She sat at the end of the sofa, her hands held together in her lap. 'Nothing,' she said. 'He was impotent. He tried for some time, but nothing happened. He was crying. At first I became very angry but then I laughed at him, made fun of him. Then he went.'

I put my arms around her. I could feel the tension in her slight body. It was some atavistic relief that Jonathan had not entered her. It was hard to find appropriate words. 'It doesn't matter, now. It doesn't matter,' I said.

She moved in my arms so that I could see one tear-puffed eye. 'If only I hadn't laughed,' she said.

I had come to see her about Jonathan. The inquest had only given official sanction to what had happened, only tidied some respectable formula away into a drawer in some filing cabinet. I knew that words broke before the truth, that things often become untrue as one is saying them, that nothing can be verified, that people lie. Despite all these knowings, the feelings culled through dark nights from my teeming brain, and heaped remorselessly upon one another time and again, I still felt the hopeless need to find some stable answer. Yet, even as I thought this, I knew that I had come for something else, beside which, to my shame, I felt at that moment no further concern for Jonathan.

'Did you ever . . .?' I asked. I couldn't finish the sentence. She moved within my arms so that her hair hung over her face, and her voice was muffled.

'Jonathan was so nice at first. He made me laugh. There was nothing for him to be jealous about . . .' I felt sick, betrayed beyond recall, as if the word 'jealous' underlined what I had dreaded; I couldn't understand how Rachel could drop this casually into the conversation, as if it had no significance. She moved away from me and went to the mirror, abstractedly moving her fingers through her hair. It was as if she were talking to herself and I was not present, and I felt again the androgynous sense of confusion which she had so often provoked in me.

I said bitterly, 'So you did sleep with him. And I suppose you slept with Mandeville, too?'

She turned away, with a defensive gesture, as if I had offered to strike her. I would have given anything to have taken the words back. She looked so defenceless, and I felt that I had taken some freedom to speak as she wished, and to be accepted, from her. When she spoke I could hardly hear her.

'Did you really think I had? Is that all you think about?' She gestured towards the door. 'Perhaps you'd better go.'

Until that moment I had felt certain that she had slept with Jonathan, that I must leave, that this was only the concluding of old business which should have been finished long ago. Now she had blurred the hard outlines of my certainty. As in a dream I began to move towards the door, gathering my coat from the arm of the sofa, while she watched me from the bedroom door. Her face was white, and she stood motionless and dry-eyed.

Suddenly I could bear the tension no longer. I walked over to her and put my arm around her. I knew, somewhere far below the level of conscious thought, that I was opening a door that I could not close; that, whatever happened, my life would be irrevocably changed by the next few moments. I knew, too, that for once I had elected to act, rather than be the passive observer, and that I could not, this time, blame the consequences, whatever they might be, on circumstances beyond my control.

We clung together, swaying, by the door. She held me so tightly that I could feel my ribs hurt where I had fractured one in a schoolboy game of rugby.

'I couldn't say anything to you,' she kept saying, covering my face in feverish and distracted kisses, passionless, and somehow more frightening for that.

Breathless, gasping, wide-eyed, silent, we undressed each other and fell upon the bed.

It was like a silent, terrible battle. There seemed nothing to say, only our bodies coming together and the musky smell of sex rising like a miasma from the rumpled bed. When she lay back, abandoned, after we had made love once, and then again, I saw the bruise of my fingers on her arm. She had not cried out, and I too felt the smart of the gashes left by her nails in my back. Her eyes were wide, her face without expression, as she stared at the ceiling. I watched her, propped on my elbow, her breasts flattening into quiescence as her breathing slowed.

I heard her say softly to herself, 'This shouldn't have happened.'

The shrilling of the telephone woke me. Rachel was already walking over towards the hall table, graceful, slender, unconscious of her beauty. I felt afraid, now the telephone had brought us back; for once, I could not dispatch what had happened to some unreal realm of denial. 'Yes,' she said, 'he's here. I'll get him.'

She walked back into the room. I felt a sick apprehension, and her calm made me feel worse. 'It's Caroline,' she said. 'She wants to speak to you.'

I wound the sheet around me, suddenly aware of my nakedness. Rachel picked up a silk dressing-gown and put it around her shoulders. What can one say in such circumstances? How Caroline had discovered where I was was beyond me. More to the immediate point, what I could say to her, freshly risen from the rank sweat of an adulterous bed. It occurred to me, in the short walk to the telephone, that we make a disproportionate fuss about extra-marital sex. That would occur to me, of course, a frail defence against the coldness of Caroline's voice, and the turmoil of my own awakening guilt.

'Hello.'

I had not misjudged the cold. The delivery carried more meaning than the words.

'We've been waiting for you. Everyone's arriving in an hour.'

'How did you know where to find me?' I asked.

There was a short pause, and I could hear the static crackle on the line. 'I rang Mandeville and he put me on to Walter. He suggested I call Rachel.'

I felt some explanation was needed. Not wholly convention, but some horror of the brutality of what was happening, some desperate desire to avoid discovery until I knew more of what was possible, of where I might go with Rachel. As I started to mumble about wanting to see Rachel to talk about Jonathan, Caroline cut across me.

'Tell me later, if you must. You'd better get home quickly.' The receiver went dead.

I went back into the bedroom. The sheets we had used were on the floor, and Rachel was remaking the bed with clean sheets. It seemed symbolic. I dressed quickly, trying to think of what to say, of how to arrange to meet again. As I was straightening my tie before the cheval mirror, she came across with a clothes brush, and brushed the shoulders of my suit. For a moment it felt as if we were an old married couple.

'I'll call tomorrow,' I said. 'I must see you again, soon.'

She looked up at me as we stood at the door.

'Was it Walter?' she said, surprising me. I nodded, and she smiled with some inward satisfaction. 'I thought so.'

I felt again the sensation of closed and inaccessible rooms, of the past in her of which I knew nothing.

She put her hand on my arm and kissed me gently on the lips. 'I hope the evening isn't too bad. Yes, call me when you have time.'

Nothing helped as I walked out into the evening. Not the knowledge of father and Frances, nor the daily casual extramarital coupling of my friends. It was hard to know for whom I felt worse: Jonathan, or Caroline, or myself.

The perversity of feelings perplexed me. I felt closer to Caroline than I had for years. With Rachel I felt an all-consuming love, and I was already dreading the thought of seeing her again. All objects seek stasis, equilibrium, which, being translated, means sanctuary, peace. Berdyaev saw the fate of man in the modern world as division, compartmentalisation, and dissonance. I could not see how to reconcile the warring factions within myself, and suspected that, like some disturbed child employing forces beyond its control, I projected the contrary forces acting upon my inner life upon those things and people surrounding me.

As I walked down the road in the twilight I passed an open window through which the powerful cadences of Beorling or de Stefanos singing 'Ness'un Dormi' flooded. For a moment, perversely, I felt happy, carried away by the control of the singing, far from the present.

I remembered Walter, at the last supper Jonathan had eaten with us, commenting on my success and suggesting that I had broken free from Jonathan. I had once talked to him about his theories on creativity; artists, he felt, must suffer to create, and must be alone. Ordinary life brought attrition and compromise, and, in his view, the artist must remain an anchorite to preserve the integrity of his vision. It had been hopeless to quote him Baudelaire, or Rimbaud, and he didn't recognise Swinburne or Dowson as true artists.

'That little pouf,' he said indignantly, referring to Swinburne. 'I am talking of real artists,' and he grandiosely mimed a painter with a brush in his hand. He had always felt that Caroline inhibited my talent, that a well-run house and regular meals dispossessed the artist of his true heritage of suffering, hunger, angst.

It occurred to me, briefly, as I waited by some red traffic lights, that he may have taken some pleasure in telling Caroline where to find me. Sometimes I felt he saw himself as a deep, revolving, witty Buckingham, with some power to play God in the lives of his friends and clients.

I remembered, too, sitting with Jonathan under an olive tree in the garden of his rented Aegean villa, thirty feet below the baked red clay of the upper terraces where Androniki was cutting the grass with a scythe. It was between Cambridge and getting married for both of us, and our mouths seemed full of laughter, and our veins with wine.

We had swum and sunbathed, taken a boat to explore the south-east of the island, climbed Pandokrator, and spent a day by the sullen, flat, inland lake of Korissia. Jonathan was in a rare mood of reflection and reminiscence; poised at this mid-way point in the holiday the daily routines had fallen away, and there were still enough nights and days in prospect for us both to remain free of the internal preparations for our returns. Jonathan surprised me by telling me he had taken on Atkinson.

'But you had that awful run-in with him at Cambridge, didn't you?' I said, and he looked across at me with a wry smile.

'I suppose that's why I took him on,' he said. 'I found the idea of employing someone I had beaten reassuring.'

Later, as the fishing boats bobbed out in convoy in the velvet darkness over the black sea, he said, 'For me it's all competition. That's what makes it work, beating the other person. I never stop to query the ends. Unlike your friend Walter, or Mark Oldroyd, I don't believe in the perfectibility of man, and I certainly don't believe that I can influence anyone else's destiny in any way whatsoever.'

'I don't think that is a fair summary of Mark or Walter.'

He laughed shortly. 'Fair and unfair are concepts I don't recognise in life. They're part of the armoury of childhood, the primitive belief in the Hebraic law of Tallion. De Sade assessed it more accurately. "Whatever is is right".' He reached forward and poured himself another glass of retsina.

'Walter, Mark Oldroyd, Deterding, they're all Gucci Socialists. Make me chaste, Lord, but not yet. Their politics are really only benevolent paternalism hiding under the guise of socialism. They live very well but when pressed, they too recognise that people are mercenary, atavistic, resistant to change if it in any measure decreases their own portion. But they won't keep looking at the skull beneath the skin.'

'What about people like Schweitzer?' I asked.

He paused for a moment. Overhead a plane traced slowly across the sky, the faint boom of its engine barely reaching us. 'It might sound as if I am reducing everything to a mercenary self-absorption. But I do feel that altruism contains a very high measure of self-satisfaction, that Richard Rolle of Hampole, and St Augustine, and all the self-denying ordinancers of our history derived a pleasure from what they did which can be compared directly to the pleasure I get from making a killing, or you get from the execution of a pleasing painting. The fact that we have imposed a series of hierarchical moral categories upon what we do doesn't alter the way in which such things operate within us.'

'You sound like Brian,' I said, and the conversation moved into other channels.

As I drove back it came back to me, seemingly regurgitated in a totally undigested form; but I felt the reality of some of the things Jonathan had said, the sympathy with Milton's 'Lucifer', his own man in exile from the rules he could not accept. And I felt a mild resentment at Walter's interference and, nascent and wavering, an unwillingness to feel guilty for what Rachel and I had just consummated with such wild and terrible passion.

There have been periods in my life which have possessed the quality of a nightmare, in which, try as I may, I can impose no order of my own. I know then that the conversations unwinding around me, and the dancers treading their absorbed minuets and stately measures, are alike, subject to some disordered law beyond human control.

Caroline and I took my parents over to Beth's a little early. Beth and her mother were supervising the last-minute arrangements, helped by a young girl and an older woman, both in black uniforms. The room had been cleaned and dusted, and there was a faint smell of lavender in the air. I was surprised to see Walter already there, as if to make up for his absence at the inquest. He had the lugubriousness of a professional mourner, his face fixed in lines of deferential gloom, through which no smile or even relaxation would dare to break. But the show seemed unconvincing beside the genuine melancholy I had seen in him before. Rona sat by him on the sofa, her carmine-tipped nails, like the talons of some great predator, lying in her black velvet-suited lap. Walter raised his glass and Rona gave a wintry, distant smile of acknowledgement.

My parents were talking to Margaret. With a slight feeling of disquiet I recognised all the symptoms of mother beginning an impassioned defence of Jonathan's upbringing. There was no need, after all these years, for me to recognise individual words; the tone, a mixture of disbelief and pathos, and the accompanying gestures, a hand on her heart as she leaned confidentially forward, were enough to indicate what was happening. While welcoming Jean and Alan who had just arrived I strained to overhear what I could, whilst still giving the impression that they had my full attention.

'He was always such a happy boy,' mother said, and father nodded in silent agreement. I remembered the locket Karam Deen had given me, wrapped in tissue in a drawer in my studio. I caught a glimpse of Beth's face, twisted by a smile which owed more to pain, to grim amusement, than to any humour.

Then father said in a loud, clear voice, 'I couldn't understand what the coroner's verdict meant,' and, in the silence that followed, I saw his bewildered gaze traversing the wall opposite.

Jean and Alan walked over to join them and Margaret said, 'I'd been with them the day before. He was planning a trip to India . . .'

I felt suddenly angry with Jonathan, with the apparent duplicity of the gesture which had cost him his life, and following hard on the anger, a twinge of unease about the note. During the day I had convinced myself of Beth's theory, put forward so pragmatically at the inquest. And his words at the last dinner party, 'I have reached a decision about what needs to be done,' had supported my idea of a melancholy decision already taken. But those words might have referred to something quite different. As I thought, I felt a slide into endless vistas of meaning, of *double entendres* and uncertainty. To stem my rising feeling of panic, I walked over to Walter.

He said guiltily, 'Sorry I couldn't make it the other day. I couldn't put off a meeting with some overseas buyers.'

'You didn't miss much,' I said. 'Just the official verdict. Nothing important.'

Too quickly he said, 'Are you painting at the moment?' and I sensed some avaricious panic in him at the thought of those percentages disappearing just as my career had peaked. I felt a desire to wound him, to worry him, a displaced urge to punish him for the sadness, the waste, the futility. Even given that awareness I surprised myself with my answer.

'I don't think I'll paint again, Walter. It doesn't seem a serious occupation any more.'

His eyes widened, and he moved forward in an involuntary gesture, dropping his glass on the carpet. As one of the maids went to get a cloth, he picked up the glass and put it on the table by his side.

'I understand how you feel at the moment, David. This thing has come as a shock to all of us —' and he gestured around the room to embrace the growing gathering, 'but to change your entire life just when you are on the threshold of real success . . .' He left the sentence unfinished.

I heard mother say '. . . so clever. He took a First at Cambridge,' followed by Beth's hard, brittle laugh.

All the familiar feelings of my nightmares were there. The room receded until it seemed far away, brilliantly clear-cut, and the voices around me sounded muffled and dissonant. As in the nightmare I was swept, by some compulsion beyond my own volition, into making compacts with fate, not even knowing what I was about to say until the moment had passed, like a stranger eavesdropping on my own conversation. I noticed that Walter held one of Rona's hands tightly, and she had fixed me with that dispassionate stare which gave nothing away.

'I might come back to painting in some way, eventually,' I said. 'But it won't be the same as it was before. It is hard to know what will seem serious or meaningful after this.'

I left him there, with Rona. Later I saw him in close discussion with Charles Deterding, and assumed from their frequent glances towards me, that I was the subject of discussion. To alleviate the pressing sensation of unreality, I walked around with canapés, filling glasses, exchanging a few words of welcome here and there. I felt within me an urge to confront my parents, to give father the locket given me by Karam Deen, the guilty symbol of old secrets, to shatter my mother's fragile illusions with the breath of truth. But despite that passionate intensity, some curb kept my feverish daemon in check, and the maids gave me uncertain smiles of thanks as I made myself helpful.

The room became stifling, the cigar smoke hung in falling strands upon the air. I saw Charles unstretch his long limbs from the sofa and walk over to the window to throw it up and, simultaneously, I heard Beth, her voice trembling on the edge of hysteria, shout, 'You don't understand, do you? He was impotent.'

She stood before Margaret and my parents, coiled ready as if to strike. Father looked bewildered. My mother looked quickly around the room, anxious that the outburst should remain contained, should not disturb the propriety of the occasion. I walked over and took Beth by the arm and she came by my side, unresisting, out of the room into the garden.

There had been a shower during the afternoon, and the air was cool and damp. A faint smell of manure and compost mixed with the smells of wet earth. We walked down the path towards the weeping willow, where the white garden bench looked over the landscaped stream, with its orfe and carp and waxen lilies floating on the surface. We had said nothing but when we sat down she turned her face into my shoulder and wept, the black mascara running in rivulets down her white face, a grotesque and ugly harlequin, and I patted her back soothingly, wishing that I were back in the drawing-room where the threadbare currency of conventional grief was accepted. After a few minutes I felt my shoulder stiffening, and took my arm away. The movement startled her from her reverie.

'Was I rude just now?' she asked.

I replied with more lightness than I felt. 'Shocks are good for the system.'

She smiled briefly. 'It was true,' she said, musingly. 'Nothing had happened for ages . . . simply ages.' Her voice was full of weariness.

I said, 'Do you think that's why he did it?' and was shocked to see her face change, the lines of sadness giving way to a lewd hardness which turned her into a stranger.

'You haven't heard the half of it yet,' she said, and her tone carried the unmistakable sound of spite and revenge gratified. 'I told him about James,' and she looked at me as if we were conspirators in some monstrous plot.

I felt, again, a sensation of unreality, a desire to avoid the obscure challenge she offered, to withdraw from the threat of whatever information she had to give me. But there was no other path open, and I asked, 'What about James?'

Behind us the lights suddenly came on in the house, and the evening began to settle darkly around us. I felt cold, as if someone had walked across my grave. Beth smiled up at me as if to say, 'There's no need to pretend with me any more,' and I felt the distant dawning of a horrified comprehension, an appalling certainty about what she was about to say.

When she spoke again her voice had a hard edge, like that of a teacher whose patience has finally given out.

'I know how vague and woolly you are when it suits you,' she said, 'but if you work out the dates of our little escapades you'll know what I mean.'

I couldn't accept what she was saying, though one part of my mind had already unwillingly confirmed the truth of it. 'Why?' I said, 'Why?' and I could just make out her features as the light drained.

'It was all I wanted. Jonathan couldn't give me a child though we had tried . . . and he must have felt that James was his. Until I told him that James is your child . . .' For the first time her voice broke and foundered into silence.

From a long way off I heard my voice, high and incredulous, 'You told him?' (God, I thought, This must be madness. It cannot be real. First she told him that we made love and then this . . .)

She got up and stood, facing into the light evening breeze. 'I hated him,' she said. 'He'd taken everything from me. I thought this might drive him away.' She made a helpless gesture, then folded her arms again, swaying her haunched shoulders against the evening chill. 'I didn't think he would go this far. You must believe me.' She must be lying, I thought desperately.

I felt a bleakness, a dispossession which left me exhausted, as if my psychic reserves had run out. It was the feeling of being a stranger in an alien land, self-exiled to a life whose rules derived from a different order of experience, in which I had no place. I had, I thought, avoided the messiness of emotions in my own life, neatly confining my tensions and distress to the canvases which bore away my pain like waste products.

Caroline's clear laugh, carrying for a moment through the open window, pierced my heart with despair. I wanted, like some fierce Dionysian satyr, to run screaming through the garden, but the message I had was wordless. I had turned a corner, expecting the sunlit vistas of hills and flowers to be as they had always been, and was confronted with rotting flowers, the dead earth, a proliferating wilderness of baneful weeds. I could not believe that James was my son. She must be lying.

It was still not over, now that I had begun to traverse this narrow, darkened defile, into the springs which lay at the heart of the tumour which was infecting us all.

'What about the letter?' I asked. 'He didn't write it, did he?' I saw her face close towards me, cloaking some secret inward comprehension with the bland features of a pretence.

'I don't know what you mean,' she said, and for a moment I was tempted to let the question lie there, unanswered, to ripen and rot and be forgotten in time. But, now that I had started I could see no other way forward. In the darkness I could only see one side of her face, the mouth a black-lipped cavern, the eyes sunken in shadow.

'You still don't understand,' she said. 'When I told him I was frightened by his reaction, he didn't shout at me, or accuse me. He was so quiet and controlled that I thought something terrible would happen. He said nothing for a bit, just walked around the lounge. I knew I'd gone too far, but there was nothing I could do to retrieve the situation. I felt, suddenly, as if I had released him from my control, like a mad dog, and I didn't know what he would do next. It seemed he must be working everything out — the dates — God knows what else.' She paused and fumbled for a cigarette and the lighter flared, briefly illuminating the pinched face.

A bat swept past above my head, wheeling in twittering

flight towards the dark trees. The lighted windows showed yellow in the darkness, and I could hear the hum of conversation, low, persistent and indistinguishable.

'Why did you tell them Jonathan was impotent?' I asked, hoping to divert the headlong rush for a moment.

She said, fiercely, 'They were all justifying themselves, all avoiding the way things really were. Your mother particularly. And I just couldn't stand it.' I nodded, grunting assent, and she resumed. 'I asked him what he was going to do, and he just looked at me for a very long while. Eventually he said, "I'm going to fix matters once and for all. It has all gone on long enough." He said it so quietly that it worried me. I thought he might plan to come over to you, to have things out. At first, when he had gone in the car, I thought I should call you. But, as I hesitated, things began to seem different, and I began to feel you deserved everything. After all, he was your brother. So I didn't do anything.'

'Aren't you doing just what they did in there?' I asked. 'Everything must be someone else's fault. You must be innocent.' I leaned forward and put my hand on her head, "*Ego te absolvo*".'

She shrugged off my hand with a violent gesture, and got up. 'Don't patronise me,' she screamed, and the conversation momentarily lulled in the lounge. She turned and walked towards the house with quick, short steps.

The garden put forward the odours of night. Warm compost, moist and rotting from the afternoon rain, and the scent of cut grass. Behind, the softer, more subtle scent of the roses. I felt dislocated, flat.

Caroline came down the garden path with a torch. 'Your mother wants to go,' she said without expression. I looked at my watch. We had stayed as long as decorum required. There was nothing more to be done here.

In the car on the way back mother said, 'Poor Beth. She certainly isn't herself at the moment. We'll all have to make allowances for her.'

Father said, 'At times like this all sorts of issues become exaggerated. We've all had our problems. They're part of any thinking marriage.' In the mirror I saw that they were holding hands. By my side Caroline looked stonily at the road ahead.

'Ask not for whom the bell tolls. It tolls for thee'. Literature has always been a comfort.

24

The days passed in grey and dreary succession. There may have been events in the external world but I was powerless to react to them with anything but stale indifference. Through some desperate clinging to habit, we still continued to arrange the social occasions which had, at one stage, seemed vital to my burgeoning career, but now had a hollow and exhausted feel. We met in changing permutations at Walter's house, or with Charles, or once at a dinner at our own house, and talked of the war between Iraq and Iran, the siting of Cruise missiles in the UK, and the possible progress of the SALT talks, the international banking crisis, and the necessity for community policing. We discussed inflation, world poverty, the development of new and incurable viruses, the ecumenical reforms of the World Council of Churches, and the latest developments in the fight against cancer. And again I recognised that we were as impotent to change the inherent trends in any of these differing subjects as we were to change the limited circumstances which affected our own small lives.

Outwardly life had resumed its normal pattern and it seemed only my own perception that the spring had been stretched until it could not resume its former shape. I had taken my parents back home two days after the funeral, and watched the preoccupations of their small community re-absorb them, as if nothing had happened. When we arrived the hall table was covered in mail, parish newsletters, invitations to coffee mornings, reminders of library duties, and the flower roster in the church. By the time I came to leave on Sunday morning they had been to Holy Communion, and I could sense their grateful resumption of the ordered lives they had left behind. I felt like an unwelcome irritant and, despite their frequent reminders that we must come down to stay soon, I knew that they were waiting for me to leave and to take with me the last remnants of Jonathan, like the cold leavings on a plate after an unsatisfying meal.

Among the mail there had been a letter from a nephew of Dr Mac, asking if he could come down to see them, and mentioning that he had met an old Sikh a few weeks before who had known us. 'Must be Bully,' said father, pouring himself a cup of coffee. 'I must find out if Charles knows where he is.'

With Caroline I felt that some door had closed. There was a certainty about her, and I could sense her watching me when she thought I was too absorbed to notice. She said nothing about Rachel, but this cool wariness had begun on the evening she telephoned and found me at the flat. The very fact that, uncharacteristically, she avoided talking of Rachel indicated, more clearly than any comment she might have made, that she harboured her own suspicions of what might have happened.

In the past, through some sympathetic symbiosis, I had permitted Caroline to treat me as if, in some sense, I were an extra limb, devoid of autonomous life. Over the years she had developed the use of the royal 'we' to add my weight to numerous opinions she held, to determine the course of what we did, and to distinguish between people we should cultivate and those we should quietly drop. The lack of opposition she had encountered had finally led her to dispense with even the show of seeking my approval, and in recent years I had even found her recounting stories of incidents that had happened to me, or correcting me or interrupting me when she felt that I was not doing sufficient justice to my narrative.

Since she had called me at Rachel's flat there had been a slow but appreciable change. As well as the wary watchfulness and the avoidance of Rachel's name, I noticed that she had begun to credit me with my own opinions again, and that she eagerly endorsed the joint ownership of our possessions whenever it was appropriate that she should do so. Strangely, it was difficult for me to adapt to this, calling as it did for a change of attitude on my part, a positive commitment to attempt to be interesting. It was hard to begin a story at the dinner table and to know that it would not be snatched from me by an exasperated Caroline, determined to extract every nuance of effort from it, waiting like a bright-eyed jackdaw to spring upon the glittering baubles I threw up for her. But as I began, resentfully at first, to venture forth on my own, and my stories and anecdotes gained in confidence, I found that these small separations suggested, hinted, whispered at the possibilities of deeper and more fundamental partings.

Since the evening of the wake I had wavered in my thoughts about Beth and the story she had told me. At times it seemed incontrovertibly true, and I felt a sense of profound depression, as if I had committed a sin so monstrous that it could never be expiated. However I turned and twisted at those times I could not escape the furies.

One evening, struck anew with the conviction that James must indeed be my son, I had gone into the studio. The locket, long since forgotten, lay amongst my oil tubes and I picked it up, remembering the words so long forgotten which I had first heard in the small church in India: 'and the sins of the fathers shall be visited upon the sons'. But even the solace of religion, the momentary wild belief that I could blame my actions on my heritage, failed to convince me now.

At other times, with no apparent logic I could discern, I would for a brief period be convinced that the story was a fantasy concocted by Beth for some unfathomable reason. I would find sudden access to an enormous reservoir of wild energy, play with Miranda, tease Ingrid, ignoring Caroline's puzzled looks, her hesitant comments about my good humour. During that entire period I was never free of these opposite poles of despair and elation, nor could I know when or why either would strike, so irrational and obscure were the processes governing the preoccupation of the moment.

One evening Beth and her mother had been among the dinner guests, and Beth had told a story about a trip she and Jonathan had made to Tenerife, walking through the pine and scrub to the lunar landscape of sullen Teide, smoking volcanically far above the sunlit plain. Unaccountably the story reminded me of happier times and I had insisted with furious gaiety on opening several bottles of champagne.

Later I heard Caroline say, sotto voce, to Margaret: 'I'm worried about him. He's either mad or gloomy and withdrawn.' I felt at the whim or caprice of chance, rudderless, directionless, Aeneas hunting without hope for his lost Dido.

Worst of all, the words I had spoken to Walter that evening carried in them a prophecy which I had dimly felt, even as I said them, but had then dismissed. I could not paint. At first I had argued to myself that this was a natural consequence of Jonathan's death, and what I saw as my own part in it. I was sure, I told myself fiercely, that I was digesting and remoulding the experiences of the last months, and in time could return to my studio. But the certainty had gone, the coherence which had, time and again, permitted me to surprise myself by laying without thinking, one paint stroke, then another, and another upon the bare canvas with the inner conviction that the final result would be satisfying to me and, in a different way, to Walter. The wasted time meant nothing beside the innate knowledge that the vision had gone beyond recall.

When Walter began to call me on some pretext every day I knew that I could no longer paint within the conventions I had built up over so many years, if indeed I could paint at all. Like a Rosicrucian I felt I privately contemplated a skull within some darkened room in my mind — my reminder of mortality. I felt no concern for Walter, whose list of clients sported many other young painters who would soon usurp my place. Once he rang as I sat in my dark studio, under the sullen light from the studio windows, looking at some paintings I had done some years before.

'You must believe me. I didn't mean to make trouble with Caroline that time,' he pleaded. I didn't answer but put down the phone and when it rang again some moments later I ignored it until silence descended once more.

Mark Oldroyd telephoned just after the funeral. I knew that he was terminally ill, but was shocked to hear the faint, ghostly voice. 'I've left you some of my paintings,' he said, and I could hear the laboured breathing and a muffled cough in the earpiece.

'I'll come to see you soon,' I said. 'There are a few things I have to sort out here first.' I couldn't tell him that I felt I didn't have the resources to see him at that moment. But he understood.

'You must be sick of death. Don't come. There's nothing more to say now, anyway.'

There was a long pause, and I thought he had gone. Then he said, 'Remember Gide. "*Si le grain ne meurt.*" Excuse me for being pompous and aphoristic, but times grows short and I feel I want to leave something real behind.' He laughed wheezily, and we talked for a few moments about trivia, to minimise the seriousness of the first few exchanges.

A week later I heard that he had haemorrhaged heavily in the night, and had died without gaining consciousness. Over the years I had met him perhaps twenty times, and knew little of the facts of his life; but I felt a sense of profound loss; some comforting and permanent feature of my life had been uprooted and destroyed.

There was still one thing left for me to do. It was both a compulsion and a means of temporarily halting the terrifying collapse I felt was taking place all around me. When I called Jonathan's office I was surprised to find the telephone answered by Miss Bowker.

Her voice sounded ghostly and far away. 'There was still some clearing up to do so I've been coming in.' I felt I had to thank her but she cut me short, as if I had presumed upon some private terrain. 'He treated me very well. It's the least I could do.'

There was one person I hadn't yet talked to. Jonathan's assistant. I remembered him slightly from Cambridge days. 'Where can I get hold of Paul Atkinson?' I asked.

There was such a long silence that I thought we had been cut off. When she spoke again her voice was markedly colder. 'I believe he is still living in Hampstead. Wait a minute, he's ex-directory . . .'

I could hear the sound of papers being shuffled for a moment, then her voice again. When she had given me the number there seemed little else to say. 'Are you hoping for a boy?' I asked, and her voice lifted immediately.

'Oh, we don't mind what it is. If it is a boy I'd like to call him Jonathan.' I wondered if Jonathan had ever really appreciated the extent of her devotion.

It took me several days to get hold of Atkinson. When I finally caught him, late one evening, he was suspicious and evasive. It was very difficult to meet, he said. He had to spend a lot of time out of the country. He was very busy. I could hear music faintly in the background, and the sound of laughter, as if I had called him away from a party. Finally I wore down his reluctance to meet, and we arranged to have a drink at the Roebuck in Pond Street the next evening at seven. I ignored Caroline's barely contained suspicions, and drove through the homegoing commuters crawling to suburbia.

The bar had been redone since I had last been there, a lifetime ago. It took me a few moments to recognise Atkinson, dressed in a grey pin-stripe suit, his camel overcoat thrown carelessly over a chair. He looked incongruously out of place, sitting in a dark corner in front of a round oak table covered in beer mats and round bleached stains.

There were very few people in the bar. An elderly man with a half-drunk pint in front of him sat reading *The Standard*. Two youths in motorbike leathers stood at the bar talking to the barmaid. The air was musty with smoke, and the thin, sharp smell of spilt beer. I bought myself a lager and made my way over to Atkinson.

At first he seemed aggressive, and I had the curious impression he was afraid of me. We talked generally, and after I had bought him two large whiskies he seemed to relax a little, leaning forward conspiratorially in his chair so that his voice couldn't be overheard.

'Look,' he said, 'I know it must be awful for you. But you must have realised there were dangers in doing what he did.' I had no idea what he meant, but some instinct persuaded me to pretend that I did, so I nodded. His eyes flicked around the room, as if he were measuring, calibrating the distance his voice would carry. He dropped his tone so that it was almost a whisper.

'It was all right while he just did what was asked . . . you know . . . arranging parties, making introductions, that sort of thing. After all, that was what he had been taken on for. But you know what he was like. He wanted more . . .' I hoped I seemed sufficiently comprehending, and looked down at my hands so that he would not detect any perplexity in my expression.

'Mandeville was asked to keep an eye on him. The other thing our people began to worry about was the possibility that he might want to sell information.' He laughed shortly. 'Not that anything he had could have brought in very much.' He paused, looking narrowly at me; the thought that I might know nothing of all this seemed to have struck him. Evidently what he saw reassured him, and he resumed.

'Anyway, Jonathan went to Cambridge to see Willey. He demanded to know why he wasn't being properly used. Hadn't he always been a good operator?'

Atkinson stopped and looked at the empty glass before him, and I came back into the present and took the glasses up to the bar. I felt a numbed certainty about what Atkinson was telling me. I remembered Jonathan saying, 'Old Willey's fixed me up with some contacts.'

I walked back carefully, absurdly concerned not to spill any drink on the stained carpet. Atkinson smiled up at me with a hint of expansiveness. 'Now, where was I?'

Before he could start I asked, 'Was Morris Cohen in with you, then?'

His mouth dropped in a derisory smile. 'Very low down,' he said. 'He was only a kennel man.' He picked a back tooth with his little finger nail. 'Kennel man . . . kept them until the quarantine period was over. Or when they were resting.'

'Do you know Walter?' I asked, and he looked at me vacantly for a moment.

'Ah, yes,' he said, 'the art dealer. What about him?' A burst of laughter from the bar greeted some remark by one of the youths, and Atkinson looked over at them.

'Was he one of yours?'

Atkinson made an indecisive move, turning his mouth down at the corners and lifting his eyebrows. 'I don't know. It could be. He knows Mandeville very well, and he's just the type they would go for. Able to travel legitimately both sides with no questions asked.'

There was a short silence while we sipped our drinks. 'And Rachel,' I said, 'what about Rachel?' I saw his face become bland, expressionless, his eyes stilling their restless movement to watch me.

'There was a rumour that she is Willey's daughter by his first marriage. I don't know how much she knew. Of course she and Mandeville . . .' He let the comment die away and looked at me questioningly, and I found myself wondering whether he knew anything about Rachel and me.

'Look!' he said (a word I was beginning to find faintly offensive coming from him, with its hint of authority), 'anything I said about Rachel would be pure speculation.'

A group of young men came through from the back bar, talking loudly about their plans for the evening ahead, and Atkinson watched them go past, his face suddenly sad, reflective. 'What about the letter?' I asked, and he looked at me without understanding. 'Jonathan's last note. It was typed on the machine in Charles Mandeville's office.'

I saw the colour drain from his face and thought, Now I have caught him. I pressed forward. 'Didn't you know?' and he shook his head mutely.

'Look,' he said, and he sounded frightened, 'Willey only put me in with him to maintain a watching brief. They did that with everyone. I did a few reports on him and that was that.' He was defensive now, and even his posture had changed, his forearms lying on his knees with both hands clamped together.

I said, 'Did anything in your reports suggest that he was becoming a security risk?' He looked away, as if a bright light had been shone in his eyes.

'I only did what was required of me,' he said, and his voice was almost pleading. 'That was the category I was conscripted into. I knew there would never be anything glamorous, but I was serving my country.' His tone carried a pathetic ring of pride, and I could feel no hatred for him. When he spoke again his voice was tired and flat. 'I had to report that Jonathan was in financial trouble and didn't seem very stable . . .' He fell silent again.

I said, 'Did Jonathan know about you and Mandeville?' and watched him closely.

He reflected for a moment, pushing a forefinger through a spill of beer which sat on the table, wobbling uncertainly like a bead of mercury. 'He shouldn't have done. His grade was the end of the cell line,' but I noticed that his voice was uncertain. He looked at his watch and said, 'I've got to go in a minute — I've got a dinner date.'

I knew it was a lie. I put a hand on his shoulder to restrain him and said, 'One for the road, then. I've only got a couple more questions.' He sank back in his chair submissively.

When I had brought the drinks back I felt sorry for him, and almost reluctant to continue. But there was no one else to ask. I said, 'You didn't like him, did you? Didn't he beat you up in Cambridge once?'

He put up his hand like a man warding off a blow. 'You must believe me. I didn't hold that against him. Yes, Willey put me in with him because he thought that might give an edge to my reports. They know everything, you know. But I didn't hate him.'

I looked at him hard, and he returned my gaze levelly. 'Look. You know that Jonathan could somehow rob his most outrageous gestures of any offence. He had the charm of the devil. That was one time Willey got it wrong. I did my duty, but I really wanted everything to work for Jonathan.'

The minutes had ticked past, but Atkinson no longer looked at his watch, nor did he bother to lower his voice from a normal conversational tone. It could have been a result of the drink, which had begun to bite into the edges of his well-modulated enunciation, to reveal a coarser, regional burr in his accent, but I felt it was because he had relaxed now that there was nothing left to hide.

I said, 'If they had decided that someone was becoming an embarrassment, how would they go about getting rid of them?'

'Oh,' he said, waving his hand open-palmed in the air between us, to emphasise some quality of these unknown men who met in secret offices and disposed of lives as others might organise business deals. 'Of course I don't know for sure, but it seems likely they do arrange such things from time to time. No Bulgarian umbrellas, nothing as crude as that. Sometimes they just ruin the operative, or use girls, family pressures . . .'

I remembered Morris Cohen leaving the inquest followed by the grotesque blonde. Atkinson said as an afterthought, almost to himself, 'The media are always co-operative when they use girls,' and I felt a moment's wry amusement at the thought. I still wanted to hear him confirm that there might be other ways in which to look at Jonathan's death.

I said, 'Surely it must be difficult to square a death with the police.'

He looked at me pityingly, as if with that one question I had revealed an unbridgeable gap between the world in which he moved and my own. 'There are people in this country who are sanctioned to do things which are beyond the law, whose right to do those things can never be questioned. They can manipulate the media, intimidate the police, evade justice. In defence of the national interest, whatever that might mean, they can kill people, destroy families, suppress information, ruin reputations. They believe they are upholding a sacred ideal in which the ends justify the means. But . . .' He caught my eye hard and looked at me as if he would force me to accept the truth of what he was saying, 'I have no evidence whatsoever to suggest they were involved in any way in this matter of Jonathan.'

I knew he was telling the truth, that our meeting was over and there was nothing further of substance he could tell me. I knew too, that I would not follow up the meeting by confronting Willey, or Mandeville. I did not think that they would lead me further towards any truth which would stand up to scrutiny; they would only open doors, and then more doors, which would lead me down featureless corridors in search of some absolute statement I knew I would never find.

Atkinson looked at me, suddenly anxious, and I touched his arm reassuringly. 'Don't worry,' I said, 'I won't mention this to anyone.'

He smiled with relief, looking suddenly far younger than his years and oddly vulnerable. 'I needn't have met you and told you all this,' he said. 'But I felt it was the honourable thing to do in the circumstances.'

On the pavement we shook hands gravely, and he hurried off towards Haverstock Hill. I walked down the hill towards the station and Parliament Hill Fields beyond where I had parked the car. Two nurses, shrouded in their blue capes, hurried past me in giggling conversation as they walked to the entrance of the Royal Free Hospital. They looked so young and fresh, a world away. When I got to the top of the hill I was breathing hard. I walked for a little while on the hill under the darkening sky. A young man walked past me with a kite under his arm, a crying child by his side.

He walked with a set face, embarrassed by the child. 'It's broken, Daddy. It won't go,' the child's voice rising in a howl of pure misery.

His father smiled an apology at me and said, 'I'll mend it, Julian. We'll come back and fly it tomorrow.' Their voices receded as they walked over the brow of the hill, the child's querulous and complaining, the father's deeper, reassuring.

There was a bench by a crooked hawthorn where I could look down into the valley. I felt a tiredness in my soul, as I sat watching the lights breaking out like pinpricks in the dark mass of houses far below. I knew that Jonathan had kept things from me, that his dark, secret nature could not abide openness. But I felt something dirty lying at the heart of his death, a secret worm destroying from within.

As I sat there I knew something had come to an end in me, but I didn't know what it was. Only that I could not control the outcome with my will alone any longer.

25

In Kafka's *Metamorphosis*, the central character slowly becomes alienated from his surroundings, and the subjective logic of events becomes strange and distorted. Like a spinning sphere I whirled, day after day, into some dark tunnel, throwing off with centripetal energy all the things and people which had seemed closest to me. Caroline and Miranda, Mrs Haddon and Thompson. It was as though I saw them, but no longer understood what they were doing. I would find myself questioning the simplest things, now that they were clad in some subtly different shape. I saw things afresh, without willing it, and each day seemed severed from the day before.

Each morning as I woke from my neurasthenic sleep I was divorced from any experience, and would once more examine the most mundane activity, the ordinary commerce of life, with the eyes and comprehension of a child. My understanding had dulled to a point where I feared I was going insane, and only felt safe following the most arcane rituals, investing them with the magic ability to deliver me some prized goal, or to destroy me utterly.

I neglected my appearance not, as Caroline thought, from some incipient laziness which had found an excuse to manifest itself, but because the effort of taking the decisions required to put on a new shirt, or to choose a matching tie, were beyond me. There was a range of activities which I could still carry out, giving, in their sophistication, the illusion that normality had returned.

I drove, I socialised, I even gave a lecture at Walter's request; and I kept secret from everyone my fear of walking between the cracks of the paving slabs, my need to wash my hands thirty or forty times a day, my overwhelming belief that I was followed by people who would push me under a tube train, or nudge me under a bus. I began to read the daily paper from end to end, convinced that I could only keep sane by marshalling an armoury of facts, which would ballast my mind against the encroachment of madness and the Eumenides.

I felt more comfortable alone and, after concocting a story over some days before I came out with it, told Caroline that I needed to be by myself in the studio for some time to feel myself back into painting. I made up a studio couch and Mrs Haddon brought up my meals on a tray, as she used to do when I was working to a deadline. Caroline seemed relieved, partly I suspect at being freed from the object of her wariness, and partly because Walter had passed on his concern. Though I felt that she had a sneaking contempt for my work, she knew that it had afforded us an opulent lifestyle which could not be financed without a considerable income.

I slept much of the day, released by exhaustion from guilt at the empty canvases, stretched upon their wooden frames, gazing across at me with white unseeing eyes. Once or twice I gathered myself together to try to paint, but each time the ritual of preparation, of cleaning the brushes, and setting out the turpentine and the white spirit in their small containers, the paints in their serried rows of tubes, took over and robbed me of any desire to go further.

In the third week of my incarceration I began to paint, hesitantly at first, seeing the dark lines take on new and puzzling shapes. It was as if I were uncovering something which was immanent in the bare canvas, for which I held no responsibility; that I was engaged as a labourer to dig up some buried artifact, under the stern controlling gaze of an overseer who had some secret knowledge of what I would find.

As I sat eating my lunch I worked in my imagination, eager to return to the work of discovery, the canvas turned away to allow myself to rest, to give me fresh insight. When I turned back to it after lunch I felt I had been hit by a monstrous blow. The shape on the canvas would have been unrecognisable to anyone else, grotesque and tortured as it was, but I knew now what I had been working at with such unknowing fingers.

A naked body, garrotted by a rope, its monstrous tongue hard with agony, slumped in the corner of a room, covered in a grey, herring-bone overcoat (such as the one which hung in my wardrobe). Attached to it with obscene probosci were shapeless homunculi, bloated and shimmering with blood. I took a knife and slashed across the canvas, until the centre was a torn, frayed hole.

All the afternoon I slept fitfully. I felt alternately cold, then hot. Faintly through the house I heard the noises of the living going about their daily business — Miranda's footsteps scuttering over the patio; the dogs barking in joyous pursuit of squirrels or the neighbourhood cat; the burr-burr of the mower (Thompson's pride and joy upon which I was sure he sat and played games such as Jonathan and I had played so long ago); the low grinding of the washing machine. And voices, always voices, dim, faint, far away, but strident, amused, plaintive.

At 6.30 the telephone rang, and I groped from sleep to pick it up.

Rachel's voice said, 'Hello, David. I haven't heard from you for so long.' (And from the Book of the Dead, I remembered all at once the pharaoh's declaration, 'I shall live, I shall live, I shall flourish, I shall flourish, I shall wake up in peace, I shall not putrefy, my intestines shall not perish. I shall not suffer injury'.)

But I could only say, 'It's nice to hear from you.'

It seemed the sun had returned after a long winter. She told me she had been away, visiting friends in Paris, and we talked of the Louvre and the Jeu de Paumes.

'I had forgotten how pleasant it is to wander around the bouquinistes and then eat at one of those little cafés in the Rue de la Huchette,' she said, and I told her how we had smuggled back *Tropic of Cancer*, bought from Maurice Girodias' bookshop, in the springs of an ancient Austin when Brian and I had gone to Paris during a university vacation.

'Of course,' she said, wonderingly, as if we were talking of ancient history, 'that was before the Chatterley trial, wasn't it? It seems like another world.' She asked after Beth and James (and I thought, then, that there was something I would have to tell her one day, when the time was right), and, as a hesitant gesture to conformity (or so I felt), after Miranda and Caroline. 'His death took some of the certainty away,' she said, and, despite the vagueness of the comment I knew immediately what she meant.

As we talked I was seized with a desire to see her. She seemed real, bright, alive, amongst the shades and shadows which had been my companions for the last months.

Before I had said anything, she asked, 'When will I see you again?' and I felt the stirring of a long-forgotten hope, a glimpse of some inviolable belief in myself. (Jonathan had once said to me, 'She is a catalyst but no one will ever possess her. And that is what constitutes the challenge, the fascination.')

There seemed to be some difference now, after all these years, as if our feverish love-making had awakened something within her that she could no longer deny. She wanted to see me; it was the first time I had ever caught a hint, a tone of her need. Though I had often thought of the last meeting at her flat it had held no reality in my mind, possessing only the substance of a dream or a fantasy. The memory had become passive, dormant, subdued to my will, powerless (or so it seemed) to work itself into my future. It had only taken her simple question to bring everything back.

I heard Mrs Haddon put the tray down outside the door and knock. 'Mr David. It's your dinner,' and I called out to thank her. I was reminded briefly of Beth and I, sprawled in the corner while the house breathed around us, like an ants' nest. It was the same covert, illicit feeling as I spoke to Rachel, but this time I did not feel, as I did then, that what I was doing would change nothing.

I said to Rachel, the plan forming in my mind as I spoke, 'I'm going to Jonathan's grave tomorrow. If you are in around lunch-time, perhaps we could have a meal together,' and felt a spasm of delight when she agreed.

Caroline suggested she should come with me, but offered no resistance when I said I wished to go alone. Clouds scudded across the sky, driven by the tormenting wind, but the sun shone fitfully. I had joined the family briefly for breakfast, noting with wry amusement how rapidly my absence had become the norm, and how my presence introduced a note of awkwardness into the meal. Nothing was said, but I felt like an intruder. The dogs and Miranda greeted me with enthusiasm unmixed with disapproval, and Thompson, catching me as I drank my coffee in the garden, took me off to look at the magnolia.

'Look at that,' he said indignantly, gesturing with his fork to a branch which had been sheared from the trunk. 'Must be those dogs. Can't have dogs and a garden.'

This last comment, said hopefully, was part of an unceasing war against animals which seemed to me merely an extension of his dislike of growing things. I agreed we would never have an ideal garden, and even maliciously reminded him of the brown patches on the lawn where the ammoniac urine of the bitch burnt great patches. But I said with grave regret that we were very fond of the animals, and were prepared to accept the compromises which keeping them entailed. Weakly I offered him the bribe of a new garden spray, and he went off, seemingly satisfied with this, to start one of his foul, yellow-smoking bonfires.

'You don't think it's a bit morbid to go so soon?' asked Caroline, and I answered sententiously, 'I can't dismiss him so readily from my mind.'

It was easier in the car, away from the need to respond to such questions. I didn't know myself why I was going, save that I felt it might lay Jonathan's ghost for me, permit me to put his memory aside from time to time. It occurred to me, not for the first time, that concern and compassion are often only oblique aspects of self-interest.

I felt fiercely angry with Jonathan, as if he were still alive: as I caned the car engine, recklessly overtaking a line of traffic edging forward past the Scilly Isles, I railed against him in my mind; above all, at the mystery and confusion surrounding his death, realising that, even in this, he had maintained his power to hurt and destroy. A car ahead of me began to nose out of the line to my left, and I slammed my hand savagely on the horn, grimacing at the white, startled face as I drove past.

When I got to the cemetery I was perspiring furiously, despite the air-conditioning in the car. I parked in the car-park, and bought an extortionately priced bunch of flowers from the old woman by the iron gates.

'Is it for a relative, dearie?' she asked, selecting a tired group of dahlias and lilies, the petals already turning brown at the edges. Ahead a funeral party, led by a vicar, moved in stately progress to a corner of the cemetery.

I realised that I needed to relieve myself. Holding the flowers tightly, I stumbled towards the olive cypresses banked by the side of the entrance, trying to look as if I had some horticultural interest in their growth. It was no good. From three sides I was visible to the traffic streaming up the road, and to the ancient lady, even now watching me with puzzled curiosity. From the other, screened from the road, I was thwarted by small groups wandering with bouquets, or standing with expressions of fond remembrance over their loved ones.

By this time, aggravated by the expectation of finding a suitable place, I was fairly hopping with pain. As I gazed wildly around, clutching my flowers like a relay runner's baton, a small man wheeling a council dustcart came slowly up the road, his jaws champing methodically on some gum, and with a spiked stick in his right hand. Hobbling towards him in extremis I asked if there was a lavatory nearby. He scratched his head and pivoted slowly on his heels, looking towards the far horizon in each direction. Removing the plug of chewing gum from his mouth for a moment he laid a grimy hand on my sleeve and pointed to a building attached to a small chapel, some hundred yards away.

'Reckon the only place is the crematorium,' he said. 'The boys won't mind.' I thanked him and began to walk, my pain easing slightly with the movement.

'See you're in trouble,' said one of the men lounging about in the dark interior. 'It's over there,' and he pointed towards a door by the end of the building.

A young man swept the floor desultorily, watching me with a half-grin on his face, and a third sat by one wall on a stained wooden bench, reading one of the tabloids with an expression of bored tiredness on his face. By his feet a grimy mug steamed. Part of the vast chamber was partitioned off with steel, and through a small door in the centre a conveyor belt moved slowly. The lavatory smelt of urine and damp, the metal-framed windows above the stalls rimed with algae, but the relief was exquisite. I washed my hands and picked up the drooping bouquet.

Outside the boy was resting on his broom, his chin on his hands, swaying from side to side. The older man who had spoken to me as I came in, and the other man, stood by his side. I had emerged in the middle of a conversation. They eyed me, and I felt like a cowboy, faced with the possibility of violence. The young man with the broom gestured towards a door in the steel sheeting, hasped and bolted like a door of a medieval castle, through whose ill-fitting side I could see the orange glow of the furnace.

'Do you want to have a look?' he gestured, and the sly challenge in his voice was unmistakable.

It struck some chord within me and I heard myself saying carelessly, 'Why not?'

The others grinned, like spectators at a bullring urging their dogs in towards the beleaguered beast, and the youth hooked the end of the broom under the door and pulled it open.

I walked to the door and looked in. At first I could only see the shimmering fires and the rollers, emerging blackly from the flames. Then I saw a shape slowly emerge into view through the vaporous heat, dimly recognisable as human. It seemed to dance to the orchestrated hiss of the flames, the limbs moving in antic glee, like a sleeper shrugging off a heavy night. The movements were slow and dreamlike, and the blackened flesh caricatured the figure. It was a child's marionette show, Pinocchio coaxed into stiff, uncontrolled life.

I turned to my would-be tormentors, grouped around me in sniggering anticipation of my reaction. The oldest was about my age and, given a few pounds, close to my bulk.

He leaned forward, his face distorted, and said, 'Like it then, Mister?' and brought back to me instantly the sour taste of my first day at school, and Jenkins towering over me and initiating me: the debased words and phrases of schoolboy humour.

I caught him by the collar and slammed him against the partition. As he brought his hands up to ward off my grip, catching my coat at the shoulder, I clenched my hands together and brought them down hard, breaking his grip. He cried out in pain and attempted, feebly, to hit me. With the heel of my right hand I hit him under the nose and felt something break, and a dribble of blood and mucus ran over his lips and down his chin. The others had backed away, and watched, open-mouthed, still as statues. I caught him by the throat and heard his head hit the metal partition with a dull thud.

As he fell I hit him twice more, one wild blow hitting him mid-chest, and the second in the face. When he was on the floor I kicked him twice, my anger abating into a feeling of ashamed foolishness. It had all been nothing to do with him, after all, and I recognised the unjust over-reaction of the attack.

For a moment we stood there in a grotesque tableau. Through the open door I could see the body still moving remorselessly forward, now dissolving and diminishing under the fierce heat. I felt in my wallet and took out three twenty pound notes. The figure on the ground was stirring slightly, moaning a bubbling song of pain. I held the notes out to the boy, but he didn't move. I took his arm and put the notes in his hand.

'I'm sorry about that. My brother died last week, and I didn't find it very funny.'

The boy put the money in his overall pocket and walked forward to help the man on the floor. None of them looked at me as I walked to the door.

It seemed a very long time had elapsed since I went in to the crematorium. But for the chance of not being able to find a sheltered place to pee I would have missed the wild happiness which had begun to rise through me, the fierce sense of life stretching ahead, and the warmth of the sun on my skin. That was all it was, a dance in the firelight. The grotesque yet pathetic image seemed to have dispelled the hoarded decades of death which lay like remains littered amongst the layers of my experience. There was no Hell, no Judgement, only a final dancing in the flames before become proud and angry dust.

I ran towards Jonathan's grave. In the distance an elderly Indian shuffled off on the arm of a younger woman. As I ran I laughed, a middle-aged man freed at last from a great tyranny of childhood. An old lady in a plum-red coat looked at me disapprovingly, moving to the side of the path to let me past. I leaped with glee, holding the flowers aloft like an Olympic torch. 'Rachel! Rachel!' I shouted and the swallows skimmed and darted across my path in joyous pursuit of insects. My ribs hurt where the attendant's fists had caught them.

Rachel was standing by the grave, the browning wreaths around her feet. She started to say, 'I came . . .' and I caught her in my arms and danced her round and round. Her bag dropped to the ground, but I whirled her on, laughing again at the half-smiling amazement on her face.

'No,' I said. 'No,' with the tears streaming down my face, 'I'm not mad.'

She said uncertainly, breathlessly, 'I know.'

I knew that there might be a way with her. As we walked away from the grave, Rachel said, 'The trouble with Jonathan was that he destroyed people and relationships, rather than preserving them.'

Something twitched in my memory, and was gone. They were the words of Jonathan's last letter. Only to be remembered later, when it could no longer be spoken of. There had been a fresh wreath on the grave. The label read 'From an Old Friend', and the flowers had come from a florist in Southall.

That afternoon we began again, Rachel and I, and I dismissed the shadows from my mind. In time, as I can now reflect, it has become another enslavement, but it was eagerly entered into. I grew wilfully careless in our meetings, and I knew that we would be discovered, and that the time of reckoning would come when the future could no longer be avoided.

The hardest part was the thought of losing Miranda, but even in her I could see, day by day, a movement towards Caroline and away from me, an indoctrination which took her towards dolls and parties and preoccupations which I barely understood, and even disapproved of. She would look at me over those weeks and months with her head on one side and say, 'You don't know anything about it, Daddy,' and her tone prophesied a contempt and assumption of superiority which I felt uncomfortably that time would only harden and mature.

Caroline and I saw Beth and James, Margaret, Walter and Rona, and even went to dinner with Mandeville and Halsbury and their wives. But some fire had swept through me, gutting the rooms of the past, destroying the associations constructed so haphazardly over the years. Like Gauguin I had reached the rim and peered over to the level plain beyond, and my Tahiti beckoned. When a concerned friend (whose identity I never discovered though I suspected Walter had put Rona up to it) confided to Caroline that she had seen Rachel and me together in circumstances which could only suggest an affair, Caroline saw that other people must know, and it was this more than any private hurt which finally brought about the long-awaited confrontation.

In the long drawing-room we dissected our past into parcels, one autumn evening as the rooks cawed and wheeled in their last flights before the night. Mark Oldroyd's generosity, the shares, and the capital I had earned and Caroline had invested so carefully, made it a comfortable settlement, and we managed without solicitors who would have complicated the last rites with their jargon and alien concepts. It was loaded in her favour; a gesture towards her hurt and my guilt.

Once, during the evening of reckoning I looked across, and some trick of the light on Caroline's bent head reminded me of that first meeting at Brian's party. I felt pierced to the heart with sadness, that the attrition of the years had brought us to this from such hopeful beginnings.

But the moment she began to talk again, her clipped tones reminded me of the distance we had come, and how long it was since our paths had diverged, and I knew that the uncertain future outside was preferable and, stronger than that, that I had no alternative. Yet I still stayed in the house, too exhausted by all that had happened to move. 'Perhaps in a month or so,' I said to Rachel.

My parents, Jean and Alan, and my friends all professed shock, and rallied round Caroline. One evening, walking hand-in-hand with Rachel by the Serpentine, I took the locket Karam Deen had given me from my pocket and threw it into the middle of the water. The setting sun had turned the water red, so that for a moment, it seemed to be burning.

'What was that?' she asked, startled, watching the curving flight into the water.

'Nothing of any importance,' I said, and we walked on together by the quiet water.

Nothing ends immediately, or is born all in a moment; at least that is how it had always been in my experience. I seemed to lack some vital faculty which would enable me to react immediately to events. It was a time of half-life, when the usages and habits of many years still persisted, depite the decisions already taken. Though it was inappropriate to feel moral guilt for this wavering I was acutely aware that I had to take some action for the sake of everyone concerned: for Caroline and Miranda, for Beth and James and, above all, for Rachel.

It was when I felt entirely abandoned that I found the resources to be decisive. All those closest to me had signalled the end of our old existence in unmistakable, if oblique, ways. But it was only when Rachel had left and then Brian, and Caroline had defiantly prevented a return to a life upon the old terms, that I, too, was reluctantly forced into making a decision. So I followed them.

26

I had felt uneasy when Brian met me at the airport in Heliopolis. He stood in the thronged hall, instantly recognisable, nearly a foot taller than most of the Egyptian travellers who ran backwards and forwards across the tiled floor, greeting each other with incomprehensible cries. He had put on a lot of weight and his cheeks bulged, echoing the vast vault of his stomach which overhung the waistband of his soiled white trousers.

When he came over to hug me in his great bearlike clasp I noticed a slight, hesitant figure behind him. The figure had the self-effacing, washing gestures of some merchant from the Rialto, and an uncertain smile which glinted with gold fillings.

Brian introduced him as Faroukh saying, rather grandiosely, that they shared a suite of rooms at the pensione. This turned out to be a dingy sitting-room with two small bedrooms off it. But that was later.

What had crystallised my unease was that Brian was unsteady on his feet, and appeared to have been drinking heavily. There was a mass of fine broken veins by his nose and on his cheekbones now. This, and the new exuberance of his gestures, the hyperbole of his conversation and the dramatic use of his hands as he indicated the passing sights while Faroukh drove us silently through the sleeping suburbs, all seemed somehow at odds with the Brian I knew. It was a slightly manic intensity, an antic gaiety which seemed to me to hint of some tremendous pressure within.

When we sat in their rooms on the first evening, after eating *Fool Mudhammas* and *Kanafa* washed down with a resinous Greek wine at a nearby restaurant, he brought out a collection of photographs to show me.

'We must take David for a cruise,' he commented to Faroukh, who was silently tidying the déshabillé of the room. 'Look at that,' he said, standing over my chair as I looked at these unfamiliar images; despite the awe in his voice I could only see umber rocks and sand under a pitiless sun, with a few pillars standing forlornly against the sky. 'We must arrange it!'

As he talked I looked around the room. The drive from the airport and the small, dirty restaurant had prepared me to a degree for the room we sat in, but it was hard to reconcile my once fastidious friend with these surroundings. The colonial rattan furniture had begun to fray, and the subtle paintwork had long since chipped and faded. The walls were covered with posters of Akhenaton, Rameses, scenes of rural life. Villagers pumped water from the Nile with a crude sling and bucket at the end of a long pole, weighted at the other end by a large stone. A tree covered (so the legend ran) in Sacred Ibis stood beneath the Aga Khan's Mausoleum. The posters were sun-faded and ragged-edged, and where the yellowing paper curled up from the wall they left paler marks on the smoke stained wallpaper.

In a pause in Brian's monologue Faroukh said, in his soft,

apologetic voice, 'So, how do you like our country?' I replied, 'It's too new for me to have any impression yet.'

He smiled gently and poured me another glass of the light red wine, and I noticed that his hands were long and slender with well-scrubbed nails. I caught Brian looking at me as I took the glass, and was surprised. It was a calculating glance, belying the garrulousness of his manner all evening.

I was unsure about Faroukh's position. I had gleaned over the evening that he was an Anglophile of that sad, ingratiating breed whose constant apology for not being British suggested that he was ashamed of his own country. Quite apart from his sharing the rooms with Brian, there was some covert understanding, some subterranean business, between them. I could not place the nature of the traffic. At times they talked together as equals, but at other times Brian showed an unconscious colonial dismissiveness.

At 10.30 I felt tired, and Brian said he would take me to my room. It was down the shadowy corridor outside, lit by one low-powered bulb.

'It must feel strange to you,' he said, and I nodded, looking out of the fifth-floor window onto the zoological gardens below, garishly lit by concealed spotlights. While Brian told me the routine of the pensione, and how to reimburse Narouz, the aged daily, and a variety of other details I would need to know, I wandered around the room. There was a battered fridge containing three cans of Stella Artois. A vast wardrobe, its veneer buckled and crackled, exuded a powerful smell of mothballs. The iron bed was pure English public school circa 1950. The second window gave out on to a small balcony, inadequately protected by a flimsy wrought-iron railing.

Brian stepped past me and pointed across the outlines of the city to where it was still possible to see the faint outlines of the Pyramids. 'I couldn't get you the next room,' he said, 'but at least you've got a view.'

He left me to unpack, pausing in the door for a few moments after we had said our goodnights. 'I'll arrange the trip. Leave it to me. You'll want to see Rachel first, I suppose.' He paused a moment. 'I'll give you a knock about nine tomorrow and we'll get some breakfast.'

When I had finished unpacking, and had hung my clothes in the wardrobe, I undressed. On the bedside table was a Guide to Egypt, well thumbed and dog-eared. I turned first to the section on telephoning, and then looked at the street map of Cairo. In the dim light it took me fifteen minutes to locate the pensione and the street where Rachel's uncle had his office. It was strange to think that we three were, once more, contained within the area of one city. There was some comfort in the thought as I fell asleep, fighting against the unfamiliar sounds of the great city.

Rachel reluctantly agreed to see me after I had been in Cairo for a week, and we met at a café on the windswept plaza under the towering spires of the Mohammed Ali Mosque, with the lights from the City of the Dead spread out below us beginning to twinkle in the gathering dusk. Occasionally a group of tourists trotted by on foot, or creaked past in an ancient fiacre, and the white dust swirled around our feet, carrying the detritus of paper and discarded cigarette packets around the concrete apron where we sat, while the corrugated-iron shade creaked and groaned above us.

At first she was cool and distant, glancing at me covertly from time to time as we spoke as if to reassure herself that I would not attempt to invade the space which had opened up between us. We talked of her work with her uncle, of the sightseeing I had done, avoiding the subjects which were uppermost in our minds, and it appeared to me that she had taken on some of the alien remoteness of the city and deliberately withdrawn from the past we had shared together.

There was no way in which I could broach the questions which lay embedded in my mind and beneath the surface of the desultory, hypocritical conversation, but I could sense the gathering tension and knew that, sooner or later, one of us must refer to the events which had driven each of us, separately, so far from home and from each other. Finally she smiled at me, as if to signal the beginning of some complicity, and raised her eyes slightly in a gesture which I knew indicated some exasperation with me.

'So, I gather you went to see Atkinson. Why?'

'How did you find out?' I countered defensively, unwilling to concede that there was any case to answer.

A savage gust of wind lodged some flapping cardboard against the leg of the table and I moved it with my foot, watching it scurry erratically down the road. The smell of mimosa briefly in the air was snatched away again by the whipping wind.

'Charles Mandeville told me.' She observed me in silence looking for a reaction. 'I got a letter from him last week.'

We sat for a moment and I sipped the bitter dregs of my coffee. I should have realised that Charles would find out about our meeting, that the perplexing and unknowable communication would continue between him and Rachel. When she spoke again I was surprised at the distress in her voice. She looked at me directly, the great dark eyes steady, her chin propped in one palm.

'You had to follow everything up, didn't you? To look in every corner, no matter what you might find.'

I said stiffly, 'I found it impossible to live with the uncertainty. It didn't actually solve anything, seeing Atkinson. But it did tell me some things I didn't know about Jonathan.' (I remembered her saying that summer so long ago, 'Facts. You always want facts.')

She sat without speaking, and I felt, again, the need to explain. 'Rachel. He was my brother. I didn't feel I could accept the official verdict. Don't you understand?'

After a pause she said bitterly, 'Does it really matter now? It's people like you who cause all the trouble, who won't let things remain decently buried, who won't accept the way things are.'

I felt the edge of her anger at my intrusion, my need to know, and faintly beyond that, some unspoken warning about the things I must not ask her. Looking at her face, set in these unaccustomed tensions, I knew that she wanted me to give in, to agree, but it was not within my power.

I said sadly, 'That's not the point,' and she made a small clicking sound of annoyance with her tongue, and picked up her bag. The taxi driver stopped picking his teeth with a matchstick and got out of the cab to hold open the back door.

I followed her to the taxi trying to keep the anxiety from my voice. 'When will I see you again?' Behind me the café owner came out and started to clear the cups and sticky sweetmeat plates from the table. I gestured to him that I was coming back, and he smiled and nodded, mopping the cracked white plastic of the table-top furiously.

She said, 'I'm surprised you still want to,' half to herself, then 'Call me in a few days,' and settled back into the darkness of the interior. The cab swept in a wide arc and turned towards the Heliopolis road, and I returned to my table.

I had another coffee and the proprietor, having served me, sat down a couple of tables away, his eyes following each car that rattled past. In the darkness under the walls opposite a scavenging cat moved like a dark shadow through the rubbish left by the stall-holders, delicately moving a decaying cabbage to reach into the space beneath.

When Faroukh and Brian came to pick me up an hour later, the night was yellow black, and the Mosque stood clear against the stars.

'Where to?' asked Faroukh, engaging the column-mounted gear-shift with difficulty and Brian said eagerly, 'What about a nightcap at the Sheraton?' looking at me pleadingly for approval.

It was impossible for me to do anything but nod, though part of me wished I was already back in my small room. It was Brian, now, who seemed to be trying to recapture the flavour of Cambridge. I had no stomach for even such a harmless deceit that evening, but I knew it was better to be in company than on my own.

As we drove past Roda Island Brian asked, 'Well, was it as you expected?'

Over the Tahrir Bridge the wheels sounded different, drumming hollowly over the macadam. On the black water I made out the shape of a long vessel moving swiftly downstream.

'She seemed angry with me,' I said. 'I don't understand it. Why should she be angry because I was trying to find out something about Jonathan's death?'

Brian half-turned in his seat so that I could see his face in the street lights flicking past. He said slowly, 'There's so much you don't know. Has it occurred to you that she might be afraid of what you may find out?'

The thought hadn't suggested itself, and I sat silently, trying to digest it. When Brian spoke again his voice had an edge of anger and exasperation.

'God knows how you have managed to retain your innocence all these years.' Faroukh glanced sideways at him, and Brian laughed reassuringly. He put his hand on my arm and said, 'Forgive me. I shouldn't have said that.'

From the Sheraton Terrace we looked out over the New City. Brian pointed out the Great Pyramid, slopping the wine from his glass carelessly down the sleeve of his pointing arm. 'Evidence has come to light which suggests that the Pyramids were primarily observatories, but there are conflicting theories, each with impressive validation. That Imhotep, Zoser's Grand Vizier and the High Priest of Heliopolis, the man who mastered the physics to produce the Step Pyramid, was providing a symbol of the Egyptian Creation myth. Yet another theory was that the conception of these vast tombs to preserve the sacred *ka* was undertaken so that the unification of the country begun by Menes would continue through the conscription of people from all over Egypt to provide their skills in building. Hollywood never got it right, anyway. The workers willingly gave their lives to preserve the soul of the Pharaoh.' He seemed embarrassed at his own pomposity for a moment as the tourist couple at the next table got up and went through the sliding glass doors, shooting us a curious glance.

We sat in silence for a while. I knew that Brian was trying to tell me something in the elliptical manner he employed when he was too embarrassed to be straightforward, and I knew that I could not question him directly.

In the car on the way back to the pensione I slept fitfully. I was convinced by now that Faroukh understood the complexities of the traffic lights, and could cope with the fatalistic bad manners of other drivers. Once I was jolted awake as we hit a pothole, and I heard Brian say in a low voice to Faroukh, 'We must see if we can take his mind off her. We'll take him out to some of those clubs . . .'

*

I woke again at three o'clock and sat, wrapped in blankets, on the balcony, watching the sleeping city come to life. First some small carts creaking down the road, and the occasional lorry. Then, ever growing, the trickle of vehicles became a steady stream and then a torrent. Released for the moment from any compulsory activity, I brooded over the past years.

Though it was fashionable in the Cambridge of the Sixties to profess atheism or agnosticism I had, nevertheless, kept my childhood faith in a furtive and ashamed way. Apart from the half-facetious discussions with Brian, which were my despairing attempt to reconcile the new freedom Cambridge offered me with some abstract and humanist ideal of good behaviour, I did see Father Gomez from time to time, though I despaired of reaching any accommodation with his unbending Jesuitical statements. ('The old heresy that Matter is Evil contained within it a grain of ecclesiastical insight, wrapped within layers of ignorance. The argument exemplified medieval theological literalism — that if Matter is Evil we should, ergo, become more evil as our physical matter increased. But it is true that as we grow, so the temptations offered to us are more freely available. For the temptations are the testing of our free will, so that we may perfect ourselves further.') And on and on in this vein, ignoring the daffodils by the path as we walked up Kings Backs under the dying light of a cloud-barred sky.

When the prospects of eternal life faded before the accumulation of mundane evidence, under the weight of the observed minutiae in the behaviour of friends who cheerfully went to Mass and to Confession after committing both mortal and venial sins, I expected a diminution of the savage and archaic laws which reminded me despairingly of how far my steps had strayed from the true paths. Yet, though the rewards became ever more evanescent until they no longer retained even the flavour of superstition, the punishments still remained. I could not appease the savage god within me.

Over twenty years later in Cairo these thoughts have suffered a sea change, but cling to their submerged rocks under the storm-dashed seas as tenaciously as limpets. There had been no ruin of my reputation in any public sense and, despite everything that had happened, I could have remained in

London and resumed the patterns of my former life. My betrayals had been private, and would only leak into the gossip columns in tentative dribs and drabs. Unlike a public servant, a renegade churchman or a cabinet minister, any further revelations of my past behaviour (which had begun to attract behind-the-hand gossip even before I left) would only have fed the popular and patronising view of the artist as a feckless, Bohemian eccentric who could not be expected to conform to the prevalent codes of social behaviour. I would have been released from any censure or accountability for my actions by society's acceptance of the peccadilloes of a long line of distinguished precedents. I would not be permitted any punishment for the wrongs I had done. ('Absolution given for true repentance purges the soul.')

Walter had sent me a copy of an article written about me in order, I suppose, to maintain the tenuous contact, and in the vain hope that I might return and resume my work as if nothing had happened. Miles Sinclair's piece was typical; its tone mildly amused and dismissive, as if nothing done by a creative artist could have much real significance.

'There is a long tradition of social irresponsibility in the artist,' he wrote in the *Mid-Atlantic Arts Review*, 'and a certain childlike pride in their flouting of the conventions of the day, as if only through such perverse behaviour can they obtain the recognition which will gratify their egos.' I noted hidden envy with a moment's mournful enjoyment, but the barb struck home. It was that article (if Walter had only known) which, almost more than any other single factor, confirmed that the path I had chosen was the only one left to me.

Neither Caroline nor Beth wrote, and the mute reproach of their silence wounded me more than the shrill disbelief in my parents' letter. It was only a matter of time before I read the inevitable phrase, 'I cannot understand how any son of mine could have done this'. The Pharisaic narcissism released me from any feeling of guilt for what I may have done to them.

I had never realised that the price of seeking freedom through action would be paralysis: that the action I had finally taken in fact, and so much against my habitually passive nature, would have left me with the frightening realisation that

I no longer needed permission to act. The paradox is that I had sought freedom in exile, in the burnt bone-white features of an alien country, when I know now it is only to be found in the familiar, experienced differently, never in the company of strangers in a harsh land.

Constantly reminded of my strangeness by a curious sideways glance from a glaucous eye, by the unfailing shock of the echoing muezzin five times a day, and by the host of minor uncertainties attendant upon my life here in the midst of this reeking secret city, I knew that I could never fully enter into the life of its pavements, its cafés, its tenebrous alleyways, as its denizens and those it loves, can. As they seethed past me in their jostling masses, intent, absorbed, I was reminded each day that this is their home, that its sights and sounds have been with them since they were born.

Once, in making some point to me that I have long forgotten, Father Gomez quoted the Jesuit maxim to me, 'Give me the child until he is seven and I will give you the man,' and I had at last unravelled its mystery. Home, that assembly of trivial ephemera, of stale habit, contains also within its aggregation of smells, of barely acknowledged sights, the sense of visceral belonging. The potency and power of the familiar, rendered seemingly dull and unimportant, is only recognised when one is in exile and it is no longer possible to return. It is nothing, after all, to do with love, and its strength often manifests itself to me in the same terms as Father Gomez' dicta: giving nothing directly, but obscurely, silently, exercising its iron grasp upon one's very soul.

In the weeks that followed, Brian and Faroukh kept such determined company with me that I began to feel mildly resentful. Faroukh worked in the administration section of Cairo Museum during the day, but Brian had nothing to do until his appointment began in the autumn, and set himself up as my guide, mentor and dragoman.

During this time I saw Rachel intermittently, but it was invariably unsatisfactory. The season had started and we only ever had time to spend a few minutes over a coffee or a Rickard before she had to leave to take a tour, or some importunate American lady would waddle up sucking an ice-cream and engage Rachel in some detailed conversation, stabbing a beringed finger at the guide book.

'It says here that we can get a flight to Abu Simbel. Where do I get tickets, and how many dawlaaars will it be?' I was amazed at Rachel's patience, her unfailing solicitude, and a little angry that she seemed to welcome these queries as a release from some obligation to me. Though she would sigh, and her manner would convey regret that we could not spend longer together, I felt uneasily sure that she was glad, at least for the moment, that no opportunity had arisen for a more intimate meeting.

Once, as I walked to the tour office, I came unexpectedly upon her and Brian having a coffee together in the nearby café. In the moment before they saw me I noticed how they sat across the table from each other, their faces almost touching as they discussed something with an urgency or passion totally lacking in my exchanges with her. I felt absurdly jealous that Brian should have such access to her feelings, and I should have none.

When I joined them Rachel said, 'Brian tells me he has arranged a tour for you. I'll see if we can meet up at one of the sites and spend a day or two together.' Her voice had the forced brightness of a professional courier. There was the sound of a horn, and her uncle's Mercedes drew up outside the window.

'I must go,' she said, and kissed me briefly on the cheek, waving to Brian as she went. When I turned back from watching her leave, Brian was looking at me intently.

'Give her time . . .' he said, as we walked out into the brilliant sunshine.

By day we scoured the sites. We went to Memphis, Gizeh, the Fatimid Necropolis, where the illustrious Mamelukes lay in their tombs beneath their seething descendants; a whole city of ragged, village life living in the tombs. I felt ill as we penetrated into Cheops, bending double to creep forward up the narrow walkway, and gagging on the stale, foetid air; a sense of awe when we entered the Pyramid of Unas where the Pyramid Texts, found by Gaston Maspero in 1881, celebrate eternal life and identify the dead pharaoh with Osiris in beautiful cartouches and chiselled pictograms; unease, as on a baking day we walked across sand, which burnt my feet through leather soles, to the serdab of Zoser's pyramid, where a facsimile of the pharaoh sits gazing with malevolent, sightless sockets at those who would disturb his rest; moved to tears to see the mummy of Nefertari, her fabled beauty shrunken and withered to an uncaring snarl.

The mystery I had felt from the moment I arrived deepened, day by day, and I felt strangely oppressed and overwhelmed by the sheer prodigality of Cairo's treasures. Brian was untiring, foraging restlessly through the museums and around the sites, his Baedeker bristling with strips of paper which marked various pages for easy reference.

When we were in the city we ate a sparing lunch at Groppi's restaurant, now so changed under the subtle Muslimisation of Mubarak's rule that my taxi driver in London would not have noticed it, or Lappas, or the Café Riche on Sharia Talaat Harb near the midan where Nasser, Sadat and other revolutionaries had plotted the coup of 1952. I would sit over an omelette or a hamam or Roz bel khalta, while Brian would eat abstractedly, his guide book open at his side, occasionally exclaiming in enlightenment or — with a finger marking the passage — giving me some item of importance about what we had seen that morning.

In stark contrast, the evenings for most of the month before we went on tour were spent in a variety of night-clubs and restaurants. It was a time of day when I felt my exile most keenly, as Faroukh would nod and exchange a few words with an acquaintance, underlining his acceptance in the city. At first we went round the most expensive and plainly the most touristically inclined establishments; the Belvedere and the Bateau Omar Khayyam, where any anticipation I might have felt was rapidly dispelled by the tasteless exteriors, followed by a sense of shock (at the prices), and by an incredulity verging on disgust at the level of entertainment.

After an enormously fat belly-dancer at the Scheherezade had undulated preposterously in front of me for the climax of her dance for a full minute, I commented mildly to Faroukh that I would like to find some indigenous entertainment, some more local way of spending my evenings. He evidently felt a mission to provide the means of my catharsis.

'You need a beautiful woman,' he said uncomprehendingly, and I shuddered to think what Brian must have told him. I realised, as he described a shape of obscene voluptuousness in the air with his slender hands, that his apparent westernisation, his love of English clothes, his knowledge of English politics and the cricket scores, were completely superficial. That, au fond, he would have been more at home in a mud-hut beside one of the tributaries of the Nile, than he was in this fictive guise. His great, liquid eyes almost filled with tears as, night after night, I failed to avail myself of the services offered in the humbler establishments we now frequented, and Brian seemed to share his genuine concern. They both appeared to see my failure to accept these prodigal daughters of the littoral and the city as an example of English reserve which prevented me from immersing myself in the ambience of Cairene society, a racist fastidiousness which condemned me to the role of passive observer.

One night Brian surprised me. Faroukh had gone into one of the cafés to assure the girl that no disrespect was offered or intended, and left us alone together. He leaned back in his chair under the cloudless night sky and fixed me with a quizzical look.

'Your trouble is that you elevate the satisfaction of a simple appetite into something of far greater importance. What do you see as intrinsically good in refusing, or bad in accepting?'

I didn't answer, angry that he had ventured so close. With a sigh he had turned away as Faroukh rejoined us, and for a brief moment I felt an unexpected warmth towards them both.

One evening, a week before we were due to set off on a tour, Rachel rang. Narouz knocked on my door at 5.30, waking me from my afternoon siesta, and I took the call in the grubby kiosk in the hall, under the curious eye of Muhammad, the desk clerk.

Rachel sounded tired and I felt overwhelmed by tenderness. 'I have some time off. Shall we have dinner tonight?'

All the coolness I had planned was instantly forgotten, and I said eagerly, 'Where shall we meet?'

There were still things she had to tidy up, she said. An

American lady had been attacked in the Old City and had lost all her money. The arrangements would take some time, so she would come round to the pensione when she had sorted everything out. 'Let's avoid the tourist restaurants tonight. We'll have a quiet evening.'

I went back to my room and tried to read Cavafy, but even her casual call, promising nothing, had made me uncertain — alternately elated and depressed. To a great extent the fine sureness I had possessed in London some two months before had faded, and I sometimes felt as if I had given up a great deal and compromised myself hopelessly, condemning myself to a lifetime of unasked questions, without gaining the object of my sacrifice.

Each time I saw her I was reconvinced, by the curve of her throat, by her profile across a room like the head on an old coin. But in this squalid hostelry, the ambivalence of my feelings, exiled from her presence, was underlined more and more. I felt that I had invested her with mythic and romantic qualities which she did not possess, the products of my hope and imagination alone.

Truth to tell I was a little ashamed of myself now. And frightened for the future. I had, after all, destroyed the images of family respectability, filial loyalty and domestic enslavement, which I had believed in for almost forty years.

Even Brian had been tired that day, and I was pleased to have some respite from his unflagging energy. I thought I had detected some movement in his room when I went past, but that may have been Narouz tidying up. As dusk was falling I went out onto the balcony. The outlines of the city began to dull over those few brief moments as the sun thrust down into the cooling sands. I could see the desert beyond the gaunt skeleton of the new apartments being built at Gizeh. Beyond the iron girders Cheops, Chephren and Mycerinus rose above the Sphinx, catching the last red rays filtering through the swirling dust raised by the light evening wind. In the street below a merchant came into view, perched on the front slats of his rickety cart whilst his emaciated donkey walked stoically forward into the cutting edge of the blast.

'Ya Abdul,' he called to an acquaintance, then leaned

forward to resume his bubbling crooning monologue to the beast, his face that of a gentle lover.

Sometimes I had heard him singing as he went past, the words indistinguishable in his cracked, high voice. Tonight it was too hot and close to sing as the cart bucked and jolted down the rutted street and out of sight. I went back to get a Stella from the fridge and sat on the balcony. Behind me Narouz came in with his broom, and started to sweep with small, ineffectual strokes.

I began to wonder if Rachel would come. She might or, hours later, call to make an excuse. She had to spend a lot of time with the police, or the fiacre got caught in the traffic, or she had to go to the airport. I could never really tell with her what was the exact and absolute truth about such arrangements.

Narouz had finished now and was shifting from foot to foot as he waited for his baksheesh. I pretended not to notice and walked over to pick up my book from the table. The pantomime of his worry varied from evening to evening, but usually consisted in his picking his nose with great ferocity or scratching his bottom with equal intensity. Though I could not avoid paying, something in his mute presence inspired this sadistic nightly charade, though I always felt ashamed later. Two filthy tens and a five. He touched his forehead with a curled forefinger and unconvincingly muttered his thanks, and that I should go with God. Perversely, I missed him when he was gone, and even toyed with the idea of going down the hall to wake Brian. But then I might miss her, so I picked up my Cavafy and sat down in the easy-chair overlooking the gardens to wait.

The night calls from the garden began to add to the muffled roar of the traffic. There had been a minor tragedy in the birds' enclosure earlier. One small duck had been repeatedly raped in the artificial lake by a flock of mallards, and her body lay limply in the reeds. The drakes swam to and fro, unconcerned, under the arc-lights, with that occasional twizzle of the tail which suggested that all was well with their world. In the gloom beyond the wire-netting the ratites quested ceaselessly.

Nine o'clock. I began to think she would not come, and a

feeling of loneliness settled over me; the evening began to feel stale, useless. My perspectives had altered already after these few weeks in Egypt. There was no point in constantly checking my watch in a country where a waiter could take fifteen minutes to bring a cruet to the table. At 9.30 I heard the lift and then the crisp click of heels over the block flooring.

She said, 'Oh God, I'm sorry. The woman was in a terrible state. I had to take her to the hospital and then to her hotel. Let's go out now.' A draught down the hall blew her hair across her mouth as I kissed her; warm musk in my mouth and her faint, elusive perfume.

She walked ahead of me to the lift and I said, 'Don't you want to look in on Brian?' but she shook her head and we creaked down in the rickety lift.

In the taxi I felt strangely breathless, like Yeats' dying animal, sick with desire. Rachel gave an address in Gezira, and we slipped into the permanent traffic jam, inching forward with the lorries, taxis and bicycles which bunched nose-to-tail, day in, day out. There was something different about her manner. The coolness had gone and she made no move to take her hand away from my clasp on the pretext of checking her make-up or fumbling in her bag.

'Is Brian tiring you out?' she asked, and laughed when I mimed exhaustion. 'He really has found his métier now. You know he wore a suit for the first two weeks?' and she laughed again, her thigh moving under our joined hands.

At the restaurant she was gay, unrestrained. She had a facility for droll mimicry. I laughed until the tears ran down my face when she told the story of an English spinster lady at Luxor on one of her tours. Standing before the place where the obelisk had stood before being removed to Paris in 1836, Rachel had quoted Cocteau's caustic comment about the plinth of the obelisk in Paris. The authorities had objected to the depiction of dog-faced baboons erect with excitement, so a sculptor had been commissioned to geld them.

Amid the ensuing laughter Rachel had become aware of a small, determined lady with white hair, making her way to the front of the crowd. Standing before an ithyphallic Amun-Re, with the Court of Rameses II with its papyriform columns straining towards the sky, the old lady had delivered a lecture on 'our sex-obsessed modern culture in which youth,' and Rachel pointed at herself, pealing with such fresh, delighted laughter that I saw several people at nearby tables turn and smile, 'had no concept of spiritual values.' Her delivery of the dry Scots Presbyterian tones was exact, prim, unforgiving. There were several such stories before she grew more silent, more thoughtful.

I almost broke the mood only once. As I began to speak she put her finger against my lips. 'Perhaps when you come back from the tour we'll talk of the old times,' she said, and her face darkened for an instant. 'If you still want to, then.' I couldn't even allay my unease by asking what she meant.

We paid off the taxi and walked the last mile to the pensione. We were both slightly drunk, navigating the broken pavement with mildly exaggerated steps. Once Rachel stumbled and for a long moment I held her as she examined the heel of her shoe. Outside the pensione the tourist police detail that night was two boys, their Lee Enfields casually leant against the paper kiosk. They lay asleep, like fugitives from a comic opera whose curtain had come down. Our laughter woke them up, and the younger boy grinned sheepishly as he straightened his cap. The elder put his hand in his pocket and pulled out a wad of Egyptian pounds.

'Change. English money. I give good rate.'

His rate was eighty per cent better than I had got at the bank that morning. But I could tell from the slight stiffening of Rachel's body at my side that she didn't want me to change money with him.

'You never know which ones are acting for the authorities,' she said, 'they like to make an example now and then.'

We tiptoed up to the room down the silent corridor. Automatically I went over to the bed and turned the pillow over, and Rachel said, 'Why do you do that?'

I explained to her, shame-facedly, that I had watched Narouz smooth the pillow with his filthy hand, so I turned it every night, and she laughed delightedly, 'I wonder what you would have made of the kitchen where we ate tonight.'

As she looked into the mirror and straightened her hair I put my arms around her waist, and she leaned back against me, moving her head against my cheek. When she turned to me there were tears in her eyes, and her mascara had run slightly down one cheek.

She said, 'Oh David, David,' as if her heart were breaking, and we kissed. When we moved apart, she began to unbutton her dress and kicked off her shoes, looking at me intently.

When I woke the sun was already high, and Rachel had gone.

27

Brian and I took the night sleeper to Aswan. I had called Rachel several times at the office, but the girl answering the phone always said, 'Miss Rachel not here. Maybe tomorrow,' in a bored sing-song way. I could imagine her cradling the phone against her ear while she painted her fingernails.

As the train meandered through the darkening landscape, I chafed that nothing had been arranged. Through the window the Nile came into view, swollen with silt, and then slid out of sight again. Once or twice we passed groups of people, with a loaded donkey or camel, walking on a mud path by the river in single file; three naked children bathed by the far bank, waving at the train; the palms stood sharply against the skyline like shredded umbrellas, each carrying a cargo of dates; an old man stumbled across a field, bent double with the weight of vegetation bound in a coarse sack upon his back. Every few moments I pressed myself against the pane to allow the tourists past on their way to the dining-car.

Faroukh had been unable to get away, but would join us later at Kom Ombo or Esna. The museum had acquired some further exhibits and he had arranged to accompany the researcher to the sites.

I lay awake much of the night, unable to sleep through the slow jolting of the carriages through the points, but Brian snored in the upper bunk. At 2.30 the tannoy system suddenly gave out a shriek of Islamic chanting, and for over a minute we scrambled sleepily around trying to turn off the switch. I rang the bell but no steward arrived, and in the corridor all the compartment lights were on, with people in pyjamas yawning hugely or talking to each other. When the steward did finally come and apologised for the noise with a wide grin, I felt I might have underestimated the Egyptian sense of humour.

In some way the sheer portentousness of what I experienced over the next few days, the massive, inchoate sense of a way of life so alien, well modulated and harmonious, all insulated me against what was to come. At first I felt disappointed, standing above the cataracts on the dam and gazing towards Nubia and the Sudan while Brian gave me a heterogeneous collection of information on the dam, the cataracts, and a party of revellers who were eaten by the crocodiles in Lake Nasser after an accident.

When we slid quietly through the glassy water in our *felucca*, steered by a Nubian arab with one tooth in his top jaw, and Philae rose from the waters like a shimmering mirage, I began then to feel a quickening sense of awe. The light was a brilliant white which hurt the eyes, and the swallows skimmed and skittered over the surface in pursuit of insects. Here the Osiris Cult had become the official religion under the Ptolemies and had continued as the centre of Isis worship until the reign of Justinian in the sixth century.

The boatman altered the rigging of the boat by moving his foot, around which the ropes were tied, and we idled, waiting for the queue before us to disembark. He lolled against the tiller for a while, watching us covertly from time to time from his trachoma-free eye. Finally he told us, in a mixture of pidgin-English, French and Italian that this was where Seth had killed his brother Osiris, and Isis who was Osiris' sister and wife, gathered together the dismembered body and remade him to live as king of the underworld.

'Did you get all that?' asked Brian, smiling, and the boatman joined in our laughter. It was only as we walked around that I felt a sense of artificiality in the place, as if in the process of moving it so precisely above the waters some vital cosmic insight had been lost.

The river-steamer restored the magic. Two days after we had arrived we nosed quietly out into the river to start our journey towards the southern source. A light wind riffled across our faces as we sat under the flapping canopy on deck, sipping orange juice and watching the banks and the huge varieties of birds wheeling and turning over the barren landscape. There were some French tourists, and a small group of Germans, shepherded and managed by a formidable, chain-smoking blonde woman with skin like fissured leather. There was only one English family, a husband who occasionally nodded a greeting, his wife and two sons.

We read and talked, without urgency, and I savoured that freedom from responsibility which every journey had given me. The broad wake moved out from the back and birds dived and vied to catch the fish thrown up by the turbulence. Occasionally we passed a ruined temple with pastel marble columns standing starkly against the hillside; or some rock tombs, cut into the stratified rock under the overhanging cliffs. Palms, bananas and vegetable gardens suddenly terminated in bleak rock, only to resume again suddenly as if the desert were blooming.

The first two nights we ate a very acceptable meal in the dining-room, served by starched-coated waiters whose movements suggested they might be more at home in a *felucca* or in reaping the harvest. After dinner we sat and talked under a violet sky, lingering long after the other passengers had gone to bed, listening to the slap of the water against the bows and the guttural exchanges of the crew below deck.

We arrived at Kom Ombo at daybreak. Brian slept on, but I was woken by the shouting of the children from the bank as we tied up against the rushy shore. While Brian slowly woke I washed and dressed, and said that I would meet him at the site. I ate a hurried breakfast and then walked over the gangplank, complete with red carpet, down to the collapsing bank. I was amused to see the captain ahead of me, walking very decorously apart from the very trim French girl he was escorting up the thin mud path. 'Captain's perks,' said Brian, cynically, on our first evening. 'Bet he ends up with that one.'

The mosquitoes hummed and sang above the field as I

walked through. The children, ragged-trousered and filthy, left the captain and his girlfriend to offer me their trinkets, and I waved them away. '*La-a, La-a.*' But I was smiling so they persisted with their scarabs and their alabaster heads of Nefertiti, and their pieces of mummified crocodile (stolen, no doubt, from Sobek's shrine) until I took a handful of coins from my pocket and threw them into the field, leaving them to search under the crops with delighted whoops while I made my way towards the road. Nubian vendors unfolded bales of cloth in front of me and jangled the bracelets hanging from their arms. A boy rushed forward with a stuffed crocodile, three feet long, and thrust the grinning jaws towards me.

I followed the captain, now discreetly holding the girl's arm at the crook of the elbow, up through the gate and into the first courtyard, past the destroyed pylon. Under the capitals, the papyriform columns showed coloured carvings, still fresh and arresting after almost two millenia. There was a Greekishness about the place which appealed to me, and I sat for some time on the north-west corner of the courtyard overlooking the birth-house and the Nile, while the sun soaked into my skin and the voices receded.

The crowds were sparser when I got up from the wall and made my way into the body of the temple, pausing here and there to look with sleepy eyes at the reliefs of various Ptolemaic pharaohs receiving blessings and the double crown. A girl with long, slender legs strode past, scouring the columns with swift, predatory glances. When she spoke in a hushed voice to her companion, a swarthy man in moss-coloured trousers and battle dress top, I was amused.

'Beats Disneyland,' she said, the American accent sounding out of place. There were no people there as I moved towards the sanctuary, the stone flooring uneven from the traffic of centuries, and paused to look at the relief of Ptolemy Philomotor and his sister-wife being presented to the gods of the temple. I heard a sound from the dark twin sanctuary, like the cry of someone in pain, and walked through the open door into the gloom.

Even before my eyes became accustomed to the darkness of the place I realised that it was no cry of pain. There were two figures, and their embrace was like a battle to the death. I was about to move away with an apology when I recognised the face of the figure which had turned to see the intruder. It was Faroukh and, as Brian's head began to turn, I ran quickly out into the main hall and down to the court.

When they came over to me twenty minutes later they walked apart and I greeted Faroukh in the English way, as if I had observed nothing. Brian was very quiet and, after we had exchanged general news about the weather in Cairo and where we were going next, I left them to have a coffee, and retraced my steps to the boat. I was surprised to find I was disapproving. Naïvely this possibility had never occurred to me; knowing Brian had lived with a couple of girls it was an aspect I would never have thought of myself. I felt uneasy about the prospect of spending the rest of the cruise with Brian, not knowing how he felt about being discovered, or how to pass the matter off as being of no concern. In the event that worry was naïve too.

I watched the child, fascinated. He was completely absorbed in his jigsaw puzzle laid on the scrubbed planking beside my deck-chair. He squatted over the pieces, freckled and red-haired, frowning with concentration as he moved the remaining segments into small piles of the same tone and colour. Each time he fitted a new piece in place he gave a small sound of satisfaction in his throat, and looked around for someone to share his pleasure.

I smiled at him and said, 'How's it going?' He looked seriously at me.

'It's very difficult,' he said, 'so many pieces look as if they should fit, but when you try to push them together you find they're wrong.'

His father came up the stairs onto the deck, blinking as he emerged into the bright sunshine. He had a pair of binoculars around his neck and an expensive camera hung over one shoulder. He looked at his son and said, in a mock-exasperated tone, obviously intended for our ears, 'We bring you out here to see the sights and you spend your time doing a puzzle.'

Brian said, 'In ten years time he'll kick himself for this,' and we all laughed, an adult and slightly condescending laugh, while the boy, unmoved, bent down over his puzzle again.

Neither Brian nor I had mentioned the incident at Kom Ombo. There had been a change in Brian's manner, a sharp astringency which made me feel ill-at-ease in his company, but that was all. It was only when we docked at Edfu that the incident which prompted Brian to enlighten me further took place.

Brian and I were following the trail of tourists up the esplanade and into the town. It was cool, and the night mists still hung in the reedy shallows by the far bank of the river. As we reached a junction where the front road suddenly plunged at right-angles between narrow, peeling tenements towards the town, a group of boys came running down the uneven pavement.

The leading child, looking over his shoulder as he ran, tripped headlong and fell against Brian's legs. Brian steadied himself and picked up the child — and a moment later the children were running again.

I looked at Brian for a moment, really to see if he was all right, and he said with uncharacteristic venom, 'I'm not a child molester, you know!' Out of sheer embarrassment I laughed, and realised my mistake immediately.

He said, 'It's about time I told you a few things, David. Let's pass up the temple and have a drink. It's pretty second-rate, anyway.'

With a sinking heart I followed him to a table at the quayside café. I remembered as a child how I had hidden under the sheets to shut out the sounds of my parents arguing. When we were sitting at the table, Brian with a brandy and I with a coffee, he said almost apologetically, 'I'm not doing this because of anything that has happened. But there are things you should know in order to make up your own mind.'

I felt trapped, miserable. 'Nothing has happened so far as I'm concerned,' I said, but Brian merely smiled sardonically, and I knew it was hopeless to try to stop him. He took a photograph from his wallet and passed it to me. With a sense of shock I saw it was a black and white group shot taken on a picnic. Willey sat at the back of the group in a folding chair and, round a tablecloth, spread with the remains of food and wine, sat Charles Mandeville, Jonathan, Rachel and, by Willey's side, Brian. Rachel was smiling, a glass of wine in her hand, her gaze fixed upon Jonathan.

Brian took the photograph back from me and put it away in his wallet. 'Atkinson took that,' he said.

'I never realised that you and Jonathan knew each other so well before I came up,' I said. Somewhere in my mind I felt the slow and unwilling dawning of comprehension.

'Willey's group,' said Brian, 'or to be more accurate, Willey's boys. Conscripted at Fenner's or the Air Squadron or at private dinners.' He moved in his chair, crossing one leg over another. 'Rachel brought us all together. She's Willey's daughter, you know,' and he slipped me a sideways look. When I said nothing he went on, 'Willey was a communist in the Thirties for a short time. Whether or not he saw the light after the war, I don't know, but he appears to have been sounding out people for intelligence work since the mid-Fifties.'

'Were you . . .' I began, and Brian laughed.

'No,' he said, 'I could never take it seriously. Not like Jonathan . . .'

A vendor appeared before us, carrying bales of brightly coloured cloth, and I waved him away. The waiter passed near the table and I signalled to him to replenish our drinks. Brian looked at me and I thought I saw pity in his quick glance. He said, 'Do you want me to go on?' and I nodded.

'Jonathan took it all seriously, too seriously. I couldn't really understand it. He was very bright, and it was all a bit of a game. Then one evening I went off with him and a few others to London. Anyway, Jonathan said he had to pay someone a visit and asked if I'd join him. We went to a place in Southall and met this old Sikh and his family. I couldn't understand much of what was said, but it was all terribly emotional, everyone shaking hands and kissing and so on . . . he was someone you'd known in India . . .'

'Bully,' I said, and Brian nodded.

'That's right.'

Jonathan and Bully had talked about old times for an hour or so, and Brian had heard odd snatches but was more interested to see how the family lived. How Jonathan had found Bully and why he had told none of us about the visit were both issues beyond knowing now. When they left Jonathan had asked Bully for forgiveness.

'The British failed you,' he had said, and Brian went on, 'I realised that he had never come to terms with what he saw as the betrayal of England over the events of Partition.'

Brian had felt vaguely concerned about what he should do, torn between loyalty to Jonathan and concern over the fact that he had been conscripted by Willey, however loose and informal such an arrangement might be. Eventually he had mentioned it to Willey who had merely laughed and said he would never entrust Jonathan with anything serious.

'I think he thought of Jonathan as the son he never had,' said Brian, taking a sip of his cognac. I noticed that he was sweating heavily, and a damp patch had appeared by each armpit and down the front of his shirt. A group of tourists went by, laden with purchases, led by an elderly man in khaki shorts and grey socks with sandals.

'So that's why Jonathan went up to see him just before . . .' I said, and Brian nodded.

'Yes,' he said cynically. 'Willey had another protégé by then. When Jonathan came round to see me about the money, he started by telling me about his visit to Willey. Willey had laughed at him, told him he could never be entrusted with anything more.' He sipped his drink slowly, looking across the river. 'He couldn't see Jonathan's need to do something important.'

We sat in silence awhile. Then Brian said, 'Shall we walk?' I left the money on the table and followed him into the crowded street. I caught up with him at a shop selling amphorae, oil lamps, and grave figures.

'Look at that,' he said, pointing at a pharaonic head carrying a substantial price tag. 'How they con the tourists.' As we walked on he resumed. 'I remember Jonathan saying "I'll show him" and feeling glad I wasn't Willey.'

'What about his death?' I asked. Somehow I couldn't bring myself to say the word suicide.

I sensed some slight evasion in Brian's manner, and he

moved almost hesitantly, like a man avoiding a blow. He was silent for some time as we walked towards the pit where the excavated temple sat, an indifferent first-century edifice, some thirty or forty feet below the surrounding houses on the level where we now stood.

'There are a number of possibilities,' he said at last. 'Suicide is the most obvious. However, that doesn't seem to account very adequately for the last letter which was typed on a machine in Charles Mandeville's office and was then sent through the post to Beth. Her explanation at the inquest was a brave try, but it doesn't really seem to me to fit.'

I suddenly remembered Rachel in the graveyard quoting from Jonathan's letter.

Brian said, 'Of course he may have made it look suspicious in order to implicate Willey's people, to make a scandal, but that, too, seems far-fetched. Or he was indulging a sexual fetish. Again, that doesn't seem likely to me. Or —,' and he paused and looked at me, as if to gauge whether or not he could venture this last suggestion, '— he was killed and they made it look like suicide.'

'They?' I said automatically, but I knew who he meant.

Brian sighed and began to walk down the steps towards the temple. An old woman toiled stolidly up, hauling herself, step by step up the railing. We pressed into the wall to let her past. The sun had risen high so that the massive pillars of the temple stood in clear relief against the dark interior. I followed Brian to a mound by the new excavations, away from the crowd. He looked heavy, melancholy.

'I had the impression it was all a little amateur,' he said, 'the whole shooting match. Oh, I've no doubt that Willey was a finder. But I think he liked to surround himself with gilded youth anyway. Being in control of the operation he could use that line — the *dulce et decorum est* — to create an exclusive set of his own. But while most of us took it as a game, Jonathan didn't. Willey reckoned without that seriousness of his.'

'So you think Willey panicked?' I asked, and Brian said heavily, 'For my money, yes.'

I sat down on the parapet running around the excavations. My chest hurt and I found it difficult to breathe. Brian put a hand on my shoulder, peering at me anxiously. 'Are you all right?'

I nodded. We sat in silence for about a minute and I felt a little better. 'What about Rachel?' I asked, 'how did she fit in?'

Brian got up abruptly and looked around him with a strangely lost expression. He looked at me as if he didn't see me, his face screwed up against the sunlight like that of a child about to cry.

'I have to spell everything out for you, don't I?' he said bitterly. 'She had the job of bringing them all in. Whatever it needed.' He gave the word 'whatever' a lewd emphasis, an embarrassed levity.

We walked back to the boat in silence. I reflected that Brian would probably have made none of these disclosures if I had not come across him and Faroukh. I was no nearer any ultimate truth, but I had the facts which Rachel had mocked me for seeking that summer so long ago. So far as Jonathan was concerned my new perspectives had already begun to form, confirming the uneasiness I had felt at the inquest. Nothing was certain about Rachel.

The magic had gone. The river seemed sullen and charmless, the scenery monotonous and stale. I listened listlessly as Brian, now seemingly restored to a ponderous good humour, expatiated at length on Egyptian mythology and culture. Seated on deck with my merciless thoughts I was glad when the boy, Rodney, came to lend me his binoculars and to point out to me the different birds which sat or soared or bathed in the prodigal river or by its banks. I was almost angry when we arrived at Luxor, and I had to wrest myself away from this pursuit.

We docked at Luxor in the evening. The smells and noises of the night were already in the air as we took an old fiacre pulled by an ancient horse, its haunches beaten raw by its remorseless owner.

'Karnak,' said Brian, and the driver nodded, waving his whip over the horse's flanks. It broke into a tired trot and then immediately slowed to a walk.

When we arrived, our guide was looking impatiently at her watch. As she remonstrated angrily with our driver, the other carriage owners, whose sleek ponies were already munching from their nosebags, grinned and made jokes with each other about our vehicle.

Along the processional way towards the main pylon the ram-headed sphinxes, each guarding their mummy-wrapped statue of Rameses II, looked stonily ahead, unmoved by two thousand years of harsh suns and scouring winds. I walked with Brian like an automaton, my mind once again pre-occupied with all that he had told me. In that one conversation he had dredged up things which I would rather have left decently buried beneath the sands of memory. Now that they were exposed once more I was forced to look at them again.

As we arrived in the hypostyle hall I felt oppressed by the weight of the pillars, the sheer gigantism of the enormous structure. I felt relieved when the group moved on, led by the shrill-voiced guide, with Brian following behind and looking up from time to time from the pages of his guidebook. It was sad to have learnt of these things in a strange land, where there was no familiar place to return for comfort. As I closed my eyes and leaned back against the pillar I was surprised to find myself longing for home: for the house, Miranda, Caroline, the dogs, rain, the smell of wet grass.

When I opened my eyes again Rodney stood before me. He tapped his camera and said, 'I've got a good shot of you . . ' I laughed.

'Was I snoring with my mouth open?'

He considered this for a moment, his head on one side. 'No,' he said, 'you looked sad.'

I asked him where the others were and he gestured vaguely in the direction of the Sacred Lake.

'It was getting so boring,' he said. 'We've spent an entire week just looking at ruins and old tombs.' He pushed the toe of his sandal into the sand and expertly flicked a rock into the air and caught it. 'D'you like football?'

'I've never had the co-ordination for those games,' I said, and he shot me a curious glance. We walked out into the open.

'There you are,' said Brian. 'Not bored, are you?'

'A bit tired, that's all.'

*

We were taken back at a brisk pace past the Gateway of Euergetes to the Luxor Temple. The sun had set and the night chill was enhanced by a thin wind. Overhead a brilliant moon and the white stars helped the spotlights to illuminate the temple. On the dome of Abu Hagagg's Mosque a brilliant green neon sign proclaimed the word Allah in the midst of the pagan ruins. The floor was uneven and rubble-strewn.

There was a slender woman talking to a group of people in the Court of Amenhopis. I watched her incuriously as a more human focus for my attention amidst all the gigantic splendour. I was too far to distinguish her voice amid the humming swell of conversations echoing from the walls, but her gestures, vivid and arresting, were accentuated by a pale suit which reflected the dim light, and gave her a ghostly, ethereal appearance. When we had almost walked past the group I realised, with a shock, that it was Rachel.

As I turned to Brian he smiled and said, 'I know,' and walked forward until he was lost in the shadows beyond. I moved into the darkness by a pillar, and watched her.

Brian had broken the pre-Raphaelite ideal for ever. She was now flesh and blood and prone to all that I, too, was heir to. I realised, as I watched her, that I had always feared that her passivity, her seemingly uncritical acceptance of people, indicated that she had no will and direction of her own. That an ardent suitor might be accepted, even without love. That she would deceive me. Not in the purely sexual sense, though that was a painful enough thought, but in some far more fundamental denial of any relationship between us. The tone of the time was uncertainty, and I felt these old fears rise silently within me as I watched.

The lassitude I had felt was gone. The long waiting was over. I knew that I could not take this half-life any more, these leavings and returns which had begun to destroy even the act of love for me. In one part of my mind I was ready to go home if it did not work this time.

She finished her talk and said goodnight to her group. Now that they had begun to walk away she seemed less sure of herself, as if she had temporarily forgotten her lines. I called her twice from the shadows where I stood, and laughed to see her startled movements.

She said, 'David? Where are you?' and her voice sounded frightened. I stepped into the light and she looked at me for a long moment without moving or speaking. I stood against the pillar, between hope and despair.

When she ran across and put her arms around my neck and her head on my chest I half-led, half-carried her to the healing dark between the columns.

'I hoped you would come,' she said, again and again.

28

I was looking through a case of old photographs and documents the other day, half-heartedly trying to throw away a few more useless bits of information, a few memories which had become outworn with time. I had steeled myself to looking at the photographs again, and found that they possessed curiously little power to move me. But at the bottom of the case I found a letter Jonathan had written to me when he first went to Cambridge and it was like seeing the face of a friend, long dead, miraculously revived and walking towards one. I read it again, and was overcome by sadness at the waste of our bright hopes and dreams. My coffee cooled by my side on the glass-topped cane table, and I was glad that I was alone.

Dear David,

I thought it might be worth giving you a few first impressions of Cambridge since you too have now been accepted. I must confess, too, that this letter stems from a (self-regarding) desire to record my first impressions before they are overlaid with familiarity.

I am stuck in digs in Jesus Lane. The landlord has sparse orange hair (appropriately enough for the district, a tonsure), and wears vivid red or blue shirts and checked trousers. He is a fervently practising homosexual, and God knows what besides. The noises emanating from his rooms would be impossibly exciting for one more prurient than I. But he serves marvellous breakfasts, in a tight-lipped and rather resentful way. So far, while the enthusiasm is still with me, I get down to the lecture theatre at Mill Lane a couple of miles away, for nine o'clock, usually with a friend — Giles — who is also in his first year. I must confess that I stray about a bit and don't stick strictly to my course. When you have Leavis on The Novel in lecture room 3, C S Lewis on The Crisis of Faith in lecture room 4, and George Steiner on The Death of Tragedy in lecture room 6, it is a little difficult to get worked up about Economic Liberalism in the 19th century. Honourable, pedestrian, worthy — it is all of those things — but it lacks the heady delights of the Literature course.

My Moral Tutor is one Algernon Charles Willey (known as A C — he hates the Swinburne connection). It is so English to have a Moral Tutor acting in loco parentis; it conjures up such delightful visions of absinthe-ruined undergraduates being rescued from dens of vice. The reality is rather more prosaic: he is a curious mixture — tall, thin, pedantic, shy — but refreshingly nice under it all. I wonder sometimes if he cultivates a deliberate eccentricity as a defence against the world. He is an Historian, specialising in Indian History 1750 to present day, and has that peculiarly Anglo-Saxon self-justifying set of attitudes about English rule in India, about the wisdom of Partition, about Gandhi. On such matters he is like a modern academic General Dyer, blinkered by chauvinism, and subtly patronising about 'the lesser breeds beneath the law'. A group of us go to his rooms at Great Court every second Monday during term time for what he refers to as 'our Socratic Symposiums'. The lights are lowered, candles lit, coffee and port are passed around and a sort of free association ensues. Last week he treated us to an extremely dubious bit of history, suggesting that the German High Command arranged sorties over Poland just prior to the invasion, during which the pilots would jettison specially prepared pornographic material over the major cities. The idea being that the Polish youth would become introverted through their unhealthy interest in this material, and would be unable to fight. The lights were too low for me to see any glimmer of expression in his face, but I suspect he throws these things in to sustain the image he feels appropriate to his station. He is curiously likeable, and I feel that he enjoys my company too, in his desiccated, colourless way.

I can't begin to communicate the febrile intense excitement of being here. You feel almost neurotic about what you might be missing — not, I hasten to add, in the flesh-pot sense, but in the sense of intellectual stimulation. Besides Union debates and numerous society activities, there is, for example, a series of guest speakers currently debating questions of faith at Saturday Matins in Great St Mary's Church. Where else could you get the Home Secretary speaking across a crowded nave in debate with the foremost philosopher of our time, arguing the provenance of The Four Gospels? The richness and variety is prodigal, every rift is loaded with ore.

After the Head's frequent quotation of '*Mens sana in corpore sano*' I have not been neglecting my exercise, either. Three afternoons a week, come rain or watery sunshine, I am shivering in my singlet at stroke in our third boat. We even have a coach, one 'Crocker' Harris, who rides a stolen lady's bike down the tow-path roaring unprintable suggestions through a megaphone — 'Give it a ten, you lazy —— You're rowing like a bunch of swans with polio,' and on and on in this would-be humorous vein. A lot of his kind around I'm afraid, ex-English schoolboy rugby players or rowers here on closed scholarships to boost their alma mater's games records. But this side of things provides a much needed continuity from school. The humour is more puerile, there are high jinks in the changing rooms, and undemanding dinners where much beer is drunk. When we won the Rugby cup I was advised to borrow a dinner jacket for the festivities; much gnomic touching of sides of noses, and 'You'll see why's.' After dinner the tables were set end to end and lined with pints of beer on either side. Two captains picked their teams, and the game started. The first two on each side drank a pint of beer each, crawled under the tables to the other end, then ran back to touch the first person in their line . . . and so on. After three rounds the weaker brethren were looking decidedly green, or were tipping half their beer on the floor. Afterwards, some bright sparks had piled a load of furniture from the Junior Combination room in the middle of the Quad and set light to it. Others — in dinner jackets and gowns — were riding their bicycles through the blazing furniture. To cap it all the Master and Willey were tenderly helping the hopelessly over-indulged to their rooms. The next morning a notice went up to say that we would all have a contribution towards the damage docked from our grants! O brave New World, that has such people in it.

As for g-u-r-l-s and l-u-r-v-e, the percentages, alas, run against us here. There is a certain animosity between Town and Gown, sometimes resulting in violence, and the net effect of all this is that female companionship tends to come from one of the ladies' colleges or one of the language schools. The former establishments tend towards the tweed-suited, bespectacled blue stockings — either shockingly etiolated or bucolically full-blown — and the latter to impossibly glossy brown-skinned girls with unpronounceable names who earnestly ask you to talk to them in English whilst very firmly removing your hand from their knee. I have spent one evening with an earnest Francesca, miming my way through a meal at the Blue Boar, before returning her at a decorously early hour to the Bell School of Languages. She looked like an angel, brown hair lightened by summer suns, and a fuzz of peachlike hair along the length of her jaw, but when she showed me a picture of her parents I could already see what she would become. A stout, Roman materfamilias, clad in outmoded cotton dresses and with a rudimentary grasp of English. I felt sad, looking at that photograph, to know that her beauty would pass, the bloom would go.

Do you remember Dr Mac? And Bulant Singh? I remember Mac most of all because he seemed to me to be looking for significance in the random workings of our lives. Without him that whole episode of Partition and after would have remained a meaningless, cruel jumble. I think that talking to him sowed the first seeds of what has finally brought me here to read History; he made the attempt to explain what was happening to us all in human terms, to appreciate why people were doing these grotesque and horrible things to neighbours they had lived with happily for years. Looking back, it seems that all the other adults merely reacted against what was happening on the basis of their biased assumptions, whereas he looked at people and events with insight and a will to understand. Bully comes back for a different reason; because he was so unconsciously funny I cannot imagine him dead — as if to me he has attained the stature of a Panurge or a sort of Babu Don Quixote. For some reason they both come to mind a lot now, and I remember them as if we had just parted, though the rest of our childhood seems to belong to some dusty, dead world.

Something rather shocking happened a week ago. One of our group at Willey's Monday evenings was a History Exhibitioner, Fergus McPhail. Very quiet, clever, with a tendency to chew on his nail furiously while he listened to you talk — watching you with a frightening intensity. One of the college bridge-playing fraternity, a server at chapel, and already settling into a premature and identifiable middle-age. The sort of chap one could confidently assume would be a pillar of his local community in twenty years. At Willey's last Monday evening, after the lights had been turned down, the tapers lit, and there was a hushed silence while we all hoped for someone else to open their mouths first, Willey ventured the opinion that someone in our midst had a death wish. This seemed to be one of his wilder essays and there was much surreptitious coughing and sniggering, but I happened to notice McPhail's face. He was looking at Willey open-mouthed, as if the old man had come up with some profound insight which would alter our lives. Anyway, the conversation shifted into other channels, and I forgot the slight uneasiness I felt about this scene until later. On Friday I arrived for breakfast to see an ambulance outside the college, and a large group of undergraduates outside McPhail's staircase. As I arrived, two stretcher-bearers came down the stairs carrying somebody covered in a blanket. The leading one made an awkward pass through the door and caught the edge of the blanket, which pulled away to reveal Fergus' face — black as night and monstrously swollen — and very dead. It transpired that he had gone along for his customary bridge-hand round at the Anchor, and had retired early with a bottle of Scotch. He had then left a note pinned to his door for his bedmaker suggesting that she did not, as was her custom, come in with a cigarette posted in her mouth, and had turned on the gas whilst drinking the entire bottle of whisky. Since then there has been much theorising, much half-informed discussion about what has happened. I haven't talked to Willey since, and I find it hard to know what I could say.

There is a rather arrogant élitism here, which bobs to the surface from time to time. Bloomsbury still enjoys a certain vogue, it seems nothing since has had the power to displace that self-satisfied ethic — that ambience of superiority. I have just been reading Maynard Keynes' letters, and am amazed at how little certain things seem to have changed at Oxbridge. He writes to Lytton Strachey about their membership of The Apostles: 'is it monomania — this colossal moral superiority that we feel? I get the feeling that most of the rest never see anything at all — too stupid or too wicked.' Here the same immature sense of effortless superiority over the hoi polloi is quite widespread, and is shamelessly upheld by the Establishment. It is pernicious, because the view is held without any redeeming trace of self-mocking humour, and one finds, time and again, a tacit — often overt — belief in the idea that intellectual brilliance is everything, that compassion, insight, emotional understanding, are as nothing compared to this pinnacle *sub-specie aeternitatis*. Sometimes (and this is my own private counterweight) I have an uneasy feeling that our tutors here are emotional pigmies who have sacrificed the most important part of themselves — the small, shared daily intimacies which balance this soaring spirit of discovery.

Yet there are nevertheless wholly unexpected and endearing solecisms: two evenings ago I went to a Humanist cocktail party held in Pembroke, and noticed we were being served South African sherry. The address — given by an earnest Fellow of Peterhouse — was, ironically enough, about the iniquitous and undemocratic régimes of some emergent nations: as if to labour the point he fairly pasted apartheid and Verwoerd. This high seriousness is one of the less positive aspects of life here, and fortunately only exists in certain sectors.

I wonder what Father would make of it now, forty years after his undergrad. days. I suspect that the changes have been smaller, more gradual, than they have been in the outside world. King's Parade, the Backs, the Market Square, the colleges, still sport the same appearance now as they did then. The archaic college servant system is still the same. There is even, I suspect (and hope), still a latent patriotism, despite the inevitable dilution produced by the foreign hordes now entering from every corner of the Commonwealth. The old system, almost amounting to primogeniture, of sons going to father's old college, is dying out, and the total stranglehold of the major public schools has been loosened. We are heading towards a meritocracy and, reactionary that I am, I believe that many of the accompanying changes are not for the best. I have a soft spot for tradition, even when it stands in the way of so-called progress. Giles says he will have to drag me screaming and struggling into the twentieth century; I'm not sure I want to come.

I hope you are going to enjoy it as much as I do. Perhaps my year of voluntary service overseas has helped. Working with the team on excavating the Mortuary Temple of Hatshepsut was an experience that will come back to me throughout my life; but so too, will the poverty, the disease, the sense of lives lived just above the surface of consciousness, where the soul has no chance to soar. I do feel that the school-leavers who have come straight up tend to miss out on the non-academic aspects of life here. After Hall they are straight off to their rooms to study, seemingly afraid of the wanton freedoms of the evenings. The group I see most of — Giles, Paul Atkinson (facetious, bright, young, ex-Eton), and Miles Sinclair (rich, waspish, good fun — but gives the impression he will always be second) — tend to go to The Eagle two or three times a week. Less sporting than the Bath Hotel, but still full of voluble sporting enthusiasts and aspiring thespians all shouting to make themselves heard. Yeats was right. 'The best lack all conviction while the worst are full of passionate intensity.'

I see I have not really caught it, as I read through these pages at two in the morning, with a hoar frost on the grass outside my window under a brilliant moon. But I feel marvellous things inside, and the growing belief that I will create, manufacture, produce something worthwhile in the future. Nothing concrete or tangible yet, but it will come. Meanwhile (as I yawn mightily), sleep beckons.

Sorry to pontificate so. You will form your own impressions, make your own connections. Selfishly I wanted to communicate the totality — insofar as it can be reduced to words — to someone. I've failed, in part because it became less important as I began to analyse it. But who better to fail with than with you, whom I have known almost all my life. Love to Jean and the parents. Tell them I will be writing separately in the near future. Write when you have time.

Your brother,
Jonathan.

Rachel found me sitting by the window, gazing at the traffic crawling along the avenue outside. She looked at me, head cocked on one side in a familiar gesture of mock-exasperation, and put her bag on the floor. From the kitchen I heard her voice, sharpened by asperity. 'He always wrote good letters, didn't he?' The implied coda might have been that his letters were more attractive than the reality; what I couldn't tell her then or ever was that I knew that her father was the invisible worm, the loving destroyer.

That is where we are now — home — a four-room apartment in Nasr City. A hundred yards across the open plaza, Anwar Sadat sits in his sarcophagus facing Mecca. The years have passed quickly and Jonathan no longer haunts me. Our daughter, Yasmin, is four — an unexpected late present. Brian, rather older and comfortably gone to seed, thinks she looks like me.

He has almost given up zibib and brandy, and has embraced the Catholic faith; his new style is to pretend to be the simple man.

'Insurance, old man,' he says. 'Can't do any harm.'

Yasmin adores him and I enjoy his company too in a slightly perverse and masochistic way. On good days he could almost be Freud's good father, wise, benevolent. Especially now, as Jonathan would say, that his gonads are taking a break. With Faroukh and his successors long gone, it will, I'm afraid, be permanent in his case.

I paint for the tourists now: the soukh, felaheen head. Sinclair wouldn't be interested but we make a living. I have no more faith in graven images, in the deceptive surfaces of things.

As for Rachel I still do not know her precise role in the events of the past. Nor will I ask her, or she tell me. That is our unspoken pact. I still find parts of her I do not know. She is my delight. I revel in her body. I long to possess her utterly; to make her see me. Sometimes, briefly, these things come together for a few moments, an hour. At my age it is enough. Like Theseus I followed the thread into the maze. Now that I have traversed the last corner I find myself overcome by pity and fear. For I know now that I can never kill the monster which I see at last to be an aspect of myself and of those I love most.